Aravind Adiga was born in Madras in 1974 and studied at Columbia and Oxford Universities. His first novel, *The White Tiger*, won the Man Booker Prize for 2008. A former Indian correspondent for *Time* magazine, his writing has also appeared in the *New Yorker*, the *Financial Times* and the *Sunday Times*, among other publications. He lives in Mumbai.

Praise for *Between the Assassinations*:

'Poverty, corruption, class and caste resentment and gross inequality are [Adiga's] big themes... There is nothing subtle about his prose or its intention. It knocks you about the head like a sledgehammer.' Chitra Ramaswamy, *Scotland on Sunday*

'*Between the Assassinations* is unified by its preoccupation with the inner lives of Indians mired in an intricate system of social control. In increments of concretely realized detail, Adiga builds his portrait of Kittur... Impassioned and involving.' Kevin Power, *Sunday Business Post*

'Adiga observes this human tragedy with compassionate detachment... The have-nots either cannot write or write for their minority and therefore go largely unheard. Has Adiga given them a voice? Of course not. Rather he has given them his own voice, which is no cheap gift.' Alan Taylor, *Glasgow Herald*

'Adiga's stories resemble those of Maupassant in depicting lives so restricted that the slightest gesture can cause disaster; and the pressure of desire is ever present, although its workings are devious... The collection has an impressive range and displays an alert, comic tenderness which can register delicate movements of indistinct feeling and the dignity of deflected lives.' Bernard Manzo, *Financial Times*

Also by Aravind Adiga

The White Tiger

Between the Assassinations

ARAVIND ADIGA

Atlantic Books
London

First published in India in 2008 by Picador India.

First published in Great Britain in 2009 in hardback by
Atlantic Books, an imprint of Grove Atlantic Ltd.

This paperback edition first published in Great Britain
in 2010 by Atlantic Books.

5 7 9 10 8 6 4

A CIP catalogue record for this book is available
from the British Library.

ISBN: 978 1 84887 207 3

Printed in Great Britain by CPI Bookmarque, Croydon

Atlantic Books
An imprint of Grove Atlantic Ltd
Ormond House
26–27 Boswell Street
London WC1N 3JZ

www.atlantic-books.co.uk

For Ramin Bahrani

CONTENTS

ARRIVING IN KITTUR

Kittur is on India's south-western coast, between Goa and Calicut, and almost equidistant from the two. It is bounded by the Arabian Sea to the west, and by the Kaliamma river to the south and east. The terrain of the town is hilly; the soil is black and mildly acidic. The monsoons arrive in June and besiege the town through September. The following three months are dry and cool and are the best time to visit Kittur. Given the town's richness of history and scenic beauty, and diversity of religion, race, and language, a minimum stay of a week is recommended.

Day One (Morning): THE RAILWAY STATION

The arches of the railway station frame your first view of Kittur as you arrive as a passenger on the Madras Mail (arrival early morning) or the West Coast Express (arrival afternoon). The station is dim, dirty, and littered with discarded lunch bags into which stray dogs poke their noses; in the evening, the rats emerge.

The walls are covered with the image of a jolly, plump, pot-bellied, and entirely naked man, his genitalia strategically covered by his crossed legs, who floats above a caption in Kannada that says: 'A SINGLE WORD FROM THIS MAN CAN CHANGE YOUR LIFE'. He is the spiritual leader of a local Jain sect that runs a free hospital and lunch-room in the town.

The famous Kittamma Devi temple, a modern structure built in the Tamil style, stands on the site where an ancient shrine to the goddess is believed to have existed. It is within walking distance of the train station and is often the first port of call of visitors to the town.

None of the other shopkeepers near the railway station would hire a Muslim, but Ramanna Shetty, who ran the Ideal Store, a tea-and-samosa place, had told Ziauddin it was okay for him to stay.

Provided he promised to work hard. And keep away from all hanky-panky.

The little, dust-covered creature let its bag drop to the ground; a hand went up to its heart.

'I'm a Muslim, sir. We *don't* do hanky-panky.'

Ziauddin was small and black, with baby fat in his cheeks and an elfin grin that exposed big, white, rabbity teeth. He boiled tea for the customers in an enormous, pitted stainless-steel kettle, watching with furious concentration as the water seethed, overspilled, and sizzled into the gas flame. Periodically, he dug his palm into one of the battered stainless-steel boxes at his side to toss black tea powder, or a handful of white sugar, or a piece of crushed ginger into the brew. He sucked in his lips, held his breath, and with his left forearm tipped the kettle into a strainer: hot tea dripped through its clogged pores into small, tapering glasses that sat in the slots of a carton originally designed to hold eggs.

Taking the glasses one at a time to the tables, he delighted the rough men who frequented the teashop by interrupting their conversations with shouts of 'One-a! Two-a! Three-a!' as he slammed the glasses down in front of them. Later, the men would see him squatting by the side of the shop, soaking dishes in a large trough filled with murky bilge water; or wrapping greasy samosas in pages ripped from college trigonometry textbooks so they could be home-delivered; or scooping the gunk of tea leaves out of the strainer; or tightening, with a rusty screwdriver, a loose nail in the back of a chair. When a word was said in English all work stopped: he would turn around and repeat it at the top of his voice ('Sunday-Monday, Good-bye, Sexy!'), and the entire shop shook with laughter.

Late in the evening, just as Ramanna Shetty was ready to close up, Thimma, a local drunk, who had bought three cigarettes every night, would roar with delight to see Ziauddin, his bum and thighs pressed against the giant fridge, shoving it back into the shop, inch by inch.

'Look at that whippersnapper!' Thimma clapped. 'The fridge is bigger than him, but what a fighter he is!'

Calling the whippersnapper close, he put a twenty-five paisa coin in his palm. The little boy looked at the shopkeeper's eyes for approval. When Ramanna Shetty nodded, he closed his fist, and yelped in English:

'*Thanks you, sir!*'

One evening, pressing a hand down on the boy's head, Ramanna Shetty brought him over to the drunk and asked: 'How old do you think he is? Take a guess.'

Thimma learned that the whippersnapper was nearly twelve. He was the sixth of eleven children from a farm-labouring family up in the north of the state; as soon as the rains ended his father had put him on a bus, with instructions to get off at Kittur and walk around the market until someone took him in. 'They packed him off without even one paisa,' Ramanna said. 'This fellow was left entirely to his own wits.'

He again placed a hand on Ziauddin's head.

'Which, I can tell you, aren't much, even for a Muslim!'

Ziauddin had made friends with the six other boys who washed dishes and ran Ramanna's shop, and slept together in a tent they had pitched behind the shop. On Sunday, at noon, Ramanna pulled down the shutters, and slowly rode his blue-and-cream-coloured Bajaj scooter over to the Kittamma Devi temple, letting the boys follow on foot. As he entered the temple to offer a coconut to the goddess, they sat on the green cushion of the scooter, discussing the bold red words written in Kannada on the cornice of the temple: 'HONOUR THY NEIGHBOUR, THY GOD.'

'That means the person in the house next door is your God,' one boy theorized.

'No, it means God is close to you if you really believe in Him,' retorted another.

'No, it means, it means—' Ziauddin tried to explain.

But they wouldn't let him finish: 'You can't read or write, you hick!'

When Ramanna shouted for them to come into the temple, he darted in with the others a few feet, hesitated, and then ran back to the scooter: 'I'm a Muslim, I can't go in.'

He had said the word in English, and with such solemnity that the other boys were silent for a moment, and then grinned.

A week before the rains were due to start, the boy collected his bundle and said: 'I'm going home.' He was going to do his duty to his family, and work alongside his father and mother and brothers, weeding or sowing or harvesting some rich man's fields for a few rupees a day. Ramanna gave him an 'extra' of five rupees (minus ten paise for each of two bottles of Thums Up he had broken), to make sure he would return from his village.

Four months later, when Ziauddin came back, he had developed vitiligo, and pink skin streaked his lips and speckled his fingers and earlobes. The baby fat in his face had evaporated over the summer; he returned lean and sunburned, and with a wildness in his eyes.

'What happened to you?' Ramanna demanded, after releasing him from a hug. 'You were supposed to come back a month and a half ago.'

'Nothing happened,' the boy said, rubbing a finger over his discoloured lips.

Ramanna ordered a plate of food at once; Ziauddin grabbed it and stuffed his face like a little animal, and the shopkeeper had to say: 'Didn't they feed you anything back home?'

The 'whippersnapper' was displayed to all the customers, many of whom had been asking for him for months; some who had drifted to the newer and cleaner teashops opening up around the train station came back to Ramanna's place just to see him. At night, Thimma hugged him several times, and then slipped him two 25-paise coins which Ziauddin accepted silently, sliding them into his trousers. Ramanna shouted to the drunk: 'Don't leave him tips! He's become a thief!'

The boy had been caught stealing samosas meant for a client, Ramanna said. Thimma asked the shopkeeper if he was joking.

'I wouldn't have believed it myself,' Ramanna mumbled. 'But I saw it with my own eyes. He was taking a samosa from the kitchen, and—' Ramanna bit into an imaginary samosa.

6

Gritting his teeth, Ziauddin had begun pushing the fridge into the shop with the back of his legs.

'But…he used to be an honest little fellow…' the drunk recalled.

'Maybe he had been stealing all along and we just never knew it. You can't trust anyone these days.'

The bottles in the fridge rattled. Ziauddin had stopped his work.

'I'm a Pathan!' He slapped his chest. 'From the land of the Pathans, far up north, where there are mountains full of snow! I'm not a Hindu! I don't do hanky-panky!'

Then he walked into the back of the shop.

'What the hell is this?' asked the drunk.

The shopkeeper explained that Ziauddin was now spouting this Pathan-Wathan gibberish all the time; he thought the boy must have picked it up from some mullah in the north of the state.

Thimma roared. He put his hands on his hips and shouted into the back of the shop: 'Ziauddin, Pathans are white-skinned, like Imran Khan; you're as black as an African!'

The next morning there was a storm at the Ideal Store. This time Ziauddin had been caught red-handed. Holding him by the collar of his shirt and dragging him out in front of the customers, Ramanna Shetty said: 'Tell me the truth – you son of a bald woman. Did you steal it? Tell me the truth this time and I might give you another chance.'

'I am telling the truth,' Ziauddin said, touching his pink, vitiligo-discoloured lips with a crooked finger. 'I didn't touch even one of the samosas.'

Ramanna grabbed him by the shoulder and pushed him to the ground, kicked him, and then shoved him out of the teashop, while the other boys huddled together and watched impassively, as sheep do when watching one of their flock being shorn. Then Ramanna howled: he raised one of his fingers, which was bleeding.

'He bit me – the animal!'

'I'm a Pathan!' Ziauddin shouted back, as he rose to his knees. 'We came here and built the Taj Mahal and the Red Fort in Delhi. Don't you dare treat me like this, you son of a bald woman, you—'

Ramanna turned to the ring of customers who had gathered around them, and were staring at him and at Ziauddin, trying to make up their minds as to who was right and who was wrong: 'There is no work here for a Muslim, and he has to fight with the one man who gives him a job.'

A few days later, Ziauddin passed by the teashop, driving a cycle with a cart attached to it; large canisters of milk clanged together in the cart.

'Look at me,' he mocked his former employer. 'The milk people trust me!'

But that job did not last long either; once again he was accused of theft. He publicly swore never to work for a Hindu again.

New Muslim restaurants were being opened at the far side of the railway station, where the Muslim immigrants were settling, and Ziauddin found work in one of these restaurants. He made omelette and toast at an outdoor grill, and shouted in Urdu and Malayalam: 'Muslim men, wherever in the world

8

you are from, Yemen or Kerala or Arabia or Bengal, come eat at a genuine Muslim shop!'

But even this job did not last – he was again charged with theft by his employer, who slapped him when he talked back – and he was next seen in a red uniform at the railway station, carrying mounds of luggage on his head and fighting bitterly with the passengers over his pay.

'I'm the son of a Pathan; I have the blood of a Pathan in me. You hear; I'm no cheat!'

When he glared at them, his eyeballs bulged and the tendons in his neck stood out in high relief. He had become another of those lean, lonely men with vivid eyes who haunt every train station in India, smoking their beedis in a corner and looking ready to hit or kill someone at a moment's notice. Yet when old customers from Ramanna's shop called him by his name, he grinned, and then they saw something of the boy with the big smile who had slammed glasses of tea down on their tables and mangled their English. They wondered what on earth had happened to him.

In the end, Ziauddin picked fights with the other porters, got kicked out of the train station too, and wandered aimlessly for a few days, cursing Hindu and Muslim alike. Then he was back at the station, carrying bags on his head again. He was a good worker; everyone had to concede that much. And there was plenty of work now for everyone. Several trains full of soldiers had arrived in Kittur – there was talk in the market that a new army base was being set up on the route to Cochin – and for days after the soldiers left, freight trains followed in their wake, carrying large crates that needed to be offloaded. Ziauddin shut his mouth, and carried the crates off the train and out of the station, where army trucks were waiting to load them.

One Sunday, he lay on the platform of the station, still asleep at ten in the morning, dead tired from the week's labour. He woke up with his nostrils twitching: the smell of soap was in the air. Rivulets of foam and bubble flowed beside him. A line of thin black bodies were bathing at the edge of the platform.

The fragrance of their foam made Ziauddin sneeze.

'Hey, bathe somewhere else! Leave me alone!'

The men laughed and shouted and pointed their lathered white fingers at Ziauddin: 'We're not all unclean animals, Zia! Some of us are Hindus!'

'I'm a Pathan!' he yelled back at the bathers. 'Don't talk to me like that.'

He began shouting at them when something strange happened – the bathers all rushed away from him, crying: 'A coolie, sir? A coolie?'

A stranger had materialized on the platform, even though no train had pulled up: a tall, fair-skinned man holding a small black bag. He wore a clean white business shirt and grey cotton trousers and everything about him smelled of money; this drove the other porters wild, and they crowded around him, still covered in lather, like men with a horrible disease gathering around a doctor who might have a cure. But he rejected them all and walked up to the only porter who was not covered in lather.

'Which hotel?' Ziauddin asked, struggling to his feet.

The stranger shrugged, as if to say: 'Your choice.' He looked with disapproval at the other porters, who were still hovering around, nearly nude and covered in soap.

After sticking his tongue out at the other porters, Zia set off with the stranger.

The two of them walked towards the cheap hotels that filled the roads around the station. Stopping at a building that was covered in signs – for electrical shops, chemists, pharmacists, plumbers – Ziauddin pointed out a red sign on the second floor.

HOTEL DECENT
BOARDING AND LODGING
ALL FOODS AND SERVICES HERE
NORTH INDIAN SOUTH INDIAN
CHINESE WESTERN TIBETAN DISHES
TAXI PASSPORT VISA XEROX TRUNK CALL
FOR ALL COUNTRIES

'How about this one, sir? It's the best place in town.' He put a hand on his heart. 'I give you my word.'

The Hotel Decent had a good deal with all the railway porters: a 'cut' of two and a half rupees for every customer they brought in.

The stranger lowered his voice confidentially. 'My dear fellow, is it a good place, though?'

He emphasized the critical word by saying it in English.

'Very good,' Zia said with a wink. 'Very, very good.'

The stranger crooked his finger and beckoned Zia closer. He spoke into Zia's ear: 'My dear fellow: I am a Muslim.'

'I know, sir. So am I.'

'Not just any Muslim. I'm a *Pathan*.'

It was as if Ziauddin had heard a magic spell. He gaped at the stranger.

'Forgive me, sir... I...didn't... I... Allah has sent you to exactly the right porter, sir! And this is not the right hotel for you at all, sir. In fact it is a very bad hotel. And this is not the right...'

Tossing the foreign bag from hand to hand, he took the stranger around the station to the other side – where the hotels were Muslim-owned and where 'cuts' were not given to the porters. He stopped at one place and said: 'Will this do?'

HOTEL DARUL-ISLAM
BOARDING AND LOGING

The stranger contemplated the sign, the green archway into the hotel, the image of the Great Mosque of Mecca above the doorway; then he put a hand into a pocket of his grey trousers and brought out a five-rupee note.

'It's too much, sir, for one bag. Just give me two rupees.' Zia bit his lip. 'No, even that is too much.'

The stranger smiled. 'An honest man.'

He tapped two fingers of his left hand on his right shoulder.

'I've got a bad arm, my friend. I wouldn't have been able to carry the bag here without a lot of pain.' He pressed the money into Zia's hands. 'You deserve even more.'

Ziauddin took the money; he looked at the stranger's face.

'Are you really a *Pathan*, sir?'

The boy's body shivered at the stranger's answer.

'Me too!' he shouted, and then ran like crazy, yelling: 'Me too! Me too!'

That night Ziauddin dreamed of snow-covered mountains and a race of fair-skinned, courteous men who tipped like gods. In the morning, he returned to the guest house, and found the stranger on one of the benches outside, sipping from a yellow teacup.

'Will you have tea with me, little Pathan?'

Confused, Ziauddin shook his head, but the stranger was already snapping his fingers. The proprietor, a fat man with a clean-shaven lip and a full, fluffy white beard like a crescent moon, looked unhappily at the filthy porter, before indicating, with a grunt, that he was allowed to sit down at the tables today.

The stranger asked: 'So you're also a Pathan, little friend?'

Ziauddin nodded. He informed the stranger of the name of the man who had told him he was a Pathan. 'He was a learned man, sir: he had been to Saudi Arabia for a year.'

'Ah,' the stranger said, shaking his head. 'Ah, I see. I see now.'

A few minutes passed in silence. Ziauddin said: 'I hope you're not staying here a long time, sir. It's a bad town.'

The Pathan arched his eyebrows.

'For Muslims like us, it's bad. The Hindus don't give us jobs; they don't give us respect. I speak from experience, sir.'

The stranger took out a notebook and began writing. Zia watched. He looked again at the stranger's handsome face, his expensive clothes; he inhaled the scent from his fingers and face. 'This man is a countryman of yours, Zia,' the boy said to himself. 'A countryman of yours!'

The Pathan finished his tea and yawned. As if he had forgotten all about Zia, he went back into his guest house and shut the door behind him.

As soon as his foreign guest had disappeared into the guest house, the owner of the place caught Ziauddin's eye and jerked his head, and the dirty coolie knew that his tea was not coming. He went back to the train station, where he stood in his usual spot and waited for a passenger to approach him with steel trunks or leather bags to be carried to the train. But his soul was shining with pride, and he fought with no one that day.

The following morning, he woke up to the smell of fresh laundry. 'A Pathan always rises at dawn, my friend.'

Yawning and stretching himself, Ziauddin opened his eyes: a pair of beautiful pale blue eyes was looking down on him: eyes such as a man might get when he gazes on snow for a long time. Stumbling to his feet, Ziauddin apologized to the stranger, then shook his hand and almost kissed his face.

'Have you had something to eat?' the Pathan asked.

Zia shook his head; he never ate before noon.

The Pathan took him to one of the tea-and-samosa stands near the station. It was a place where Zia had once worked, and the boys watched in astonishment as he sat down at the table and cried: 'A plate of your best! Two Pathans need to be fed this morning!'

The stranger leaned over to him and said: 'Don't say it aloud. They shouldn't know about us: it's our *secret*.'

And then he quickly passed a note into Zia's hands.

Uncrumpling the note, the boy saw a tractor and a rising red sun. Five rupees!

'You want me to take your bag all the way to Bombay? That's how far this note goes in Kittur.'

He leaned back in his chair as a serving-boy put down two cups of tea, and a plate holding a large samosa, sliced into two and covered with watery ketchup, in front of them. The Pathan and Zia each chewed on his half of the samosa. Then the man picked a piece of the samosa from his teeth and told Ziauddin what he expected for his five rupees.

Half an hour later, Zia sat down at a corner of the train station, outside the waiting room. When customers asked him to carry their luggage, he shook his head and said: 'I've got another job today.' When the trains came into the station, he counted them. But since it was not easy to remember the total, he moved further away and sat under the shade of a tree that grew within the station; each time an engine whistled past he made a mark in the mud with his big toe, crossing off each batch of five. Some of the trains were packed; some had entire carriages full of soldiers with guns; and some were almost entirely empty. He wondered where they were going to, all these trains, all these people...he shut his eyes and began to doze; the engine of a train startled him, and he scraped another mark with his big toe. When he got up to his feet to go for lunch, he realized he had been sitting on some part of the markings and they had been smudged under his weight; and then he had to try desperately to decipher them.

In the evening, he saw the Pathan sitting on one of the benches outside the guest house, sipping tea. The big man smiled when he saw Ziauddin and slapped a spot on the bench next to him three times.

'They didn't give me tea yesterday evening,' Ziauddin complained, and he explained what had happened. The Pathan's face darkened; Ziauddin saw that the stranger was righteous. He was also powerful: without saying a word he turned to the proprietor and glowered at him; within a minute a boy came running out of the hotel holding a yellow cup and put it down in front of Zia. He inhaled the flavours of cardamom and sweet steaming milk, and said: 'Seventeen trains came into Kittur. And sixteen left Kittur. I counted every one of them just like you asked.'

'Good,' the Pathan said. 'Now tell me: how many of these trains had Indian soldiers in them?'

Ziauddin stared.

'How-many-of-them-had-Indian-soldiers-in-them?'

'All of them had soldiers... I don't know...'

'Six trains had Indian soldiers in them,' the Pathan said. 'Four going to Cochin, two coming back.'

The next day, Ziauddin sat down at the tree in the corner of the station half an hour before the first train pulled in. He marked the earth with his big toe; between trains he went to the snack-shop inside the station.

'You can't come here!' the shopkeeper shouted. 'We don't want any trouble again!'

'You won't have any trouble from me,' Zia said. 'I've got money on me today.' He placed a one-rupee note on the table. 'Put that note into your money-box and then give me a chicken samosa.'

That evening Zia reported to the Pathan that eleven trains had arrived with soldiers.

'Well done,' said the man.

The Pathan, reaching out with his weak arm, exerted a little pressure on each of Ziauddin's cheeks. He produced another five-rupee note, which the boy accepted without hesitation.

'Tomorrow I want you to notice how many of the trains had a red cross marked on the sides of the compartments.'

Ziauddin closed his eyes and repeated: 'Red cross marked on sides.' He jumped to his feet, gave a military salute, and said: *'Thanks you, sir!'*

The Pathan laughed; a warm, hearty, foreign laugh.

The next day, Ziauddin sat under the tree once again, scrawling numbers in three rows with his toe. One, number of trains. Two, number of trains with soldiers in them. Three, number of trains marked with red crosses.

Sixteen, eleven, eight.

Another train passed by; Zia looked up, squinted, then moved his toe into position over the first of the three rows.

He held his toe like that, in mid-air, for an instant, and then let it fall to the ground, taking care that it not smudge any of the markings. The train left, and immediately behind it another one pulled into the station, full of soldiers, but Ziauddin did not add to his tally. He simply stared at the scratches he had already made, as if he had seen something new in them.

The Pathan was at the guest house when Ziauddin got there at four. The tall man's hands were behind his back, and he had been pacing around the benches. He came to the boy with quick steps.

'Did you get the number?'

Ziauddin nodded.

But when the two of them had sat down, he asked: 'What're you making me do these things for?'

The Pathan leaned all the way across the table with his weak arm and tried to touch Ziauddin's hair.

'At last you ask. At last.' He smiled.

The guest house proprietor with the beard like the moon came out without prompting; he put two cups of tea down on the table, then stepped back and rubbed his palms and smiled. The Pathan dismissed him with a movement of his head. He sipped his tea; Ziauddin did not touch his.

'Do you know where those trains full of soldiers and marked with red crosses are going?'

Ziauddin shook his head.

'Towards Calicut.'

The stranger brought his face closer. The boy saw things he had not seen before: scars on the Pathan's nose and cheeks, and a small tear in his left ear.

'The Indian army is setting up a base somewhere between Kittur and Calicut. For one reason and one reason only...' – he held up a thick finger. 'To do to the Muslims of South India what they are doing to Muslims in Kashmir.'

Ziauddin looked down at the tea. A rippled skin of milk-fat was congealing on its surface.

'I'm a Muslim,' he said. 'The son of a Muslim too.'

'Exactly. Exactly.' The foreigner's thick fingers covered the surface of the teacup. 'Now listen: each time you watch the trains, there will be a little reward for you. Mind – it won't always be five rupees, but it will be something. A Pathan takes care of other Pathans. It's simple work. I am here to do the hard work. You'll–'

Ziauddin said: 'I'm not well. I can't do it tomorrow.'

The foreigner thought about this, and then said: 'You are lying to me. May I ask why?'

A finger passed over a pair of vitiligo-discoloured lips. 'I'm a Muslim. The son of a Muslim, too.'

'There are fifty thousand Muslims in this town.' The foreigner's voice crackled with irritation. 'Every one of them seethes. Every one of them is ready for action. I was only offering this job to you out of pity. Because I see what the Indians have done you. Otherwise I would have offered the job to any of these other fifty thousand fellows.'

Ziauddin kicked back his chair and stood up.

'Then get one of those fifty thousand fellows to do it.'

Outside the compound of the guest house, he turned around. The Pathan was looking at him; he spoke in a soft voice.

'Is this any way to repay me, little Pathan?'

Ziauddin said nothing. He looked down at the ground. His big toe slowly scratched a figure into the earth: a large circle. He sucked in fresh air and released a hoarse, wordless hiss.

Then he ran. He ran out of the hotel, ran around the train station to the Hindu side, ran all the way to Ramanna Shetty's teashop, and then ran around the back of the shop and into the blue tent where the boys lived. There he sat with his mottled lips pressed together and his fingers laced tightly around his knees.

'What's got into you?' the other boys asked. 'You can't stay here, you know. Shetty will throw you out.' They hid him there that night for old times' sake. When they woke up he was gone. Later in the day he was once again seen at the railway station, fighting with his customers and shouting at them:

'—*don't* do hanky-panky!'

HOW THE TOWN IS LAID OUT

In the geographical centre of Kittur stands the peeling stucco façade of Angel Talkies, a pornographic cinema theatre; regrettably, when the townsfolk give directions, they use Angel Talkies as a reference point. The cinema lies halfway down Umbrella Street, the heart of the commercial district. A significant chunk of Kittur's economy consists of the manufacture of hand-rolled beedis; no wonder, then, that the tallest building in town is the Engineer Beedi Building on Umbrella Street, owned by Mabroor Engineer, reputed to be the town's richest man. Not far from it lies Kittur's most famous ice-cream shop, The Ideal Traders Ice Cream and Fresh Fruit Juice Parlour; White Stallion Talkies, the town's only exclusively English-language film theatre, is another nearby attraction. Ming Palace, the first Chinese restaurant in Kittur, opened on Umbrella Street in 1986. The Ganapati Temple in this street is modelled on a famous temple in Goa and is the site of an annual pooja to the elephant-headed deity. Continue on Umbrella Street north of Angel Talkies and you will reach, via the Nehru Maidan and the train station, the Roman Catholic suburb of Valencia, whose main landmark is the Cathedral of Our Lady of Valencia. The Double Gate, a colonial-era arched gateway at the far end of Valencia, leads into Bajpe, once a forest, but today a fast-expanding suburb. To the south of Angel Talkies, the road goes uphill into the Lighthouse Hill, and down to the Cool Water Well. From a busy junction near the Well begins the road that leads to the Bunder, or the area around the port. Further south from the Bunder may be seen Sultan's Battery, a black fort, which overlooks the road that leads out over the Kaliamma river into Salt Market Village, the southernmost extension of Kittur.

Day One (Afternoon): THE BUNDER

You have walked down the Cool Water Well Road, past Masjid Road, and you have begun to smell the salt in the air and note the profusion of open-air fish stalls, full of prawns, mussels, shrimps and oysters; you are now not far from the Arabian Sea.

The Bunder, or the area around the port, is now mostly Muslim. The major landmark here is the Dargah, or tomb-shrine, of Yusuf Ali, a domed white structure to which thousands of Muslims from across southern India make pilgrimage each year. The ancient banyan tree growing behind the saint's tomb is always festooned in ribbons of green and gold and is believed to have the power to cure the crippled. Dozens of lepers, amputees, geriatrics, and victims of partial paralysis squat outside the shrine begging alms from visitors.

If you walk to the other end of the Bunder, you will find the industrial area, where dozens of textile sweatshops operate in dingy old buildings. The Bunder has the highest crime rate in Kittur, and is the scene of frequent stabbings, police raids, and arrests. In 1987, riots broke out between Hindus and Muslims near the Dargah, and the police shut down the Bunder area for six days. The Hindus have since been moving out to Bajpe and Salt Market Village.

Abbasi uncorked the bottle – Johnnie Walker Red Label blended, the second-finest whisky known to God or man – and poured a small peg each into two glasses embossed with the Air India *maharajah* logo. He opened the old fridge, took out a bucket of ice, and dropped three cubes by hand into each glass. He poured cold water into the glasses, found a spoon and stirred. He bent his head low and prepared to spit into one of the glasses.

Oh, too simple, Abbasi. Too simple.

He swallowed spittle. Unzipping his cotton trousers, he let them slide down. Pressing the middle and index fingers of his right hand together, he stuck them deep into his rectum; then he dipped them into one of the glasses of whisky and stirred.

He pulled up his trousers and zipped them. He frowned at the tainted whisky; now came the tricky part – things had to be arranged so that the right man took the right glass.

He left the pantry carrying the tray.

The official from the State Electricity Board, sitting at Abbasi's table, grinned. He was a fat, dark man in a blue safari suit, a steel ballpoint pen in his jacket pocket. Abbasi carefully placed the tray on the table in front of the gentleman.

'Please,' Abbasi said, with redundant hospitality; the official had taken the glass closer to him, and was sipping and licking his lips. He finished the whisky in slow gulps, and put the glass down.

'A man's drink.'

Abbasi smiled ironically.

The official placed his hands on his tummy.

'Five hundred,' he said. 'Five hundred rupees.'

Abbasi was a small man, with a streak of grey in his beard which he did not attempt to disguise with dye, as many middle-aged men in Kittur did; he thought the white streak gave him a look of ingenuity, which he felt he needed, because he knew that his reputation among his friends was that of a simple-minded creature prone to regular outbreaks of idealism.

His ancestors, who had served in the royal darbars of Hyderabad, had bequeathed him an elaborate sense of courtesy and good manners, which he had adapted for the realities of the twentieth century with touches of sarcasm and self-parody.

He folded his palms into a Hindu's namaste and bowed low before the official. 'Sahib, you know we have just reopened the factory. There have been many costs. If you could show some—'

'Five hundred. Five hundred rupees.'

The official twirled his glass around and gazed at the Air India logo with one eye, as if some small part of him were embarrassed by what he was doing. He gestured at his mouth with his fingers: 'A man has to eat these days, Mr Abbasi. Prices are rising so fast. Ever since Mrs Gandhi died, this country has begun to fall apart.'

Abbasi closed his eyes. He reached towards his desk, pulled out a drawer, took out a wad of notes, counted them, and placed the money in front of the official. The fat man, moistening his finger for each note, counted them one by one; producing a blue rubber band from a pocket of his trousers, he strapped it around the notes twice.

But Abbasi knew the ordeal was not over yet. 'Sahib, we

have a tradition in this factory that we never let a guest depart without a gift.'

He rang the bell for Ummar, his manager, who entered almost at once with a shirt in his hands. He had been waiting outside the whole time.

The official took the white shirt out of its cardboard box: he looked at the design: a golden dragon whose tail spread round onto the back of the shirt.

'It's gorgeous.'

'We ship them to the United States. They are worn by men who dance professionally. They call it "ballroom dancing". They put on this shirt and swirl under red disco lights.' Abbasi held his hands over his head, and spun round, shaking his hips and buttocks suggestively; the official watched him with lascivious eyes.

He clapped and said: 'Dance for me one more time, Abbasi.'

Then he put the shirt to his nose and sniffed it three times.

'This pattern' – he pressed on the outlines of the dragon with his thick finger – 'it is wonderful.'

'That dragon is the reason I closed,' Abbasi said. 'To stitch the dragon takes very fine embroidery work. The eyes of the women doing this work get damaged. One day this was brought to my attention; I thought, I don't want to answer to Allah for the damage done to the eyes of my workers. So I said to them, go home, and I closed the factory.'

The official smiled ironically. Another of those Muslims who drink whisky and mention Allah in every other sentence.

He put the shirt back in its box and tucked it under his arm. 'What made you reopen the factory, then?'

Abbasi bunched his fingers and jabbed them into his mouth. 'A man has to eat, sahib.'

They went down the stairs together, Ummar following three steps behind. When they reached the bottom, the official saw a dark opening to his right. He took a step towards the darkness. In the dim light of the room, he saw women with white shirts on their laps, stitching threads into half-finished dragons. He wanted to see more, but Abbasi said: 'Why don't you go in, sahib. I'll wait out here.'

He turned and looked at the wall, while Ummar took the official around the factory floor, introduced him to some of the workers, and led him back out. The official extended his hand to Abbasi just before he left.

I shouldn't have touched him, Abbasi thought, the moment he closed the door.

At 6 p.m., half an hour after the women left the stitching room for the day, Abbasi closed the factory, got into his Ambassador car, and drove from the Bunder towards Kittur; he could think about one thing only.

Corruption. There is no end to it in this country. In the past four months, since he had decided to reopen his shirt factory, he had had to pay off:

The electricity man; the water board man; half the income tax department of Kittur; half the excise department of Kittur; six different officials of the telephone board; a land tax official of the Kittur City Corporation; a sanitary inspector from the Karnataka State Health Board; a health inspector from the Karnataka State Sanitation Board; a delegation of the All India Small Factory Workers' Union; delegations of the Kittur

Congress party, the Kittur BJP, the Kittur Communist Party, and the Kittur Muslim League.

The white Ambassador car went up the driveway of a large, whitewashed mansion. At least four evenings a week Abbasi came to the Canara Club, to a small air-conditioned room with a green billiards table, to play snooker and drink with his friends. He was a good shot, and his aim deteriorated after his second whisky, so his friends liked to play long sets with him.

'What's bothering you, Abbasi?' asked Sunil Shetty, who owned another shirt factory in the Bunder. 'You're playing very rashly tonight.'

'Another visit from the electricity department. A real bastard this time. Dark-skinned fellow. Lower-caste of some kind.'

Sunil Shetty purred in sympathy; Abbasi missed his shot.

Halfway through the game, the players all moved away from the table, while a mouse scurried across the floor, running along the walls until it found a hole to vanish into.

Abbasi banged his fist on the edge of the table.

'Where does all our membership money go? They can't even keep the floors clean! You see how corrupt the management of the club is?'

After that, he sat quietly with his back to the sign that said 'RULES OF THE GAMES MUST BE FOLLOWED AT ALL TIMES' and watched the others play, while resting his chin on the end of his cue stick.

'You are tense, Abbasi,' said Ramanna Padiwal, who owned a silk-and-rayon store on Umbrella Street and was the best snooker-shark in town.

To dispel this myth, Abbasi ordered whiskies for everyone,

and they stopped playing and held their glasses wrapped in paper napkins as they sipped. As always, what they talked about first was the whisky itself.

'You know that chap who goes around from house to house offering to pay twenty rupees if you sell him your old cartons of Johnnie Walker Red Label,' Abbasi said. 'To whom does he sell those cartons in turn?'

The others laughed.

'For a Muslim, you're a real innocent, Abbasi,' Padiwal, the used-car salesman, said with a laugh. 'Of course he sells them to the bootlegger. That's why the Johnnie Walker Red you buy from the store, even if it comes in a genuine bottle and genuine carton, is bootlegged.'

Abbasi spoke slowly, drawing circles in the air with his finger: 'So I sold the carton...to the man who will sell it to the man who will bootleg the stuff and sell it back to me? That means I've cheated myself?'

Padiwal shot a look of wonderment at Sunil Shetty and said: 'For a Muslim, this fellow is a real...'

This was a sentiment that was widespread among the industrialists – ever since Abbasi had shut down his factory because the work was damaging the eyesight of his employees. Most of the snooker-players owned, or had invested in, factories that employed women in the same manner; none had dreamed of closing a factory down because a woman here or a woman there went blind.

Sunil Shetty said: 'The other day I read in the *Times of India* that the chief of Johnnie Walker said, there is more Red Label consumed in the average small Indian town than is produced in all of Scotland. When it comes to three things' – he counted them off – 'black-marketing, counterfeiting, and corruption, we are the world champions. If they were included in the Olympic Games, India would always win gold, silver, and bronze in those three.'

After midnight, Abbasi staggered out of the club, leaving a coin with the guard who got up from his chair to salute him and help him into his car.

Drunk by now, he raced out of the town and up to the Bunder, finally slowing down when the smell of sea breeze got to him.

Stopping by the side of the road when his house came into view, he decided he needed one more drink. He always kept a small bottle of whisky under his seat, where his wife would not find it; reaching down, he slapped his hand around the floor of the car. His head banged against the dashboard. He found the bottle, and a glass.

After the drink, he realized he couldn't go home; his wife would smell the liquor on him the moment he got past the threshold. There would be another scene. She never could understand why he drank so much.

He drove up to the Bunder. He parked the car next to a rubbish dump and walked across to a teashop. Beyond a small beach the sea was visible; the smell of roasted fish wafted through the air.

A blackboard outside the teashop proclaimed, in letters of white chalk: 'WE CHANGE PAKISTANI MONEY AND CURRENCY'. The walls of the shop were adorned with a photograph of the Great Mosque of Mecca along with a poster of a boy and a girl bowing to the Taj Mahal. Four benches had been arranged in an outdoor verandah. A dappled white-and-brown goat was tied to a pole at one end of the verandah; it was chewing on dried grass.

Men were sitting on one of the benches. Abbasi touched one of the men on his shoulder; he turned around.

'Abbasi.'

'Mehmood, my brother. Make some room for me.'

Mehmood, a fat man with a fringe beard and no moustache, did so, and Abbasi squeezed in next to him. Abbasi had heard that Mehmood stole cars; he had heard that Mehmood's four sons drove them to a village on the Tamil Nadu border, a village whose only business was the purchase and sale of stolen cars.

Alongside Mehmood, Abbasi recognized Kalam, who was rumoured to import hashish from Bombay and ship it to Sri Lanka; Saif, who had knifed a man in Trivandrum; and a small, white-haired man who was only called the Professor – and who was believed to be the shadiest of the lot.

These men were smugglers, car thieves, thugs, and worse; but while they sipped tea together, nothing would happen to Abbasi. It was the culture of the Bunder. A man might be stabbed in daylight, but never at night, and never while sipping tea. In any case, the sense of solidarity among the Muslims at the Bunder had deepened ever since the riots.

The Professor was finishing up a story of Kittur in the twelfth century, about an Arab sailor named bin Saad who sighted the town, just when he had given up hope of finding land. He had raised his hands to Allah and promised that if he arrived safely on land, he would never again drink liquor or gamble.

'Did he keep his word?'

The Professor winked. 'Take a guess.'

The Professor was always welcome at late-night chit-chats at the teashop because he knew many fascinating things about the port; how its history went back to the Middle Ages, for instance, or how Tippu Sultan had once installed a battery of French-made cannon here to scare away the British. He pointed a finger at Abbasi: 'You're not your usual self. What's on your mind?'

'Corruption,' Abbasi said. 'Corruption. It's like a demon sitting on my brain and eating it with a fork and knife.'

The others drew closer to listen. Abbasi was a rich man; he must have an intimacy with corruption that exceeded theirs. He told them about the morning.

Kalam, the drug-dealer, smiled and said: 'That's nothing, Abbasi.' He gestured towards the sea. 'I have a ship, half full of cement and half full of something else, that has been waiting two hundred metres out at sea for a month. Why? Because this inspector at the port is squeezing me. I pay him and he wants to squeeze me even more, too much more. So the ship is just drifting out there, half full of cement and half full of something else.'

'I thought things would get better with this young fellow Rajiv taking over the country,' Abbasi said. 'But he's let us all down. As bad as any other politician.'

'We need one man to stand up to them,' the Professor said. 'Just one honest, brave man. That fellow would do more for this country than Gandhi or Nehru did.'

The remark was greeted by a chorus of agreement.

'Yes,' Abbasi agreed, stroking his beard. 'And the next morning he would be floating in the Kaliamma river. Like this.'

He mimicked a corpse.

There was general agreement over this too. But even as the words left his mouth, Abbasi was already thinking: is it really true? Is there nothing we can do to fight back?

Tucked into the Professor's trousers, he saw the glint of a knife. The effect of the whisky was wearing off, but it had carried him to a strange place, and his mind was filling up with strange thoughts.

Another round of tea was ordered by the car thief, but Abbasi, yawning, crossed his hands in front of him and shook his head.

The next day, he turned up to work at ten-forty, his head throbbing with pain.

Ummar opened the door for him. Abbasi nodded and took the mail from him. With his head down to the floor, he moved to the stairs that led up to his office; then he stopped. At the threshold of the door that led to the factory floor, one of the stitching women was standing staring at him.

'I'm not paying you to waste time,' he snapped.

She turned and fled. He hurried up the stairs.

He put on his glasses, read the mail, read the newspaper, yawned, drank tea, and opened a ledger bearing the logo of the Karnataka Bank; he went down a list of customers who had paid and not paid. He kept thinking of the previous evening's game of snooker.

The door creaked open; Ummar's face popped in.

'What?'

'They're here.'

'Who?'

'The government.'

Two men in polyester shirts and ironed blue bell-bottoms pushed Ummar aside and walked in. One of them, a burly fellow with a big pot belly and a moustache like that of a wrestler in a village fair, said: 'Income Tax Department.'

Abbasi got up. 'Ummar! Don't just stand there! Get one of the women to run and bring tea from the teashop by the sea. And some of those round Bombay biscuits as well.'

The big taxman sat down at the table without being invited. His companion, a lean fellow with arms tied together, hesitated in a fidgety kind of way, until the other gestured him to sit down too.

Abbasi smiled. The taxman with the moustache talked.

'We have just walked around your factory floor. We have just seen the women who work for you, and the quality of the shirts they stitch.'

Abbasi smiled and waited for it.

It came quickly this time.

'We think you are making a lot more money than you have declared to us.'

Abbasi's heart beat hard; he told himself to calm down. There is always a way out.

'A lot, lot, lot more.'

'Sahib, sahib,' Abbasi said, patting the air with conciliatory gestures. 'We have a custom in this shop. Everyone who comes

34

in will receive a gift before they leave.' Ummar, who knew already what he had to do, was waiting outside the office with two shirts. With a fawning smile, he presented them to the two tax officers. They accept the bribes without a word, the lean fellow looking to the big one for approval before snatching his gift.

Abbasi asked: 'What else can I do for you two sahibs?'

The one with the moustache smiled. His partner also smiled. The one with the moustache held up three fingers.

'Each.'

Three hundred per head was too low; real pros from the income tax office wouldn't have settled for anything under five hundred. Abbasi guessed that the two men were doing this for the first time. In the end, they would settle for a hundred each, plus the shirts.

'Let me offer you a little boost first. Do the sahibs take Red Label?'

The fidgety fellow almost jumped out of his seat in excitement, but the big one glared at him.

'Red Label would be acceptable.'

They've probably never been offered anything better than hooch, Abbasi realized.

He walked into the pantry, took out the bottle. He poured into three glasses with the Air India *maharajah* logo. He opened the fridge. He dropped two ice cubes into each glass and added a thin stream of ice water from a bottle. He spat in two of the glasses and arranged them furthest away on the tray.

The thought fell into his mind like a meteor from a purer heaven. No. Slowly it spread itself across his mind. No, he could not give this whisky to these men. It might be counterfeit stuff, sold in cartons bought under false premises, but it was still a thousand times too pure to be touched by their lips.

He drank one whisky, and then the second, and then the third.

Ten minutes later, he came back into the room with heavy steps. He bolted the door behind him, and let his body fall heavily against it.

The big taxman turned sharply: 'Why are you closing the door?'

'Sahibs. This is the port city of the Bunder, which has ancient traditions and customs, dating back centuries and centuries. Any man is free to come here of his own will, but he can only leave with the permission of the locals.'

Whistling, Abbasi walked to his desk and picked up the phone; he shoved it, like a weapon, right in the face of the bigger taxman.

'Shall I call the income tax office right now? Shall I find out if you have been authorized to come? Shall I?'

They looked uncomfortable. The lean man was sweating. Abbasi thought: my guess is right. They are doing this for the first time.

'Look at your hands. You have accepted shirts from me, which are bribes. You are holding the evidence in your hands.'

'Look here—'

'No! You look here!' Abbasi shouted. 'You are not going to leave these premises alive, until you sign a confession of what you were trying to do. Let us see how you get out. This is the port city. I have friends in all four directions. You will both be dead and floating in the Kaliamma river if I snap my fingers now. Do you doubt me?'

The big taxman looked at the ground, while the other fellow produced an extraordinary amount of sweat.

Abbasi unbolted the door and held it open. 'Get out.' Then, with a wide smile, he bowed down to them: 'Sahibs.'

The two men scurried out without a word. He heard the thump of their feet on the staircase; and then a cry of surprise from Ummar, who was walking up the stairs with a tray of tea and Britannia biscuits.

He let his head rest on the cool wood of the table and wondered what he had done. Any moment soon, he was expecting that the electricity would be cut off; the income tax officials would return, with more men and an arrest warrant.

He walked round and round the room, thinking: what is happening to me? Ummar stared at him silently.

After an hour, to Abbasi's surprise, there had been no call from the income tax office. The fans were still working. The light was still on.

Abbasi began to hope. These guys were raw – tyros. Maybe they'd just gone back to the office and got on with their work. Even if they had complained, the government officials had been wary of the Bunder ever since the riots; it was possible they would not want to antagonize a Muslim businessman at this point. He looked out of the window at the Bunder: this violent, rotten, garbage-strewn port, crawling with pickpockets and knife-carrying thugs – it seemed the only place where a man was safe from the corruption of Kittur.

'Ummar!' He shouted. 'I'm leaving early today for the club

– give Sunil Shetty a call to say that he should come today too. I have great news for him! I beat the income tax office!'

He came running down the stairs and stopped at the last step. To his right, the doorway opened onto the factory floor. In the six weeks since his factory had reopened, he had not once gone through this doorway; Ummar had handled the affairs of the factory floor. But now the doorway to his right, black and yawning, had become inescapable.

He felt he had no option but to go in. He realized now that the morning's events had all been, somehow, a trap: to bring him to this place, to make him do what he had avoided doing since reopening his factory.

The women were sitting on the floor of the dimly lit room, pale fluorescent lights flickering overhead, each at a work station indicated by a numeral in red letters painted on the wall. They held the white shirts close to their eyes and stitched gold thread into them; they stopped when he came in. He flicked his wrist, indicating that they should keep working. He didn't want their eyes looking at him: those eyes that were being damaged, as their fingers created golden shirts that he could sell to American ballroom dancers.

Damaged? No, that was not the right word. That was not the reason he had shunted them into a side room.

Everyone in that room was going blind.

He sat down on a chair in the centre of the room.

The optometrist had been clear about that; the kind of detailed stitchwork needed for the shirts scarred the women's retinas. He had used his fingers to show Abbasi how thick the scars were. No amount of improved lighting would reduce the impact on the retinas. Human eyes were not meant to stare for hours at designs this intricate. Two women had already gone blind; that was why he had shut down the factory. When he reopened, all his old workers came back at once. They knew their fate; but there was no other work to be had.

Abbasi closed his eyes. He wanted nothing more than for Ummar to shout that he was urgently needed upstairs.

But no one came to release him and he sat in the chair, while the women around him stitched, and their stitching fingers kept talking to him: we are going blind; look at us!

'Does your head hurt, sahib?' a woman's voice was asking him. 'Do you want me to get you some Disprin and water?'

Unable to look at her, Abbasi said: 'All of you please go home. Come back tomorrow. But please go home today. You'll all be paid.'

'Is sahib unhappy with us for some reason?'

'No, please. Go home now. You'll all be paid for the whole day. Come back tomorrow.'

He heard the rustle of their feet and he knew, they must be gone now.

They had left their shirts at their work stations and he picked one up; the dragon was half-stitched. He kneaded the cloth between his fingers. He could feel, between his fingers, the finespun fabric of corruption.

'The factory is closed,' he wanted to shout out to the dragon. 'There – you happy with me? The factory is closed.'

And after that? Who would send his son to school? Would he sit by the docks with a knife and smuggle cars like Mehmood? The women would go elsewhere, and do the same work.

He slapped his hand against his thigh.

Thousands, sitting in teashops and universities and workplaces every day and every night, were cursing corruption. Yet not one fellow had found a way to slay the demon without giving up his share of the loot of corruption. So why did he – an ordinary businessman given to whisky and snooker and listening to gossip from thugs – have to come up with an answer?

But just a moment later, he realized he already had an answer.

He offered Allah a compromise. He would be taken to jail, but his factory would go on with its work: he closed his eyes and prayed to his God to accept this deal.

But an hour passed and still no one had come to arrest him.

Abbasi opened a window in his office. He could see only buildings, a congested road, and old walls. He opened all the windows, but still he saw nothing but walls. He climbed up to the roof of his building and ducked under a clothesline to walk out onto the terrace. Coming to the edge, he placed a foot on the tiled roof that protruded over the front of his shop.

From here, a man could see the limits of Kittur. At the very edge of the town, one after the other, stood a minaret, a church steeple, and a temple tower, like signposts to identify the three religions of the town to voyagers from the ocean.

Abbasi saw the Arabian Sea stretching away from Kittur. The sun was shining over it. A ship was slowly leaving the Bunder, edging to where the blue waters of the sea changed colour and turned a deeper hue. It was about to hit a large patch of brilliant sunshine, an oasis of pure light.

Day Two (Morning): LIGHTHOUSE HILL

After a lunch of prawn curry and rice at the Bunder, you may want to visit the Lighthouse Hill and its vicinity. The famous lighthouse, built by the Portuguese and renovated by the British, is no longer in use. An old guard in a blue uniform sits at the foot of the lighthouse. If visitors are poorly dressed, or speak to him in Tulu or Kannada, he will say: 'Can't you see it's closed?' If visitors are well-dressed or speak English, he will say: 'Welcome.' He will take them into the lighthouse and up the spiral staircase to the top, which affords a spectacular view of the Arabian Sea. In recent years, the Corporation has begun running a reading room inside the lighthouse; the collection includes Father Basil d'Essa, S.J.'s *Short History of Kittur*. The Deshpremi Hemachandra Rao Park around the lighthouse is named in honour of the freedom-fighter who hung a Congress tricolour from the lighthouse during British rule.

It happens at least twice a year. The prisoner, handcuffs on his wrists, is striding towards the Lighthouse Hill police station with his head held high and a look of insolent boredom on his face; whilst following him, almost scampering to catch up, are the two policemen holding a chain attached to the handcuffs. The odd part is that the man in handcuffs seems to be dragging along the policemen, like a fellow taking two monkeys out for a walk.

In the past nine years, the man known as 'Xerox' Ramakrishna has been arrested twenty-one times on the granite pavement in front of Deshpremi Hemachandra Rao Park for the sale, at discounted rates, of illegally photocopied or printed books to the students of St Alfonso's college. A policeman comes in the morning, when Ramakrishna is sitting with his books spread out on a blue bedsheet; he places his lathi on the books and says: 'Let's go, Xerox.'

The bookseller turns to his eleven-year-old daughter, Ritu, who sells books with him, and says: 'Go home and be a good girl, dear.' Then he holds his hands out for the cuffs.

In jail, Xerox is unchained and put in a cell. Holding on to the bars, he regales the policemen with ingratiating stories. He may tell them a smutty tale about some college girl whom he saw that morning wearing blue jeans in the American style, or a new swear-word in Tulu he has heard on the bus while going to Salt Market Village, or perhaps, if they are in the mood for longer entertainment, he will narrate to them, as he has done so many times before, the story of what his father did for a living all his life – taking the crap out of the houses of rich landlords, the traditional occupation of people of his caste. All day long, his old man would hang around the back wall of the landlord's house, waiting for the smell of human shit; as soon as he smelled that smell, he came up to the house and waited, with bent knees, like a wicket-keeper waits for the ball. (Xerox bent his knees and showed how.) Then, as soon as he heard the 'thud' of the boom-box being shut, he had to pull out the chamber pot through a hole in the wall, empty it into the rose-bushes, wipe it clean with his loincloth and insert it back before the next person came to use the toilet. That was the job he did his whole life, can you believe it!

The jailers will laugh.

They bring Xerox samosas wrapped in paper, they offer him chai. They consider him a decent fellow. They let him out at midday; he bows low to them and says: 'Thank you.' Then Miguel D'Souza, the lawyer for the publishers and booksellers on Umbrella Street, will call the station and yell: 'Have you let him off again? Doesn't the law of the land mean anything to you?' The inspector of the station, Ramesh, keeps the receiver at a distance from his ear and reads the newspaper, looking at the Bombay stock-market quotes. That is all Ramesh really wants to do in life: read the stock-market quotes.

By late afternoon, Xerox is back at it. Photocopied or cheaply printed copies of Karl Marx, *Mein Kampf*, published books – and films and albums – and others, are arranged on the blue cloth spread out on the pavement on Lighthouse Hill, and little Ritu sits stiff-backed, with her long unbroken nose and faint moustache, watching as the customers pick up the books and flip through them.

'Put that back in place,' she will say, when a customer has

rejected a book. 'Put it back exactly where you picked it up from.'

'*Accounting for Entrance Exams*?' one customer shouts at Xerox. '*Advanced Obstetrics*?' cries another.

'*The Joy of Sex*?'

'*Mein Kampf*?'

'Lee Iacocca?'

'What's your best price?' a young man asks, flipping through the book.

'Seventy five rupees.'

'O, you're *raping* me! It's too much.'

The young man walks away, turns around, comes back, and says, 'What's your final best price, I have no time to waste.'

'Seventy two rupees. Take it or leave it. I've got other customers.'

The books are photocopied, or sometimes printed, at an old printing press in Salt Market Village. Xerox loves being around the machinery. He strokes the photocopier; he adores the machine, the way it flashes like lightning as it works, the way it whirrs and hums. He cannot read English, but he knows that English words have power, and that English books have aura. He looks at the image of Adolf Hitler from the cover of *Mein Kampf* and he feels his power. He looks at the face of Kahlil Gibran, poetic and mysterious, and he feels the mystery and poetry. He looks at the face of Lee Iacocca, relaxed with his hands behind his head, and he feels relaxed. That's why he once told Inspector Ramesh: 'I have no wish to make any trouble for you or for the publishers, sir; I just love books: I love making them, holding them and selling them. My father took out shit for a living, sir: he couldn't even read or write. He'd be so proud if he could see that I make my living from books.'

Only one time has Xerox really been in trouble with the police. That was when someone called the station and said that Xerox was selling copies of Salman Rushdie's *The Satanic Verses* in violation of the laws of the Republic of India. This time when he was brought to the station in handcuffs there were no courtesies, no cups of chai.

Ramesh slapped him.

'Don't you know, the book is banned, you son of a bald woman? You think you are going to start a riot among the Muslims? And get me and every other policeman here transferred to Salt Market Village?'

'Forgive me,' Xerox begged. 'I had no idea that this was a banned book, really... I'm just the son of a man who took out shit, sir. He waited all day long for the boom-box to make a noise. I know my place, sir. I wouldn't dream of challenging you. It was just a mistake, sir. Forgive me, sir.'

D'Souza, the booksellers' lawyer, a small man with black oily hair and a neat moustache, heard what had happened and came to the station. He looked at the banned book – a massive paperback with an image of an angel on the front – and shook his head in disbelief.

'That fucking untouchable's son, thinking he's going to photocopy *The Satanic Verses*. What balls.'

He sat at the inspector's desk and shouted at him: 'I told you this would happen, if you didn't punish him! You're responsible for all this.'

Ramesh glared at Xerox, who was lying penitently on a bed, as he had been ordered to do.

'I don't think anyone saw him selling it. Things will be fine.'

To calm the lawyer down, Ramesh asked a constable to go fetch a bottle of Old Monk rum. The two of them talked for a while.

Ramesh read passages out from the book and said: 'I don't get what the fuss is all about, really.'

'Muslims,' D'Souza said, shaking his head. 'Violent people. Violent.'

The bottle of Old Monk arrived. They drank it in half an hour and the constable went to fetch another. In his cell, Xerox lay perfectly still, looking at the ceiling. The policeman and the lawyer went on drinking. D'Souza told Ramesh his frustrations, and the inspector told the lawyer his frustrations. One had wanted to be a pilot, soaring in the clouds and chasing stewardesses, and the other – he had never wanted anything but to dabble in the stock market. That was all.

At midnight, Ramesh asked the lawyer: 'Do you want to know a secret?' Stealthily, he walked the lawyer to the prison and showed him the secret. One of the bars of the cell could be removed. The policeman removed it, and swung it, and then put it back in place. 'That's how the evidence is hidden,' he said. 'Not that that kind of thing happens often at this station, mind you – but that's how it is done, when it is done.'

The lawyer giggled. He loosened the bar and slung it over his shoulder, and said: 'Don't I look like Hanuman now?'

'Just like on TV,' the policeman said.

The lawyer asked that the cell door be opened, and it was.

The two of them saw the sleeping prisoner lying on his cot, an arm over his face to keep out the jabbing light of the naked bulb above him. A sliver of naked skin was exposed beneath his cheap polyester shirt; a creeper of thick black hair, which looked to his two onlookers like an outgrowth from his groin, was just about visible.

'That fucking son of an untouchable. See him snoring.'

'His father took out the shit – and this fellow thinks he's going to dump shit on us!'

'Selling *The Satanic Verses*. He'll sell it under my nose, will he?'

'These people think they own India now. Don't they? They want all the jobs, and all the university degrees, and all the...'

Ramesh pulled down the snoring man's trousers; he lifted the bar high up, while the lawyer said: 'Do it like Hanuman does, on TV!' Xerox woke up screaming. Ramesh handed the bar to D'Souza. The policeman and the lawyer took turns: he smashed the bar against Xerox's legs, just at the knee-joint, like the monkey god did on TV, and then he smashed the bar against Xerox's legs, just below the knee-joint, like the monkey-god did on TV, and then he smashed it into Xerox's legs, just above the knee-joint, and then, laughing and kissing each other, the two staggered out, shouting for someone to lock the station up behind them.

Periodically through the night, when he woke up, Xerox resumed his screaming.

In the morning, Ramesh came back, was told by a constable about Xerox and said: 'Shit, it wasn't a dream then.' He ordered the constables to take the man in the prison to the

Havelock Henry General Hospital, and asked for a copy of the morning paper, so he could check the stock-market prices.

The next week, Xerox arrived, noisily, because he was on crutches, at the police station, with his daughter behind him.

'You can break my legs, but I can't stop selling books. I'm destined to do this, sir,' he said. He grinned.

Ramesh grinned too, but he avoided the man's eyes.

'I'm going up the hill, sir,' Xerox said, lifting up one of his crutches. 'I'm going to sell the book.'

Ramesh and the other cops gathered around Xerox and his daughter and begged. Xerox wanted them to phone D'Souza, which they did. The lawyer came with his wig, along with two assistants, also in black gowns and wigs. When he heard why the policeman had summoned him, D'Souza burst into laughter.

'This fellow is just teasing you,' he told Ramesh. 'He can't possibly go up the hill with his leg like that.'

D'Souza pointed a finger at the middle part of Xerox's body.

'And if you do try to sell it, mind – it won't be just your legs that we break next time.'

A constable laughed.

Xerox looked at Ramesh with his usual ingratiating smile. He bent low with folded palms and said: 'So be it.'

D'Souza sat down to drink Old Monk rum with the policemen, and they settled into another game of cards. Ramesh said he had lost money on the market the past week; the lawyer sucked at his teeth and shook his head, and said that in a big city like Bombay everyone was a cheat or a liar or a thug.

Xerox turned around on his crutches and walked out of the

station. His daughter came behind him. They headed for the Lighthouse Hill. The climb took two hours and a half, and they stopped six times for Xerox to drink tea, or a glass of sugarcane juice. Then his daughter spread down the blue sheet in front of Deshpremi Hemachandra Rao Park, and Xerox lowered himself. He sat on the sheet, stuck his legs out slowly, and put a large paperback down next to him. His daughter sat down too, keeping watch over the book, her back stiff and upright. The book was banned throughout the Republic of India and it was the only thing that Xerox intended to sell that day: *The Satanic Verses*, by Salman Rushdie.

Day Two (Afternoon): ST ALFONSO'S BOYS' HIGH SCHOOL AND JUNIOR COLLEGE

A short walk from the park rises a massive grey Gothic tower on which is painted a coat of arms and the slogan 'LUCET ET ARDET'. This is the St Alfonso's Boys' High School and Junior College, established 1858, one of the oldest educational establishments in the state of Karnataka. The Jesuit-run school is Kittur's most famous, and many of its alumni have gone on to the Indian Institute of Technology, the Karnataka State Regional Engineering College, and other prestigious universities in India and abroad.

Several seconds, perhaps even a full minute, had passed since the explosion, but Lasrado, the chemistry professor, had not moved. He sat at his desk, his arms spread apart, his mouth open. Smoke was billowing from the bench at the back of the room, a yellow dust like pollen had filled the room, and the stench of fireworks was in the air. The students had all left the classroom by now; they watched from the safety of the door.

Gomati Das, the calculus teacher, arrived from next door with most of his class; then came Professor Noronha, the English and Ancient History man, bringing his own flock of curious eyes. Father Almeida, the principal, pushed his way through the crowd and entered the acrid classroom, his palm over his nose and mouth. He lowered his hand and cried: 'What is the meaning of this nonsense?'

Only Lasrado was left in the classroom; he stood at his desk like the heroic boy who would not leave the burning deck. He replied in a monotone.

'A bomb in class, *Pather*. The bench all the way in the back. It went *opp* during the lecture. About one minute *apter* I began talking.'

Father Almeida squinted at the thick smoke and then turned to the boys: 'The youth of this country have gone to hell and will ruin the names of their fathers and grandfathers!'

Covering his face with his arm, he walked gingerly to the bench, which had toppled over from the blast.

'The bomb is still smoking,' he shouted. 'Shut the doors and call the police.'

He touched Lasrado on the shoulder. 'Did you hear me? We must shut the doors and—'

Red-faced with shame, quivering with wrath, Lasrado turned suddenly, and – addressing principal, teachers, students – yelled: 'You *Puckers! Puckers!*'

In moments the entire Junior College emptied; the boys gathered in the garden, or in the corridor of the Science and Natural History wing, where the skeleton of a shark that had washed up on the beach some decades ago had been suspended from the ceiling as a scientific curiosity. Five of the boys kept apart from all the others, under the shade of a large banyan tree. They were distinguishable from the others by the pleated trousers that they wore, brand-name labels visible on the back-pockets or at the side, and by their general air of cockiness. They were Shabbir Ali, whose father owned the only video rental store in town; the Bakht twins Irfan and Rizwan, children of the black marketeer; Shankara P. Kinni, whose father was a plastic surgeon in the Gulf; and Pinto, the scion of a coffee-estate family.

One of them had planted the bomb. Each of this group had been subjected to multiple periods of suspension from classes for bad behaviour, had been kept back a year because of poor marks, and had been threatened with expulsion for insubordination. If anyone would plant a bomb, it had to be one of this lot.

They seemed to think so themselves.

'Did you do it?' Shabbir Ali asked Pinto, who shook his head.

Ali looked at the others, silently repeating the question. 'I didn't do it either,' he stated at the end.

'Maybe God did it,' Pinto said, and all of them giggled. Yet they were aware that everyone in the school suspected them. The Bakht twins said they would go down to the Bunder to eat mutton biryani and watch the waves; Shabbir Ali would go to his father's video store, or watch a pornographic movie at home; Pinto would probably tag along with him.

Only one of them remained at the school.

He could not leave yet; he loved it too much, the smoke and confusion. He kept his fist clenched.

He mingled among the crowd, listening to the hubbub, drinking it in like honey. Some of the boys had gone back into the building; they stood out on the balconies of the three floors of the college and shouted down to those on the ground; and this added to the hum, as if the college were a beehive struck with a pole. He knew that it was his hubbub – the students were talking about him, the professors were cursing him. He was the god of the morning.

For so many years the institution had spoken to him – spoken rudely: teachers had caned him, headmasters had suspended and threatened to expel him. (And, he was sure, behind his back, it had mocked him for being a Hoyka, a lower-caste.)

Now he had spoken back to it. He kept his fist clenched.

'Do you think it's the terrorists…?' he heard some boy say. 'The Kashmiris, or the Punjabis…?'

No, you morons! he wanted to shout. It's me! Shankara! The lower-caste!

There – he watched Professor Lasrado, his hair still dishevelled, surrounded by his favourite students, the 'good boys', seeking support and succour from them.

Oddly enough, he felt an urge to go up to Lasrado and touch him on the shoulder, as if to say: 'Man, I feel your grief, I understand your humiliation, I sympathize with your rage', and thus end the long strife between him and the chemistry professor. He felt the desire to be one of the students whom Lasrado trusted at such moments, one of his 'good boys'. But this was a lesser desire.

The main thing was to exult. He watched Lasrado's suffering and smiled.

He turned to his left; someone in the crowd had said: 'The police are coming.'

He hurried to the back yard of the college, opened a gate, and walked down the long flight of stone steps that led to the Junior School. After the new passageway had been opened through the playground, hardly anyone used this route any more.

The road was called Old Court Road. The court had long relocated and the lawyers had moved, and the road had been closed down for years – after the suicide of a visiting businessman here. Shankara had been coming down this road ever since he was a boy; it was his favourite part of town. Even though he could summon his chauffeur up to the college, the man was instructed to wait for him down at the bottom of the steps.

The road was lined with banyan trees; but even strolling in the shade, Shankara had worked up a terrific sweat. (He was always like that, quick to sweat, as if some irrepressible heat were building up inside him.) Most boys had handkerchiefs placed in their pockets by their mothers, but Shankara had never carried one, and to dry himself he had adopted a savage method: he tore large leaves off a nearby tree, and scraped his arms and legs over and over, until the skin was red and raw.

Now he felt dry.

About halfway down the hill, he left the road, parting a growth of trees, and walked into a clearing that was completely hidden except to those who knew it. Inside this bower was a statue of Jesus, made of dark bronze. Shankara had known of this statue for years, ever since stumbling upon it as a boy while playing hide-and-seek. There was something wrong with the statue; with its dark skin, the lopsided expression on its lips, its bright eyes, it seemed more like an icon of the devil than of the Saviour. Even the words at the base – 'I AM THE RESURRECTION AND THE LIFE' – seemed like a taunt to God.

He saw that there was still some fertilizer around the foot of the statue – the remains of the same powder that he had used to detonate his bomb. Quickly he covered the powder with dry leaves. Then he leaned against the base of the Jesus statue. 'Puckers,' he said – and giggled.

But as he did so, he felt as if his great triumph had been reduced to that one giggle.

He sat at the foot of the dark Jesus, and the tension and thrill slowly left him. He always relaxed around images of Jesus. There was a time when he had thought about converting to Christianity; among Christians there are no castes. Every man was judged by what he had done with his own life. But after the way the Jesuit priests had treated him – caning him once on a Monday morning in the assembly grounds, in full view of the entire school – he had sworn never to become a Christian. There was no better institution to stop Hindus from converting to Christianity than the Catholic boys' school.

Waving goodbye to the Jesus, and having checked that there was no fertilizer visible around the base of the statue, he continued downhill.

His chauffeur, a small dark man in a bedraggled khaki uniform, was waiting for him, halfway down the road.

'What are you doing here?' he shouted. 'I told you: wait at the bottom of the hill for me. Never come up this road!'

The driver bent low with his palms folded.

'Sir...don't be angry... I heard...a bomb...your mother asked me to make sure you were...'

How quickly news had spread. It was bigger than him; it was taking on a life of its own.

'The *bomb* – oh, it was nothing important,' he told the driver, as they walked down. Was that a mistake, he wondered – should he have exaggerated instead?

It was not an appealing irony. His mother had sent the driver to look for him, as if he were a little baby – he, who had exploded the bomb! He gritted his teeth. The driver opened the door of the white Ambassador car for him, but instead of getting into the car, he began shouting.

'You bastard! Son of a bald woman!'

He paused for breath, and then said: 'You *pucker*! You *pucker*!'

Laughing hysterically, he got into the car, while the driver stared at him.

On the way home, he thought how any other master could

expect loyalty from his chauffeur. Yet Shankara expected nothing; he suspected his chauffeur of being a Brahmin.

As they paused at a red light, he heard two ladies in an adjacent Ambassador talking about the bomb-blast: '—the police have sealed off the entire school and college now, they say. No one can leave until they find the terrorist.'

It occurred to him he had had a lucky escape; had he stayed any longer, he would have fallen into the trap of the police.

When he got to his mansion, he ran in through the back door and bounded up the steps to his room. He had thought, at one point, of sending a manifesto to the *Dawn Herald*: 'The man Lasrado is a fool and the bomb was burst in his class to prove this to the whole world.' He could not believe he had left it lying on his desk; he tore it up at once. Then, uncertain whether the pieces could be reassembled and the message re-created, he thought about swallowing them all, but decided instead to swallow only some of the key syllables – 'rado', 'bo', 'm', 'class'. The rest he set fire to, with his pocket lighter.

Besides, he thought, slightly sick from the sensation of paper settling into his stomach, that was not the right message to send to the press, because ultimately his anger was not solely directed at Lasrado; it went much deeper. If the police asked him for a statement, what he would say was this: 'I have burst a bomb to end the 5,000-year-old caste system that still operates in our country. I have burst a bomb to show that no man should be judged, as I have been, merely by the accident of his birth.'

And the lofty sentences made him feel better. He was sure he would be treated differently in prison, as a martyr of some kind. The Hoyka Self-Advancement committees would organize marches for him, and the police would not dare touch him. Perhaps, when he was released, large crowds would greet him – he would be launched on a political career.

Now he felt he had to send an anonymous letter to the newspaper at all costs. He took a fresh piece of paper and began writing, even as his stomach was churning from the paper he had swallowed.

There! He was done. He read it over.

'The Manifesto of a Wronged Hoyka. Why the Bomb was Burst Today!'

But then he reconsidered. It was well-known that he was a Hoyka. Everyone knew it. They gossiped about it, and their gossip was like that faceless buzz out of the black doors of the classrooms today. Everyone in his school, in this entire town, knew that as rich as Shankara Prasad Kinni was, he was only a Hoyka woman's son. If he sent that letter, they would know it was he who had planted the bomb.

He jumped. It was only the cry of the vegetable seller, who had brought his cart right up outside the back wall of the house: 'Tomatoes, tomatoes, ripe red tomatoes, come get your ripe red tomatoes.'

He wanted to go down to the Bunder, book into a cheap hotel, and say he was someone else. No one would ever find him there.

He paced around his room and then slammed the door; he dived into his bed and pulled the sheet over him. Inside the darkness of the bedsheet he could still hear the vendor shouting: 'Tomatoes, ripe red tomatoes, hurry before they all rot!'

*

In the morning, his mother was watching an old black-and-white Hindi film which she had rented from Shabbir Ali's father's video store. This was how she spent every morning these days, addicted to old melodramas.

'Shankara, I heard there was some brouhaha in school,' she said, turning as she heard him come down. He ignored her and sat at the table. He could not remember the last time he had spoken a full sentence to his mother.

'Shankara,' his mother said, putting toast on the table before him. 'Your Urmila Aunty is coming. Please stay around the house today.'

He bit into the toast, saying nothing to his mother. He found her possessive, and pesky, and hectoring. But he knew that she was in awe of her half-Brahmin son; she felt beneath him, because she was a full-blooded Hoyka.

'Shankara! Please tell me: will you stay around? Will you be nice to me just today?'

Dropping his toast onto his plate, he got to his feet and headed for the stairs.

'Shan-ka-ra! Come back!'

Even as he cursed her, he understood her fears. She did not want to face the Brahmin woman alone. Her sole claim to acceptance, to respectability, was the production of a male child, an heir – and if he wasn't in the house, then she had nothing to show. She was just a Hoyka trespassing into a Brahmin's household.

He thought: it is her own fault if she feels wretched in their presence. Again and again he had told her, mother, ignore our

Brahmin relatives. Don't continually humiliate yourself in front of them. If they don't want us, let us not want them.

But she could not do that; she still wanted to be accepted. And her ticket of acceptance was Shankara. Not that he himself was fully acceptable to the Brahmins. They viewed him as the product of a buccaneering adventure on the part of his father; they associated him (he was sure) with an entire range of corruptions. Mix one part premarital sex and one part caste violation in a black pot and what do you get? This cute little satan: Shankara.

Some Brahmin relatives, like Urmila Aunty, had visited him for years, although they never seemed to enjoy fondling his cheeks, or sending flying kisses his way, or doing the other repellent things aunties did to nephews. He got the feeling, around her, that he was being tolerated.

Fuck, he did not like being tolerated.

He had the driver take him to Umbrella Street, gazing blankly out of the window as the car passed its furniture shops and sugarcane juice stands. He got off at White Stallion Talkies. 'Don't wait for me; I'll call you when I'm done with the movie.'

As he was climbing the steps, he saw the owner of a store nearby waving at him vigorously. A relative, on his mother's side. The man flashed him enormous smiles; then he began gesturing for him to come sit in his shop. Shankara was always treated as someone special among his Hoyka relatives; because he was half-Brahmin, and hence so much higher than them in caste terms; or because he was so rich, and hence so much higher than them in class terms. Swearing to himself, he kept going up the stairs. Didn't these stupid Hoykas understand? There was nothing he hated more than their grovelling to him, because of his half-Brahmin-ness. If they had been contemptuous to him, if they had forced him to crawl into their shops to expiate the sin of being half-Brahmin, then wouldn't he have come to see them every day!

There was another reason for him not to visit this particular relative. He had heard a rumour that the plastic surgeon Kinni had kept a mistress in this part of town – another Hoyka girl. He suspected that the relative would know of this woman, that he would be thinking constantly: this fellow Shankara – poor, poor Shankara, little does he know of his father's treachery. Shankara knew all about his father's treachery – this father, whom he had not seen for six years, who no longer even wrote or called over the phone, although he still sent home packages of candies and foreign-made chocolates. Yet, somehow, he felt that his father knew what life was about. A Hoyka mistress near the theatre and another beautiful Hoyka woman for a wife. Now he was leading a life of ease and luxury in the Gulf, fixing the noses and lips of rich Arab women. Another mistress there, for sure. Fellows like his father belonged to no caste or religion or race; they lived for themselves. They were the only real men in this world.

The box office was shuttered up. 'NEXT SHOW 8.30 P.M.' He came down the stairs quickly, avoiding eye-contact with his relative. Turning down a couple of streets in a hurry, he went into the Ideal Traders Ice Cream Shop and ordered a chikoo milkshake.

He sucked it down quickly, and with the sugar in his brain

he leaned back and chuckled and said to himself: 'Pucker!'

So he had done it; he had humiliated Lasrado for having humiliated him.

'One more chikoo milkshake!' he shouted. 'With double ice cream!'

Shankara had always been one of the rotten apples at school. Since the age of eight or nine, he had been in trouble. But the most trouble he had ever had was with this chemistry teacher with the speech impediment. One morning, Lasrado had caught him smoking a cigarette in the sugarcane juice stand outside the college.

'Smoking *bepore* the age of twenty will arrest your development as a normal human being,' Mr Lasrado had shouted. '*Ip* your *pather* were here, and not in the *Gulp*, he would do exactly what I am doing now…'

For the rest of that day, Shankara was made to kneel outside the Chemistry class. He kneeled with his eyes to the ground, and thought, over and over again: he is doing this to me because I am a Hoyka. If I were a Christian or a Bunt he would never have humiliated me like this.

That night, he lay in bed, and the thought had come to him: since he has hurt me, I will hurt him back. And it came to him, so clearly and succinctly, like a ray of sunlight, like a credo for his entire life. The initial euphoria turned into a restlessness, and he turned from side to side in the bed, saying: Mustafa, Mustafa. He had to meet Mustafa now.

The bomb-maker.

He had heard the name several weeks ago, at Shabbir Ali's place.

They had just – all five of the 'bad boys' gang' – watched another porno at Shabbir Ali's place that night. The woman had been entered from behind; the big black man had stuck his cock into her again and again. Shankara had no idea it could be done that way too; nor did Pinto, who kept squealing with pleasure. Shabbir Ali watched his friends' amusement with detachment; he had seen this video many times and it no longer excited his lust. He lived with such familiarity with evil that nothing excited him any more – neither scenes of fornication nor rape nor even bestiality; a constant exposure to vice had nearly returned him to a state of innocence.

After the video, the boys lay on Shabbir Ali's bed, threatening to jerk off right there, while their host warned them not even to think about it.

Shabbir Ali produced a condom to keep them happy, and they took turns sticking fingers into it.

'Who's this for, Shabbir?'

'My girlfriend.'

'Shut up, you homo.'

'You're the homo!'

The others talked about sex, and Shankara, staring at the ceiling, pretending to be absorbed in himself, listened. He felt he was always being kept out of such discussions, because the others knew he was a virgin. There was a girl in the college who 'talked' to men. Shabbir Ali had 'talked' to her; he implied that he had done much more. Shankara had tried to pretend that he too had 'talked' to women; maybe even screwed a whore on Old Court Road. He knew that the others saw through him.

Ali began passing things around; the condom was followed by a dumb-bell that he kept under his bed; copies of *Hustler*, *Playboy*, and the official NBA magazine.

'Guess what this is,' he said. It was something small and black, with a timer attached to it.

'It's a detonator,' he said, when no one could guess.

'What does it do?' Shankara asked, standing up on the bed and holding the thing to the light.

'It detonates, you idiot.' There was laughter. 'You use it in a bomb.'

'It's the easiest thing on earth, to make a bomb,' Shabbir said. 'Take a bag of fertilizer, and then put this detonator in it, and that's it.'

'Where would you get it?' someone, not Shankara, asked. 'Mustafa gave it to me,' Shabbir Ali said, almost in an aside.

Mustafa, Mustafa. Shankara clung tightly to the name.

'Where does he live?' asked one of the twins.

'Down by the Bunder. In the pepper market. Why?' Shabbir Ali poked his questioner. 'You planning on making a bomb?'

'Why not?'

More giggling. And Shankara had said nothing more that evening, saying Mustafa, Mustafa to himself, terrified he would forget the name unless he said nothing else all evening.

As he was stirring his third chikoo shake, two men came and sat down next to him: two policemen. One ordered an orange juice, and the other wanted to know how many types of tea were served at the shop. Shankara got up; then sat down. He knew they would start talking about him. His heart beat faster.

'Only the detonator went off and it blew the fertilizer all round the room. That idiot who made it thought making a bomb is as simple as sticking a detonator into a bag of fertilizer. It's a good thing, otherwise some of those boys would have been killed.'

'What is the youth of this country coming to?'

'These days, it's all sex, sex, and violence. The whole country is going the Punjab way.'

One of the cops caught him staring and stared back. He turned away. Maybe I should have stuck around with Urmila Aunty. Maybe I should have kept indoors today.

But what guarantee that she – even though she was his aunty – wouldn't betray him? You never knew with Brahmins. As a boy, he had been taken to a wedding of one of his Brahmin relatives. His mother never came to such events, but his father put him in the car, and then told him to play with his cousins. The Brahmin boys invited him to join in a competition. An inch of salt sat on a slab of vanilla ice cream; the challenge was for someone to eat it. 'You idiot,' one of the others shouted, when Shankara put his spoon down, a scoop of salty ice cream in his mouth. 'It was just a joke!'

As the years passed, it was always the same. Once, a Brahmin boy in school had invited him home. He took a chance, he liked the fellow, he said yes. The boy and his mother invited Shankara into the drawing room. It was a 'modern' family – they had lived abroad. He saw miniature Eiffel Towers and porcelain milkmaids in the drawing room, and he felt reassured that he would not be ill-treated here.

He was given tea and biscuits and made to feel perfectly at

home. But as he left, he turned and saw his friend's mother with a cleaning rag in her left hand. She had begun wiping the sofa where he had been sitting.

His caste seemed to be common knowledge to people who had no business knowing it. One day, when he had gone to play cricket at Nehru Maidan, an old man had stood watching him from the wall of the playground. In the end, he called Shankara over and examined his face, neck, and wrists for several minutes. Shankara had stood helpless during the examination: he just looked at the wrinkles that radiated from the old man's eyes.

'You're the son of Vasudev Kinni and the Hoyka woman, aren't you?'

He insisted that Shankara walk along with him.

'Your father always was a headstrong man. He would never agree to an arranged marriage. One day he found your mother, and he told all the Brahmins: to hell with you. I am marrying this beautiful creature, whether you like it or not. I knew what would happen; you would be a bastard. Neither a Brahmin nor a Hoyka. I told your father this. He would not listen.'

The man patted him on the shoulder. The unselfconscious way in which he touched Shankara suggested that he was not a bigot, not caste-obsessed, but just someone speaking the sad truth of life.

'You too belong to a caste,' said the old fellow. 'The Brahmo-Hoykas, in between the two. They are mentioned in the scriptures and we know that they exist somewhere. They are a people separate entirely from other humans. You should talk to them, and marry one of them. That way everything will be normal again.'

'Yes, sir,' Shankara said, not knowing why he said it.

'Today, there is no such thing as caste,' the man said, with regret. 'Brahmins eat meat. Kshatriyas get educated and write books. And lower-castes convert to Christianity and Islam. You heard what happened at Meenakshipuram, didn't you? Colonel Gaddafi is trying to destroy Hinduism, and the Christian priests are hand in glove with him.'

They walked along for a while, until they came to the bus stop.

'You must find your own caste,' said the man. 'You must find your people.' He lightly embraced Shankara and boarded the bus, where he began to jostle with young men for a seat. Shankara felt sorry for this old Brahmin. He had never in his life had to catch a bus; there was always the chauffeur.

Shankara thought: he is of a higher caste than me, but he is poor. What does this thing mean then, caste?

Is it just a fable for old men like him? If you just said to yourself, caste is a fiction, would it vanish like smoke; if you said, 'I am free', would you realize you had always been free?

He had finished his fourth chikoo milkshake. He felt sick.

As he left the ice-cream shop, all he wanted to do was to go visit Old Court Road. To sit by that statue of the dark Jesus.

He looked around to see if the police were following him. Of course on a day like this he could not go anywhere near the Jesus statue. It was suicide. They would be watching all routes into the school.

He thought of Daryl D'Souza. That was the man to go see! In twelve years in the schooling system, Daryl D'Souza was the only one who had been decent to Shankara.

Shankara had first seen the professor at a political rally. This was the 'Hoyka Pride and Self-Expression Day Rally' held at the Nehru Maidan – the greatest political event in the history of Kittur, the newspaper would say the following day. Ten thousand Hoykas had filled the maidan to demand their rights as a full-fledged community, and to ask for retribution for the five millennia of injustice done to them.

The warm-up speaker talked about the language issue. The official language of the town should be declared Tulu, the language of the common man, and not Kannada, which was the Brahmin language.

A thunderclap of applause followed.

The professor, although not himself a Hoyka, had been invited as a sympathetic outsider; he was sitting next to the guest of honour, Kittur's Member of Parliament, who was a Hoyka, the pride of his community. A three-time MP, and also a junior member of the Cabinet of India – a sign to the entire community of how high they could aim.

Eventually, after many more preliminary speakers, the Member of Parliament got up. He began to shout: 'We, brother and sister Hoykas, were not even allowed into the temple in the old days, did you know? The priest stood at the door, saying: "You low-caste!"'

He paused, to let the insult reverberate among his listeners.

'"Low-caste! Go back!" But ever since I was elected to parliament – by you, my people – do the Brahmins dare do that to you? Do they dare call you "low-caste"? We are ninety per cent of this town! We *are* Kittur! If they hit us, we will hit them back! If they shame us, we will—'

After the speech, someone recognized Shankara. He was led into a small tent where the Member of Parliament was relaxing after the speech, and was introduced as the plastic surgeon Kinni's son. The great man, who was sitting on a wooden chair, a drink in his hand, set his glass down firmly, spilling his drink. He took Shankara's hand in his hand and gestured for him to squat down on the ground beside him.

'In the light of your family situation, your high status in society, you are the future of the Hoyka community,' the MP said. He paused, and belched.

'Yes, sir.'

'You understand what I said?' asked the great man.

'Yes, sir.'

'The future is ours. We are ninety per cent of this town. All that Brahmin shit is finished,' he said, flicking his wrist.

'Yes, sir.'

'If they hit you, you hit them back. If they...if they...' The great man made circles with his hand, to complete the slurred statement.

Shankara wanted to shout out in joy. 'Brahmin shit!' Yes, that was exactly how he would put it himself; and here was a Member of Parliament, a Cabinet minister in the government of Rajiv Gandhi, talking just as he would!

Then an aide led Shankara from the tent. 'Mr Kinni.' The aide squeezed Shankara's arm. 'If you could make a small donation towards this evening's function. Just a small amount...'

Shankara emptied his pockets. Fifty rupees. He gave it all to the aide, who bowed deeply and told him once more that he was the future of the Hoyka community.

Shankara watched. Already hundreds of men were getting into lines, where beer and quarter-litre bottles of rum were being distributed to them, as a bribe for having attended the rally and cheered the speakers. He shook his head with disapproval. He didn't like the idea that he was part of 90 per cent of his town. Now it seemed to him that the Brahmins were defenceless – a former elite of Kittur who now lived in constant fear of being robbed of their homes and their wealth by the Hoykas, the Bunts, the Konkanas, and everyone else in town. The sheer averageness of the Hoykas – whatever they did became the average at once, by definition – repulsed him.

The following morning, he read the newspaper and thought he had been too harsh on the Hoykas. He remembered the professor who had been up on stage and found out from his chauffeur where he lived. He paced backwards and forwards outside the front gate of the professor's house for a while. Finally he opened the gate, approached the house, and pressed the front doorbell.

The professor opened the door. Shankara said: 'Sir, I am a Hoyka. You are the only man in this town whom I trust. I wish to talk with you.'

'I know who you are,' Professor D'Souza said. 'Come in.'

Professor D'Souza and Shankara sat in the living room and had a long talk.

'Who is that Member of Parliament? What is his caste?' the professor asked.

The question confused Shankara.

'He is one of us, sir. A Hoyka.'

'Not quite,' the professor said. 'He is a Kollaba. Have you heard the term? There is no such thing as a Hoyka, my dear fellow. The caste is sub-divided into seven sub-castes. You understand the term? Sub-caste? Good. The Member of Parliament is a Kollaba, the top of the seven sub-castes. The Kollabas have always been millionaires. The British anthropologists of Kittur noted this fact with interest even in the nineteenth century. The Kollabas have exploited the other six Hoyka castes for years. And now once again, this man is playing the Hoyka card to get himself re-elected, so he can sit in an office in New Delhi and accept large envelopes filled with cash from businessmen who want to set up garment factories in the Bunder.'

Seven sub-castes? The Kollabas? Shankara had never heard any of this. He gaped.

'This is the big problem with you Hindus,' the professor said. 'You are mysteries to yourselves!'

Shankara felt ashamed to be a Hindu; what a repulsive thing, this caste system that his ancestors had devised. But at the same time he was annoyed with Daryl D'Souza. Who was this man to lecture him on caste? How dare the Christians do this? Hadn't they been Hindus too, at some point? Shouldn't they have remained Hindus and defeated the Brahmins from within, instead of taking the easy way out by converting?

He crushed his annoyance into a smile.

'What do we do about the caste system, sir? How do we get rid of it?'

'One solution is what the Naxalites have done, just to blow

up the upper castes entirely,' said the professor. He had a quaint, woman-like habit of dipping his large round biscuit in milk, and then hurrying to eat it before it got too soggy. 'They blow up the entire system; that way you can start from scratch.'

'From scratch' – the American idiom excited Shankar. 'I too think we should start from scratch, sir. I think we should destroy the caste system and start from scratch.'

'My dear boy: you are a nihilist,' the professor said, with an approving smile. He bit into his soggy biscuit.

They had not met after that; the professor had been travelling, and Shankara had been too shy to barge in on him a second time. But he had never forgotten the conversation. Now, wandering around town in a daze, the sugar from the milkshakes upsetting his stomach, he thought: he's the only man who'd understand what I've done. I'll confess everything to him.

The professor's house was packed with students. A reporter from the *Dawn Herald* was there, asking the big man questions about terrorism. A black tape recorder sat on the desk. Shankara, who had come to the professor's house by autorickshaw, waited with the students and watched.

'It is an absolute act of nihilism on the part of some student,' the professor was saying, his eyes on the tape recorder. 'He should be caught and thrown into jail.'

'Sir, what does this episode say about today's India, sir?'

'This is an example of the nihilism of our youth,' said Professor D'Souza. 'They are lost and directionless. They have...' – a pause – '...lost the moral standards of our nation. Our traditions are being forgotten.'

Shankara felt himself choke with rage. He stormed out.

He caught an autorickshaw to Shabbir Ali's house and rang the bell. A bearded man in a North Indian-style kurta, with his chest hair sticking out, opened the door. It took Shankara some time to recognize him as Shabbir Ali's father, whom he had never before seen.

'He is not allowed to talk to any of his friends,' he said. 'You fellows have corrupted my son.' And he slammed the door in Shankara's face.

So, the great Shabbir Ali, the man who 'talked' to women and played with condoms, was locked up in his house. By his father. Shankara wanted to laugh.

He was tired of moving in autorickshaws; so he called home from a pay-phone and asked for the car to be sent to Shabbir Ali's house to pick him up.

Back home, he bolted the door to his room. He lay in bed. He picked up the phone and put it down and counted to five and then picked it up again. Eventually it worked. In Kittur, that was all you had to do to enter into someone else's world.

He was listening to a crossed line.

The phone line crackled and came to life. A man and woman, possibly husband and wife, were talking. They were speaking in a language he couldn't understand; he thought it might be Malayalam – the speakers must be Muslim, he thought. He wondered what they were talking about – was the man complaining about his health, was she asking for more money for the household? Why were they on the phone, he wondered? Was the man living away from Kittur? Whatever their situation, whatever they were saying in that foreign language, he felt the intimacy of their conversation. It would be nice to have a wife or a girlfriend, he thought. Not to be so alone all the time. Even a single real friend. Even that would have kept him from planting the bomb and getting into all this trouble.

The man's tone changed suddenly. He began to whisper.

'I think someone's breathing on the line,' the man said – or so Shankar imagined.

'Yes, you're right. Some pervert is listening to us,' the woman replied – or so Shankara imagined.

Then the man hung up.

I have the worst of both castes in my blood, Shankara thought, lying in bed, the receiver of the phone still at his ear. I have the anxiety and fear of the Brahmin, and I have the tendency to act without thinking of the Hoyka. In me the worst of both has fused and produced this monstrosity which is my personality.

He was going mad. Yes, he was convinced of that. He wanted to get out of the house again. He worried that the chauffeur was noticing his restlessness.

He went out of the back door and slipped away from the house without the driver observing him.

But he probably doesn't suspect me, he thought. He probably thinks I'm a useless rich brat, like Shabbir Ali.

All these rich fellows like Shabbir Ali, he told himself bitterly, lived out a kind of code. They talked things, but did not do them. They had condoms at home, but did not use them;

they kept detonators but did not explode him. Talk, and talk, and talk. That was their life. It was like the salt on the ice cream. The salt was smeared on the slab of vanilla and left there in the open; but no one was meant to lick it! That was only a joke! It was meant to be talk only, all this bomb-exploding stuff. If you knew the code, you understood it was just talk. Only he had taken them seriously; he had thought that they fucked women and blew up bombs. He did not know about the code, because he did not really belong – either to the Brahmins, or to the Hoykas, or even to the gang of spoiled brats.

He was in a secret caste – a caste of Brahmo-Hoykas, of which he had found only one representative so far, himself, and which put him apart from all the other castes of humankind.

He took another autorickshaw to the Junior School, and from there, making sure no one was watching him, walked up Old Court Road with his head to the ground and his hands in his pockets.

He parted the trees, came up to the statue of Jesus, and sat down. The smell of fertilizer was still strong in the air. Closing his eyes, he tried to calm himself. Instead, he began to think about the suicide that had taken place on this road many years ago. He had heard about it from Shabbir Ali. A man had been found hanging from a tree by this road – perhaps even in this spot. A suitcase lay at his feet, broken open. Inside, the police found three gold coins and a note. 'In a world without love, suicide is the only transformation possible.' Then there was a letter, addressed to a woman in Bombay.

Shankara opened his eyes. It was as if he could see the man

from Bombay, hanging in front of him, his feet dangling in front of the dark Jesus.

He wondered: was that going to be his fate? Would he end up condemned and hanged?

He remembered again the fateful events. After the conversation at Shabbir Ali's house, he had gone down to the Bunder. He had asked for Mustafa, describing him as a man who sold fertilizers; he had been directed to a market. He found a row of vegetable sellers, asked for Mustafa, and was told: 'Go upstairs.' He climbed stairs. He found himself in a pitch-black space where a thousand men seemed to be coughing at once. He too began to cough. As his eyes got used to the dark he realized he was in a pepper market. Giant gunnybags were stacked up against the grimy walls, and coolies, coughing incessantly, were hauling them around. Then the darkness ended and he arrived in an open courtyard. Once again he asked: 'Where is Mustafa?'

He was directed by a man lying on a cart of old vegetables towards an open door.

He went in and found three men at a round table playing cards.

'Mustafa's not in,' said a man with narrow eyes. 'What do you want?'

'A bag of fertilizer.'

'Why?'

'I am growing lentils,' Shankara said. The man laughed.

'What kind?'

'Beans. Green gram. Horse gram.'

The man laughed again. He put his cards down, went into

a room and hauled out an enormous gunnybag, and put it down by Shankara's feet.

'What else do you need to grow your beans?'

'A detonator,' Shankara said.

The men at the table all put down their cards together.

In the inner room of the house, he was sold a detonator; he was told how to turn the dial and set the timer. It would cost more than Shankara had on him at that moment, so he came back the next week with the money, and took the bag and the detonator back with him by autorickshaw, and got off at the bottom of Old Court Road. He had hidden it all near the statue of Jesus.

One Sunday, he went around the school. It was like the movie *Papillon*, one of his favourites, the scene where the hero plans how to escape from jail – it was as exciting as that. He was seeing his school as if for the first time, with all the keenness of a fugitive's eye. After that, on that fateful Monday, he took the bag of fertilizer with him to school, and attached the detonator to it, turned the timer to one hour, left it under the back row, where he knew no one would sit.

Then he waited, counting off the hour minute by minute, like the hero in *Papillon*.

At midnight, the phone began ringing.

It was Shabbir Ali.

'Lasrado wants to see us all in his office, man! Tomorrow, first thing!'

All five of them had to be there in his office. The police would be present.

'He's going to have a lie-detector.' Shabbir paused. Then he shouted: 'I know you did it! Why don't you confess? Why don't you confess at once!'

Shankara's blood went chill. 'Fuck you!' he yelled back and slammed down the phone. But then he thought: my god, so Shabbir knew all along. Of course! Everyone knew all along. Everyone in the bad boys' gang must have known; and by now they must have told the whole town. He thought: let me confess right now. It would be best. Perhaps the police would give him some credit for having turned himself in. He dialled '100', which he thought was the police number.

'I want to speak to the Deputy Inspector General, please.'

'Ha?'

The voice was followed by a shriek of incomprehension.

Thinking he'd get better results, he spoke in English: 'I want to confess. I planted the bomb.'

'Ha?'

'The bomb. It was me.'

'Ha?'

Another pause. The phone was transferred.

He repeated his message to another person on the other line.

Another pause.

'Sorrysorrysorry?'

He put the phone down in exasperation. Damn Indian police – can't even answer a phone call properly; how the hell were they going to catch him?

Then the phone rang again; Irfan, calling on behalf of the twins.

'Shabbir just called us; he says we did it, man. I didn't do it! Rizwan didn't do it, either! Shabbir is lying!'

Then he understood: Shabbir had called everyone and accused them all – hoping to extract a confession! Relief mingled with anger. He had almost been trapped! Now he felt anxious that the police might trace his '100' call back to his phone. He needed a plan, he thought, a plan. Yes, he'd got it; he would say, if they asked, that he was calling to report Shabbir Ali for the crime. 'Shabbir is a Muslim,' he would say. 'He wanted to do this to punish India for Kashmir.'

The following morning, Lasrado was in the principal's office, sitting next to Father Almeida, who was at his desk. The two men stared at the five suspects.

'I have *scientipic* evidence,' Lasrado said. '*Pinger*-prints survive on the black stub of the bomb.' He sensed incredulity among the accused, so he added: '*Pingerprints* have survived even on the loaves of bread *lept* behind in the *Paraoh's* tomb. They are indestructible. We will *pind* the *pucker* who has done this, rest assured.'

He pointed a finger.

'And you, Pinto, a Christian boy – shame on you!'

'I didn't do it, sir,' Pinto said.

Shankara wondered: should he also throw in an interjection of his innocence, just to be safe?

Lasrado looked at them piercingly, waiting for the guilty part to turn himself in. Minutes passed. Shankara understood: he has no fingerprints. He has no lie-detector. He is desperate. He has been humiliated, mocked, and rendered a joke in college, and he wants revenge.

'You *puckers*!' Lasrado shouted. And then, again, in a

trembling voice: 'Are you *lapping* at me? Are you *lapping* because I cannot say the letter "*epp*"?'

Now the boys could barely control themselves. Shankara saw that even the principal, having turned his face to the ground, was trying to suppress his laughter. Lasrado knew this; you could see it on his face. Shankara thought: this man has been mocked his whole life because of his speech impediment. That's why he has been such a jerk in class. And now his entire life's work has been destroyed by this bomb; he will never be able to look back on his life with the pride, however false, that other professors do; never be able to say, at his farewell party, 'My students, although I was strict, loved me.' Always there would be someone whispering at the back – yes, they loved you so much they exploded a bomb in your class!

At that moment, Shankara thought, I wish I had just left this man alone. I wish I had not humiliated him, as so many have humiliated me and my mother.

'I did it, sir.'

Everyone in the room turned to Shankara.

'I did it,' he said. 'Now stop bothering these other boys and punish me.'

Lasrado banged his hand on the desk. 'Mother-*pucker*, is this a joke?'

'No, sir.'

'*Op* course it is a joke!' Lasrado shouted. 'You are mocking me! You are mocking me in public!'

'No, sir—'

'Shut up!' Lasrado said. 'Shut up!' He flexed a finger and pointed it wildly around the room.

'*Puckers! Puckers!* Get out!'

Shankara walked out with the four innocent ones. He could see that they did not believe his confession: they too thought he had been mocking the teacher to his face.

'You went too far there,' Shabbir Ali said. 'You really have no respect for anything in this world, man.'

Shankara waited outside the college, smoking. He was waiting for Lasrado. When the door to the staff room opened, and the chemistry professor walked out, Shankara threw the cigarette to the ground and stubbed it out with a scrape of his shoe. He watched his teacher for a while. He wished there were some way he could go up to him and say he was sorry.

Day Two (Evening): LIGHTHOUSE HILL (THE FOOT OF THE HILL)

You are on a road surrounded by ancient banyan trees; the smell of neem is in the air, an eagle glides overhead. Old Court Road – a long, desolate road with a reputation as a hang-out for prostitutes and pimps – leads down from the top of the hill to St Alfonso's Boys' High School and Junior College.

Next to the school you will find a whitewashed mosque dating back to the time of Tippu Sultan; according to local legend, Christians from Valencia suspected of being British sympathizers were tortured here. The mosque is the focus of a legal tussle between the school authorities and a local Islamic organization, both of which claim possession of the land on which it stands. Muslim students from the school are allowed, every Friday, to leave classes for an hour to offer namaaz at this mosque, provided they bring a signed note from their fathers, or in case of boys whose fathers are working in the Gulf, from a male guardian. From a bus stop in front of the mosque, express buses go to Salt Market Village.

At least four stalls stand outside the mosque, selling sugarcane juice and Bombay-style bhelpuri and charmuri to passengers at the bus stop.

A flurry of alarm bells rang at ten to nine, warning that this was no ordinary morning. It was a Morning of Martyrs, the thirty-seventh anniversary of the day Mahatma Gandhi had sacrificed his life so that India might live.

Thousands of miles away, in the heart of the nation, in chilly New Delhi, the President was about to bow his head before a sacred torch. Echoing through the massive Gothic edifice of St Alfonso's Boys' High School and Junior College – through thirty-six classrooms with vaulted ceilings, two outdoor lavatories, a chemistry-cum-biology laboratory, and a refectory where some of the priests were still finishing breakfast – the alarm bells announced that it was time for the school to do the same.

In the staff room, Mr D'Mello, assistant headmaster, folded his copy of the newspaper, noisily, like a pelican folding its wings. Tossing the paper on a sandalwood table, Mr D'Mello struggled against his paunch to get to his feet. He was the last to leave the staff room.

Six hundred and twenty-three boys, pouring out of class-rooms and eventually merging into one long line, proceeded into the Assembly Square. In ten minutes they had formed a geometrical pattern, a tight grid around the flagpole at the centre of the square.

By the flagpole stood an old wooden platform. And next to the platform stood Mr D'Mello, drawing the morning air into his lungs and shouting: 'A-ten-shannn!'

The students shuffled in concert. *Thump!* Their feet knocked the chatter out of the square. Now the morning was ready for the sombre ceremony.

The guest of honour had fallen asleep. From the top of the

flagpole, the national tricolour hung, limp and crumpled, entirely uninterested in the events organized for its benefit. Alvarez, the old school peon, tugged on a blue cord to goad the recalcitrant piece of cloth into a respectable tautness.

Mr D'Mello sighed and gave up on the flag. His lungs swelled again: 'Sa-loot!'

The wooden platform began to creak noisily: Father Mendonza, junior school headmaster, was ascending the steps. At a sign from Mr D'Mello, he cleared his throat into the booming mike and launched into a speech on the glories of dying young for your country.

A series of black boxes amplified his nervous voice across the square. The boys listened to their headmaster spellbound. The Jesuit told them the blood of Bhagat Singh and Indira Gandhi fertilized the earth on which they stood, and they brimmed with pride.

Mr D'Mello, squinting fiercely, kept an eye on the little patriots. He knew that the whole humbug would end any moment. After thirty-three years in an all-boys' school, no secret of human nature was hidden from him.

The headmaster lumbered towards the crucial part of the morning's speech.

'It is of course customary on Martyrs' Day for the government to issue every school in the state with Free Film Day tickets for that following Sunday,' he said. It was as if electric current had jolted the square. The boys became breathless with anticipation.

'But this year' – the headmaster's voice quivered – 'I regret to announce that there will be no Free Film Day.'

For a moment, not a sound. Then, the entire square let out one big, aching, disbelieving groan.

'The government has made a terrible mistake,' the headmaster said, trying to explain. 'A terrible, terrible mistake... They have asked you to go to a House of Sin...'

Mr D'Mello wondered what the headmaster was prattling on about. It was time to bring the speech to an end and send the brats back to class.

'I cannot even find the words to tell you...it has been a terrible mix-up. I am sorry. I...am...'

Mr D'Mello was looking around for Girish, when a movement at the back of the square caught his eye. Trouble had begun. The assistant headmaster, hindered by his massive paunch, struggled to descend from the podium, but then, with a surprising litheness, he slipped through the rows of boys and homed in on the danger zone. Students turned on their toes to watch him as he made his way to the back. His right hand trembled.

A brown dog had climbed up from the playground below the Assembly Square and was loping about behind the boys. Some trouble-makers were trying to persuade it to draw nearer with soft whistles and clicks of their tongue.

'Stop that at once!' D'Mello – he was gasping for breath already – stamped his foot towards the dog. The indulged animal mistook the fat man's advance for another blandishment. The teacher lunged at the dog and it pulled back, but as he stopped to breathe, it raced back towards him.

The boys were laughing openly now. Waves of confusion spread throughout the square. Over the speaker system the headmaster's voice wobbled, with a hint of desperation.

'… you boys have no right to misbehave…the Free Film Day is a privilege, not a right…'

'*Stone it! Stone it!*' someone shouted at D'Mello.

In a moment of panic, the teacher obeyed. Whack! The stone caught the dog on the belly. The animal yelped in pain – he saw a gleam of betrayal in its eyes – before it bounded out of the square and ran down the steps of the playground.

A sensation of sickness tightened in Mr D'Mello's gut. The poor animal had been hurt. Turning around, he saw a sea of grinning boys. One of them had goaded him to stone the animal; he swung around, picked a boy at random – only hesitating for a split second to make sure that it wasn't Girish – and slapped him hard, twice.

When Mr D'Mello walked into the staff room, he found all the other teachers gathered around the sandalwood table. The men were dressed alike, in light-coloured half-sleeve shirts, closely checked, with brown or blue trousers that widened into bell-bottoms, while the few women wore peach or yellow polyester-and-cotton-blended saris.

Mr Rogers, the biology-cum-geology teacher, was reading aloud a schedule of the Free Film Day from the Kannada-language newspaper:

'**Film One:** Save the Tiger
Film Two: The Importance of Physical Exercise
Bonus Reel: The Advantages of Native Sports
(with special attention to Kabbadi and Kho-Kho).'

After that harmless listing, came the bombshell:

'Where to send your son or daughter on Free Film Day
(1985):
1. St Milagres Boys' High School; Surnames A to N,
   White Stallion Theatre, O to Z Belmore Theatre.
2. St Alfonso's Boys' High School; Surnames A to N,
   Belmore Theatre, O to Z Angel Talkies.'

'Half our school!' Mr Rogers' voice whistled in excitement.
'Half our school to Angel Talkies!'

Young Mr Gopalkrishna Bhatt, only a year out of the
teachers' college in Belgaum, tended to supply the chorus on
such occasions. He raised his arms fatalistically: 'What a mix-
up! Sending our children to *that* place!'

Mr Pundit, senior Kannada language teacher, scoffed at the
naivety of his colleagues. He was a short silver-haired man of
startling opinions.

'This is no mix-up, it's deliberate! The Angel Talkies has
bribed all those bloody politicians in Bangalore, so they'd send
our boys to a House of Sin!'

Now the teachers were divided between those who thought
it was a mix-up and those who thought it was a deliberate ploy
to corrupt the youth.

'What do you think, Mr D'Mello?' young Mr Bhatt called out.

Instead of replying, Mr D'Mello dragged a cane chair from
the sandalwood table towards an open window at the far end
of the staff room. It was a sunny morning: he had a blue sky,
rolling hills, a private vista of the Arabian sea.

The sky was a dazzling light blue, a thing meant for meditation. A few perfectly formed clouds, like wishes that had been granted, floated through the azure. The arc of Heaven deepened in colour as it stretched towards the horizon and touched a crest of the Arabian Sea. Mr D'Mello invited the morning's beauty into his agitated mind.

'What a mix-up, eh, Mr D'Mello?'

Gopalkrishna Bhatt hopped onto the window ledge, blocking the view of the sea. Dangling his legs gleefully, the young man flashed a gap-toothed smile at his senior colleague.

'The only mix-up, Mr Bhatt,' said the assistant headmaster, 'was made on 15 August 1947, when we thought this country could be run by a people's democracy instead of a military dictatorship.'

The young teacher nodded his head. 'Yes, yes, how true. What about the Emergency, sir – wasn't that a good thing?'

'We threw that chance, away,' Mr D'Mello said. 'And now they've shot dead the only politician we ever had who knew how to give this country the medicine it needed.' He closed his eyes again and concentrated on an image of an empty beach in an attempt to dispel Mr Bhatt's presence.

Mr Bhatt said: 'Your favourite's name is in the paper this morning, Mr D'Mello. Page 4, near the top. You must be a proud man.'

Before Mr D'Mello could stop him, Mr Bhatt had begun reading:

'The Mid-Town Rotary Club announces the Winners of its Fourth Annual Inter-School English Elocution Contest.

Theme: Science – A Boon or Curse for the Human Race?
First Prize: Harish Pai, St Milagres High School
(Science as a Boon).
Second Prize: Girish Rai, St Alfonso's High School
(Science as a Curse).'

The assistant headmaster pulled the newspaper from the hands of his junior colleague. 'Mr Bhatt—' he snarled, 'I have often said this publicly: I have no favourites among the boys.'

He closed his eyes, but now his peace of mind was gone.

'Second prize' – the words stung him once again. He had worked with Girish all last evening on the speech – its content, its delivery, the boy's posture at the mike, everything! And only second prize? His eyes filled with tears. The boy had got into a habit of losing these days.

There was commotion in the staff room now, and through his closed eyes Mr D'Mello knew that the headmaster had arrived, and all the teachers were running around him sycophantically. He remained in his seat, though he knew his peace would not last long.

'Mr D'Mello,' came the nervous voice. 'It is a terrible mix-up...one half of the boys won't get to see the free film this year.'

The headmaster was gazing at him from near the sandalwood table. Mr D'Mello ground his teeth. He folded his copy of the newspaper violently; he took his time getting to his feet, and he took his time turning around. The headmaster was mopping his forehead. Father Mendonza was a very tall, very bald man, with strands of heavily oiled hair combed over his naked pate. His large eyes stared out through thick glasses and an enormous forehead glittered with beads of sweat, like a leaf spotted with dew after a shower.

'May I make a suggestion, Father?'

The headmaster's hand paused with his handkerchief at his brow.

'If we don't take the boys to Angel Talkies, they'll see it as a sign of weakness. We'll only have more trouble with them.'

The headmaster bit his lips.

'But...the dangers...one hears of terrible posters...of evils that cannot be put into words...'

'I will take care of the arrangements,' Mr D'Mello said, gravely. 'I will take care of the discipline. I give you my word.'

The Jesuit nodded hopefully. As he left the staff room, he turned to Gopalkrishna Bhatt and the depth of gratitude in his voice was unmistakable: 'You too should go along with the assistant headmaster when he takes the boys to Angel Talkies...'

Father Mendonza's words echoing in his mind, he walked to his 11 a.m. class, his first of the morning. *Assistant headmaster.* He knew that he had not been the Jesuit's first choice. The insult still smarted after all this time. The post was his by right of seniority. For thirty years he had taught Hindi and arithmetic to the boys of St Alfonso's, and maintained order in the school. But Father Mendonza, who had recently come down from Bangalore with an oily comb-over and six trunks full of 'modern' ideas, stated his preference for someone 'smart' in appearance. Mr D'Mello had a pair of eyes and a mirror at home. He knew what that remark meant.

He was an overweight man entering the final phase of middle age, he breathed through his mouth, and a thicket of hair poked out of his nose. The centrepiece of his body was a massive pot belly, a hard knot of flesh pregnant with a dozen cardiac arrests. To walk, he had to arch his lower back, tilt his head, and screw his brow and nose together in a foul-looking squint. 'Ogre,' the boys chanted as he passed. 'Ogre! Ogre! Ogre!'

At noon, he ate a dish of red fish curry out of a stainless-steel tiffin-carrier, at his favourite window in the staff room. The smell of the curry did not please his colleagues, so he ate alone. Done, he slowly took his tiffin-carrier to the public tap outside. The boys stopped their games. Since it was out of the question for him to bend forward (the paunch, of course), he had to fill his tiffin-carrier with water and raise it to his mouth. Gargling loudly, he belched out a saffron torrent several times. The boys shrieked with pleasure each time. When he was back in the staff room, they crowded by the tap: little skeletons of fish had piled up at its base, like deposits of a nascent coral reef. Awe and disgust commingled in the voices of the boys and they chanted, in a unison that grew louder and louder: '*Ogreogreogre!*'

'The main problem with selecting Mr D'Mello as my assistant is that he has an excessive penchant for old-fashioned violence,' the young headmaster wrote to the Jesuit Board. Mr D'Mello caned too often, and too much. Sometimes, even as he wrote on the blackboard, his left hand would reach for the duster. He would turn around and send it flying at the last row, and there would be a scream and the bench would topple over under the weight of diving boys.

He had done worse. Father Mendonza reported in detail a shocking story he had heard. Once, many years ago, a small boy had been talking in the front row, right in front of D'Mello. The teacher said nothing. He just sat still and let his anger stew. Suddenly, it was said, there was a moment of blackness in his brain. He snatched the boy from his seat and hoisted him into the air and took him to the back of the class: there he shut him in a cupboard. The boy beat on the insides of the cupboard with his fists for the rest of the class. 'I can't breathe in here!' he shouted. The beating inside the cupboard grew louder and louder; then fainter, and fainter. When the cupboard was finally opened, a full ten minutes later, there was a stench of fresh urine, and the boy fell out in an unconscious heap.

Then there was the little matter of his past. Mr D'Mello had been in training at the Valencia Seminary to be a priest for six years, before leaving suddenly, and on bad terms with his superiors. The rumour was that he had challenged the holy Dogma, and declared that the polices of the Vatican on the matter of family planning were illogical in a country like India – and so walked out, abandoning six years of his life. Other rumours suggested that he was a free-thinker, who did not attend church regularly.

The weeks went on. The Jesuit Board inquired by mail if Father Mendonza had made a decision yet. The young headmaster confessed he had had no time for that. Every morning the padre found that his first duty was to discipline a long line of recalcitrants. The same faces appeared morning after morning. Talking in class. Disfiguring school property. Pinching studious boys.

One day, a foreigner, a Christian woman from Britain who was a generous donor to worthy causes in India, paid a visit to the school. Father Mendonza oiled his surviving strands of hair with special care that morning. He solicited Mr Pundit's assistance in guiding the British lady around the school. With great courtesy, the Kannada teacher explained to the foreigner the proud history of St Alfonso's, its celebrated alumni, its role in civilizing the savage nature of this part of India, once a bare wilderness overrun by elephants. Father Mendonza began to feel that Mr Pundit was as smart a fellow as he was likely to find in this part of the world. Then, all at once, the foreigner began shrieking. The fingers of her hand spread out with horror. Julian D'Essa, the coffee-plantation scion, was standing on the last bench of a giggling classroom, exposing his privates to the world. Mr Pundit rushed at the crazy boy, but the damage had been done. The Jesuit saw the foreign donor step back from him with terror-struck eyes: as if he were the exhibitionist.

An old member of the Board called Father Mendonza from Bangalore that evening to console him. Did the 'reformer' not finally see the truth? Modern ideas of education were fine in Bangalore. But in a backwater like Kittur, miles and miles and miles away from civilization?

'To manage a school filled with six hundred little animals' – the old member of the Board told the sobbing young headmaster – 'you need an ogre now and then.'

Two months after his arrival at St Alfonso's, Father Mendonza summoned Mr D'Mello over to his office one morning. He told Mr D'Mello that he had no option but to ask him to serve as the assistant headmaster. To handle a school like this, the Jesuit declared, he needed a man like Mr D'Mello.

Stop for a moment, D'Mello told himself. Catch your breath. He was about to go into the classroom – about to declare war. The plan had worked well so far; he had come the way of the rear entrance. A surprise attack. He had figured that the news of Mendonza's change of mind on Angel Talkies was by now common knowledge. The boys had of course construed it as cowardice on the part of the school authorities. The danger was highest now, but also the opportunity to teach them a lasting lesson.

The class was quiet – too quiet.

D'Mello went in on tiptoe. The last row, where the tall, over-developed boys sat, were clumped together, a soundless knot around a magazine. D'Mello hovered over the boys. The magazine was the usual kind of magazine. 'Julian,' he said gently.

The boys turned around and the magazine dropped to the floor. Julian stood up with a grin. He was the tallest of the tall, the most over-developed of the over-developed. An inverted triangle of chest hair jutted out of his open shirt already, and when he rolled up a sleeve and made a muscle, D'Mello could see his biceps swelling into pale, thick tubers. As the son of a coffee-planting dynasty, Julian D'Essa could never be expelled from the school. But he could be punished. The little demon looked up at D'Mello, with a lecherous grin pasted on his face. In his mind Mr D'Mello heard D'Essa's voice; it goaded him on to do his worst: *Ogre! Ogre! Ogre!*

He heaved the boy out of the seat by his collar. Rip – the collar came off the shirt. D'Mello's shaking elbow straightened out – it connected with the side of the boy's face.

'Get out of the class, you animal…and kneel down…'

After shoving Julian out of the class, he put his hands on his knees and caught his breath. He picked up the magazine and flipped its pages about for public view.

'So this is the sort of thing you boys want to read, huh? Now you want to go to Angel Talkies? You think you'll see the posters on the wall: those Murals of Sin?'

He walked around the class with his shaking elbow and thundered: even the lechers were ashamed to go into Angel Talkies. They covered themselves in blankets and pushed rupee notes shamefully to the desk attendants. Inside, the walls of the theatre were papered with posters of X-rated films, purveyors of every known depravity. To see a movie in such a theatre was a corruption of body and soul alike.

He hurled the magazine against a wall. Did they think he was frightened to beat them? No! He was not one of these 'new-fashioned' teachers trained in Bangalore or Bombay! Violence was his staple, and his dessert. Spare the rod and spoil the child.

He collapsed onto his chair. He was horribly out of breath. A dull pain spread its roots across his chest. He saw with satisfaction that his speech had had some effect. The boys were sitting without a squeak. The sight of Julian with his torn collar kneeling outside the class had a quieting effect. But Mr D'Mello knew it was just a matter of time, just a matter of time. At the age of fifty-seven he had no more illusions about human nature. Lust would inflame the boys' hearts with rebellion again.

He ordered them to open the Hindi textbooks. Page 168.

'Who will read the poem?'

The class was silent around one raised arm.

'Girish Rai, read.'

A boy wearing comically large spectacles got to his feet from the first bench. His hair was thick and parted down the middle; his small face was overpowered by pimples. He did not need the textbook, for he knew the poem by heart:

'Nay, said the flower:
Cast me, said the flower,
Not on the virgin's bed
Nor in the bridal carriage
Nor in the Merry Village square.

Nay, said the flower
Cast me but on that lonely path
Where the heroes walk
For their nation to die.'

The boy sat down. The entire class was silent, humbled for a moment by the purity of his enunciation in Hindi, that alien language. 'If only all of you could be like this boy,' Mr D'Mello said quietly.

But he had not forgotten that his favourite had let him down in the Rotary competition. Ordering the class to copy out the poem six times in their notebooks, he ignored Girish for two or three minutes. Then he summoned him with his fingers.

'Girish.' His voice faltered. 'Girish…why didn't you get first prize in the Rotary competition? How will we ever get to Delhi unless you win more first prizes?'

'Sorry, sir…' the boy said. He hung his head in shame.

'Girish…lately you haven't been winning so many first prizes…is something the matter?'

There was a worried look on the boy's face. Mr D'Mello panicked.

'Is someone troubling you? One of the boys? Has D'Essa threatened you?'

'No, sir.'

He looked at the tall boys in the back row. He turned to his right and glanced at the kneeling D'Essa, who was grinning hard. The assistant headmaster came to a quick decision.

'Girish…tomorrow…I don't want you to go to Angel Talkies. I want you to go to Belmore Talkies.'

'Why, sir?'

Mr D'Mello recoiled.

'What do you mean why? Because I say so, that's why!' he yelled. The class looked at them; had Mr D'Mello raised his voice to his favourite?

Girish Rai reddened. He seemed on the verge of tears, and Mr D'Mello's heart melted. He smiled and patted the small boy on the back.

'Now, now, Girish, don't cry… I don't care about the other boys. They've been to the talkies many times – they've read magazines. There isn't anything left to be corrupted. But not you. I won't let you go there. Go to Belmore.'

Girish nodded and went back to his seat in the front bench. He was still on the verge of tears. Mr D'Mello felt his heart melting out of pity; he had been too harsh on the poor boy.

When the class ended, he went up to the front bench and tapped on the desk: 'Girish – do you have any plans for this evening?'

What a terrible day, what a terrible day. Mr D'Mello was walking along the mud road that led from the school to his home in the teachers' colony. That awful *whack* of the stone echoed over and over again in his head…the look in the poor animal's eyes…

He walked back with his poetry books beneath his armpit. His shirt was now speckled with red curry, and the tips of his collars were curled in, like sunburned leaves. Every few minutes, he stopped to straighten his aching back and catch his breath.

'Are you ill, sir?'

Mr D'Mello turned around: Girish Rai, with a huge khaki schoolbag strapped to his back, was following him.

Teacher and pupil walked a few yards side by side, and then Mr D'Mello stopped. 'Do you see that, boy?' he pointed.

Halfway between the school and the teacher's house ran a brick wall with a wide crack yawning down the middle. Both the wall and the crack had been there for years, in that road where no detail had significantly changed since Mr D'Mello had moved to the neighbourhood thirty years ago to take up the quarters assigned to him as a young teacher. Three lamp-posts along the adjacent road were visible through the crack in the wall, and for nearly twenty years now Mr D'Mello had stopped every evening and squinted hard at the three lamp-posts. For twenty years, he had been searching the lamp-posts for the explanation of a mystery. One morning, about two decades ago, while passing the crack he had seen a sentence in white chalk marked on all three lamp-posts:

'Nathan X must die.'

He had squeezed through the crack in the wall to get to the three lamp-posts, and scraped the words with his umbrella, to decipher their mystery. What did the three signs mean? An old man pulled along a cart of vegetables. He tried asking him who Nathan X was, but the vegetable man just shrugged. Ernest D'Mello stood there, with the mist in the trees, and wondered.

The next morning the signs were gone. Intentionally wiped out. When he got to school, he scanned the obituary column of the newspaper and couldn't believe his eyes – a man called 'Nathan Xavier' had been murdered the previous night at the Bunder! He was convinced at first that he had come upon some secret society planning a murder. A darker anxiety beset him soon. Maybe Chinese spies had written those words? Years had passed, but the mystery remained, and he thought about it each time he passed that crack.

'Do you think Pakistani spies did it, sir?' Girish said. 'Did they kill Nathan X?'

Mr D'Mello grunted. He felt he shouldn't have revealed the memory to Girish; he felt, somehow, he had compromised himself. Teacher and student walked on.

Mr D'Mello watched as the rays of sunset fell through the banyan leaves in large patches on the ground, like the puddles left behind by a child after a bath. He looked to the sky, and involuntarily spoke a line of Hindi poetry: '*The golden hand of the sun as it grazes the clouds...*'

'I know that poem, sir,' a little voice said. Girish Rai repeated the rest of the couplet: '*... is like a lover's hand as it grazes its beloved.*'

They walked on.

'So you have an interest in poetry?' D'Mello asked. Before the boy could reply, he confessed another secret to him. In his youth he had wanted to be a poet – a nationalist writer, no less, a new Bharathi or Tagore.

'Then why didn't you become a poet, sir?'

He laughed. 'In this little hole of Kittur, my learned friend, how could a man make a living from poetry?'

The lamps came on, one by one. It was almost night now. In the distance Mr D'Mello saw a lighted door, his quarters. As they got closer to the house, he stopped talking. He could hear the brats from here. What have they smashed today, he wondered.

Girish Rai watched.

Mr D'Mello took off his shirt and left it on a hook on the wall. The boy saw the assistant headmaster in his singlet, slowly setting himself down on a rocking chair in his living room. Two girls in identical red frocks were running in circles round the room, bellowing their lungs out. The old teacher ignored them completely. He gazed at the boy for a while, again wondering why, for the first time in his career as a teacher, he had invited a student home.

'Why did we let the Pakistanis get away, sir?' Girish blurted out.

'What do you mean, boy?' Mr D'Mello screwed his nose and brow together and squinted.

'Why did we let the Pakistanis get away in 1965? When we had them in our clutches? You said it in class one day, but you didn't explain.'

'Oh, that!' Mr D'Mello slapped his hand against his thigh with relish. Another of his favourite topics. The great screw-up of the war of 1965. The Indian tanks had rolled into the outskirts of Lahore when our own government cut the ground beneath their feet. Some bureaucrat had been bribed; the tanks came back.

'Ever since Sardar Patel died, this country has gone down the drain,' he said, and the little boy nodded. 'We live in the midst of chaos and corruption. We can only do our jobs, and go home,' he said, and the little boy nodded.

The teacher exhaled contentedly. He was deeply flattered; in all these years at the school, no student had ever felt the same outrage he had, at that colossal blunder of '65. Lifting himself off the rocking chair, he pulled out a volume of Hindi poetry from a bookshelf. 'I want this back, huh? And in perfect shape. Not one scratch or blotch on it.'

The boy nodded. He looked around the house furtively. The poverty of his teacher's house surprised him. The walls of the living room were bare, save for a lighted picture of the Sacred Heart of Jesus. The paint was peeling, and stout-hearted geckos ran all over the walls.

As Girish flicked through the book, the two girls in red dresses took turns at shrieking into his ears, before screaming away into another room.

A woman in a flowing green dress, patterned with white flowers, approached the boy with a glass of red cordial. The boy was confused by her face and could not answer her questions. She looked very young. Mr D'Mello must have married very late in life, the boy thought. Perhaps he had been too shy to go near women in his young days.

D'Mello frowned and drew nearer to Girish.

'Why are you grinning? Is something funny?'

Girish shook his head.

The teacher continued. He spoke of other things that made his blood boil. Once India had been ruled by three foreigners: England, France, and Portugal. Now their place was taken by three native-born thugs: Betrayal, Bungling, and Backstabbing. 'The problem is here...' – he tapped his ribs. 'There is a beast inside us.'

He began to tell Girish things he had told no one – not even his wife. His innocence of the true nature of schoolboys had lasted just three months into his life as a teacher. In those early days, he confessed to Girish, he stayed back after class to read up on the collection of Tagore's poetry in the library. He read the pages carefully, stopping sometimes to close his eyes and fantasize that he were alive during the freedom struggle – in any one of those holy years when a man could attend a rally and see Gandhi spinning his wheel and Nehru addressing a crowd.

When he got out of the library his head would be buzzing

with images from Tagore. At that hour, electrolysed by the setting sun, the brick wall around the school became a long plane of beaten gold. Banyan trees grew along the length of the wall; within their deep, dark canopies, tiny leaves glittered in long strings of silver, like rosaries held by the meditating tree. Mr D'Mello passed. The whole earth seemed to be singing Tagore's verses. He passed by the playground, which was set into a pit below the school. Debauched shouts jarred his reveries.

'What is that shouting in the evenings?' he asked a colleague naively. The older teacher helped himself to a pinch of snuff. Inhaling the vile stuff from the edge of a stained handkerchief, he had grinned.

''tripping. That is what is going on.'

''*tripping*?'

The more experienced teacher winked.

'Don't tell me it didn't happen when you were at school…'

From D'Mello's expression he gathered that this was, indeed, not the case.

'It's the oldest game played by boys,' the old teacher said. 'Go down and see for yourself. I don't have the language to describe it.'

He went down the next evening. The sounds became louder and louder as he descended the steps into the playground.

The next morning, he summoned all the boys involved – all of them, even the victims – to his desk. He kept his voice calm with an effort. 'What do you think this is, a moral school run by Catholics, or a whorehouse?' He hit them with such violence that morning.

When he was done, he noticed that his right elbow was still shaking.

The next evening, there was no noise from the playground. He recited Tagore out loud to protect himself from evil: '*Where the head is held high and the mind is without fear*...'

A few days later, passing the playground, he saw his right elbow trembling again in recognition. The old, familiar, black noise was rising from the playground.

'That was when the scales fell off my eyes,' Mr D'Mello said. 'I had no more illusions about human nature.'

He looked at Girish with concern. The little boy was stirring a large grin into the red cordial.

'They haven't done it to you, have they, Girish – when you play cricket with them in the evening? 'tripping?'

(Mr D'Mello had already let D'Essa and his over-developed gang know: if they ever tried that on Girish, he would skin them alive. They would see what an ogre he really was.)

He watched Girish with anxiety. The boy said nothing.

Suddenly he put his cordial down, stood up, and advanced to his teacher with a folded piece of paper. The assistant headmaster opened it, prepared for the worst.

It was a gift: a poem, in chaste Hindi.

Monsoon:
  This is the wet and fiery season,
  When lightning follows after thunder.
  Each night, the sky shakes, and I wonder,
  What could be the reason
  God gave us this wet and fiery season?

'Did you write this yourself? Is this what you were blushing about?'

The boy nodded happily.

Good Lord! he thought. In thirty years as a teacher no one had done anything like this for him.

'Why is the rhyming scheme uneven?' D'Mello frowned. 'You should be careful about such things…'

The teacher pointed out the flaws of the poem one by one. The boy nodded his head attentively.

'Shall I bring you another one tomorrow?' he asked.

'Poetry is good, Girish, but…are you losing interest in quizzes?'

The boy nodded.

'I don't want to go any more, sir. I want to play cricket after class. I never get to play, because of the—'

'You have to go to the quizzes!' Mr D'Mello got up from his rocking chair. He explained: any opportunity for fame in this small town had to be seized at once. Didn't the boy understand?

'First go to the quizzes, become famous, then you'll get a big job, and then you can write poetry. What will your cricket get you, boy? How will it make you famous? You'll never write poetry if you don't get out of here, don't you understand?'

Girish nodded. He finished his cordial.

'And, tomorrow, Girish… You're going to Belmore. I don't want any more discussion about that.'

Girish nodded.

After he left, Mr D'Mello sat in his rocking chair and thought for a long time. It was no bad thing, he was thinking, Girish Rai's newfound interest in poetry. Perhaps he could look out for a poetry contest for Girish to enter. The boy would win, of course – he would come back heaped in gold and silver. The *Dawn Herald* might put a picture of him on the back page. Mr D'Mello would stand with his arms proudly on Girish's shoulders. 'The teacher who nourished the budding genius.' They would conquer Bangalore next, the teacher-and-pupil team that won the all-Karnataka state poetry contest. After that, what else – New Delhi! The president himself would award the two of them a medal. They would take an afternoon off, take a bus to Agra, and visit the Taj Mahal together. Anything was possible with a boy like Girish. Mr D'Mello's heart leaped up with joy, as it had not done for years, since his days as a young teacher. Just before he went to sleep in his chair he pressed his eyes shut and prayed fervently: 'Lord, only keep that boy pure.'

Next morning, at ten past ten, by the express order of the state government of Karnataka, a throng of innocent schoolboys from St Alfonso's with surnames from O to Z rushed into the welcoming arms of a theatre of pornography. An old stucco angel crouched over the doorway of the theatre, showering its dubious benediction on the onrushing boys.

Once they got inside, they found they had been tricked.

The walls of Angel Talkies – those infamous murals of depravity – had been covered in black cloth. Not a single picture remained visible to the human eye. A deal had been struck between Mr D'Mello and the theatre management. The children would be shielded from the Murals of Sin.

'Do not stand close to the black cloth!' Mr D'Mello shouted

out. 'Do not touch the black cloth!' He had everything planned. Mr Alvarez, Mr Rogers, and Mr Bhatt went among the students to keep them away from the posters. Two attendants from the theatre – presumably the dispensers of tickets to the blanket-covered men – helped in the arrangements. The boys were split into two groups. One group was marched to the upstairs auditorium, one herded downstairs. Before they could react, the boys would be sealed off inside the auditoriums. And so it was done: the plan worked perfectly. The boys were inside Angel Talkies, and they were going to watch nothing but the government films; Mr D'Mello had won.

The lights cut out inside the upstairs auditorium; a buzz of excitement from the boys. The screen glowed.

A scratched and fading reel flickered into life.

SAVE THE TIGER!

Mr D'Mello stood behind the seated boys along with the other teachers. He wiped his face with relief. It looked like everything was going to be okay, after all. Leaving him alone in peace for a few minutes, young Mr Bhatt then moved up to the assistant headmaster and tried to make small-talk.

Ignoring young Mr Bhatt, he kept his eyes to the screen. Photos of tiger cubs frolicking together flashed on the screen, and then a caption said: 'If you don't protect these cubs today, how can there be tigers tomorrow?'

He yawned. Stucco angels stared at him from the four corners of the auditorium, long peels of faded paint rising from their noses and ears, like heat-blisters. He hardly went to the films any more. Too expensive; he had to get tickets for the wife and the two little screamers too. But as a boy, hadn't films been his whole life? This very theatre, Angel Talkies, had been one of his favourite haunts; he would cut class and come here and sit alone and watch movies and dream. Now look at it. Even in the darkness the deterioration was unmistakable. The walls were foul, with large moisture-stains. The seats had holes in them. The simultaneous advance of decay and decadence: the story of this theatre was the story of the entire country.

The screen went black. The audience tittered. 'Silence!' Mr D'Mello shouted.

The title-shot of the 'bonus reel' came on.

The Importance of Physical Well-Being
in the Development of Children

Images of boys showering, bathing, running, and eating, each appropriately captioned, began flashing one by one. Mr Bhatt came up to the assistant headmaster once again. This time he whispered deliberately: 'It's your turn to go now, if you want.'

Mr D'Mello understood the words, but not the hint of secrecy in the young man's voice. At his own suggestion, the teachers were taking turns to patrol the black-clothed corridor to make sure none of the over-developed boys slipped out to take a peek at the pornographic images. It had just been Gopalkrishna Bhatt's turn to patrol the Murals of Sin. For a moment he was lost – then it all made sense. From the way the young man was grinning, Mr D'Mello realized that he had taken a quick peek himself. He looked around: each of the teachers was suppressing a grin.

Mr D'Mello walked out of the auditorium full of contempt for his colleagues.

He walked past the black-cloth-covered walls without feeling the slightest urge. How could Mr Bhatt and Mr Pundit have been so base to have done it? He walked past the whole length of the black cloth without the least temptation to lift it up.

A light flickered on and off in a stairwell that led to an upper gallery. The walls of this gallery too were covered with black cloth. Mr D'Mello dropped his mouth open and squinted at the upper gallery. No, he was not dreaming. Up there, he could make out a boy, his face averted, walking on tiptoe towards the black cloth. Julian D'Essa, he thought. Naturally. But then the boy's face came into view, just as he lifted up a corner of the black cloth and peered.

'Girish! What are you doing?'

At the sound of Mr D'Mello's voice the boy turned. He froze. Teacher and student stared at each other.

'I'm sorry, sir... I'm sorry...they...they...'

There was giggling behind him; and suddenly he vanished, as if someone had dragged him away.

Mr D'Mello rushed up the stairs at once, to the upper gallery. He could climb only two steps. His chest burned. Stomach heaving and hands clutching the balustrade, he rested there for a moment. The naked bulb in the stairwell sputtered on and off, on and off. The assistant headmaster felt dizzy. In his chest the heartbeat felt fainter and fainter, a dissolving tablet. He tried to call to Girish for help, but the words would not come out. Reaching out a hand for help, he caught a corner of the black cloth on the wall. It ripped, and split open: hordes of copulating creatures frozen in postures of rapes, unlawful pleasures, and bestialities, swarmed out and danced around his eyes in a taunting cavalcade, and a world of angelic delights that he had scorned until now flashed at him. He saw everything, and he understood everything, at last.

Young Mr Bhatt found him like that, lying on the stairs.

Day Three (Morning): MARKET AND MAIDAN

The Jawaharlal Nehru Memorial Maidan (formerly King George V Memorial Maidan) is an open ground in the centre of Kittur. In the evenings, it fills up with people playing cricket, flying kites, and teaching their children to ride bicycles. At the edges of the maidan, ice-cream and ice-candy sellers peddle their wares. All major political rallies in Kittur are held there. The Hyder Ali Road leads from the maidan to Central Market, Kittur's largest market for fresh produce. The Town Hall of Kittur, the new law court, and the Havelock Henry General Hospital, and both the premier hotels in Kittur – the Hotel Premier Intercontinental and the Taj Mahal International – are within walking distance of the market. In 1988, the first temple meant exclusively for the use for Kittur's Hoyka community opened for worship in the vicinity of the maidan.

With hair like that, and eyes like those, he could easily have passed himself off as a holy man and earned a living sitting cross-legged on a saffron cloth near the temple. That was what the shopkeepers at the market said. Yet all this crazy fellow did, morning and evening, was crouch on the central railing of the Hyder Ali Road and stare at the passing buses and cars. In the sunset, his hair – a gorgon's head of brown curls – shone like bronze, and his irises glowed. While the evening lasted, he was like a Sufi poet, full of mystic fire. Some of the shopkeepers could tell stories about him: one evening they had seen him on the back of a black bull, riding it down the main road, swinging his hands and shouting, as if the Lord Shiva himself were riding into town on his bull Nandi.

Sometimes, he behaved like a rational man, crossing the road carefully, or sitting patiently outside the Kittamma Devi temple with the other homeless, as they waited for the leftovers of meals from weddings or thread-ceremonies to be scraped into their clustered hands. At other times he would be seen picking through piles of dog shit.

No one knew his name, religion, or caste, so no one made any attempt to talk to him. Only one man, a cripple with a wooden leg who came to the temple in the evenings once or twice a month, would stop to give him food.

'Why do you pretend not to know this fellow?' the cripple would shout, pointing one of his crutches at the fellow with the brown curls. 'You've seen him so many times before! He used to be the king of the number 5 bus!'

For a moment the attention of the market would turn to the

wild man; but he would only squat and stare at a wall, his back to them and the city.

Two years ago, he had come to Kittur with a name, a caste, and a brother.

'I am Keshava, son of Lakshminarayana, the barber of Gurupura village,' he had said, at least six times on his way to Kittur, to bus conductors, toll-gatherers, and strangers who asked. This formula, a bag of bedding tucked beneath his arm, and the light pressure of his brother's fingers at his elbow whenever they were in a crowd, were all he had brought with him.

His brother had ten rupees, a bag of bedding that he too tucked under his right arm, and the address of a relative written on a paper chit that he kept crushed in his left hand.

The two brothers had arrived in Kittur on the 5 p.m. bus. They got off at the bus station; it was their first visit to a town. Right in the middle of the Market–Maidan road, in the centre of the biggest road in all of Kittur, the conductor had told them that their six rupees and twenty paise would take them no further. Buses charged around them, with men in khaki uniforms hanging from their doors, whistles in their mouths that they blew on screechingly, shouting at the passengers: 'Stop gaping at the girls, you sons of bitches! We're running late!'

Keshava held on to the hem of his brother's shirt. Two cycles swerved around him, nearly running over his feet; in every direction, cycles, autorickshaws, cars, threatened to crush his toes. It was as if he were at the beach, with the road shifting beneath him like sand beneath the waves.

After a while, they summoned up the courage to approach a bystander, a man whose lips were discoloured by vitiligo.

'Where is Central Market, uncle?'

'Oh, that... It's down by the Bunder.'

'How far is the Bunder from here?'

The stranger directed them to an autorickshaw driver, who was massaging his gums with a finger.

'We need to go to the market,' Vittal said.

The driver stared at them, his finger still in his mouth, revealing his long gums. He examined the moist tip of his finger. 'Lakshmi Market or Central Market?'

'Central Market.'

'How many of you?'

And then: 'How many bags?'

And then: 'Where are you from?'

Keshava assumed that these questions were standard in a big city like Kittur, that an autorickshaw driver was entitled to such inquiries.

'Is it a long distance away?' Vittal asked, desperately. The auto driver spat right at their feet.

'Of course. This isn't a village, it's a city. Everything's a long distance from everything else.'

He took a deep breath and sketched a series of loops with his damp finger in the air, showing them the circuitous path that they would have to take. Then he sighed, giving the impression that the market was incalculably far away. Keshava's heart sank; they had been swindled by the bus driver. He had promised to drop them off within walking distance of Central Market.

'How much, uncle, to take us there?'

The driver looked at them from head to toe, and then from toe to head, as if gauging their height, weight, and moral worth: 'Eight rupees.'

'Uncle, it's too much! Take four!'

The autorickshaw driver said: 'Seven twenty-five', and motioned for them to get in. But then he kept them waiting in the rickshaw, their bundles on their laps, without any explanation. Two other passengers negotiated a destination and a fare and crammed in; one of them sat on Keshava's lap without any warning. Still the rickshaw did not move. Only after another passenger joined them, sitting in the front beside the driver, and with six people crammed into the tiny vehicle that had space for three, did the driver start kicking on his engine's pedal.

Keshava could barely see where they were going, and thus his first impressions of Kittur were of the man who was sitting on his lap; of the scent of castor oil which had been used to grease his hair and the hint of shit that he produced when he squirmed. After dropping off the rider in the front seat, and then the two men at the back, the autorickshaw meandered for some time through a quiet, dark area of town, before turning into another cacophonous street, lit by the glaring white light of powerful paraffin lamps.

'Is this Central Market?' Vittal shouted at the driver, who pointed to a sign:

KITTUR MUNICIPALITY CENTRAL MARKET:
ALL MANNER OF VEGETABLES AND FRUIT AT FAIR PRICES
AND EXCELLENT FRESHNESS

'Thank you, brother,' Vittal said, overwhelmed with gratitude, and Keshava thanked him too.

When they got out, they found themselves once again in a vortex of light and noise; they kept very still, waiting for their eyes to make sense of the chaos.

'Brother,' Keshava said, excited at having found a landmark that he recognized. He pointed: 'Brother, isn't this where we started out?'

And when they looked round, they realized that they were only a few feet away from where the bus driver had set them down. Somehow they had missed the sign, which had been right behind them all the time.

'We were cheated!' Keshava said, in an excited voice. 'That autorickshaw driver cheated us, brother! He—'

'Shut up!' Vittal whacked his younger brother on the back of his head. 'It's all your fault! You're the one who wanted to take an autorickshaw!'

The two of them had been brothers for only a few days.

Keshava was dark and chubby; Vittal was tall and lean and fair, and five years older. Their mother had died years ago, and their father had abandoned them; an uncle had raised them and they had grown up amongst their cousins (whom they also called 'brothers'). Then their uncle had died, and their aunt called Keshava and told him to go with Vittal, who was being dispatched to the big city to work for a relative who ran a grocery shop. And that was, really, how they had come to realize that there was a bond between them deeper than that between cousins.

They knew that their relative was somewhere in the Central Market of Kittur: that was all. Taking timid steps, they went into a dark market area where vegetables were being sold, and then, through a back door, they went into a well-lit market where fruits were being sold. Here they asked for directions. Then they walked up steps that were covered in rotting garbage and moist straw to the second floor. Here they asked again: 'Where is Janardhana the store owner from Salt Market Village? He's our kinsman.'

'Which Janardhana – Shetty, Rai, or Padiwal?'

'I don't know, uncle.'

'Is your kinsman a Bunt?'

'No.'

'Not a Bunt? A Jain, then?'

'No.'

'Then of what caste?'

'He's a Hoyka.'

A laugh.

'There are no Hoykas in this market. Only Muslims and Bunts.'

But the two boys looked so lost that the man took pity and asked someone, and found out that there were indeed some Hoykas who had set up shop near the market.

They walked down the steps and went out of the market. Janardhana's shop, they were told, displayed a large poster of a muscular man in a white singlet. They couldn't miss it. They walked from shop to shop and then Keshava cried: 'There!'

Beneath the image of the man with the big muscles sat a lean shopkeeper, unshaven, who was reading a notebook with his glasses down on the bridge of his nose.

'We are looking for Janardhana, from Gurupura village,' Vittal said.

'Why do you want to know where he is?'

The man was looking at them suspiciously.

Vittal burst out: 'Uncle, we're from your village. We're your kin.'

The shopkeeper stared. Moistening a tip of his finger, he turned another page in his book.

'Why do you think you're my kin?'

'We were told this, uncle. By our aunty. One-eyed Kamala.'

The shopkeeper put the book down.

'One-eyed Kamala's…ah, I see. And what happened to your parents?'

'Our mother passed away many years ago, after Keshava's – this fellow's – birth. And four years ago, our father lost interest in us and just wandered away.'

'Wandered away?'

'Yes, uncle,' Vittal said. 'Some say he's gone to Varanasi, to do yoga by the banks of the Ganga. Others say he's in the holy city of Rishikesh. We haven't seen him in many years; we were raised by our uncle Thimma.'

'And he…?'

'Died last year. We stayed on, and then it was too much for our aunt to support us. The drought was very bad this year.'

The shopkeeper was amazed that they had come all this way, without any prior word, on so thin a connection, just expecting that he would take care of them. He reached down into a counter, bringing out a bottle of arrack, which he uncapped and put to his lips. Then he capped the bottle and hid it again.

'Every day people come from the villages, looking for work. Everyone thinks that we in the towns can support them for nothing. As if we have no stomachs of our own to feed.'

The shopkeeper took another swig of his bottle; his mood improved. He had rather liked their naïve recounting of that story of daddy having gone to 'the holy city of Rishikesh…to do yoga'. Old rascal is probably shacked up with a mistress somewhere, and taking care of a brood of bastards, he thought, smiling in approval; how you can get away with anything in the villages. Stretching his hands high above his head as he yawned, he brought them down onto his stomach with a loud whack.

'Oh, so you're orphans now! You poor fellows. One must always stick to one's family – what else is there in life?' He rubbed his stomach: look at the way they are staring at me, as if I were a king, he thought, feeling suddenly important. It was not a feeling he had had often since coming to Kittur.

He scratched his legs. 'So, how are things in the village these days?'

'Except for the drought, everything's the same, uncle.'

'You got here by bus?' the shopkeeper asked. And then: 'From the bus station, you walked over here, I take it?' He got up from his seat: 'Autorickshaw? How much did you pay? Those fellows are total crooks. Seven rupees!' The shopkeeper turned red. 'You imbeciles! Cretins!'

Apparently holding the fact that they had been cheated against them, the shopkeeper ignored them for half an hour.

Vittal stood in a corner, his eyes to the ground, crushed by humiliation. Keshava looked around. Red-and-white stacks of Colgate–Palmolive toothpaste and jars of Horlicks were piled behind the shopkeeper's head, shiny packets of malt-powder hung from the ceiling like wedding bunting; blue bottles of kerosene and red bottles of cooking oil were stacked in pyramids up the front of the shop.

Keshava was a small, lean, dark-skinned boy, with enormous eyes that stared lingeringly. Some of those who knew him insisted he had the energy of a hummingbird and was always flapping around, making a nuisance of himself; others found him lazy and melancholic, liable to sit and stare at the ceiling for hours at a time. He smiled and turned his head away when he was scolded for his behaviour, as if he had no conception of himself and no opinion on the matter.

Again the store owner took out the bottle of arrack, and he sipped a little more. Again this affected his mood for the better.

'We don't drink here like they do in the villages,' he said, returning Keshava's big stare. ' Only a little sip at a time. The customer never finds out that I am drunk.' He winked. 'That's how it is in the city: you can do anything you want, as long as no one finds out.'

After drawing the shutters on his shop, he took Vittal and Keshava around the market. Everywhere men were sleeping on the ground, covered in thin bedsheets; after asking some questions, Janardhana led the boys to an alley behind the market. Men and women and children were sleeping in a long line all the way down the alley. Keshava and Vittal stood back as the store owner began negotiations with one of the sleepers.

'If they sleep here, they will have to pay the Boss,' the sleeper complained.

'What do I do with them, they have to sleep somewhere!'

'Well, you're taking a risk, but if you have to leave them here try the far end.'

The alley ended in a wall that leaked continuously; the drainage pipes had been badly fitted. A large rubbish bin at this end of the alley emitted a horrible stench.

'Isn't uncle going to take us to his house, brother?' Keshava whispered, when the store owner, having given them some advice about how to sleep out in the open, vanished.

Vittal pinched him.

'I'm hungry,' Keshava said, after a few minutes. 'Can we find uncle and ask him for food?'

The two brothers were lying side by side, wrapped in their bedding, next to the garbage bin.

In response, his brother entirely covered himself in his sheet and lay inside, still, like a cocoon.

Keshava could not believe he was expected to sleep here – and on an empty stomach. However bad things had been at home, at least there had always been something to eat. Now all the frustrations of the evening, the fatigue, and confusion combined, and he kicked the shrouded figure hard. His brother, as if he had been waiting for just such a provocation, tore the blanket off; caught Keshava's head in his hands and slammed it twice against the ground.

'If you make one more sound, I swear, I will leave you all alone in this city.' Then he covered himself with his bedding once more and turned his back to his brother.

And though his head had begun to hurt, Keshava was frightened by what his brother had said. He shut up.

Lying there, his head stinging, Keshava wondered, dully, where it was decided that this fellow and this fellow would be brothers; and about how people came into the earth, and how they left it. It was a dull curiosity. Then he began thinking about food. He was in a tunnel, and that tunnel was his hunger, and at the end of the tunnel, if he kept going, he promised himself, there would be a huge heap of rice, covered with hot lentils, with big chunks of chicken.

He opened his eyes; there were stars in the sky. He looked up at them to block the stench of garbage.

When they arrived at the shop the following morning, the shopkeeper was using a long stick to hang plastic bags of malt-powder on hooks in the ceiling.

'You,' the shopkeeper said, pointing to Vittal. He showed the boy how each plastic bag was to be fitted to the end of the pole, and then lifted up and snared on a hook in the ceiling.

'It takes forty-five minutes every morning to do this; some-times an hour. I don't want you to rush the work. You don't mind working, do you?'

Then, with the redundancy of speech typical of the rich, he said: 'If a man doesn't work, he doesn't eat in this world.'

While Vittal hung the plastic bags from the hooks, the shopkeeper told Keshava to sit behind the counter. He gave him six sheets of paper with the faces of film actresses printed on them, and six boxes of incense-sticks. The boy was to cut out the pictures, put them on the incense-stick boxes, cover them with cellophane quickly, and Scotch-tape the cellophane to the box.

'With pretty girls on them, you can charge ten paise more,' said the storekeeper. 'Do you know who this is?' He showed Keshava the picture he had just cut from the sheet. 'She's famous in Hindi films.'

Keshava began cutting out the next actress from the sheet. In front of them, below the counter, he could see where the store owner had hidden his bottle of hooch.

At noon, the shopkeeper's wife came with lunch. She looked at Vittal, who avoided her gaze, and at Keshava, who stared at her, and said: 'There's not enough food for both of them. Send one of them to the barber.'

Keshava, following instructions he had memorized, made his way through the unfamiliar streets and came to a part of town where he found a barber working on the street. He had set up his barber's stall against a wall, hanging his mirror from a nail hammered between a family planning sign and an anti-tuberculosis poster.

A customer sat in a chair in front of the mirror, draped in a white cloth, and the barber was shaving him. Keshava waited till the customer had left.

The barber scratched his head and inspected Keshava from head to foot.

'What kind of work can I offer you, boy?'

At first the barber could think of nothing for him to do but hold the mirror for his customers to examine themselves after they had been shaved. Then he asked Keshava to clip the toenails and calluses from the customers' feet as he shaved them. Then he told the boy to sweep the hair from the pavement.

'Serve him some food too, he's a good boy,' the barber told his wife, when she arrived with tea and biscuits at four o'clock.

'He's the shopkeeper's boy, he can get food himself. And he's a Hoyka, you want him eating with us?'

'He's a good boy, let him have some food. Just a little.'

It was only as the barber watched the boy wolf down the biscuits that he realized why the shopkeeper had sent the boy to him. 'My God! You haven't eaten all day?'

The next morning, when Keshava showed up, the barber patted him on the back. He still didn't know exactly what to do with Keshava, but that no longer seemed to be a problem; he knew he could not let this boy, with his sweet face, starve all day at the shopkeeper's place. In the afternoon, Keshava was given lunch. The barber's wife grumbled, but her husband splashed Keshava's plate with large helpings of fish curry.

'He's a hard worker, he deserves it.'

That evening, Keshava accompanied the barber on a round of house-calls; they went from house to house, and waited in the back yards for their customers to come outside. While Keshava set up a small wooden chair in the back yard, the barber threw a white cloth around the customer's neck and asked him how he wanted his hair cut that day. After each appointment, the barber would flap the white cloth hard, dusting off the curlets of hair; as they left the house and went to the next, the barber passed a commentary on the customer.

'That customer can't get it up, you can tell from how limp his moustache is.' Seeing Keshava's blank stare, he said: 'I guess you don't know about that bit of life yet, eh, boy?' Then, regretting that confidence, he whispered to the boy: 'Don't repeat that to my wife.'

Each time they crossed the road, the barber seized the boy's hand by the wrist.

'It's *dangerous* out here,' he said, pronouncing the key word in English, in a tremulous manner, bringing out all the drama in that foreign word. 'One moment of not watching out in this city and your whole life is gone. *Dangerous.*'

In the evening Keshava came back to the alley behind the market. His brother was lying face down on the ground, fast asleep, too tired even to lay out his bedding. Keshava turned Vittal over, unfolded the sheet and covered his face up to his nose.

Since Vittal was already asleep, he pulled his mattress right next to his brother's, so that their arms would touch. He fell asleep gazing at the stars.

A horrible noise woke him in the middle of the night: three kittens, chasing each other, right around his body. In the morning, he saw their neighbour feeding the kittens a bowl of milk. They had yellow flesh, and their pupils were elongated, like claw-marks.

'Have you got the money ready?' the neighbour asked him, when he came over to pet the kittens. He explained that Vittal and Keshava would have to pay a fee to a local 'boss' – one of those who collected payments from the homeless of the streets of Kittur in return for 'protection' – mainly from himself.

'But where is this Boss? My brother and I have never seen him here.'

'You'll see him tonight. That was the word we received. Have the money ready; or he'll beat you.'

Over the next few weeks, Keshava developed a routine. In the mornings, he worked at the barber's; after his work at the barber's, he was free to do as he wished. He wandered about the market, which seemed to him to be bursting with shining things, expensive things. Even the cows that ate the garbage seemed so much larger in this market than they were back home. He wondered what there was in the garbage here that made the cows so fat. One black cow, an animal with extra-ordinary horns, walked about like a magical animal from some other land; back in the village he used to ride cows and he wanted to mount this animal, but he was frightened of doing so here in the city. Food seemed to be everywhere in Kittur; even the poor did not starve here. He saw food being scraped into the hands of the poor by the Jain temple. He saw a shop-keeper, trying to sleep in the hubbub of the market, covering his head with a scooter helmet. He saw shops selling glass bangles, white shirts and undershirts in cellophane bags, maps of India with her states marked out.

'Hey! Move out of the way, you village hick!'

He turned. The man was driving a bullock cart laden with cardboard boxes stacked into a pyramid; the boy wondered what was in the boxes.

He wished he had a cycle, to ride fast up and down the main road and stick his tongue out at these haughty fellows riding the bullock carts, who were always rude to him. But most of all he wished he were a bus conductor. They hung from the sides of the buses, shouting at people to get in faster, cursing when a rival bus overtook them; they had their khaki uniforms and their black whistles hanging from the red cords around their necks.

One evening, nearly every bystander around the market looked up to see a monkey walking on a telephone wire that went over their heads. Keshava stared at the monkey in wonder. Its pink scrotum dangled between its legs, and huge red balls whacked against the sides of the wire. It leaped onto a building with a blue sun and spreading rays painted on it, and sat there, looking down indifferently at the crowd.

Suddenly an autorickshaw hit Keshava, flinging him down onto the road. Before he could scramble to his feet, he saw the rickshaw driver in front of him, yelling furiously.

'Get up! You son of a bald woman! Get up! Get up!' The driver had made a fist already, and Keshava covered his face with his hands and begged.

'Leave the boy alone.'

A fat man in a blue sarong stood over Keshava, pointing a stick at the autorickshaw driver. The driver grumbled, but turned away and returned to his vehicle.

Keshava wanted to catch the hands of the man in the blue sarong and kiss them, but the man had melted away into the crowd.

Once again, the cats woke Keshava in the middle of the night. Before he could go back to sleep, there was a loud whistle from the far end of the alley. 'Brother's here!' someone cried. A shuffling of clothes and bedsheets followed; men were getting up all around him. A pot-bellied man in a white singlet and a blue sarong was standing at the head of the alley, his hands on his hips. He bellowed:

'So my little darling dumplings, you thought you could avoid payments to your poor bereaved Brother by coming here to this alley, did you?'

The fat man – the one who called himself Brother – went up to each of the men sleeping in the alley one by one. Keshava started: it was his saviour from the market. With his stick Brother poked every sleeping person and asked.

'How long has it been since you paid me? Huh?'

Vittal was terrified; but a neighbour whispered: 'Don't worry, he'll only make you do some squats, and say sorry, and then he'll be off. He knows there's no money in this lane.'

When he reached Vittal, the fat man stopped and inspected him carefully.

'And you sir, my Maharajah of Mysore, if I may bother you a second,' he said. 'Your name?'

'Vittal, son of the barber from Gurupura village, sir.'

'Hoyka?'

'Yes, sir.'

'When did you arrive in this lane?'

'Four months ago,' Vittal said, blurting out the truth.

'And how many payments have you made to me in that period?'

Vittal said nothing.

The fat man slapped him and he staggered back, tripped on his bedding, and fell on the ground hard.

'Don't hit him, hit me!'

The man in the blue sarong turned to Keshava.

'He's my brother, he's my only relative in the world! Hit me instead. Please!'

The fat man down put his stick; with narrowed eyes he examined the little boy.

'A Hoyka who is so brave? That's unusual. Your caste is full of cowards, that's been Brother's experience in Kittur.'

He pointed at Keshava with his stick and addressed the entire lane: 'Everyone: notice the way he sticks by his brother. Wah, wah. Young fellow, for your sake, I spare your brother's hide tonight.'

He touched Keshava's head with the stick. 'On Thursday, you'll come see me. At the bus station. I have work for brave boys like you there.'

The next morning, the barber was aghast when Keshava told him of his tremendous good fortune.

'But who's going to hold the mirror?' he said.

He caught the boy by the wrist.

'It's *dangerous* with those people in the buses. Stay with me, Keshava. You can come and sleep in my house, so this Brother doesn't bother you any more; you'll be like a son to me.'

But Keshava had lost his heart to the buses. Every day, he went straight to the bus station at the end of Central Market to scrub the buses clean with a mop and a bucket of water. He was the most enthusiastic of the cleaners. When he was inside the bus, he would take the wheel and pretend he was driving, vroom-vroom!

'A nice little catch here for us,' Brother told them – and the conductors and drivers laughed and agreed.

As long as he was at the wheel, pretending to be driving, he was loud, and used the coarsest language; but if anyone stopped him and asked: 'What's your name, loudmouth?', he would get confused, and roll his eyes, and slap the top of his skull, before saying: 'Keshava – yes, that's it. Keshava. I think that's my name.' They roared and said: 'He's a bit touched in the head, this fellow!'

One conductor took a liking to him and told him to come along on his 4 p.m. round on the bus. 'Only one round, you understand?' he warned the boy sternly. 'You'll have to get off the bus at 5.15 p.m.'

The conductor returned to the station with Keshava at half past ten.

'He brings good luck,' he said, ruffling the boy's hair. 'We beat all the Christian buses today; a clean sweep.'

Soon all the conductors began inviting him on their buses. Brother, who was a superstitious man, observed this development and declared that Keshava had brought good luck with him from his village.

'A young fellow like you, with ambition!' He tapped Keshava's bottom with his stick. 'You might even become the conductor of a bus one day, loudmouth!'

'Really?' Keshava's eyes widened.

He went with the buses when they roared down the market road at five o'clock, the rush hour, with the number 77 bus right ahead of them.

He was seated up the front, near the driver's seat, a cheering squad of one. 'Are you going to let them beat us?' He asked the driver. 'Let the Christians overtake the Hindu buses?'

The conductor waded his way through the crowd, issuing tickets, collecting money, his whistle in his mouth all the time. The bus picked up speed, just missing a cow. Tearing down the road, the number 5 bus drove parallel to the number 243, as a frightened scooter driver veered leftward for his life, and then – a big cheer from the passengers! – overtook its rival. The Hindu bus had won!

In the evenings, he washed the buses and fixed incense-sticks to the portraits of the gods Ganapati and Krishna by the drivers' rear-view mirrors.

On Sundays, he was free after noon. He explored Central Market from the vegetable sellers at one end, to the clothes sellers at the other end.

He learned to notice what people noticed. He learned what was good value for money in shirts; what was a rip-off; what made for a good dosa, and a bad one. He acquired the connois-seurship of the market. He learned to spit; not like he had in the past, simply to clear his throat or nose, but with some arrogance – some style. When the rains failed again, and more fresh faces arrived at the market from villages, he mocked them: 'O, you hicks!' He came to master life in the market; learned how to cross the road despite the continuous traffic, simply by holding his hand as a stop sign and moving briskly, ignoring the loud honks from the irritated drivers.

When there was a cricket match, the entire market would be abuzz. He went from store to store; each shopkeeper had a small black transistor that emitted a crackly noise of cricket commentary. The entire market was buzzing as if it were a hive, whose every cell secreted cricket commentary.

At night people ate by the side of the road. They chopped firewood and fed it into the stoves, and sat around the fires, burnished by the flickering flames, looking haggard and hard. They cooked broth and sometimes fried fish. He did petty favours for them, like carrying empty bottles, bread, rice, and blocks of ice to nearby shops on the back of his bicycle, and for this he was invited to eat with them.

He hardly saw Vittal any more. By the time he got back to the alley, his brother was wrapped up in his bedsheet and was snoring softly.

One evening, he had a surprise: the barber, who worried that Keshava was falling into the influence of the 'dangerous' fellows at the bus station, took him to see a film, holding his hand tightly the whole way to the cinema. When they emerged from the theatre, the barber told him to wait as he went to chat up a friend who sold paan-leaves outside the cinema. As he waited, Keshava heard a drum-beat and yelling, and followed the noise around the corner to the source. A man stood beating a long drum outside a playground; next to him was a metal board painted with the images of fat men in blue underwear grappling with each other.

The drum-beater would not let Keshava in. Two rupees admission, he said. Keshava sighed and turned towards the cinema. On his way back, he saw a group of boys climbing over the side of a wall into the playground; he followed them.

Two wrestlers were in the sandpit in the middle of the

playground, one wore grey shorts, the other wore yellow. Six or seven other wrestlers stood by the pit, shaking their legs and arms. He had never seen men with such slender waists and such enormous shoulders before; it was so exciting just to watch their bodies. 'Govind Pehlwan fights Shamsher Pehlwan,' announced a man with a megaphone.

The man with the megaphone was Brother.

Both wrestlers touched the ground and then raised their fingers to their foreheads; then they charged into one another like rams. The one with the grey shorts stumbled and slipped, and the one with the yellow shorts pinned him down; then the situation was reversed. Things continued like this, for some more time, until Brother separated them, saying: 'What a fight that was!'

The wrestlers, covered in dirt, came to the side and washed themselves clean. Under their shorts, to Keshava's surprise, they each wore another pair of shorts and they bathed in these. Suddenly, one of the wrestlers reached over and squeezed the other's buttock. Keshava rubbed his eyes to make sure he had seen what he had seen.

'Next up: Balram Pehlwan fights Rajesh Pehlwan,' came the announcement from Brother.

The pale mud in the pit was now dark in the centre, where the wrestling and fighting had been most intense. Spectators sat on a grassy bank near the pit. Brother walked around the pit, offering commentary on the action. 'Wah, wah,' he cried, whenever a wrestler pinned another one down. A cloud of mosquitoes swirled overhead, as if they too were excited by the match.

Keshava walked among the crowd of spectators; he saw

boys who were holding each other's hands, or resting their heads on another's chest. He was envious; he wished he had a friend here too, so he could hold his hand.

'Sneaked in, did you?' Brother had come up to him. He put an arm on Keshava's shoulder and winked. 'Not a good idea – the ticket money comes to me, so you've been swindling me, you rascal!'

'I have to go,' Keshava said, squirming. 'The barber is waiting for me.'

'To hell with the barber!' Brother roared. He sat Keshava next to him and returned to his commentary with the megaphone.

'I too was like you,' Brother told him, during the next break in his commentary. 'A boy with nothing; I wandered here from my village with empty hands. And look what I've done for myself—'

He spread his arms wide, and Keshava saw them embrace the wrestlers, the sellers of peanuts, the mosquitoes, the man with the drum at the gate: Brother seemed like the ruler of all that was important in the world.

That night the barber came down the alley and embraced Keshava, who had lain down to sleep. 'Hey! Where did you vanish after the movies? We thought you were lost.' He put his hand on Keshava's head and ruffled his hair.

'You're like my son, now, Keshava. I'll tell my wife, we must take you into our house. Let her agree, then you come with me. This is your last night here.'

Keshava turned to Vittal, who had pulled down a corner of his blanket to overhear them.

Vittal pulled his blanket over his head and turned the other way. 'Do what you want with him,' he mumbled. 'I have enough work to do, looking after myself.'

One evening, as Keshava was scrubbing the bus, a stick tapped the ground next to him.

'Loudmouth!' It was Brother, in his white singlet. 'We need you for the rally.'

A whole gang of the boys from the bus station were being taken by a number 5 bus to the Nehru Maidan. An enormous crowd had gathered there. Poles had been stuck up over the ground and miniature Congress party flags hung from them.

A huge stage had been erected in the middle of the ground, and above the stage hung the enormous painted image of a man with a moustache and thick black glasses, his arms raised as if in universal benediction. Six men, in white clothes, sat on the stage beneath the painting. A speaker was at a mike: 'He is a Hoyka sits next to the prime minister Rajiv Gandhi and gives him advice! And so the entire world can see that the Hoykas are trustworthy and reliable, despite the falsehoods that the Bunts and other upper castes spread about us!'

After a while, the MP himself – the same man whose face was on the painting – got to the mike.

At once, Brother hissed: 'Start shouting.'

The dozen boys who were standing together at the back of the crowd filled their lungs and bellowed: 'Long live the hero of the Hoyka people!'

They shouted six times, and then Brother told them to shut up.

The great man spoke for over an hour.

'There will be a Hoyka temple. No matter what the Brahmins say; no matter what the rich say; there will be a Hoyka temple in this town. With Hoyka priests. And Hoyka gods. And Hoyka goddesses. And Hoyka doors, and Hoyka bells, and even Hoyka doormats and doorknobs! And why? Because we are ninety per cent of this town! We have our rights here!'

'We are ninety per cent of this town! We are ninety per cent of this town.' Brother instructed the boys to shout. The other boys did as told; Keshava came close to Brother and yelled into his ear: 'But we are not ninety per cent of this town. That isn't true.'

'Shut up and shout.'

After the procession, bottles of liquor were being handed out from trucks, and men jostled each other to grab them.

'Hey,' Brother signalled to Keshava. 'Have a drink, come on, you deserve it.' He slapped him on the back; the others forced the liquor down his throat and he coughed.

'Our star slogan-shouter!'

That night, when Keshava finally got back to the alley, Vittal was waiting for him with his arms folded.

'You're drunk.'

'So what?' Keshava thumped his chest. 'Who are you, my father?'

Vittal turned to the neighbour, who was playing with his cats, and shouted: 'This guy is losing all sense of morality in this city. He can't tell right from wrong any longer. He hangs out with drunks and thugs.'

'Don't say things like that about Brother, I warn you,' Keshava said, in a low voice.

But Vittal continued: 'What the hell do you think you are doing, roaming around the city this late? You think I don't know what kind of animal you've become?'

He swung his fist at Keshava; but his younger brother caught his hand.

'Don't touch me.'

Then, without being entirely aware of what he was doing, he picked up his bedding and walked down the alley.

'Where do you think you're going?' Vittal shouted.

'I'm leaving.'

'And where will you sleep tonight?'

'With Brother.'

He was almost out of the alley, when he heard Vittal shouting his name. Tears were streaming down his face. Calling his name was not enough; he wanted Vittal to come running down, to touch him, to embrace him, to beg for him to come back.

A hand touched his shoulder; his heart leaped. But when he turned around, he saw not Vittal, but the neighbour. A second later, the cats had also come to him and were licking his feet and meowing ferociously.

'You know Vittal didn't mean that! He's worried about you, that's all: you have been mixing with a dangerous crowd. Just forget everything he said and come back.'

Keshava only shook his head.

It was ten o'clock at night. He walked into the bus-repair shop. In the darkness, two men with masks were cutting metal with a blue flame; fumes, sparks, the smell of acrid smoke, and loud noise.

After a while, one man in a mask gestured upwards with his hand, and not knowing what that meant, Keshava walked right past the buses. He saw a woman crouching on the floor, whom he had never seen before. She was pressing the feet of Brother, who sat bare-chested in a cane chair.

'Brother, take me in, I have nowhere to stay. Vittal has thrown me out.'

'Poor boy!' Without getting up from the chair, Brother turned to the woman pressing his feet. 'You see what is happening to the family structure in our country? Brothers casting brothers out on the street!'

He led Keshava to a nearby building, which, he explained, was a hostel he ran for the best workers at the bus station. He opened a door; inside were rows of beds, and on each bed lay a boy. Brother tore the cover off one bed. A boy was lying asleep with his head on his hands.

Brother slapped the boy awake.

'Get up and get out of this house.'

Without any protest, the boy began scrambling to collect his stuff. He moved into a corner and crouched; he was too confused to know where to go. 'Get out! You haven't showed up to work in three weeks!' Brother shouted.

Keshava felt sorry for the crouching figure, and he wanted to shout out: no, don't throw him out, Brother! But he understood: it was either this boy or him in this bed tonight.

A few seconds later, the crouching figure had vanished.

A long clothesline had been fixed between two of the crossbeams of the ceiling, and the white cotton sarongs of the boys hung from it, overlapping each other like ghosts stuck together. Posters of film actresses and the god Ayappa, sitting on his peacock, covered the walls. The boys were clustered around the beds, staring at him and taunting him.

Ignoring them, he took out his things: a spare shirt, a comb, half a bottle of hair oil, some Scotch tape, and six pictures of film actresses that he had stolen from his relative's shop. He stuck the pictures up over his bed with the Scotch tape.

At once, the other boys gathered round.

'Do you know the names of these Bombay chicks? Tell us.'

'Here's Hema Malini,' he said. 'Here's Rekha, she's married to Amitabh Bachchan.'

The statement provokes giggles from the boys around him.

'Hey, boy, she's not his wife. She's his *girlfriend*. He sticks it to her every Sunday in a house in Bombay.'

He felt so angry when they said this that he got to his feet and shouted incoherently at them. He lay his face down in bed for an hour after that.

'Moody fellow. Like a lady, so delicate and moody.'

He pulled the pillow over his head; he began thinking of Vittal, wondering where he was right now, why he was not sleeping at his side. He began to cry into the pillow.

Another boy came over: 'Are you a Hoyka?' He asked.

Keshava nodded.

'Me too,' the boy said. 'The rest of these boys are Bunts. They look down on us. You and I, we should stick together.'

He whispered: 'There's something I have to warn you about. In the night, one of the boys walks around tapping guys' cocks.'

Keshava started. 'Which one does that?'

He stayed awake all night, sitting up whenever anyone came anywhere near his bed. Only in the morning, watching the other boys giggling hysterically as they brushed their teeth, did he realize that he had been had.

Inside a week, it seemed as though he had always lived at the hostel.

Some weeks later, Brother came for him.

'It's your big day, Keshava,' he said. 'One of the conductors was killed last night in a fight at a liquor-shop.' He held Keshava's arm up high, as if he had won a wrestling match.

'The first Hoyka bus conductor in our company! He's a pride to his people!'

Keshava was promoted to chief conductor of one of the twenty-six buses that plied the number 5 route. He was issued a brand-new khaki uniform, his own black whistle on a red cord, and books of tickets, marked in maroon, green, and grey, all bearing the number 5.

As they drove, he stood leaning out of the bus, holding on to a metal bar, with his whistle in his mouth, blowing sharply once to tell the driver to stop and twice to tell him not to. As soon as the bus stopped, he jumped down onto the road and shouted at the passengers: 'Get in, get in.' Waiting until the bus moved again, he jumped onto the metal steps that led down from the entrance and hung from the bus, holding on to the rail. Shoving and yelling and pushing his way inside the packed bus, he collected money and gave out tickets. There was no need for tickets – he knew every customer by sight; but it was the tradition for tickets to be issued, and he did so, ripping them out and handing them to the customers, or sending them through the air to inaccesible customers.

In the evenings, the other cleaning boys, awed by his swift promotion, gathered around him at the bus station.

'Fix this thing!' He shouted, pointing to the metal bar by which he hung from the bus. 'I can hear it rattling all day long, it's so loose.'

'It's not so much fun,' he said when the work was done and the boys crouched around, gazing at him with star-struck eyes. 'Sure there are girls on the bus, but you can't pester them – you're the conductor, after all. Then there's the constant worry about whether those Christian bastards will beat us and steal the customers. No, sir, it's not all fun at all.'

When the rains started, he had to lower the leather canvas above the windows so that the passengers would remain dry; but water always seeped in anyway and the bus became dank. The front glass of the bus was besmirched with rain; blotches of silvery water clung to the screen like blobs of mercury; the world outside became hazy, and he would grip the bar and lean outside to make sure the driver could find his way.

In the evening, as he lay on his bed in the hostel, having his hair dried with a white towel by one boy and getting his feet massaged by another (these were his new privileges), Brother came to the dormitory, bringing in a rusty old bike behind him.

'You can't go walking around town any more, you're a bigshot now. I expect my conductors to travel in style.'

Keshava pulled the bike to his bed; that night, to the amusement of the other boys, he went to sleep with the bike next to him.

One evening, at the bus station, he saw a cripple sitting and blowing at his tea with his legs crossed, exposing the wooden stub of his artificial leg.

One of the boys chuckled.

'Don't you recognize your patron?'

'What do you mean?'

The boy said: 'That's the man whose bike you ride these days!'

He explained that the cripple had himself once been a bus conductor, like Keshava; but he had fallen from the bus, crushing his legs under a passing lorry, and had to have an amputation.

'And thanks to that, you now have a bike of your own!' he guffawed, slapping Keshava heartily on the back.

The cripple drank his tea slowly, staring at it intensely, as if it were the only pleasure in his life.

When Keshava was not conducting the bus, Brother had a string of bicycle delivery jobs for him; once he had to strap a block of ice on the back of his cycle and ride all the way downtown to drop it off at the house of Mabroor Engineer, the richest man in town, who had run out of ice for his whisky. But in the evenings, he was allowed to ride the bike for his pleasure; which meant, usually, taking it at full speed down the main road next to Central Market. On either side, the shops glowed with the light of paraffin lamps, and all the lights and colour got him so excited that he took both hands off the handlebars and whooped for joy, braking just in time to stop himself running into an autorickshaw.

Everything seemed to be going so well for him; yet one morning his neighbours found him lying in bed, staring at the picture of the film actresses and refusing to move.

'He's being morose again,' his neighbours said. 'Hey, why don't you jerk off, it'll make you feel better?'

The next morning he went back to see the barber. The old man was not in. His wife was sitting in the barber's chair, combing her hair. 'Just wait for him, he's always talking about you. He misses you very much, you know.'

Keshava nodded; he cracked his knuckles and walked round the chair three or four times.

That night at the dormitory, the other boys seized him as he was brushing his hair and dragged him out the door.

'This fellow's been morose for days now. It's time for him to be taken to a woman.'

'No,' he said. 'Not tonight. I have to visit the barber. I promised I'd come for—'

'We'll take you to a barber, all right! She'll shave you good!'

They put him in an autorickshaw and drove him down to the Bunder. A prostitute was 'seeing' men in a house by the shirt factories, and though he shouted at them and said he didn't want to do it, they told him that doing it would cure his moods and make him normal like everyone else.

He did seem more normal in the days that followed. One evening, at the end of his shift, he saw a new cleaning boy, one of Brother's recent hires, spit on the ground as he was cleaning the bus; calling him over, Keshava slapped him.

'Don't spit anywhere near the bus, understood?'

That was the first time he ever slapped anyone.

It made him feel good. From then on, he regularly hit the cleaning boys, like all the other conductors did.

On the number 5, he got better and better at his job. No

trick escaped him any more. To the schoolboys who tried to get free rides back from the movie theatre on their school passes, he'd say: 'Nothing doing. The passes work only when you're going to class, or going back from class. If it's a joy ride, you pay the full fare.'

One boy was a consistent problem – a tall, handsome fellow, whose friends called him Shabbir. Keshava watched people staring at the shirt enviously. He wondered why this boy was taking the bus at all; people like him had their own cars and drivers.

One evening, when the bus stopped at the women's college, the rich boy went down to the seats earmarked for women and leaned over to one of the girls.

'Excuse me, Miss Rita. I just want to talk to you.'

The girl turned her face towards the window; shifting her body away from him.

'Why won't you just talk to me?' the boy with the Bombay shirt asked, with a rakish grin. His friends up the back whistled and clapped.

Keshava bounded up to him. 'Enough!' He seized the rich boy by the arm and pulled him away from the girl. 'No one pesters women on my bus.'

The boy called Shabbir glared. Keshava glared back at him.

'Did you hear me?' he tore a ticket and flicked it at the rich boy's face to underline the warning. 'Did you hear me?'

The rich boy smiled. 'Yes, sir,' he said, and put out his hand to the conductor as if for a handshake. Confused, Keshava took his hand; the boys in the back row howled with laughter.

When the conductor withdrew his hand, he found a five-rupee note in it.

Keshava flung the note at the rich boy's feet.

'Try it again, you son of a bald woman and I'll send you flying out the bus.'

As she stepped down from the bus, the girl looked at Keshava: he saw the gratitude in her eye, and he knew he had done the right thing.

One of the passengers whispered: 'Do you know who that boy is? His father owns that video-lending store and he's best friends with the Member of Parliament. See that insignia that says "CD" on the pocket of his shirt? His father buys those shirts from a shop in Bombay and brings them for his son. Each shirt costs a hundred rupees, or maybe even two hundred rupees, they say.'

Keshava said: 'On my bus, he'd better behave. There's no rich or poor here; everyone buys the same ticket. And no one troubles the women.'

That evening, when Brother heard this story, he embraced Keshava: 'My valiant bus conductor! I'm so proud of you!'

He raised Keshava's hand up high, and the others applauded. 'This little village boy has shown the rich of this town how to behave on a number 5 bus!'

The following morning, as Keshava was hanging from the metal bar of the bus and blowing his whistle to encourage the driver, the bar creaked—and then it snapped. Keshava fell from the speeding bus, hit the road, rolled, and slammed his head into the side of the kerb.

For some days afterwards, the boarders at the hostel would

find him hunched over his bed, on the verge of tears. The bandage had come off his head and the bleeding had stopped. But he was still silent. When they gave him a good shake, Keshava would nod his head and smile, as if to say, yes, he was okay.

'Then why don't you get out and go back to work?'

He said nothing.

'He's morose all day long. We've never seen him like this.'

But then after not turning up at work for four days, they saw him leaning out of the bus, and yelling at the passengers, looking every bit his old self.

Two weeks passed. One morning, he felt a heavy hand on his shoulder. Brother himself had come to see him.

'I hear that you've turned up for work only one day in the last ten. This is very bad, my son. You can't be morose.' Brother made a fist. 'You have to be full of life.' He shook his fist at Keshava, as if to demonstrate the fullness of life.

A boy nearby tapped his head. 'Nothing gets to him. He's touched. That blow on the head has turned him into an imbecile.'

'He always was an imbecile,' said another boarder, combing his hair at a mirror. 'Now he just wants to sleep and eat for free in the hostel.'

'Shut up!' Brother said. He swished his stick at them. 'No one talks about my star slogan-shouter like that!'

He gently tapped his stick on Keshava's head. 'You see what they're saying about you, Keshava? That you're putting on this act just to steal food and bed from Brother? You see the insults they spread about you?'

Keshava began to cry. He drew his knees up to his chest and put his head in them, and cried.

'My poor boy!' Brother himself was almost in tears. He got onto the bed and hugged the boy.

'Someone's got to tell the boy's family,' he said, on the way out. 'We can't keep him here if he's not working.'

'We did tell his brother,' the neighbours replied.

'And?'

'He's not interested in hearing about Keshava. He says there's no connection between them any more.'

Brother slammed his fist against the wall.

'You see the extent to which family life has deteriorated these days!' He shook his fist, which was aching from the blow. 'That fellow has to take care of his brother. He has no other option!' He shouted. He whipped his stick through the air: 'I will show that piece of shit! I will force him to remember his duty to his younger brother!'

Although no one actually threw him out, one evening when Keshava came back, someone else was sitting on his bed. The fellow was tracing his finger along the outlines of the actresses' faces, and the other boys were teasing him: 'O, so she's his *wife*, is she? She's not, you idiot!'

It was as if he had always been there, and they had always been his neighbours.

Keshava simply wandered away. He felt no desire to fight to get his bed back.

He sat by the closed doors of the Central Market that night, and some of the streetside sellers recognized him and fed him. He did not thank them; did not even say hello. This went on for a few days. Finally, one of them said to him: 'In this world, a fellow who doesn't work doesn't eat. It's not too late; go to Brother and apologize and beg him to give you your old job back. You know he thinks of you as family…'

For a few nights, he wandered outside the market. One day he drifted back to the hostel. Brother was sitting in the drawing room again, as his feet were massaged by the woman. 'That was a lovely dress Rekha wore in the movie, don't you think…' Keshava wandered into the room.

'What do you want?' Brother asked, getting up. Keshava tried to put it into words. He held his arms out to the man in the blue sarong.

'This Hoyka idiot is mad! And he stinks! Get him out of here!'

Hands dragged him for some distance and pushed him to the ground. Leather shoes kicked him in the ribs.

A little later, he heard footsteps, and then someone lifted him up. Wooden crutches tapped on the earth, and a man's voice said: 'So Brother's got no use for you either, eh…?'

He vaguely sensed that he was being offered something to eat. He sniffed; it reeked of castor oil and shit, and he rejected it. He smelled garbage around him, and turned his head towards the sky; his eyes were full of the stars when they closed.

THE HISTORY OF KITTUR
(abridged from *A Short History of Kittur* by Father Basil d'Essa, S.J.)

'The word "Kittur" is a corruption either of "Kiri Uru", "Small Town", or of "Kittamma's Uru" – Kittamma being a goddess specializing in repelling smallpox whose temple stood near today's train station. A letter from a Syrian Christian merchant written in 1091 recommends to his peers the excellent natural harbour of the town of Kittur, on the Malabar Coast. During the entire twelfth century, however, the town appears to have vanished; Arab merchants who visited Kittur in 1141 and 1190 record only wilderness. In the fourteenth century a dervish named Yusuf Ali began curing lepers at the Bunder; when he died, his body was entombed in a white dome, and the structure – the Dargah of Hazrat Yusuf Ali – has remained an object of pilgrimage to the present day. In the late fifteenth century, "Kittore, also known as the citadel of elephants", is listed in the tax-collection records of the Vijayanagara rulers as one of the provinces of their empire. In 1649, a four-man Portuguese missionary delegation led by Father Cristoforo d'Almeida, S.J., trekked down the coast from Goa to Kittur; it found "a deplorable mess of idolators, Mohameddans, and elephants". The Portuguese drove out the Mohammeddans, pulverized the idols, and distilled the wild elephants into a rubble of dirty ivory. Over the next hundred years, Kittur – now renamed Valencia – passed back and forth between the Portuguese, the Marathas, and the kingdom of Mysore.

In 1780, Hyder Ali, the ruler of Mysore, defeated an army of the East India Company near the Bunder; by the Treaty of Kittur, signed that year, the Company renounced its claims on "Kittore, also called Valencia or The Bunder". The Company violated the treaty after Hyder Ali's death in 1782, by setting up a military camp near the Bunder; in retaliation, Tippu, the son of Hyder Ali, constructed the Sultan's Battery, a formidable fortress of black stone, mounted with French guns. After Tippu's death in 1799, Kittur became Company property and was annexed into the Madras Presidency. The town, like most of South India, took no part in the great anti-British mutiny of 1857. In 1921, an activist of the Indian National Congress raised a tricolour at the old lighthouse: the freedom struggle had come to Kittur.'

Day Three (Afternoon): ANGEL TALKIES

Nightlife in Kittur centres on the Angel Talkies cinema. Every Thursday morning, the walls of the town are plastered with hand-painted posters featuring a sketch of a full-bodied woman brushing her hair with her fingers; below is the title of the movie: HER NIGHTS, WINE AND WOMEN, MYSTERIES OF GROWTH, UNCLE'S FAULT. The words 'Malayalam Colour' and 'Adults Only' are prominently featured on the posters. By 8 a.m., a long line of unemployed men has queued outside Angel Talkies. Show times are 10 a.m., noon, 2 p.m., 4 p.m. and 7.10 p.m. Seat prices range from Rs 2.20 for a seat at the front to Rs 4.50 for a 'Family Circle' seat up in the balcony. Not far from the theatre is the Hotel Woodside, whose attractions include a famous Paris cabaret, featuring Ms Zeena from Bombay, every Friday, and Ms Ayesha and Ms Zimboo from Bahrain, every second Sunday. A travelling sexologist, Dr Kurvilla, MBBS, MD, M.Ch., MS, DDBS, PCDB, visits the hotel on the first Monday of every month. Less expensive and seedier in appearance than the Woodside are a nearby series of bars, restaurants, hostels, and apartments. Thanks to the presence of a YMCA in the neighbourhood, however, men of decency also have the option of a moral and clean hostel.

The door of the YMCA swung open at two in the morning; a short figure walked out.

He was a small man with a huge protruding forehead, which gave him the look of a professor in a caricature. His hair, thick and wavy like a teenager's, was oiled and firmly pressed down; it was greying around the temples and in the sideburns. He had walked out of the YMCA looking at the ground; and now, as if noticing for the first time that he was in the real world, he stopped for a moment, looked this way and that, and then headed towards the market.

A series of whistles assaulted him at once. A policeman in uniform, cycling down the street, slowed to a halt and put a foot on the pavement.

'What is your name, fellow?'

The man who looked like a professor said: 'Gururaj Kamath.'

'And what work do you do that makes you walk alone at night?'

'I look for the truth.'

'Now don't get funny, all right?'

'Journalist.'

'For which paper?'

'How many papers do we have?'

The policeman, who may have been hoping to uncover some irregularity associated with this man, and hence either to bully or to bribe him, both acts which he enjoyed, looked disappointed, and then rode away. He had hardly gone a few yards when a thought hit him and he stopped again and turned towards to the little man.

'Gururaj Kamath. You wrote the column on the riots, didn't you?'

'Yes,' said the little man.

The policeman looked down at the ground.

'My name is Aziz.'

'And?'

'You've done every minority in this town a great service, sir. My name is Aziz. I want to…to thank you.'

'I was only doing my job. I told you: I look for the truth.'

'I want to thank you anyway. If more people did what you do, there wouldn't be any more riots in this town, sir.'

Not a bad fellow after all, Gururaj thought, as he watched Aziz cycle off. Just doing his job.

He continued his walk.

No one was watching him, so he let himself smile with pride.

In the days after the riots, the voice of this little man had been the voice of reason in the midst of chaos. In precise, biting prose he had laid out for his readers the destruction caused by the Hindu fanatics who had ransacked the shops of Muslim shopkeepers; in a calm, unemotional tone he had blasted bigotry and stood up for the rights of religious minorities. He had wanted nothing more from his columns than to help the victims of the riots: instead, Gururaj now found himself something of a celebrity in Kittur. A star.

A fortnight ago, he had suffered the greatest blow of his life. His father had passed away from pneumonia. The day after Gururaj returned to Kittur from his ancestral village, having shaved his head and sat with a priest by the water-tank in his ancestral temple to recite Sanskrit verses to bid his father's soul farewell, he discovered that he had been promoted to Deputy Executive Editor, the number two position at the newspaper where he had worked for twenty years.

It was life's way of evening things out, Gururaj told himself.

The moon shone brightly, with a large halo around it. He had forgotten how beautiful a nocturnal walk could be. The light was strong and clean, and it laminated the earth's surface; every object carved sharp shadows in it. He thought it might be the day after a full moon.

Even at this hour of the night, work continued. He heard a low, continuous sound, like the audible respiration of the nocturnal world: an open-back truck was collecting mud, probably for some construction site. The driver was asleep at the wheel; his arm stuck out of one window, his feet out of the other one. As if ghosts were doing the work behind, morsels of mud came flying into the truck from behind. The back of Gururaj's shirt became damp, and he thought: but I will catch a cold. I should go back. That thought made him feel old, and he decided to go on; he took a few steps to his left and began to walk right down the middle of Umbrella Street; it had been a childhood fantasy of his to walk down the middle of a main road, but he had never been able to sneak away from his father's watchful eyes long enough to fulfil the fantasy.

He came to a halt, right in the middle of the road. Then he quickly went into a side alley.

Two dogs were mating. He crouched down and tried to see exactly what was happening.

After completing the act, the dogs separated. One went

down the alley and the other headed towards Gururaj, running with postcoital vigour and almost brushing his trousers as it went past. He followed.

The dog came into main road and sniffed at a newspaper. Taking the newspaper in its mouth, it ran back into the alley, and Gururaj ran behind it. Deeper and deeper the dog ran into the side alleys, as the editor followed. Finally, it dropped its bundle; turning, it snarled at Gururaj and then tore the newspaper to shreds.

'Good dog! Good dog!'

Gururaj turned to his right to confront the speaker. He found himself face to face with an apparition; a man in khaki, carrying an old Second World War-era rifle, his yellowish, leathery face covered with nicks and scars. His eyes were narrow and slanting. Drawing closer, Gururaj thought: of course. He's a Gurkha.

The Gurkha was sitting on a wooden chair out on the pavement, in front of a bank's rolled-down shutter.

'Why do you say that?' said Gururaj. 'Why are you praising the dog for destroying a paper?'

'The dog is doing the right thing. Because not a word in the newspaper is true.'

The Gurkha – Gururaj took him for an all-night security guard for the bank – rose from his chair and took a step to the dog.

At once it dropped the paper and ran away. Picking up the torn and mangled and saliva-stained paper with care, the Gurkha turned the pages.

Gururaj winced.

'Tell me what you're looking for: I know everything that's in that newspaper.'

The Gurkha let the dirty paper go.

'There was an accident last night. Near Flower Market Street. A hit and run.'

'I know the case,' Gururaj said. It had not been his story, but he read the proofs of the entire paper every day. 'An employee of Mr Engineer's was involved.'

'The newspaper said that. But it was not the employee who did it.'

'Really?' Gururaj smiled. 'Then who did it?'

The Gurkha looked right into Gururaj's eyes. He smiled and then pointed the barrel of the ancient gun at him. 'I can tell you, but I'd have to shoot you afterwards.'

Looking at the barrel of the rifle, Gururaj thought: I'm talking to a madman.

The next day, Gururaj was in his office at 6 a.m. First to get there, as always. He began by checking the telex machine, inspecting the reels of badly smudged news it was printing out from Delhi and Colombo and other cities he would never visit in his life. At seven he turned on the radio and began jotting down the main points of the morning's column.

At eight o'clock, Ms D'Mello arrived. The chattering of a typewriter broke the peace of the office.

She was writing her usual column, 'Twinkle Twinkle'. It was a daily beauty column; a women's hair salon owner sponsored it and Ms D'Mello answered readers' questions about hair care, offering advice and gently nudging her correspondents in the direction of the salon owner's products.

Gururaj never spoke to Ms D'Mello. He resented the fact that his newspaper ran a paid-for column, a practice he considered unethical. But there was another reason to be cool towards Ms D'Mello: she was an unmarried woman and he didn't want anyone to assume that he might have the slightest interest in her.

Relatives and friends of his father had told Guru for years that he ought to move out of the YMCA and marry, and he had almost given in, thinking that the woman would be needed to nurse his father in his growing senility, when the need for a wife was removed entirely. Now he was determined not to lose his independence to anyone.

By eleven, when Gururaj came out of his room again, the office was full of smoke – the only aspect of his workplace that he disliked. The reporters were at their desks, drinking tea and smoking. The teleprinter machine, off to the side, was vomiting out rolls of smudged and misspelled news reports from Delhi.

After lunch, he sent the office boy to find Menon, a young journalist and a rising star at the paper. Menon came into his room with the top two buttons of his shirt open, a shiny gold necklace flashing at his neck. 'Sit down,' Gururaj said.

He showed him two articles about the car crash on Flower Market Street, which he had dug out of the newspaper's archives that morning. The first (he pointed to it) had appeared before the trial; the second after the verdict.

'You wrote both articles, didn't you?'

Menon nodded.

'In the first article, the car that hits the dead man is a red

Maruti Suzuki. In the second, it is a white Fiat. Which one was it, really?'

Menon inspected the two articles.

'I just filed according to the police reports.'

'You didn't bother looking at the vehicle yourself, I take it?'

That night he ate the dinner that the caretaker at the YMCA brought up to his room; she talked a lot, but he was worried she was trying to marry him off to her daughter and he said as little as possible to her.

As he went to sleep he set the alarm for two o'clock.

He woke up with his heart racing fast; he turned on the lights, left his room, and squinted at his clock. It was twenty minutes to two. He put on his trousers, patted his wavy strands of hair back into place, and almost ran down the stairs and out of the gate of the YMCA, and in the direction of the bank.

The Gurkha was there at his chair, with his ancient rifle.

'Listen here, did you see this accident with your own eyes?'

'Of course not. I was sitting right here. This is my job.'

'Then how the hell did you know the cars had been changed in the police—'

'Through the grapevine.'

The Gurkha talks quietly. He explains to the newspaper editor that a network of nightwatchmen passes information around Kittur; every nightwatchman comes to the next for a cigarette and tells him something, and that one visits the next one for a cigarette in turn. In this way, word gets around. Secrets get spread. The truth – what really happened during the daytime – is preserved.

This is insane, this is impossible – Gururaj wipes the sweat from his forehead.

'So what actually happened – Engineer hit a man on his way back home?'

'Left him for dead.'

'It can't be true.'

The Gurkha's eyes flashed. 'You've lived here long enough, sir. You know it *can be*. Engineer was drunk; he was coming back from his mistress's home; he hit the fellow like some stray dog and drove away, leaving him there, with his guts spilled out on the street. In the morning the newspaper boy found him like that. The police know perfectly who drives down that road at night drunk. So the next morning two constables go to his house. Hasn't even washed the blood off the front wheels of the car.'

'Then why—'

'He is the richest man in this town. He owns the tallest building in this town. He cannot be arrested. He gets one of the employees at his factory to say that he was driving the car when it happened. The guy gives the police a sworn affidavit. I was driving under the influence on the night of 12 May when I hit the unfortunate victim. Then Mr Engineer gave the judge six thousand rupees, and the police something less, perhaps four thousand or five, because the judiciary is of course more noble than the police, to keep quiet. Then he wants his Maruti Suzuki back, because it's a new car and a fashion statement and he likes driving it, so he gives the police another thousand to change the identity of the killer car to a Fiat, and he has his car back and he's driving around town again.'

'My God.'

'The employee got four years. The judge could have given him a harsher sentence, but he felt sorry for the bugger. Couldn't let him off for free, of course. So' – the nightwatchman brought down an imaginary gavel – 'four years.'

'I can't believe it,' Gururaj said. 'Kittur isn't that kind of place.'

The foreigner narrowed his cunning eyes and smiled. He looked at the glowing tip of his beedi for a while and then offered the beedi to Gururaj.

In the morning Gururaj opened the only window in his room. He looked down on Umbrella Street, on the heart of the town where he was born, and where he had grown to maturity and where he would almost certainly die. He sometimes thought he knew every building, every tree, every tile on the roof of every house in Kittur. Glowing in the morning light, Umbrella Street seemed to say: *No, the Gurkha's story can't be true*. The clarity of the stencilling on an advertisement, the glistening spokes of the bicycle wheel ridden by the man delivering newspapers, said: *No, the Gurkha is lying*. But as Gururaj walked to his office, he saw the dense dark shade of the banyan tree lying across the road, like a patch of night left unswept by the morning's broom, and his soul was in turmoil again.

Work began. He calmed down. He avoided Ms D'Mello.

That evening, the editor-in-chief of the newspaper summoned him to his room. He was a plump old man, with sagging jowls and thick white eyebrows that looked like frosting and hands that trembled as he drank his tea. The tendons on his neck stood out in deep relief, and every part of his body seemed to be calling out for retirement.

If he did retire, Gururaj would inherit his chair.

'Regarding this story you've asked Menon to reinvestigate...' said the editor-in-chief, sipping the tea. 'Forget it.'

'There was a discrepancy over the cars—'

The old man shook his head. 'The police made a mistake on the first filing, that was all.' His voice changed into the quiet, casual tone Gururaj had come to recognize as final. He sipped more tea, and then some more.

The slurping sound of the tea being sipped, the abruptness of the old man's manner, the fatigue of so many nights of broken sleep got on Gururaj's nerves and he said: 'A man might have been sent to jail for no good reason; a guilty man might be walking free. And all you can say is, let's drop the matter.'

The old man sipped his tea; Gururaj thought he could detect his head move, as if in the affirmative.

He went back to the YMCA and walked up a flight of stairs to his room. He lay down on the bed with his eyes open. He was still awake at two in the morning, when the alarm went off. When he emerged, he heard a whistling sound; the policeman, passing by him, waved heartily, as if to an old friend.

The moon was shrinking fast; in a few days it would be entirely dark at night. He walked the same route now, as if it were a ritual formula: first slowly, then crossing to the centre of the road, and then dashing into the side alley until he reached the bank. The Gurkha was in his chair, his rifle on his shoulder, a glowing beedi in his fingers.

'What does the grapevine tell you tonight?'

'Nothing tonight.'

'Then tell me something from a few nights ago. Tell me what else the paper has published that is untrue.'

'The riots. The newspaper got that wrong, completely.'

Gururaj thought his heart would skip a beat. 'How so?'

'The newspaper said that it was Hindus fighting Muslims, see?'

'It was Hindus fighting Muslims. Everyone knows that.'

'Ha.'

The next morning Gururaj did not turn up at the office. He went straight down to the Bunder, the first time since he had come there to talk to the shopkeepers in the aftermath of the riots. He traced every restaurant and fish market that had been burned down in the riots.

He went back to the newspaper, rushed into the office of the editor-in-chief and said: 'I heard the most incredible story last night about the Hindu–Muslim riots. Shall I tell you what I heard?'

The old man sipped his tea.

'I heard that our MP along with the mafia down at the Bunder instigated the riots. And I heard that the hoodlums and the MP have transferred all the burned and destroyed property into the hands of their own men, under the name of a fictitious trust called the New Kittur Port Development Trust. The violence was planned. Muslim goons burned Muslim shops and Hindu goons burned Hindu shops. It was a real-estate transaction masquerading as a religious riot.'

The editor stopped sipping.

'Who told you this?'

'A friend. Is it true?'

'No.'

Gururaj smiled and said: 'I didn't think so, either. Thanks.'
He walked out of the room while his boss watched him with
concern.

The next morning, he arrived at the office late once again.
The office boy turned up at his desk and shouted: 'Editor-in-
chief wants to see you.'

'Why didn't you turn up at the City Corporation Office
today?' the old man asked him, as he sipped another cup of tea.
'The mayor asked for you to be there; he released a statement
on Hindu–Muslim unity and attacking the BJP that he wanted
you to hear. You know he respects your work.'

Gururaj pressed his hair down; he had not oiled it this
morning and it was unruly.

'Who cares?'

'Excuse me, Gururaj?'

'You think anyone in this office doesn't know that all this
political fighting is just make-believe? That in reality the BJP
and the Congress cut each other deals and share the bribe
money they take on construction projects in Bajpe? You and I
have known for years that this is true and yet we pretend to
report things otherwise. Doesn't this strike you as bizarre?
Look here. Let's just write nothing but the truth and the whole
truth in the newspaper today. Just today. One day of nothing
but the truth. That's all I want to do. No one may even notice.
Tomorrow we'll go back to the usual lies. But for one day I
want to report, write, and edit the truth. One day in my life I'd
like to be a proper journalist. What do you say to that?'

The editor-in-chief frowned, as if thinking about it, and then said: 'Come to my house after dinner tonight.'

At nine o'clock, Gururaj walked up Rose Lane, to a home with a big garden and a blue statue of Krishna with his flute in a niche in the front, and rang the bell.

The editor let him into the drawing room and closed the door. He asked Gururaj to sit down, gesturing at a brown sofa.

'You'd better tell me what's bothering you.'

Gururaj told him.

'Let's assume you have proof of this thing. You write about it. You're not only saying that the police force is rotten, but also that the judiciary is corrupt. The judge will call you for contempt of court. You will be arrested – even if what you are saying is true. You and I and people in our press pretend that there is freedom of press in this country but we know the truth.'

'What about the Hindu–Muslim riots? Can't we write the truth about that, either?'

'What is the truth about it, Gururaj?'

Gururaj told him the truth and the editor-in-chief smiled. He put his head in his hands and, in a laugh that seemed to rock the entire night, he laughed his heart out.

'Even if what you're saying is indeed the truth,' the old man said, regaining control of himself, 'and observe that I neither admit nor contradict any of it, there would be no way for us to publish it.'

'Why not?'

The editor smiled.

'Who do you think owns this newspaper?'

164

'Ramdas Pai,' Gururaj said, naming a businessman in Umbrella Street whose name appeared as proprietor on the front page.

The editor shook his head. 'He doesn't own it. Not all of it.'

'Who does?'

'Use your brains.'

Gururaj looked at the editor-in-chief with new eyes. It was as if the old man had a nimbus around him, of all the things he had learned over the length of his career and could never publish; this secret knowledge glowed around his head like the halo around the nearly full moon. This is the fate of every journalist in this town and in this state and in this country and maybe in this whole world, thought Gururaj.

'Had you never guessed any of this before, Gururaj? It must come from the fact that you are not yet married. Not having had a woman, you have never understood the ways of the world.'

'And you have understood the ways of the world far too well.'

The two men stared, each feeling tremendously sorry for the other.

The following morning, as he walked to the office, Gururaj thought: it is a false earth I am walking on. An innocent man is behind bars and a guilty man walks free. Everyone knows that this is so and not one has the courage to change it.

From then on, every night, Gururaj went down the dirty stairwell of the YMCA, gazing blankly at the profanities and graffiti scribbled on the walls, and walked down Umbrella Street, ignoring the barking and skulking and copulating stray dogs, until he got to the Gurkha, who would lift up his old rifle in recognition and smile. They were friends now.

The Gurkha told him how much rottenness there could be in a small town; who had killed whom in the past few years; how much the judges of Kittur had asked for in bribe money, how much the police chiefs had asked. They talked until it was nearly dawn and it was time for Gururaj to leave, so he could get some sleep before going to work. He hesitated: 'I still don't know your name.'

'Gaurishankar.'

Gururaj waited for him to ask him his name; he wanted to say: 'Now that my father has died, you are my only friend, Gaurishankar.'

The Gurkha sat with his eyes closed.

At four in the morning, walking back to the YMCA, he was thinking: who is this man, this Gurkha? From some reference he had made to being a manservant in the house of a retired general, Gururaj deduced that he had been in the army, in the Gurkha regiment. But how he ended up in Kittur, why he hadn't gone back home to Nepal, all this was still a mystery. Tomorrow I should ask him all this. Then I can tell him about myself.

There was an Ashoka near the entrance to his YMCA, and Gururaj stopped to look at the tree. The moonlight lay on it, and it seemed different somehow tonight; as if it were on the verge of growing into something else.

'They are not my fellow workers; they are lower than animals.'

Gururaj could no longer stand the sight of his colleagues; he averted his eyes as he came into the office, scurrying into his room and slamming his door shut as soon as he got to work. Although he continued to edit the copy he was given, he could no longer bear to look at the newspaper. What especially terrified him was catching his own name in print; for this reason he asked to be relieved from what had been his greatest pleasure, writing his column, and insisted only on editing. Although in the old days he used to stay up to midnight, now he left the office at five o'clock every evening, hurrying back to his apartment to fall on his bed.

At two o'clock sharp, he woke up. To save himself the trouble of finding his trousers in the dark, he had taken to sleeping in all his clothes. He almost ran down the stairs and thrust open the door of the YMCA, so he could speak to the Gurkha.

Then one night, at last, it happened. The Gurkha was not sitting outside the bank. Someone else had taken his chair.

'What do I know, sir?' the new nightwatchman said. 'I was appointed to this job last night; they didn't tell me what happened to the old fellow.'

Gururaj ran from shop to shop, from house to house, asking every nightwatchman he met what had happened to the Gurkha.

'Gone to Nepal,' one nightwatchman finally told him. 'Back to his family. He was saving money all these years, and now he's gone.'

Gururaj took the news like a physical blow. Only one man had known what was happening in this town, and that one man had vanished to another country. Seeing him gasping for air, the nightwatchmen gathered around him, made him sit down, and brought him cool, clean water in a plastic bottle. He tried explaining to them what had happened between him and the Gurkha all these weeks, what he had lost.

'That Gurkha, sir?' One watchman shook his head. 'Are you sure you talked about these things with him? He was a complete idiot. His brain had been damaged in the army.'

'What about the grapevine? Is it still working?' Gururaj asked. 'Will one of you tell me what you hear now?'

The nightwatchmen stared. In their eyes, he could see doubt turning into a kind of fear. They seem to think I'm mad, he thought.

He wandered at night, passing by the dim buildings, by the sleeping multitudes. He passed by large, still, darkened buildings, each containing hundreds of bodies lying in a stupor. 'I am the only man who is awake now,' he told himself. Once, up on a hill to his left, he saw a large housing block burning with light. Seven windows were lit up and the building blazed; it seemed to him to be a living creature, a kind of monster of light, shining from its entrails.

Gururaj understood: the Gurkha had not abandoned him at all. He had not done what everyone else in his life had done. He had left something behind; a gift. Gururaj would now hear the grapevine on his own. He lifted his arms towards the building burning with lights; he felt full of occult power.

One day as he came into work, late again, he heard a whisper behind him: 'It happened to the father too, in his last days…'

He thought: I must be careful that others do not notice this change that is happening inside me.

When he reached his office, he saw that the peon was removing his nameplate from the door. I am losing everything I worked for so many years for, he thought. But he felt no regret or emotion; it was as if these things were happening to someone else. He saw the new nameplate on the door:

KRISHNA MENON
Deputy Editor
Dawn Herald
Kittur's only and finest newspaper

'Gururaj! I didn't want to do it, I—'

'No explanation is necessary. In your position, I'd have done the same.'

'Do you want me to speak to someone, Gururaj? We can arrange it for you.'

'What are you talking about?'

'I know you have no father now... But we can arrange a wedding for you, with a girl of a good family.'

'What are you talking about?'

'We think you are ill. You ought to know that many of us in this office have been saying that for some time. I insist that you take a week off. Or two weeks. Go somewhere on holiday. Go to the Western Ghats and watch the clouds for a while.'

'Fine. I'll take three weeks off.'

For three weeks he slept through the day and walked through the night. The late-night policeman no longer said 'Hello, editor' as he had before, and Gururaj could see the man's head, as he cycled past, turn and stare at him. The

nightwatchmen also looked at him oddly; and he grinned –
even here, even in this Hades of the middle of the night, I have
become an outsider, a man who frightens others. The thought
excited him.

He bought a child's square blackboard one day, and a piece
of chalk. That night he wrote at the top of the blackboard:

THE TRUTH ALONE SHALL TRIUMPH.
A NOCTURNAL NEWSPAPER
SOLE CORRESPONDENT, EDITOR, ADVERTISER, AND
SUBSCRIBER:
GURURAJ MANJESHWAR KAMATH, ESQ

Copying out the headline from the morning's newspaper,
'BJP City Councillor blasts Congressman', he rubbed and
scratched and rewrote it:

2 October 1989
BJP City Councillor, who needs money in a hurry
to build a new mansion on Rose Lane, blasts
Congressman. Tomorrow he will receive a brown
bag full of cash from the Congress party, and then
he will stop blasting the Congressman.

Then he lay in bed and closed his eyes, eager for the darkness
to arrive and make his town a decent place again.

One night he thought: there is only one night of my vacation
left. The dawn was breaking already and he hurried back to the
YMCA. He stopped. He was sure that he was seeing an

170

elephant outside the building. Was he dreaming? What on earth would an elephant be doing, at this hour, in the middle of his town? It was beyond the bounds of reason. Yet it looked real and tangible to his eyes; only one thing that made him think it was not a real elephant – it was absolutely still. He said to himself: elephants move and make some noise all the time, therefore you are not really seeing an elephant. He closed his eyes and walked up to the entrance of the YMCA; and when he opened them again he was staring at a tree. He touched the bark and thought: this is the first hallucination I have had in my life.

When he returned to the office the next day, everyone said Gururaj was back to his old self. He had missed his office life; he had wanted to come back.

'Thank you for your offer to arrange a marriage,' he told the editor-in-chief, as they had tea together in his room. 'But I'm married to my work anyway.'

Sitting in the newsroom with young men just out of college, he edited stories with all his old cheer. After all the young men were gone, he stayed back, digging through the archives. He had come back to work with a purpose. He was going to write a history of Kittur. An infernal history of Kittur – in it every event in the past twenty years would be reinterpreted. He took out old newspapers and carefully read each front page. Then, a red pen in hand, he scratched out and rewrote words, which fulfilled two purposes – one, it defaced the newspapers of the past, and two, it allowed him to figure out the true relationship between the words and the characters in the news events. At first, designating Hindi – the Gurkha's language – as the language of the truth, he rewrote the Kannada-language headlines of the newspaper in Hindi; then he switched to English; and finally he adopted a code in which he substituted each letter of the Roman alphabet for the one immediately after it – he had read somewhere that Julius Caesar had invented this code for his army – and, to complicate matters further, he invented symbols for certain words; for instance, a triangle with a dot inside represented the word 'Bank'. Other symbols were ironically inspired; for instance, a Nazi Swastika represented the Congress party, and the Nuclear Disarmament Symbol the BJP, and so on. One day, looking back over the past week's notes, he found that he had forgotten half the symbols, and he no longer understood what he had written. Good, he thought, that is the way it should be. Even the writer of the truth should not know the truth entire. Every true word, upon being written, is like the full moon, and daily it wanes and then passes entirely into obscurity. That is the way of all things.

When he was done reinterpreting each issue of the newspaper, he deleted the words 'The Dawn Herald' from the headline and wrote in their place: 'THE TRUTH ALONE SHALL TRIUMPH'.

'What the hell are you doing to our newspapers?'

It was the editor-in-chief. He and Menon had sneaked up on Gururaj in the office one evening.

The editor-in-chief turned page after page of defaced newspaper in the archives without a word, while Menon tried to peek over his shoulder. They saw pages covered in squiggles, red marks, slashes, triangles, pictures of girls with pigtails and bloody teeth, images of copulating dogs. Then the old man slammed the archive shut.

'I told you to get married.'

Gururaj smiled. 'Listen, old friend, those are symbolic marks. I can interpret—'

The editor-in-chief shook his head.

'Get out of this office. At once. I'm sorry, Gururaj.'

Gururaj smiled, as if to say that no explanation was necessary. The editor-in-chief's eyes were teary, and the tendons of his neck moved up and down as he swallowed again and again. The tears came to Guru's eyes as well. He thought: how hard it has been for this old man to do this. How hard he must have protected me. He imagined a closed-door meeting where colleagues had been baying for his blood and this decent old man alone had defended him to the end. 'I am sorry, my friend, for letting you down,' he wanted to say.

That night, Gururaj walked, telling himself he was happier than he ever been in his life. He was a free man now. When he got back, just before dawn, to the YMCA, he saw the elephant again. This time it did not melt into an Ashoka tree, even when he came close. He walked right up to the beast, saw its constantly flapping ears, which had the colour and shape and movement of a pterodactyl's wing; he walked around and saw that from the back, each of its ears had a fringe of pink and was striped with veins. How can this wealth of detail be unreal? he thought. This creature was real, and if the rest of the world could not see it, then the rest of the world was the poorer for that.

Just make one sound! he pleaded with the elephant. So I

know for sure that I am not deluded, that you are for real. The elephant understood; it raised its trunk and roared so loudly that he thought he had been deafened.

'You are free now,' the elephant said, in words so loud they seemed like newspaper headlines to him. 'Go and write the true history of Kittur.'

Some months later, there was news of Gururaj. Four young reporters went to investigate.

They muffled their giggles as they pushed open the door to the municipal reading room in the lighthouse. The librarian had been waiting for them; he ushered them in with a finger to his lips.

The journalists found Gururaj sitting at a bench, reading a newspaper which partially covered his face. The old editor's shirt was in tatters, but he seemed to have gained weight, as if idleness had suited him.

'He won't say a word any more,' the librarian said. 'He just sits there till sunset, holding the paper to his face. The only time he said anything was when I told him I admired his articles on the riots, and then he shouted at me.'

One of the young journalists put his finger on the top edge of the newspaper and lowered it slowly; Gururaj offered no resistance. The journalist yelped and stepped back.

There was a moist dark hole in the innermost sheet of the paper. Pieces of newsprint stuck to the corners of Gururaj's mouth, and his jaw was moving.

THE LANGUAGES OF KITTUR

Kannada, one of the major languages of South India, is the official language of the state of Karnataka, in which Kittur is located. The local paper, the *Dawn Herald*, is published in Kannada. Although understood by virtually everyone in the town, Kannada is the mother tongue only of some of the Brahmins. Tulu, a regional language that has no written script – although it is believed to have possessed a script centuries ago – is the lingua franca. Two dialects of Tulu exist. The 'upper-caste' dialect is still used by a few Brahmins, but is dying out as Tulu-speaking Brahmins switch to Kannada. The other dialect of Tulu, a rough, bawdy language cherished for the diversity and pungency of its expletives, is used by the Bunts and Hoykas – this is the language of the Kittur street. Around Umbrella Street, the commercial centre, the dominant language changes to Konkani: this is the language of the Gaud-Saraswat Brahmins, originally from Goa, who own most of the shops here. (Although Tulu- and Kannada-speaking Brahmins began intermarrying in the 1960s, the Konkani-Brahmins have so far rejected all marriage proposals from outsiders.) A very different dialect of Konkani, corrupted with Portuguese, is spoken in the suburb of Valencia by the Catholics who live there. Most of the Muslims, especially those in the Bunder, speak a dialect of Malayalam as their mother tongue; a few of the richer Muslims, being descendants of the old Hyderabad aristocracy, speak Hyderabadi Urdu. Kittur's large migrant worker population, which floats around the town from construction site to construction site, is mostly Tamil-speaking. English is understood by the middle class.

It must be noted that few other towns in India can match Kittur's street language for the richness of its expletives, which come from Urdu, English, Kannada and Tulu. The most commonly heard term, 'son of a bald-headed woman', requires explanation. Upper-caste widows were once forbidden to remarry and forced to shave their heads to prevent them from attracting men. A child born of a bald woman was very likely to be an illegitimate one.

Day Four (Morning): UMBRELLA STREET

If you wish to do some shopping while in Kittur, allow yourself a few hours to wander through Umbrella Street, the commercial centre of town. Here you will find furniture stores, pharmacies, restaurants, sweet-shops, and book-stores. (A few sellers of hand-made wooden umbrellas can still be found here, although most have gone out of business because of cheap metal umbrellas imported from China.) The street houses Kittur's most famous restaurant, the Ideal Traders Ice Cream and Fresh Fruit Juice Parlour, and also the office of the *Dawn Herald*, 'Kittur's only and finest newspaper'.

Every Thursday evening, an interesting event takes place in the Ramvittala Temple near Umbrella Street. Two traditional minstrels sit on the verandah of this temple and recite verses from the Mahabharatha, the great Indian epic of heroism and endurance, all through the night.

All the employees of the furniture shop had gathered in a semi-circle around Mr Ganesh Pai's table. It was a special day: Mrs Engineer had come to the shop in person.

She had chosen her TV table and now she was approaching Mr Pai's desk to finalize the deal.

His face was smeared with sandalwood and he wore a loose-fitting silk shirt over which a dark triangle of his chest hair stuck out. On the wall behind his chair, he had hung gold tin-foil images of Lakshmi, goddess of wealth, and the fat elephant-god Ganapati. An incense-stick smoked below the images.

Mrs Engineer sat down slowly at the desk. Mr Pai reached into a drawer and then held out four red cards to her. Mrs Engineer paused, bit her lip, and snatched at one of the four cards.

'A set of stainless-steel cups!' Mr Pai said, showing her the bonus card she had selected. 'A truly wonderful gift, Madam. Something you'll treasure for years and years.'

Mrs Engineer beamed. She took out a small red purse, counted off four 100-rupee notes, and put them on the desk before Mr Pai.

Mr Pai, moistening the tip of his finger in a small bowl of water that he kept on his desk for just this purpose, counted the notes afresh; then he looked at Mrs Engineer and smiled, as if expecting something more.

'The balance on delivery,' she said, getting up from her chair. 'And don't forget to send the bonus gift.'

'She may be the wife of the richest man in town, but she's still a stingy old cunt,' Mr Pai said, after he had seen her out of the store, and an assistant laughed behind him. He turned and glared at the assistant – a small, dark, Tamilian boy.

'Get one of the coolies to deliver it, quickly,' Mr Pai said. 'I want the balance before she forgets about it.'

The Tamilian boy ran out of the shop. The cycle-cart pullers were in their usual position – lying on their carts, staring into space, smoking beedis. Some of them were staring with dull avarice at the store on the other side of the road, the Ideal Traders Ice Cream Parlour; fat kids in T-shirts were licking vanilla cones outside the shop.

The boy stuck out his index finger and motioned to one of the men.

'Chenayya – your number is up!'

Chenayya pedalled hard. He had been told to take the direct route to Rose Lane, so he had to go over Lighthouse Hill; he struggled to move the cart with the TV table, which was attached to his cycle. Once he was over the hump of the hill, he let the cycle glide. He slowed down in Rose Lane, found the house number, which he had memorized, and rang the bell.

He was expecting to see a servant, but when a plump, fair-skinned woman opened the door, he knew it was Mrs Engineer herself.

Chenayya carried the TV table into the house and put it down where she indicated.

He went out and returned with a saw. He had walked in holding the thing close to his side, but when he got to the dining room, where he had left the table in two separate pieces, Mrs Engineer watched as he held the tool at an arm's length and suddenly it seemed enormous: eighteen inches long, with a serrated edge, rusty, but with patches of the original metal-grey colour still showing through, like a sculpture of a shark made by a tribal artist.

Chenayya saw the anxiety in the woman's eyes. To dispel her fear, he grinned ingratiatingly – it was the exaggerated, death-mask grin of a person not used to grovelling – then he looked around as if to remind himself where he had left the table.

The legs were not of equal length. Chenayya closed an eye and examined the legs one by one; then he took the saw to each of the legs, creating a fine dust on the ground. He moved the saw so slowly, so precisely that it seemed he was just rehearsing his actions; only the accumulation of wood-dust on the ground was evidence to the contrary. He examined the four legs again with one eye closed to make sure they were even and then dropped his saw. He searched the dirty white sarong he was wearing, which was the only garment on his body, for a relatively clean corner and wiped down the table.

'The table is ready, Madam.' He folded his hands and waited.

With an ingratiating smile, he wiped the table again, to make sure that the lady of the house had noticed the care he had taken with her furniture.

Mrs Engineer had not been watching; she had retreated into an inner room. She returned and counted off seven hundred and forty-two rupees.

Hesitating a moment, she added three rupee notes to it.

'Give me something more, Madam?' Chenayya blurted. 'Give me three more rupees?'

'Six rupees? Nothing doing,' she said.

'It's a long way, Madam.' He picked up his saw and gestured at his neck. 'I had to carry it all that way, Madam, on my cycle-cart. It hurts my neck very much.'

'Nothing doing. Get out – or I'll call the police, you thug – get out and take your big knife with you!'

As he walked out of the house, grumbling and sulking, he folded the money into a wad; then tied it into a knot on the loose dirty white sarong he wore. A neem tree grew near the gate of the house, and he had to duck not to scrape his head against its branches. He had left the cycle-cart near the tree. He threw the saw into the cart. Around his cycle seat he had wrapped a white cotton cloth; he unfastened it and tied it around his head.

A cat went running past his leg; two dogs followed it in full flight. The cat leaped up the neem tree and bounded up the limbs; the dogs waited at the foot of the tree, scraping the base of the tree and barking. Chenayya, who had got onto his seat, lingered to watch the scene. The moment he started pedalling, he would no longer notice such things around him; he would turn into a pedalling machine that was headed straight back to his boss-man's shop. He stood there, watching the animals, enjoying consciousness. He picked up a rotting banana skin and left it draped on the leaves of the neem tree, so that it would startle the owners when they came out.

He was so pleased with himself for this that he smiled.

But he still did not want to start pedalling again, which was like handing over the keys of his personality to fatigue and routine.

About ten minutes later, he was on his bike again, heading back to Umbrella Street. He was cycling, as always, with his butt elevated off the seat, his spine inclined at sixty degrees. Only at crossroads did he straighten himself, relax, and ease back onto the seat. The road, as he drew near to Umbrella Street, was jammed once again; pushing his front wheel into the car ahead of him, Chenayya yelled: 'Son of a bitch, move!'

At last he saw to his right the sign 'GANESH PAI FAN AND FURNITURE STORE' and stopped his cycle.

Chenayya felt the money was burning a hole in his sarong; he wanted to hand it over to his employer as soon as possible. He wiped his palm against his sarong, pushed the door open, went into the store, and crouched by a corner of Mr Pai's table. Neither Mr Pai nor the Tamilian assistant paid any attention to him. Untying the bundle in his sarong, he put his hands between his legs and stared at the floor.

His neck was hurting again; he moved it from side to side to relieve the stress.

'Stop doing that.'

Mr Pai motioned for him to hand over the cash. Chenayya got up.

He moved slowly towards to the boss-man's desk and handed the notes over to Mr Ganesh Pai, who moistened his finger in the water bowl and counted off seven hundred and forty-two rupees. Chenayya stared at the water bowl; he noticed how its sides were scalloped to make them look like lotus-petals, and how the artisan had even traced the pattern of a trellis around the bottom of the bowl.

Mr Pai snapped his fingers. He had tied a rubber band around the notes and was holding out his palm in Chenayya's direction.

'Two rupees short.'

Chenayya undid the knot in the side of his sarong and handed over two one-rupee notes.

That was the sum he was expected to hand over to Mr Pai at the end of every delivery; one rupee for the dinner he would be given at around nine o'clock, and one rupee for the privilege of having been chosen to work for Mr Ganesh Pai.

Outside, the Tamilian boy from Mr Pai's shop was giving instructions to one of the cyle-cart pullers, a strong young fellow who had recently joined. He was about to start pedalling a cart with two cardboard boxes on it, and the boy from the store was saying, tapping the two boxes: 'It's a mixie in one box and a four-blade fan in the other. When you take it to the house, you've got to make sure they both get plugged in before you return.' He told the cart puller the address he was to go to; then he made the coolie say it aloud, like a teacher with a slow pupil.

It would be some time before Chenayya's number was called again, so he walked down the road to a spot where a man was sitting at a desk on the pavement, selling bundles of small rectangular tickets that were as colourful as pieces of candy. He smiled at Chenayya; his fingers began flipping through one of the bundles.

'Yellow?'

'First tell me if my number won last time,' Chenayya said. He brought out a dirty piece of paper from the knot on his sarong. The seller found a newspaper and glanced down to the bottom right-hand corner.

He read aloud: 'Winning Lottery Numbers. 17-8-9-9-643-455.'

Chenayya had learned enough about English numerals to recognize his own ticket number; he squinted for several moments and then let the ticket float to the ground.

'People buy for fifteen, sixteen years before they win, Chenayya,' the lottery seller said, by way of consolation. 'But in the end, those who believe always win. That is the way the world works.'

Chenayya hated it when the seller tried to console him like this; that was when he felt he was being ripped off by the men who printed the lottery tickets.

'I can't go on this way for ever,' he said. 'My neck hurts. I can't go on like this.'

The lottery seller nodded. 'Another yellow?'

Tying the ticket into his bundle, Chenayya staggered back; He collapsed onto his cart. For a while he lay like that, not feeling refreshed from the rest, but only numb.

Then a finger tapped on his head.

'Number's up, Chenayya.'

It was the Tamilian boy from the store.

To be delivered to 54 Suryanarayan Rao Lane. He repeated it aloud: '54, Suryanarayan...'

'Good.'

This route took him uphill over the Lighthouse Hill again. Riding his cart halfway up the hill, he alighted and began dragging the cart. His sinews bulged from his neck like webbing; and as he inhaled, the air burned through his chest and lungs. You can't go on, said his tired limbs, his burning chest. You can't go on. But at the same time, this was when his sense of resistance to his fate waxed greatest within him: and as he pushed, the restlessness and anger that had been within him all day became articulate at last:

You will not break me, motherfuckers! You will never break me!

If the thing to be delivered was light, like a mattress, he was not allowed to take a cycle-cart; it had to be carried on his head. Repeating the address to the Tamilian boy from the shop, he set off with a slow, light step, like a fat man jogging. In a short while, the weight of the mattress had seemed unbearable; it compressed his neck and spine and sent a shaft of pain down his back. He was virtually in a trance.

This morning he was taking a mattress to the railway station. The client turned out to be a North Indian family that was leaving Kittur; the owner, as he had guessed beforehand (from his demeanour, his manner – you can tell which of these rich people have a sense of decency and which don't), refused to pay him the tip.

Chenayya stood his ground. 'You motherfucker! Give me my money!'

It was a triumph for him; the man relented and gave him three rupees. On the way out of the station, he thought: I feel elated, but my customer has done no more than pay me what he owes me. This is what my life has been reduced to.

The odours and the noise of the train station made him feel

sick. Turning around, he squatted down by the tracks and pulled his sarong up and held his breath. As he was squatting there, the train roared by. He turned around; he wanted to shit into the faces of the people on the train. Yes, that would be good; as the train thundered over the motions, he forced out the turds into the faces of the passers-by.

Next to him, he saw a pig, which was doing the same thing.

At once, he thought, God, what am I becoming? He walked to a corner, crawled behind a bush, and defecated there. He told himself: I will never again defecate like this, in a place where I can be seen. There is a difference between man and animal; there is a difference.

He closed his eyes.

The scent of basil from near him seemed like evidence that there were good things in the world. But when he opened his eyes, the earth around was one of thorns and shit and stray animals.

He looked up and took a deep breath. The sky is clean, he thought. There is purity up there. He tore off a few leaves, wiped himself clean with them, then rubbed his left hand against the earth in a bid to neutralize the smell.

At two o'clock, he got his next 'number': the delivery of a giant stack of boxes to an address in Valencia. The Tamilian boy made sure he understood the address exactly: beyond the hospital and down by the Seminary where the Jesuit priests stayed.

'There's a lot of work today, Chenayya,' he said. 'Make sure you go the quick way – over the Lighthouse Hill.'

Chenayya grunted, rose out of the seat, shifted his weight

186

onto the pedals, and was on his way. The rusty iron chain that double-locked the cart to the front wheels of the bicycle began to make a noise as he cycled.

Down the main road, he was stuck in a traffic jam. He stopped, and became aware of his body once again. His neck hurt; the sun seared his back. Once he was conscious of pain, he began to think.

Why are some mornings difficult, some mornings simple? The other cart pullers never had 'good' or 'bad' days; they just did their work like machines. Only he had his moods. He looked down, to relieve his painful neck, and stared at the rusty chain by his feet, wound around the metal rod that joined the cycle to the cart. Time to oil the chain, he told himself. Must not forget.

Uphill again. Leaning forward out of his seat, Chenayya was straining hard; the breath entered his lungs like a hot poker. Halfway up the hill, he saw an elephant walking down towards him with a small bundle of leaves on his back, and a mahout poking its ear with an iron rod.

He stopped; this was unbelievable. He began to shout at the elephant: 'Hey, you, what are you doing with these leaves, take this load from me! It's more your size, motherfucker!'

Cars honked behind him. The mahout turned and gesticulated at him with his iron rod. A passer-by yelled at him not to obstruct the traffic.

'Don't you see that something is wrong with this world,' he said turning around to the driver of the car behind him, who was jabbing at his horn with the fleshy part of his palm. 'When an elephant gets to lounge downhill doing virtually no work at all, and a human being has to pull such a heavy cart?'

They honked and the cacophony grew.

'Don't you see something is wrong here?' he shouted. They honked back. The world was furious at his fury. It wanted him to move out of its way; but he was enjoying being exactly where he was, blocking all these rich and important people.

That evening there were great streaks of pink in the sky. After the shop closed, the coolies moved to the alley behind the store; they took turns buying small bottles of country liquor which they shared amongst themselves, getting giddy and belting out off-key Kannada film songs.

Chenayya never joined them. 'You're wasting your money, you idiots!' he sometimes shouted at them; they simply jeered back.

He would not drink; he had promised himself he would not squander the hard-earned fruits of his labour on alcohol. Yet the smell of liquor in the air made his mouth water; the good humour and bonhomie of the other cart pullers made him lonely. He closed his eyes. A tinkling noise made him open them.

Nearby, on the steps of an unused building, as was usual, a fat prostitute had emerged to ply her trade. She clapped her hands and advertised her presence by striking two coins together. A customer came up; they began haggling over a price. The deal was not concluded; and the man left cursing.

Chenayya, lying in his cart with his feet sticking out, watched the action with a dull grin.

'Hey, Kamala!' he shouted at the prostitute. 'Why not give me a chance this evening?'

She turned her face from him and kept clinking the coins together. He stared at her plump breasts, at the dark tip of her cleavage that showed through the blouse, at her garishly painted lips.

He turned his eyes to the sky: he had to stop thinking of sex. Streaks of pink amidst the clouds. Isn't there a God, or someone there, Chenayya wondered, watching down on this Earth? One evening, at the train station to deliver a parcel, he had heard a wild Muslim dervish talking in a corner of the station about the Mahdi, the last of the Imams, who would come for this Earth and give the evil their due. 'Allah is the Maker of all men,' the dervish had mumbled. 'The poor and the rich alike. And he observes our hurt, and when we suffer He suffers with us. And He will send, at the end of the Days, the Mahdi, on a white horse with a sword of fire, to put the rich in their place and correct all that is wrong with the world.'

A few days later, when Chenayya went to a mosque, he found that Muslims stank, so he did not stay there long. Yet he had never forgotten about the Mahdi; each time he saw a streak of pink in the sky, he thought he could detect some God of Fairness watching over the Earth and glowering with anger.

Chenayya closed his eyes and heard again the tinkling of coins. He turned about restlessly and then covered his face in a rag so the sun wouldn't sting him awake and went to sleep. Half an hour later, he woke up with a sharp pain in his ribs. The police jabbed their lathis into the bodies of the cycle pullers. A truck was entering this part of the market.

All you cycle-cart pullers! Get up and move your carts!

*

The kite-flying contest took place between two nearby houses. The owners of the kites were hidden; all Chenayya saw, as he brushed his teeth with the stick of neem, were the black and red kites fighting each other in the sky. As always, the kid with the black kite was winning; he was flying his kite the highest. Chenayya wondered about the poor kid with the red kite: why couldn't he ever win?

He spat, and then walked a few feet so he could urinate into the side of a wall.

Behind him he heard jeers. The other pullers were urinating right where they had slept.

He said nothing to them. Chenayya never talked to his fellow cart pullers. He could barely stand the sight of them – the way they bent and grovelled to Mr Ganesh Pai; yes, he might do the same, but he was furious, he was angry inside. These other fellows seemed incapable of even thinking badly of their employer; and he could not respect a man in whom there was no rebellion.

When the Tamilian boy brought out the tea, he reluctantly rejoined the pullers; he heard them talking once again, as they did just about every morning, about the autorickshaws they were going to buy once they got out of here; or the small teashop they were going to open.

'Think about it,' he wanted to tell them, 'just think about it.'

Mr Ganesh Pai allowed them only two rupees for each trip; meaning that, at the rate of three trips a day, they were making six rupees; once you deducted for lotteries, and liquor, you were lucky to save two rupees; Sundays were off, as were Hindu holidays; so at the month's end, they saved forty or forty-five rupees only. A trip to the village, an evening with a whore, an extra-long drinking binge, and your whole month's savings will be dust. Assuming you save everything you can, you're lucky to earn four hundred a year. An autorickshaw would cost twelve, fourteen thousand. A small teashop four times as much. That meant thirty, thirty-five years of such work before they could do anything else. But did they think their bodies would last that long? Did they find a single cart puller above the age of forty around them?

Don't you ever think about such things, you baboons?

Yet when he had once tried to get them to understand this, they had refused to demand more collectively. They thought they were lucky; thousands would take their jobs at a moment's notice. He knew they were right, too.

Despite their logic, despite their valid fears, their sheer spinelessness grated on him. That is why, he thought, Mr Ganesh Pai could be confident that a customer could hand over a cart puller thousands of rupees in cash and know that it will all come to him, every last rupee, without the cycle puller taking a note of it.

Naturally, Chenayya had long planned on stealing the money that a customer gave him one day. He would take the money and leave the town. This much he was certain he would do – someday very soon.

That evening, the men were huddled around. A man in a blue safari suit, an important educated man, was asking them questions; he had a small notepad in his hands. He said he had come from Madras.

He had asked one of the cart pullers for his age. No one

was sure; when he said, 'Can you make a rough guess?' they simply nodded. When he said: 'Are you eighteen, or twenty, or thirty – you must have *some* idea', they simply nodded again.

'I'm twenty-nine,' Chenayya called out from his cart.

The man nodded. He wrote something down in his notepad.

'Tell me, who are you?' Chenayya asked. 'Why are you asking us all these questions?'

He said he was a journalist and the cart pullers were impressed; he worked for an English-language newspaper in Madras, and that impressed them even more.

They were amazed that a smartly dressed man was talking to them with courtesy and they begged him to sit down on a cot, which one of them wiped clean with a side of his palm. The man from Madras pulled at the knees of his trousers and sat down.

Then he wanted to know what they were eating. He made a list of everything they ate every day in his notepad; then he went silent and scratched a lot on the pad with his pen, while they waited expectantly.

At the end, he put the notepad down, and, with a wide, almost triumphant grin, he declared: 'The work you are doing exceeds the amount of calories you consume. Every day, every trip you take – you are slowly killing yourselves.'

He held his notepad, with its squiggles and zig-zags and numbers, as proof of his claim.

'Why don't you do something else, like work in a factory? Anything else? Why don't you learn to read and write?'

Chenayya jumped off his cart.

'Don't patronize us, you son of a bitch!' he shouted. 'Those who are born poor in this country are fated to die poor. There is no hope for us, and no need of pity. Certainly not from you, who has never lifted a hand to help us; I spit on you. I spit on your newspaper. Nothing ever changes. Nothing will ever change. Look at me.' He held out his palms. 'I am twenty-nine years old. I am already bent and twisted like this. If I live to forty, what is my fate? To be a twisted black rod of a man. You think I don't know this? You think I need your notepad and your English to tell me this? You keep us like this, you people from the cities, you rich fucks. It is in your interest to treat us like cattle! You fuck! You English-speaking fuck!'

The man put away his notepad. He looked at the ground and seemed to be groping for a response.

Chenayya felt a tapping on his shoulder. It was the Tamilian boy from Mr Ganesh Pai's shop.

'Stop talking so much! Your number has come up!'

Some of the other cart pullers began chuckling, as if to say to Chenayya: 'Serves you right.'

You see! He glared at the English-speaker from Madras as if to say: 'Even the privilege of speech is not ours. Even if we raise our voices, we are told to shut up.'

Strangely, the man from Madras was not grinning; he had turned his face away, as if he were ashamed.

As he went up Lighthouse Hill that day, as he forced his cart over the hump, he felt none of his usual exultation. I am not really moving forward, he thought. Every turn of the wheel undid him and slowed him down. Each time he cycled, he was working the wheel of life backwards, crushing muscle and fibre into the pulp from which they were made in his mother's womb; he was unmaking himself.

All at once, right in the middle of traffic, he stopped and got off his cart, possessed by the simple and clear thought: I can't go on like this.

Why don't you do something, work in a factory, anything, to improve yourself?

After all, for years you have delivered things to the gates of factories – it is just a question of getting inside.

The next day, he went to the factory. He saw thousands of men reporting for work and he thought: what a fool I have been, never even to try and get work here.

He sat down and none of the guards asked any questions, thinking he was waiting to collect a delivery.

He waited till noon and then a man came out. From the number of people following him Chenayya thought he must be the big man. He went running past the guard and got down on his knees: 'Sir! I want to work.'

The man stared at him. The guards came running up to drag Chenayya back, but the big man said: 'I have two thousand workers and not one of them wants to work, and here is this man, down on his knees, begging for work. That's the attitude we need to move this country forward.'

He pointed at Chenayya.

'You won't get offered any long-term contract. Understand. Day by day.'

'Anything, anything you want.'

'What kind of work can you do?'

'Anything, anything you want.'

'All right, come back tomorrow. We don't need a coolie right now.'

'Yes, sir.'

The big man took out a pack of cigarettes and lit one.

'Hear what this man has to say,' he said, as a group of other men, who were also smoking, gathered around him.

And Chenayya repeated that he would do anything, under any conditions, for any sort of pay.

'Say it again!' the big man ordered and another group of men came up and listened to Chenayya.

That evening, he came back to Mr Ganesh Pai's shop and shouted at the other workers: 'I've found a real job, you motherfuckers. I'm out of here.'

The Tamilian boy alone cautioned him.

'Chenayya, why don't you wait a day and make sure the other job is good? Then you can quit here.'

'Nothing doing, I quit!' he yelled and walked away.

The next day at dawn, he was back at the factory gate. 'I want to see the big man,' he said, shaking the bars of the gate for attention. 'He told me to come today.'

The guard, who was reading the newspaper, looked up at him fiercely.

'Get out!'

'Don't you remember me? I came—'

'Get out!'

He waited near the gate; after an hour they opened and a car with tinted windows pulled out. Running side by side with the car, he banged on the windows. 'Sir! Sir! Sir!' A dozen hands seized him from behind; he was shoved to the ground and kicked.

When he wandered back to Mr Pai's shop that evening, the Tamilian boy was waiting for him. He said: 'I never told the boss you quit.'

The other rickshaw pullers did not tease Chenayya that night. One of them left him a bottle of liquor, still half full.

The rain fell without pause. He rode his cycle through the downpour, splashing down the road. He wore a long white plastic sheet over his body like a shroud; around the head, a black cloth tied it around his head, giving it the look of an Arab's cape and caftan.

This was the most dangerous time for the coolies. Whenever the road had broken up into a pothole, he had to slow down to avoid tripping his cycle-cart over.

Waiting at the crossroads, he saw to his left a fat kid sitting on the seat of an autorickshaw. The rain made him playful; he stuck his tongue out at the fellow. The boy did likewise, and the game went on for several turns, until the autorickshaw driver chided the boy and glared at Chenayya.

The pain in his neck began biting again. I can't go on like this, he thought.

From across the road, one of the other cart pullers, a young boy, drove his cart alongside Chenayya's. 'Have to deliver this fast and get back,' he said. 'Boss said he's depending on me to be back within an hour.' He grinned and Chenayya wanted to shove his fist into the grin. God, how full of suckers the world is, he thought, counting to ten to calm himself. How happy this man seems to be, to destroy himself with overwork. *You baboon!* he wanted to shout. *You and all the others! Baboons!*

He put his head down and suddenly it seemed a great strain to move the cart.

'You've got no air in one tyre!' the baboon shouted. 'You'll have to stop!' He grinned and rode on.

Stop? Chenayya thought. No, that is what a baboon would do: not me. Putting his head down, he pedalled on, forcing his flat tyre along:

Move!

And slowly and noisily, rattling its old wheels and its unoiled chains, the cart moved.

It's raining now, Chenayya thought, lying in his cart that night, a plastic sheet over him to protect him from the rain. That means half the year is over. It must be June or July. I must be nearly thirty now.

He pulled the sheet down and lifted his head to relieve the pain in his neck. He could not believe his eyes: even in this rain, some motherfucker was flying a kite! It was the kid with the black kite. As if taunting the heavens, the lightning, to come strike him. Chenayya watched and forgot his pain.

In the morning, two men in khaki uniforms came into the alley: autorickshaw drivers. They had come to wash their hands at the tap at the end of the alley. The cart pullers instinctively moved to one side and let the two men in uniforms through. As they washed their hands, Chenayya heard them talk about an autorickshaw driver who had been locked up by the police for hitting a customer.

'Why not?' one autorickshaw driver said to the other. 'He had every right to hit that man! I only wish he had gone further and killed that bastard before the police got to him!'

After brushing his teeth, Chenayya went to the lottery seller. A boy, a total stranger, was sitting at the desk, kicking his legs merrily.

'What happened to the old fellow?'

'Gone.'

'Gone where?'

'Gone into politics.'

The boy described what had happened to the old seller. He had joined the campaign of a BJP candidate for the Corporation elections. His candidate was likely to win in the elections. Then he would sit on the verandah of the candidate's house; if you wanted to see the politician, you would have to pay him fifty rupees first.

'That's the politician's life – it's the fastest way to get rich,' the boy said. He flipped through his coloured paper pieces. 'What'll you have, uncle? A yellow? Or a green?'

Chenayya turned away without buying any of the coloured tickets.

Why, he thought at night, can't that be me – the fellow who goes into politics to get rich? He did not want to forget what he had just heard, so he pinched himself sharply at the ankle.

It was Sunday again. His free day. Chenayya woke up when it got too hot, then brushed his teeth lazily, looking up to see if kites were flying in the sky. The other pullers were going to see the new Hoyka temple that the Member of Parliament had opened, just for Hoykas, with their own Hoyka deity and Hoyka priests.

'Aren't you coming, Chenayya?' the others shouted to him.

'What has any god ever done for me?' he shouted back; they giggled at his recklessness.

Baboons, he thought, as he lay down in the cart again. Going to worship some statue in a temple, thinking it'll make them rich.

Baboons!

He lay with one arm over his face; then he heard the tinkling of coins.

'Come over, Kamala,' he called out to the prostitute, who was in her usual spot, playing with the coins. When he taunted her for the sixth time, she snapped: 'Get lost, or I'll call Brother.'

At this reference to the kingpin who ran the brothels in this part of town, Chenayya sighed and turned over in his cart.

He thought: perhaps it is time for me to get married.

He had lost contact with all his relatives; plus he did not actually want to get married. Bring children – into what future? That was the most baboon-like thing the other coolies did; to procreate, as if to say, they were satisfied with their fate, they were happy to replenish the world that had consigned them to this task.

There was nothing in him but anger, and if he married he thought he would lose his anger.

As he turned around in his cart, he noticed the welt on his foot. He frowned, trying hard to remember how he had got it.

The next morning, returning from a delivery, he made a

diversion and rode his cart to the office of the Congress party in Umbrella Street. He crouched on the verandah of the office and waited for someone important-looking to come out.

A sign outside showed Indira Gandhi raising her hand, with the slogan: 'Mother Indira will protect the poor.' He smirked.

Were they completely nuts? Did they really think that anyone would believe a politician would protect the poor?

But then he thought: maybe this woman, Indira Gandhi, had been someone special; maybe they were right. In the end, she was shot dead, wasn't she? That seemed evidence to him that she had wanted to help people. Suddenly it seemed that the world did have good-hearted men and women – he felt he had cut himself off from all of them by his bitterness. Now he wished he hadn't been so rude to that journalist from Madras...

A man in loose white clothes appeared, followed by two or three hanger-ons; Chenayya rushed up to him and got down on his knees with his palms folded.

All the following week, whenever he knew his number was not going to be called for a while, he rode around on his cycle, sticking up posters of the Congress candidates in all the Muslim-dominated streets, shouting: 'Vote for Congress – the party of Muslims! Defeat the BJP!'

The week passed. The elections took place, the results were declared. Chenayya rode his cycle to the Congress party, parked it outside, went to the doorkeeper and asked to see the candidate.

'He's a busy man now; just wait out here a moment,' said the doorkeeper. He placed a hand on Chenayya's back. 'You really helped us do well in the Bunder, Chenayya. The BJP defeated us everywhere else, but you got the Muslims to vote for us!'

Chenayya beamed. He waited outside the party headquarters and watched the cars arrive and disgorge rich and important men, who hurried in to see the candidate. He saw them and thought: this is where I will wait to collect money from the rich. Not much. Just five rupees from everyone who comes to see the candidate. That should do.

His heart beat from excitement. An hour passed.

Chenayya decided to go into the waiting room, to make sure that he too got to see the Man when he finally emerged. There were benches and stools in the waiting room; a dozen other men were waiting. Chenayya saw an empty chair and wondered if he should sit down. Why not, had he not worked for the victory too? He was about to sit down, when the doorkeeper said: 'Use the floor, Chenayya.'

Another hour passed. Everyone in the waiting room was told to go in and see the Big Man; but Chenayya was still squatting outside, his face between his palms, waiting.

Finally, the doorkeeper came up to him with a box full of round yellow sweets. 'Take one.'

Chenayya took a sweet, almost put it in his mouth, and then put it back. 'I don't want a sweet.' His voice rose quickly. 'I hung posters all over this town! Now I want to see the Big Man! I want to get a job with—!'

The doorkeeper slapped him.

I am the biggest fool here, Chenayya thought, back at his alley: the other pullers were lying in their carts, snoring hard.

It was late that night and he was the only one who could not sleep. *I am the biggest fool; I am the biggest baboon here.*

On the way to his first assignment the next morning, there was another traffic jam in front of Umbrella Street – the biggest one he had ever seen.

He slowed down, spitting on the road every few minutes to help himself pass the time.

When he finally got to his destination, he found that he was delivering to a foreign man. He insisted on helping Chenayya unload the furniture, which confused Chenayya terribly. The whole time, the foreigner spoke to Chenayya in English, as if he expected everyone in Kittur to be familiar with the language.

He held his hand out at the end to shake Chenayya's hand, and gave him a fifty-rupee note.

Chenayya was in a panic – where was he expected to get change? He tried to explain, but the European just grinned and shut the door.

Then he understood. He bowed deeply to the closed door.

When he returned to the alley with two bottles of liquor, the other cart pullers jeered at him.

'Where did you get money for that from, Chenayya?'

'None of your business.'

He drank a bottle dry; then drank the second. Then he went over to the liquor shop and bought another bottle of hooch; when he woke next morning he realized he had spent all his money on liquor.

All of it.

He put his face in his hands and began to cry.

On an assignment to the train station, he went to the tap to drink; nearby, he overheard autorickshaw drivers talking about that driver who had hit his customer.

'A man has a right to do what he has to do,' one said. 'The condition of the poor is becoming intolerable here.'

But they were not poor themselves, Chenayya thought, slathering his dry forearm with water; they lived in houses, they owned their vehicles. You have to attain a certain level of richness before you can complain about being poor, he thought. When you are this poor, you are not given the right to complain.

'Look – that's what the rich of this town want to turn us into!' the autorickshaw man said, and Chenayya realized that he was being pointed at. 'They want to swindle us out of our money until we turn into that!'

He cycled out of the train station, but he could not stop hearing their words. He could not switch off his mind. Like a tap it dripped. Think, think, think. He passed by a statue of Gandhi and he began thinking again. Gandhi dressed like a poor man – he dressed like Chenayya did. But what did Gandhi do for the poor?

Did Gandhi even exist? he wondered. These things – India, the river Ganga, the world beyond India – were they even real?

How would he ever know?

Only one group was lower than he was. The beggars. One misstep and he would be down with them, he thought. One accident. And that would be him. How did the others deal with this? They did not. They preferred not to think.

When he stopped at a crossroads that night, an old beggar put his hands in front of Chenayya.

He turned his face away and rode down the road back to Mr Ganesh Pai's shop.

The following morning, he was going over the hill again, with five cardboard crates piled up one above the other in his cart, thinking: because we let them. Because we do not dare run away with that wad of fifty thousand rupees – because we know other poor people will catch us and drag us back before the rich man. We poor have built the prison around ourselves.

In the evening, he lay down exhausted. The others had built a fire. Someone would come and give him some rice. He was the hardest worker, so the boss-man had let it be known that he ought to be fed regularly.

He saw two dogs humping. There was no passion in what they were doing: it was just a release. That is all I want to do right now, he thought: hump something. But instead of humping, I have to lie here, thinking.

The fat prostitute sat outside. 'Let me come up,' he said. She did not look at him; she shook her head.

'Just one time. I'll pay you next time.'

'Get out of here, or I'll call Brother,' she said, referring to the don who ran the brothel and took a cut from the women every night. He gave in; he bought a small bottle of liquor and he began drinking.

Why do I think so much? These thoughts are like thorns

inside my head; I want them out. And even when I drink, they're there. I wake up in the night, my throat burning, and I find all the thoughts still in my head.

He lay awake, lying in his cart. He was sure he had been hounded by the rich even in his dreams, because he woke up furious and sweating. Then he heard the noise of coitus nearby. Looking around, he saw another cart puller humping the prostitute. Right next to him. He wondered: why not me? why not me? He knew the fellow had no money; so she was doing it out of charity. Why not me?

Every sigh, every groan of the coupling pair was like a chastisement; and Chenayya couldn't take it any more.

He got off his cart, walked around till he found a puddle of cowdung on the ground, and scooped a handful. He flung the shit at the lovers. There was a cry; he rushed up to them and dabbed the whore's face with shit. He put his shit-smeared fingers into her mouth and kept them there, even though she bit them; the harder she bit the more he enjoyed it, and he kept his fingers there until the other pullers descended on him and dragged him away.

One day he was given an assignment that took him right out of the city limits, into Bajpe; he was delivering a doorframe to a construction site.

'There used to be a big forest here,' one of the construction workers told him. 'But now that's all that's left.' He pointed to a distant clump of green.

Chenayya looked at the man and asked: 'Is there any work here for me?'

On his way back, he took a detour off the road and went to the patch of green. When he got there, he left his bike and walked around; seeing a high rock, he climbed up and looked at the trees around him. He was hungry, because he had not eaten all day, but he felt all right. Yes, he could live out here. If only he had a little food, what more would he want? His aching muscles could be rested. He put his head on the rock and looked at the sky.

He dreamed of his mother. Then he remembered the thrill with which he had come to Kittur from his village, at the age of seventeen. That first day, he was taken around by a female cousin who pointed out some of the main sights to him, and he remembered the whiteness of her skin, which doubled the charms of the city. He never saw that cousin again. He remembered what came next: the terrible contraction, the life that got smaller and smaller by the day in the city. The realization came to him now, that the first day in a city was destined to be the best: you had already been expelled from paradise, the moment you walk into the city.

He thought: I could be a sanyasi. Just eat bushes and herbs and live with the sunrise and sunset. The wind picked up; the trees nearby rustled, as if they were chuckling at him.

It was night-time when he cycled back. To get to the shop faster, he took the route down the Lighthouse Hill.

As he was coming down, he saw a red light and then a green light attached to the back of a large silhouette moving down the road; a moment later he realized it was an elephant.

It was the same elephant he had seen earlier; only now it had red and green traffic lights tied with string to its rump.

'What's the meaning of this?' he shouted to the mahout.

The mahout shouted back: 'Well, I have to make sure no one bumps into us from behind at night – there are no lights anywhere!'

Chenayya threw his head up and laughed; it was the funniest thing he had ever seen: an elephant with traffic lights on its rump.

'They didn't pay me,' the mahout said. He had tied the beast to the side of the road and was chatting to Chenayya. He had some peanuts and he didn't want to eat them alone, so he was glad to share a few with Chenayya.

'They made me take their kid on a ride and they didn't pay me. You should have seen them drink and drink. And they wouldn't pay me fifty rupees, which was all I asked for.'

The mahout slapped the side of his elephant. 'After all that Rani did for them—'

'That's the way of the world,' Chenayya said.

'Then it's a rotten world.' The mahout chewed a few more peanuts. 'A rotten world.' He slapped the side of his elephant. Chenayya looked up at the beast.

The behemoth's eyes gazed sidelong at him; they glistened darkly, almost as if they were tearing. The beast also seemed to be saying: 'Things should not be this way.'

The mahout pissed against the wall, turning his head up, arching his back, and exhaling in relief, as if it were the happiest thing he had done all day.

Chenayya kept looking at the elephant, its sad wet eyes. He thought: I am sorry I ever cursed you brother, as he rubbed its trunk.

The mahout stood at the wall, watching Chenayya talking to the elephant, a sense of apprehension rising within him.

Outside the ice-cream shop, two kids were licking ice lollies and staring right at Chenayya. He lay sprawled on his cart, dead tired after another day's work.

'Don't you see me?' Chenayya wanted to shout out over the traffic. His stomach was grumbling; he was tired and hungry, and there was still an hour before the Tamilian boy from Mr Ganesh Pai's shop would come out with dinner.

One of the kids across the street turned away, as if the fury in the cycle puller's eyes had become tangible; but the other one, a fat light-skinned fellow, stayed put, licking his tongue up and down his ice-cream stick, staring nonchalantly at Chenayya.

Don't you have any shame, any sense of decency, you fat fuck?

He turned around in his cart and began talking aloud to calm his nerves. His gaze fell on the rusty saw lying at the end of his cart. What stops me now, he said aloud, crossing the street and slashing that boy into shreds?

Just the thought made him feel powerful.

A finger began tapping on his shoulder. If it is the fat motherfucker with his ice-cream stick, I will pick up that saw and slice him in two, I swear to God.

It was the Tamilian assistant from the store.

'Your turn, Chenayya.'

He took his cart to the entrance of the store, where the boy handed him a small package, wrapped in newspaper and tied in white string.

'It's to the same place you went a while back to deliver the rose table. Mrs Engineer's house. We forgot to send the bonus gift and she's been complaining.'

'Oh, no,' he groaned. 'She doesn't tip at all. She's a complete cunt.'

'You have to go, Chenayya. Your number came up.'

He cycled there slowly. At every crossroads and traffic light he looked at the saw in his cart.

Mrs Engineer opened her door herself: she said she was on the phone and told him to wait outside.

'The food at the Lion's Club is so fattening,' he heard her saying. 'I've put on ten kilos in the past year.'

He looked around quickly. No lights were on in the neighbours' houses. There seemed to be a nightwatchman's shed at the back of the house, but that too was dark.

He snatched the saw and went in. She had her back to him; he saw the whiteness of her flesh in the gap between her blouse and her skirt; he smelled the perfume of her body. He went closer.

She turned round; then covered the receiver with her hand. 'Not in here, you idiot! Just put it on the floor and get out!'

He stood confused.

'On the floor!' she screamed at him. 'Then get out!'

He nodded and dropped the saw on the floor and ran out.

'Hey! Don't leave that in here! O, my God!'

He ran back, picked up the saw, then left the house, ducking low, to avoid the neem tree leaves. He tossed the saw into the cart: a loud clatter. The bonus gift...where was it? He grabbed the package, ran into the house, left it somewhere and slammed the door.

There was a startled meow. A cat was sitting up on a branch of the tree, watching him closely. He went close to it. How beautiful its eyes were, he thought. Like a jewel that had fallen off the throne, a hint of a world of beauty beyond his knowledge.

He reached up to it and it came to him.

'Kitty, kitty,' he said, stroking its fur. It wriggled in his arms, restless already.

Somewhere, I hope, a poor man will strike a blow against the world. Because there is no God watching over us. There is no one coming to release us from the jail in which we have locked ourselves.

He wanted to tell all this to the cat; maybe it could tell it to another cart puller; the one who would be brave enough to strike the blow.

He sat down by the wall, still holding on to the cat and stroking its fur. Maybe I can take you along, kitty. But how would he feed it? Who would take care of it when he was not around? He released it. He sat with his back to the wall and watched it walking cautiously up to a car, and then slinking under it; he craned his neck to see what it was doing down there, when he heard a shout from above. It was Mrs Engineer, yelling at him from a window at the top of her mansion: 'I know what you're up to, you thug – I can read your mind! You won't get another rupee out of me! Get moving!'

He was no longer angry; and he knew she was right. He had to go back to the store. His number would come up again soon. He got on his cart and pedalled.

There was a traffic jam in the city centre and Chenayya had

to go over the Lighthouse Hill again. Traffic was bad here too. It moved a few inches at a time, and then Chenayya had to stop mid-hill and clamp his foot down on the road to hold his cart in its place. When the horns began to sound, he rose from his seat and pedalled; behind him, a long line of cars and buses moved, as if he were pulling the traffic along with an invisible chain.

Day Four (Afternoon): THE COOL WATER WELL JUNCTION

The old Cool Water Well is said never to dry up, but it is now sealed and serves only as a traffic roundabout. The streets around the Well house a number of middle-class colonies. Professional people of all castes – Bunts, Brahmins, and Catholics – live side by side here, although the Muslim rich keep to the Bunder. The Canara Club, the most exclusive club in town, is located here, in a large white mansion with lawns. The neighbourhood is the 'intellectual' part of town: it boasts a Lion's Club, a Rotary Club, a Freemasons' Lodge, a Baha'i educational group, a Theosophist Society, and a branch of the Alliance Française of Pondicherry. Of the numerous medical institutions located here, the two best-known are the Havelock Henry General Hospital and Dr Shambhu Shetty's Happy Smile orthodontic clinic. The St Agnes Girls' High School, Kittur's most sought-after girls-only school, is also located close by the junction. The poshest part of the Cool Water Well Junction area is the hibiscus-lined street known as Rose Lane. Mabroor Engineer, believed to be Kittur's richest man, and Anand Kumar, Kittur's Member of Parliament, have mansions here.

It's one thing to take a little ganja, roll it inside a chappati and chew it at the day's end, just to relax the muscles – I can forgive that in a man, I really can. But to smoke this drug – this *smack* – at seven in the morning, and then lie in a corner with your tongue hanging out, I tolerate that in no man on my construction site. You understand me? Or do you want me to repeat this in Tamil or whatever language your people speak?'

'I understand, sir.'

'What did you say? What did you say, you son of…?'

Holding her brother by the hand, Soumya watched as the foreman chastized her father. The foreman was young, so much younger than her father – but he wore a khaki uniform that the construction company had given him, and twirled a lathi in his left hand, and she saw that the workers, instead of defending her father, were listening quietly to the foreman. He was sitting in a blue chair on an embankment of mud; a gas lamp buzzed noisily from a wooden pole driven into the ground next to the chair. Behind him was the crater around the half-demolished house; the inside of the house was filled with rubble, its roof had mostly fallen in, and its windows were empty. With his baton and his uniform, and his face harshly illuminated by the incandescent paraffin lamp, the foreman looked like a ruler of the underworld, at the gate of his kingdom.

A semi-circle of construction workers had formed below him. Soumya's father stood apart from the others, looking furtively at Soumya's mother, who was muffling her sobs in a corner of her sari. In a tear-racked voice she said: 'I keep telling him to give up this *smack*. I keep telling–'

Soumya wondered why her mother had to complain about her father in front of everyone. Raju pressed her hand.

'Why are they all scolding Daddy?'

She pressed back. Quiet.

All at once the foreman got up from his chair, took a step down the embankment, and raised his stick over Soumya's father. 'Pay attention, I said' – he brought his stick down.

Soumya shut her eyes and turned away.

The workers had returned to their tents, which were scattered about the open field around the dark, half-demolished house. Soumya's father was lying on his blue mat, apart from everyone else; he was snoring already, his hands over his eyes. In the old days she would have gone to him and snuggled against his side.

Soumya went up to her father. She shook him by his big toe, but he did not respond. She went to where her mother was making rice and lay down beside her.

Mallets and sledgehammers woke her up in the morning. Thump! Thump! Thump! Bleary-eyed, she wandered over to the house. Her father was up on the bit of the roof that remained, sitting on one of the black iron crossbeams; he was cutting it with a saw. Two men swung at the wall below with sledgehammers; clouds of dust rose up and covered her father as he sawed. Soumya's heart leaped.

She ran to her mother and cried: 'Daddy's working again!'

Her mother was with the other women; they were coming down from the house, carrying large metal saucers on their heads filled to the brim with rubble. 'Make sure Raju doesn't get wet,' she said, as she passed Soumya.

Only then did Soumya notice it was drizzling.

Raju was lying on the blanket where his mother had been; she woke him up and took him into one of the tents. Raju began whimpering, saying he wanted to sleep some more. She went to the blue mat; her father had not touched the rice from last night. Mixing the dry rice with the rainwater, she squeezed it into a gruel and stuffed morsels into Raju's mouth. He said he didn't like it and bit her fingers each time.

The rain fell harder and she heard the foreman roar: 'You sons of bald women, don't slow down!'

The moment the rain stopped, Raju wanted to be pushed on the swing. 'It's going to start raining again,' she said, but he wouldn't change his mind. She carried him in her arms to the old truck tyre swing near the compound wall and put him on it, and gave him a push, shouting: 'One! Two!'

As she pushed, a man appeared before her.

His dark, wet skin was coated in white dust and it took an instant for her to recognize him.

'Sweetie,' he said, 'you must do something for Daddy.'

Her heart was beating too fast for her to say a word. She wanted him to say 'sweetie' not like he was saying it now – as if it were just a word, air that he were breathing out – but like before, when it came from his heart, when it was accompanied by his pulling her to his chest and hugging her deeply and whispering madly into her ear.

He went on speaking, in the same strange, slow, slurred way, and told her what he wanted her to do; then he walked back to the house.

She found Raju, who was cutting an earthworm into smaller

bits with a piece of glass he had stolen from the demolition site, and said: 'We have to go.'

Raju could not be left alone, even though he would be a real nuisance on a trip like this. Once she had left him alone and he had swallowed a piece of glass.

'Where are we going?' he asked.

'To the Bunder.'

'Why?'

'There is a place by the Bunder, a garden, where Daddy's friends are waiting for him to come. Daddy cannot go there – because the foreman will hit him again. You don't want the foreman to beat Daddy again in front of all the world, do you?'

'No,' Raju said. 'And when we get to this garden, what do we do?'

'We give Daddy's friends at this garden ten rupees and they will give us something Daddy *really* needs.'

'What?'

She told him.

Raju, already shrewd with money, asked: 'How much will it cost?'

'Ten rupees, he said.'

'Did he give you ten rupees?'

'No. Daddy said we'll have to get it ourselves. We'll have to beg.'

As the two of them walked down Rose Lane, she kept her eyes on the ground. Once she had found five rupees on the ground – yes, five! You never know what you'd find in a place where rich people live.

They moved to the side of the lane; a white car paused for

a moment to go over a bump on the road and she shouted at the driver: 'Where is the port, uncle?'

'Far from here,' he shouted back. 'Go to the main road and take a left.'

The tinted windows in the back of the car were rolled up, but through the driver's window Soumya caught a glimpse of a passenger's hand covered with gold bangles; she wanted to knock on the window. But she remembered the rule that the foreman had laid down for all the workers' children. No begging in Rose Lane. Only on the main road. She controlled herself.

All the houses were being demolished and rebuilt in Rose Lane. Soumya wondered why people wanted to tear down these fine, large, whitewashed houses. Maybe houses became uninhabitable after some time, like shoes.

When the lights on the main road turned red, she went from autorickshaw to autorickshaw, opening and closing her fingers.

'Uncle, have pity, I'm starving.'

Her technique was solid. She had got it from her mother. It went like this: even as she begged, for three seconds she kept eye contact; then her eye would begin to wander to the next autorickshaw. 'Mother, I'm hungry' (rubbing her tummy) 'give me food' (closing her fingers and bringing them to her mouth).

'Big brother, I'm hungry.'

'Grandpa, even a small coin would—'

While she did the road, Raju sat on the ground and was meant to whimper when anyone well-dressed passed by. She did not count on him to do much; at least if he sat down he would stay out of other kinds of trouble, like running after cats, or trying to pet stray dogs that might be rabid.

Towards noon, the roads filled with cars. The windows had been rolled up against the rain, and she had to raise both her hands to the glass and scratch like a cat, to get attention. The windows in one car were rolled down and she thought her luck had improved.

A woman in one of the cars had beautiful patterns of gold painted on her hands and Soumya gaped at them. She heard the woman with the gold hands say to someone else in the car: 'There are beggars everywhere these days in the town. It never used to be like this.'

The other person leaned forward and stared for a moment. 'They're so *dark*... Where are they from?'

'Who knows?'

Only fifty paise, after an hour.

Next she tried to get on the bus when it stopped at the red light and beg there, but the conductor saw her coming and stood at the door: 'Nothing doing.'

'Why not, uncle?'

'Who do you think I am, a rich man like Mr Engineer? Go ask someone else, you brat!'

Glaring at her, he raised the red cord of his whistle over his head as if it were a whip. She scrambled out.

'He was a real cock-sucker,' she told Raju, who had something to show her: a sheet of wrapping plastic, full of round buttons of air that could be popped.

Making sure the conductor couldn't see, she got down on

her knees and put it on the road right in front of the wheel. Raju crouched: 'No, it's not right. The wheels won't go over it,' he said. 'Push it to the right a little.'

When the bus moved again, the wheels ran over the plastic sheets and the buttons exploded, startling the passengers; the conductor poked his head out of the window to see what had happened. The two children ran away.

It began raining again. The two of them crouched under a tree; coconuts came crashing down and a man who had been standing next to them with an umbrella jumped up and swore at the tree, and ran. She giggled, but Raju was worried they would get hit by a falling coconut.

When the rain stopped, she found a twig and scratched on the ground, drawing a map of the city, as she imagined it. Here – was Rose Lane. Here – was where they had come, still close to Rose Lane. Here – was the Bunder. And here – the garden inside the Bunder that they were looking for.

'Do you understand all of this?' she asked Raju. He nodded, excited by the map.

'To get to the Bunder, we have to go' – she drew another arrow – 'through the big hotel.'

'And then?'

'And then we go to the garden inside the Bunder…'

'And then?'

'We find the thing Daddy wants us to get.'

'And then?'

The truth was, she had no idea if the hotel was on the way to the port or not: but the rain had driven the vehicles away from the road, and the hotel was the only place where she might be able to beg for the money right now.

'You have to ask for money in English from the tourists,' she teased Raju as they walked to the hotel. 'Do you know what to say in English?'

They stopped outside the hotel to watch a group of crows bathing in a puddle of water. The sun was shining on the water, and the black coats of the crows turned glossy as scintillas of water flew from their shaking bodies; Raju declared it was the most beautiful thing he had ever seen.

The man with no arms and legs was sitting in front of the hotel; he yelled curses from the other side of the road.

'Go away, you devil's children! I told you never to come back here!'

She shouted back: 'To hell with you, monster! We told you: never come back here!'

He was sitting on a wooden board with wheels. Whenever a car slowed down at the traffic light in front of the hotel, he rolled up on his wooden board and begged from one side; she begged from the other side of the car.

Raju, sitting on the pavement, yawned.

'Why do we need to beg? Daddy is working today. I saw him cutting those things…' He moved his legs apart and began sawing at an imaginary crossbeam below him.

'Quiet.'

Two taxis slowed down near the red light. The man with no arms and legs rushed on his wooden board to the first taxi; she ran to the second one and put her hands into the open window. A foreigner was sitting inside. He stared at her with an open mouth: she saw his lips making a perfect pink 'O'.

'Did you get any money?' Raju asked, when she came back from the car and the white man.

'No. Get up,' she said and dragged the boy to his feet.

By the time they had crossed two red lights, however, Raju had figured it out. He pointed to her clutched fist.

'You got money from the white man. You have the money!'

She went up to an autorickshaw parked by the side of the road: 'Which way is the Bunder?'

The driver yawned. 'I don't have any money. Go away.'

'I'm not asking for money. I'm asking for directions to the Bunder.'

'I told you, I'm not giving you anything!'

She spat at his face. Then she grabbed Raju by the wrist and they ran like mad.

The next autorickshaw driver they asked was a kind man. 'It's a long, long way. Why don't you take a bus? The number 343 will get you there. Otherwise, it'll be a couple of hours at least, by foot.'

'We don't have money, uncle.'

He gave them a rupee coin and asked: 'Where are your parents?'

They got onto a bus and paid the conductor. 'Where are you getting off?' he shouted.

'The port.'

'This bus doesn't go to the port. You need the number 343. This is the number—'

They got out and walked.

They were near the Cool Water Well Junction now. They found the one-armed, one-legged boy working there, as he always did; he went hopping about from car to car, begging before she could get to them. Someone had given him a radish today, so he went about begging with a large white radish in his hand, tapping it on the windscreens to get the attention of the passengers.

'Don't you dare do your begging here, you sons of bitches!' he shouted at them, waving the radish threateningly.

The two of them stuck their tongues out at him and shouted: 'Freak! Disgusting freak!'

Raju began crying after an hour and refused to walk any more, so she picked in a rubbish can for some food. There was a carton with two biscuits and they had one each.

They walked some more. After a while, Raju's nostrils began bubbling.

'I can smell the sea from here.'

She could, too.

They walked faster. They saw a man painting a sign in English by the side of the road; two cats fighting on the roof of a white Fiat; a horse-cart, loaded with chopped wood; an elephant, walking down the road with a mound of neem leaves; a car that had been smashed up in an accident; and a dead crow with its claws drawn in stiffly to its chest, its belly open and swarming with black ants.

Then they were at the Bunder.

The sun was setting over the sea and they went past the packed markets, looking for a garden.

'There are no gardens here in the Bunder. That's why the air is so bad here,' an old Muslim peanut-seller told them. 'You've got the wrong directions.'

Looking at their crestfallen faces, he offered them a handful of peanuts to munch on.

Raju whined. He was hungry…to hell with the peanuts! He thrust them back at the Muslim man, who called him a devil.

That made Raju so angry he left his sister and ran, and she ran after him until Raju came to a stop.

'Look!' he shrieked, pointing at a row of mutilated men with bandaged limbs, sitting in front of a building with a white dome.

Gingerly they walked around the lepers. And then she saw a man lying down on a bench, his palms crossed over his face, breathing heavily. She came near the bench and saw, right at the water's edge, fenced off by a small stone wall, a little green park.

Raju was quiet now.

When they got to the park, there was shouting. A policeman was slapping a very dark man. 'Did you steal the shoes? Did you?'

The very dark man shook his head. The policeman hit him harder. 'Son of a bald woman, you take these drugs and then you steal things, and you – son of a bald woman, you–!'

Three white-haired men, hiding in a bush near her, gestured to Soumya to come and hide with them. She took Raju into the bush and they waited there for the policeman to leave.

She whispered to the three white-haired men: 'I'm the daughter of Ramachandran, the man who smashes rich people's houses in Rose Lane.'

None of the three knew her father.

'What do you want, little girl?'

She said the word, as well as she could remember: '... *ack*.'

One of the men, who appeared to be their leader, frowned: 'Say it again.'

He nodded when she said the strange word the second time. Taking a pouch made of newspaper-skin out of his pocket, he tapped it: white powder, like crushed chalk, poured out. He took out a cigarette from another pocket, sliced it open, tapped out the tobacco, filled the paper with the white powder, and rolled it tight. He held the cigarette up in the air and gestured with his other hand to Soumya.

'Twelve rupees.'

'I've got only nine,' she said. 'You'll have to take nine.'

'Ten.'

She gave them the money; she took the cigarette. A horrible doubt seized her.

'If you're robbing me, if you're cheating me – Raju and I'll come back with Daddy – and beat you all.' The three men crouched together. They began shaking, and they were laughing together. Something was wrong with them. She grabbed Raju by the wrist and they ran.

Glimpses of the scene to come flashed through her mind. She would show Daddy what she had brought for him from so far away. 'Sweetie,' he would say – the way he used to say it – and hold her in a frenzy of affection, and the two would go mad with love for each other.

Her left foot began to burn after a while, and she flexed her toes and stared at them. Raju insisted on being carried; but fair enough, she thought – the little fellow had done well today.

It began raining again. Raju cried. She had to threaten to

leave him behind three times; once she actually left him and walked a whole block before he came running after her, telling her of a giant dragon that was chasing him.

They got onto a bus.

'Tickets,' the driver shouted, but she winked at him and said: 'Big brother, let us on for free, please…'

His face softened and he let them stay near the back.

It was pitch black when they got back to Rose Lane. They saw the lamps lit up in all the mansions. The foreman was sitting under his gas lamp, talking to one of the workers. The house looked smaller: all the crossbeams had been sawed off.

'Did you go begging in this neighbourhood?' the foreman shouted, when he saw the two of them.

'No, we didn't.'

'Don't lie to me! You were gone all day – and doing what? Begging on Rose Lane!'

She raised her upper lip in contempt.

'Why don't you ask if we begged here, before accusing us!'

The foreman glared at them, but kept quiet, defeated by the girl's logic.

Raju ran ahead, screaming for his mother. They found her asleep, alone, in her rain-dampened sari. Raju ran up to her, butted his head into her side, and began rubbing against her body for warmth, like a kitten; the sleeping woman groaned and turned over to the other side. One of her arms began swatting Raju away.

'Amma,' he said, shaking her. 'Amma! I'm hungry! Soumya gave me nothing to eat all day! She made me walk and walk and take this bus and that, and no food! A white man gave her a hundred rupees but she never gave me anything to eat or drink.'

'Don't lie!' Soumya hissed. 'What about the biscuits?'

But he kept shaking her: 'Amma! Soumya gave me nothing to eat or drink all day!'

The two children began wrestling each other. Then a hand lightly tapped Soumya's shoulder.

'Sweetie.'

When he saw their father, Raju began to simper; he turned and ran away to his mother. Soumya and her father walked to one side.

'Do you have it, sweetie? Do you have the thing?'

She drew air. 'Here,' she said and put the packet into his hands. He lifted it up to his nose, sniffed, and then put it under his shirt: she saw his hands reach through his sarong into his groin. He took his hand out. She knew it was coming now: his caress.

He caught her wrist; his fingers cut into her flesh.

'What about the hundred rupees that the white man gave you? I heard Raju.'

'No one gave me a hundred rupees, Daddy. I swear. Raju is lying, I swear.'

'Don't lie. Where is the hundred rupees?'

He raised his arm. She began screaming.

When she came to lie down next to her mother, Raju was still complaining that he had not eaten all day long, and had been forced to walk from here to there and then from there to another place and then back to here. Then he saw the red marks on his sister's face and neck and went silent. She fell to the ground, and went to sleep.

KITTUR: BASIC FACTS

TOTAL POPULATION (1981 CENSUS): 193,432
residents

CASTE AND RELIGIOUS BREAKDOWN
(as percentage of total population)

HINDUS
Upper castes
Brahmins:
 Kannada-speaking: 4 per cent
 Konkani-speaking: 3 per cent
 Tulu-speaking: less than 1 per cent
Bunts: 16 per cent
Other upper castes: 1 per cent

Backward castes
Hoykas: 24 per cent
Miscellaneous backward castes and tribals: 4 per cent

Dalits (formerly known as untouchables): 9 per cent

MINORITIES
Muslims
Sunni: 14 per cent
Shia: 1 per cent
Ahmediya, Bohra, Ismaili: less than 1 per cent
Catholics: 14 per cent
Protestants (Anglicans, Pentecostals, Jehovah's
Witnesses, Mormons): 3 per cent

Jains: 1 per cent

Other religions (including Parsi, Jew, Buddhist, Brahmo Samaji, and Baha'i): less than 1 per cent

89 residents declare themselves to be without religion or caste.

Day Five (Morning): VALENCIA
(TO THE FIRST CROSSROADS)

Valencia, the Catholic neighbourhood, begins with Father Stein's Homeopathic Hospital, which is named after a German Jesuit missionary who began a hospice here. Valencia is the largest neighbourhood of Kittur; most of its inhabitants are educated, employed, and owners of their homes. The handful of Hindus and Muslims who have bought land in Valencia have never encountered any trouble, but Protestants looking to live here have sometimes been attacked with stones and slogans. Every Sunday morning, men and women in their best clothes pour into the Cathedral of Our Lady of Valencia for mass. On Christmas Eve, virtually the entire population crams into the cathedral for midnight mass; the singing of carols and hymns continues well into the early hours.

When it came to troubles seen and horrors experienced, Jayamma, the advocate's cook, wanted it known that her life had been second to none. In the space of twelve years her dear mother had given birth to eleven children. Nine of them had been girls. Yes, nine! Now *that's* trouble. By the time Jayamma was born, number eight, there was no milk in her mother's breasts – they had to feed her an ass's milk in a plastic bottle. An ass's milk, yes! Now *that's* trouble. Her father had saved enough gold only for six daughters to be married off; the last three had to remain barren virgins for life. Yes, for life. For forty years she had been put on one bus or the other, and sent from one town to the next to cook and clean in someone else's house. To feed and fatten someone else's children. She wasn't even told where she would be going next; it would be night, she'd be playing with her nephew – that roly-poly little fellow Brijju – and what would she hear in the living room but her sister-in-law tell some stranger or the other: 'It's a deal, then. If she stays here, she eats food for nothing; so you're doing us a favour, believe me.' The next day Jayamma would be put on the bus again. Months would pass before she saw Brijju again. This was Jayamma's life, an instalment plan of troubles and horrors. Who had more to complain about on this earth?

But at least one horror was coming to an end. Jayamma was about to leave the advocate's house.

She was a short, stooped woman in her late fifties, with a glossy silver head of hair that seemed to give off light. A large black wart over her left eyebrow was the kind that is taken for an auspicious sign in an infant. There were always pouches of

230

dark skin shaped like garlic cloves under her eyes, and her eyeballs were rheumy from chronic sleeplessness and worry.

She had packed up her things: one big brown suitcase, the same one she had arrived with. Nothing more. Not a paise had been stolen from the advocate, although the house was sometimes in a mess and there surely had been the opportunity. But she had been honest. She brought the suitcase to the front porch and waited for the advocate's green Ambassador. He had promised to drop her off at the bus station.

'Goodbye, Jayamma. Are you leaving us for real?'

Shaila, the little lower-caste servant girl at the advocate's house – and Jayamma's principal tormentor of the past eight months – grinned. Although she was twelve and would be ready for marriage the following year, she looked only seven or eight. Her dark face was caked with Johnson and Johnson's Baby Powder, and she batted her eyelids mockingly.

'You lower-caste demon!' Jayamma hissed. 'Mind your manners!'

An hour late, the advocate's car pulled into the garage.

'Haven't you heard yet?' he said, when Jayamma came towards him with her bag. 'I told your sister-in-law we could use you a bit longer, and she agreed. I thought someone would have informed you.'

He slammed his car door shut. Then he went to take his bath, and Jayamma took her old brown suitcase back into the kitchen and began preparing for dinner.

'I'm never going to leave the advocate's house, am I, Lord Krishna?'

The next morning, the old woman was standing over the gas burner in the kitchen, stirring a lentil stew. As she worked, she sucked in air with a hiss, as if her tongue were on fire.

'For forty years I've lived among good Brahmins, Lord Krishna: homes in which even the lizards and the toads had been Brahmins in a previous birth. Now you see my fate, stuck among Christians and meat-eaters in this strange town, and each time I think I'm leaving, my sister-in-law tells me to stay on some more...'

She wiped her forehead and went on to ask: what had she done in a previous life – had she been a murderess, an adulteress, a child-devourer, a person who was rude to holy men and sages – to have been fated to come here, to the advocate's house, and live next to a lower-caste?

She sizzled onions, chopped coriander and threw them in, then stirred in red curry powder and monosodium glutamate from little plastic packets.

'Hai! Hai!'

Jayamma started and dropped her ladle into the broth. She went to the grill that ran along the rear end of the advocate's house and peered.

Shaila was at the outer wall of the compound, clapping her hands, while next door in the Christian neighbour's back yard, thick-lipped Rosie, a cleaving knife in her hand, was running after a rooster in her background. Slowly unbolting the door, Jayamma crept out into the back yard, to take a better look. 'Hai! Hai! Hai!' Shaila was shouting in glee, as the rooster clicked and clucked, and jumped on the green net over the well, where Rosie finally caught the poor thing and began cutting its neck. The rooster's tongue stuck out and its eyes almost popped out. 'Hai! Hai! Hai!'

Jayamma ran through the kitchen, straight into the dark prayer room, and bolted the door behind her. 'Krishna… My Lord Krishna…'

The prayer room doubled as a storage room for rice, and also as Jayamma's private quarters. The room was seven feet by seven feet; the little space in between the shrine and the rice bags, just enough to curl up in and go to sleep at night, was all Jayamma had asked from the advocate. (She had refused point-blank to take up the advocate's initial suggestion that she share a room with the lower-caste in the servants' quarters.)

She reached into the prayer shrine and took out a black box which she opened slowly. Inside was a silver idol of a child god – crawling, naked, with shiny buttocks – the god Krishna, Jayamma's only friend and protector.

'Krishna, Krishna,' she chanted softly, holding the baby god in her hands again and rubbing its silver buttocks with her fingers. 'You see what goes on around me – me, a high-born Brahmin woman!'

She sat down on one of three rice bags lined up against the wall of the prayer room, and surrounded by yellow moats of DDT. Folding her legs up on the rice bag, and leaning her head against the wall, she took in deep breaths of the DDT – a strange, relaxing, curiously addictive aroma. She sighed; she wiped her forehead with the edge of a vermilion sari. Spots of sunlight, filtering through the plantain trees outside, played along the ceiling of the little room.

Jayamma closed her eyes. The fragrance of DDT made her

drowsy; her body uncoiled, her limbs loosened, she was asleep in seconds.

When she woke up, fat little Karthik, the advocate's son, was shining a torchlight on her face. This was his way of rousing her from a nap.

'I'm hungry,' he said. 'Is anything ready?'

'Brother!' The old woman sprang to her feet. 'There's black magic in the back yard! Shaila and Rosie have killed a chicken – and they're doing black magic.'

The boy switched off the torchlight. He looked at her sceptically.

'What are you talking about, you old hag?'

'Come!' The old cook's eyes were large with excitement. 'Come!'

She coaxed the little master down the long hallway into the servants' quarters.

They stopped by the metal grille which gave them a view of the back yard. There were short coconut trees, and a clothesline, and a black wall beyond which began the compound of their Christian neighbour. There was no one around. A strong wind shook the trees, and a loose sheet of paper was swirling around the back yard, like a dervish. The boy saw the white bedsheets on the clothesline swaying eerily. They too seemed to suspect what the cook suspected.

Jayamma motioned to Karthik: be very, very quiet. She pushed the door to the servants' quarters. It was bolted shut.

When the old woman unlocked it, a stench of hair oil and baby powder wafted out, and the boy clamped his nostrils.

Jayamma pointed to the floor of the room.

A triangle in white chalk had been marked inside a square in red chalk, dried coconut flesh crowned the points of the triangle. Withered, blackening flowers were strewn about inside a circle. A blue marble gleamed from its centre.

'It's for black magic,' she said, and the boy nodded.

'Spies! Spies!'

Shaila stood athwart the door of the servants' room. She made a finger at Jayamma.

'You – you old hag! Didn't I tell you never to snoop around my room again?'

The old lady's face twitched.

'Brother!' she shouted. 'Did you see how this lower-caste speaks to us Brahmins?'

Karthik made a fist at the girl. 'Hey! This is my house and I'll go wherever I want to, you hear!'

Shaila glared at him: 'Don't think you can treat me like an animal, okay…'

Three loud honks ended the fighting. Shaila flew out to open the gate; the boy ran into his room and opened a textbook; Jayamma raced around the dining room in a panic, laying the table with stainless-steel plates.

The master of the house removed his shoes in the entrance hall and threw them in the direction of the shoe rack. Shaila would have to rearrange them later. A quick wash in his private bathroom and he emerged into the dining room, a tall, mustachioed man who cultivated flowing sideburns in the style of an earlier decade. At dinner he was always bare-chested, except for the Brahmin caste-string winding around his flabby torso. He ate quickly and in silence, pausing only once to gaze into a corner of the ceiling. The house was put in order by the motions of the master's jaws. Jayamma served. Karthik ate with his father. In the car shed, Shaila hosed down the master's green Ambassador and wiped it clean.

The advocate read the paper in the television room for an hour, and then the boy began searching for the black remote control in the mess of papers and books on the sandalwood table in the centre of the room. Jayamma and Shaila scrambled into the room and squatted in a corner, waiting for the television to come on.

At ten o'clock, all the lights in the house went out. The master and Karthik slept in their rooms.

In the darkness, a vicious hissing continued in the servants' quarters:

'Witch! Witch! Black-magic-making lower-caste witch!'

'Brahmin hag! Crazy old Brahmin hag!'

A week of non-stop conflict followed. Each time Shaila passed by the kitchen, the old Brahmin cook showered vengeful deities by the thousand down on that oily lower-caste head.

'What kind of era is this when Brahmins bring lower-caste girls into their household?' she grumbled as she stirred the lentils in the morning. 'Where have the rules of caste and religion fallen today, O Krishna?'

'Talking to yourself again, old virgin?' The girl had popped her head into the kitchen; Jayamma threw an unpeeled onion at her.

Lunch. Truce. The girl put out her stainless-steel plate outside the servants' living room and squatted on the floor, while Jayamma served out a generous portion of the lentil soup over the mounds of white rice on the girl's plate. She wouldn't starve anyone, she grumbled as she served, not even a sworn enemy. That's right: not even a sworn enemy. It wasn't the Brahmin way of doing things.

After lunch, putting on her glasses, she spread a copy of the newspaper just outside the servants' quarters. Sucking air in constantly, she read loudly and slowly, piecing letters into words and words into sentences. When Shaila passed by, she thrust the paper at her face.

'Here – you can read and write, can't you? Here, read the paper!'

The girl fumed; she went back into the servants' quarters and slammed the door.

'Do you think I've forgotten the trick you played on the advocate, you little Hokya? He's a kind-hearted man, so that's why, that evening you went up to him with your simpering lower-caste face and said, Master, I can't read. I can't write. I want to read. I want to write. Doesn't he, immediately, drive out to Shenoy's Book Store in Umbrella Street and buy you expensive reading-and-writing books? And all for what? Were the lower-castes meant to read and write?' Jayamma demanded of the closed door. 'Wasn't that all just a trap for the advocate?'

Sure enough, the girl lost all interest in her books. They lay in a heap in the back of her room, and one day when she was chatting up the thick-lipped Christian next door, Jayamma sold them all to the scrap-paper Muslim. Ha! Showed her!

As Jayamma narrated the story of the infamous reading-and-writing scam, the door to the servants' quarters opened;

Shaila's face popped out and she screamed at Jayamma at the top of her voice.

That evening the advocate spoke during dinner: 'I hear there's been some disturbance or other in the house every day this week...it's important to keep things quiet. Karthik has to prepare for his exams.'

Jayamma, who had been carrying away the lentil stew using the edge of her sari against the heat, put the stew down on the table.

'It's not me making the noise, Master – it's that Hoyka girl! She doesn't know our Brahmin ways.'

'She may be a Hoyka...' – the advocate licked the rice grains clinging to his fingers – '... but she is clean and works well.'

As she cleared the table after dinner, Jayamma trembled at the reproach.

Only once the lights were off in the house, and she lay in the prayer room with the familiar fumes of DDT about her, and opened the little black box, did she calm down. The baby God was smiling at her.

O, when it came to troubles and horrors, Krishna, who had seen what Jayamma had seen? She told the patient deity the story of how she first came to Kittur; how her sister-in-law had commanded her: 'Jayamma, you have to leave us and go, the advocate's wife is in a hospital in Bangalore, someone has to take care of little Karthik' – that was supposed to be just a month or two. Now, it had been eight months since she had seen her little nephew Brijju, or held him in her arms, or played cricket with him. Oh yes, these were troubles, Baby Krishna.

The next morning, she dropped her ladle in the lentils again. Karthik had poked her midriff from behind.

She followed him out of the kitchen and into the servants' room. She watched the boy as he looked at the diagram on the floor and the blue marble at the centre of it.

In his eyes the old servant saw the gleam – the master's possessive gleam that she had seen so many times in forty years.

'Look at that,' Karthik said. 'The nerve of that girl, drawing this thing in my own house...'

The crouching pair sat down by the yellow grille and watched Shaila move along the far wall of the compound towards the Christian's house. A wide well, covered with green netting, made a bump in the back of the house. Hens and roosters, hidden by the wall, ran around the well and clucked incessantly. Rosie was standing at the wall. Shaila and the Christian talked for a while. It was a brilliant, flickering afternoon. As the light emerged and retreated at rapid intervals, the glossy green canopies of the coconut trees blazed and dimmed like bursts of fireworks.

The girl wandered aimlessly after Rosie left. They saw her bending by the jasmine plants to tear off a few flowers and put them in her hair. A little later, Jayamma saw Karthik begin to scratch his leg in long, shearing strokes, like a bear scratching the sides of a tree. From his thighs, his rasping fingers moved upward towards his groin. Jayamma watched with a sense of disgust. What would the boy's mother say, if she could see what he was doing right now?

The girl was walking by the clothesline. The thin cotton sheets hung out to dry turned incandescent, like cinema screens, when the light emerged from the clouds. Inside one of the glowing sheets, the girl made a round, dark bulge, like a thing inside a womb. A keening noise rose from the white sheet. She had begun singing:

'A star is whispering
Of my heart's deep longing
To see you once more,
My baby-child, my darling, my king.'

'I know that nursery rhyme... My brother's wife sings it to Brijju...my little nephew...'

'Quiet. She'll hear you.'

Shaila had re-emerged from the hanging clothes. She drifted towards the far end of the back yard, where neem trees mingled with coconut palms.

'Does she think about her mother and sisters often, I wonder...' Jayamma whispered. 'What kind of a life is this for a girl, away from her family?'

'I'm tired of this waiting!' Karthik grumbled.

'Brother, wait!'

But he was already in the servants' room. A triumphant shriek: Karthik came out with the blue marble.

In the evening, Jayamma was on the threshold of the kitchen, winnowing rice. Her glasses had slid halfway down her nose and her brow was furrowed. She turned towards the servants' room, which was bolted from the inside, and from which came the sound of sobbing, and shouted: 'Stop crying. You've got to

240

get tough. Servants like us, who work for others, have to learn to be tough.'

Swallowing her tears audibly, Shaila shouted back through the bolted door: 'Shut up, you self-pitying Brahmin hag! You told Karthik I had black magic!'

'Don't accuse me of things like that! I never told him you did black magic!'

'Liar! Liar!'

'Don't call me a liar, you Hoyka! Why do you draw triangles on the ground, if not to practise black magic! You don't fool me for a minute!'

'Can't you see those triangles were just part of a game? Are you losing your mind, you old hag?'

Jayamma slammed down the winnow; the rice grains were splattered about the threshold. She went into the prayer room and closed the door.

She woke up and overheard a sob-drenched monologue: it was coming from the servants' quarters, and so loud that it had penetrated the wall of the prayer room.

'I don't want to be here... I didn't want to leave my friends, and our fields, and our cows, and come here. But my mother said: "You have to go to the city and work for the advocate Panchinalli, otherwise, where will you get the gold necklace? And who will marry you without a gold necklace?" But ever since I came, I've seen no gold necklace – just trouble, trouble, trouble!'

Jayamma shouted into the wall at once: 'Trouble, trouble, trouble – see how she talks like an old woman! This is nothing, your misfortune. I've seen real trouble!'

The sobbing stopped. Jayamma told the lower-caste a few of her own troubles. At dinner, Jayamma came with the trough of rice to the servants' living room. She banged on the door, but Shaila would not open.

'Oh, what a haughty little miss she is!'

She kept banging on the door, until it opened. Then she served the girl rice and lentil stew, and watched to make sure that it was eaten.

The next morning, the two servants were sitting at the threshold together.

'Say, Jayamma, what's the news of the world?'

Shaila was beaming. Flowers in her hair, and Johnson's powder on her face again. Jayamma looked up from the paper with a scornful expression.

'Oh, why do you ask me, you can read and write, can't you?'

'C'mon, Jayamma, you know we lower-castes aren't meant to do things like that…' The little girl smiled ingratiatingly. 'If you Brahmins don't read for us, where will we learn anything…'

'Sit down,' the old woman said haughtily. She turned the pages over slowly and read out from the news items that interested her.

'They say that in Tumkur district, a holy man has mastered the art of flying through willpower, and can go seventeen feet up in the air and bring himself down too.'

'Really?' The girl was sceptical. 'Has anyone actually seen him do this, or are they simply believing him?'

'Of course they saw him do it!' Jayamma retorted, tapping on the news item as proof. 'Haven't you ever seen magic?'

Shaila giggled hysterically; then she ran into the back yard and dashed into the coconut trees; and then Jayamma heard the song again.

She waited till Shaila came back to the house and said: 'What will your husband think, if he sees you looking like a savage? Your hair is a mess.'

So the girl sat down on the threshold, and Jayamma oiled her hair and combed it into gleaming black tresses that would set any man's heart on fire.

At eight o'clock the old lady and the girl went together to watch TV. They watched till ten, then returned to their rooms when Karthik switched it off.

Halfway through the night, Shaila woke up to see the door to her room pushed open.

'Sister...'

Through the darkness Shaila saw a silver-haired head peering in.

'Sister...let me spend the night here...there are ghosts outside the storage room, yes...'

Almost crawling into the servants' quarters, Jayamma, breathing hard and sweating profusely, propped herself against a wall of the room and sank her head between her knees. The girl went out to see what was happening in the storage room; she came back giggling.

'Jayamma...those aren't ghosts, those are just two cats, fighting in the Christian's house...that's all...'

But the old lady was already asleep, her silver hair spread out on the ground.

From then on, Jayamma began to come to sleep in Shaila's

room whenever she heard the two screeching cat-demons outside her room.

It was the day before the Navaratri festival. Still no word from home, nor from the advocate, about when she might be going home. The price of jaggery had gone up again. So had kerosene. Jayamma read in the papers that a holy man had learned to fly from tree to tree in a grove in Kerala – but only if the trees were arecanut trees. There was going to be a partial solar eclipse the following year, and that might signal the end of the earth. V. P. Singh, a member of the Union Cabinet, had accused the prime minister of corruption. The government could fall any day and there was going to be chaos in Delhi.

That night, after dinner, Jayamma proposed to the advocate that on the holy day she take Karthik to the Kittamma Devi temple near the train station.

'He should not fall out of the habit of prayer now that his mother is no more, should he?' she said meekly.

'That's a good idea…' The advocate picked up his newspaper.

Jayamma breathed in for courage.

'If you could give me a few rupees towards the rickshaw…'

She knocked at the little girl's room. She opened her fist triumphantly.

'Five rupees! The advocate gave me five rupees!'

Jayamma took a bath in the servants' toilet, lathering herself thoroughly in sandalwood soap. Changing from her vermilion sari to her purple one, she walked up to the boy's room relishing the fragrance of her own skin, feeling like someone important.

'Get dressed, brother – we'll miss the five o'clock pooja.'

The boy was on his bed, punching at the buttons of a small hand-held electronic game – Bip! Bip! Bip!

'I'm not coming.'

'Brother – it's a temple. We should go!'

'No.'

'Brother... What would your mother say if she were...'

The boy put his game down for a second. He walked up to the door of his room and slammed it in Jayamma's face.

She lay in the storage room, seeking comfort in the fumes of DDT and the sight of the baby Krishna's silver buttocks. The door creaked open. A small black face, coated in Johnson and Johnson's Baby Powder, smiled at her.

'Jayamma – Jayamma – take me to the temple instead...'

The two of them sat quietly in the autorickshaw.

'Wait here,' Jayamma said at the entrance to the temple. She bought a packet of flowers with fifty paise of her own money.

'Here.' She guided the girl to place the basket in the hands of the priest when they were in the temple.

A throng of devotees had gathered around the silver linga. Little boys jumped high to strike the temple bells around the deity. They struggled in vain and then their fathers hoicked them up. Jayamma caught Shaila leaping high at a bell.

'Shall I lift you up?'

At five, the pooja got under way. A bronze plate; flames rose from camphor cubes. Two women blew giant conches; a brass gong was struck, faster and faster. Then, one of the Brahmins rushed out with a copper plate that burned at one end and

Jayamma dropped a coin into it, while the girl reached forward with her palms for the holy fire.

The two of them sat out on the verandah of the temple, on whose walls hung the giant drums that were played at weddings. Jayamma remarked on the scandal of a woman decked in a sleeveless blouse heading towards the temple gate. Shaila thought the sleeveless style was quite 'sporty'. A screaming child was being pulled along by her father to the temple door. She quietened down when Jayamma and Shaila both began to pet her.

The two servants left the temple reluctantly. Birds rose up from the trees as they waited for a rickshaw. Bands of incandescent cloud piled up one above the other like military decorations as the sun set. Jayamma began fighting with the rickshaw driver over the price to go home, and Shaila giggled the whole time, infuriating the old woman and the driver alike.

'Jayamma – have you heard the Big News?'

The old lady looked up from the newspaper spread out on the threshold. She removed her glasses and blinked at the girl.

'About the price of jaggery?'

'No, not that.'

'About the man in Kasargod who gave birth?'

'No, not that, either.' The girl grinned shyly. 'I'm getting married.'

Jayamma's lips parted. She turned her head down, took off her glasses, rubbed her eyes.

'When?'

'Next month. The marriage has been fixed. The advocate

told me this yesterday. He will send my gold necklace directly to my village.'

'So you think you're a queen now, huh?' Jayamma snapped. 'Because you're getting hitched to some village bumpkin!'

She saw Shaila run to the compound wall to spread the tidings to the thick-lipped Christian. 'I'm getting married, I'm getting married,' the girl sung sweetly all day long.

Jayamma cautioned her from the kitchen: 'You think it's any big deal being married? Don't you know what happened to my sister, Ambika?'

But the girl was too full of herself to listen. She just sang all day: 'I'm getting married, I'm getting married!'

So at night, it was the baby Krishna who got to hear the story of the luckless Ambika, punished for her sins in a previous life:

Ambika, the sixth daughter and the last to be married, was the family beauty. A rich doctor wanted her for his son. Excellent news! When the groom came to see Ambika, he left for the bathroom repeatedly. 'See how shy he is,' the women all giggled. On the wedding night, he lay with his back turned to Ambika's face. He coughed all night. In the morning, she saw blood on the sheets. He notified her that she had married a man with advanced tuberculosis. He had wanted to be honest, but his mother would not let him. 'Someone has put black magic on your family, you wretched girl,' he said, as his body was racked by fits of coughing. A month later, he was dead on a hospital bed. His mother told the village that the girl, and all her sisters, were cursed; and no one would agree to marry any of the other children.

'And that's the true story of why I'm a virgin,' Jayamma wanted the infant Krishna to know. 'In fact, I had such thick hair, such golden skin, I was considered a beauty, you know that?' She raised her eyebrows archly, like a film actress, suspecting that the little god did not entirely believe her. 'Sometimes I thank my stars I never married. What if I too had been deceived, like Ambika? Better a spinster than a widow, any day... And yet that little lower-caste can't stop singing about it every minute of the morning...' Lying in the dark, Jayamma mimicked the little lower-caste's voice for the baby god's benefit: 'I'm getting married, I'm getting married...'

The day came for Shaila's departure. The advocate said he would himself drive the girl home in his green Ambassador.

'I'm going, *Jayamma*.'

The old lady was brushing her silver hair on the threshold. She felt that Shaila was pronouncing the name with deliberate tartness. 'I'm going to get married.' The old lady kept brushing her hair. 'Write to me sometime, won't you, Jayamma? You Brahmins are such fine letter writers, the best of the best...'

Jayamma tossed the plastic comb into a corner of the storage room. 'To hell with you, you little lower-caste vermin!'

The weeks passed. Now she had to do the girl's work too. By the time dinner was served and the dishes cleaned, she was spent. The advocate made no mention of hiring a new servant. She understood that, from now on, it was up to her to perform the lower-caste's work too.

In the evenings, she took to wandering in the back yard with her long silver hair down at the sides. One evening, Rosie, the thick-lipped Christian, waved at her.

'What happened to Shaila? Did she get married?'

Thrown into confusion, Jayamma grinned.

She started to watch Rosie. How carefree those Christians were – eating whatever they wanted, marrying and divorcing whenever they felt like it.

One night the two demons came back. She lay paralysed for many minutes, listening to the screeching of the spirits, which had disguised themselves as cats once again. She clutched the idol of baby Krishna, rubbing its silver buttocks while sitting on a bag of rice surrounded by the moat of DDT; she began to sing:

> 'A star is whispering
> Of my heart's deep longing
> To see you once more,
> My baby-child, my darling, my king...'

That next evening, the advocate spoke to her at dinner. He had received a letter from Shaila's mother.

'They said they were not happy with the size of the gold necklace. After I spent two thousand rupees on it, can you believe it?'

'Some people are never satisfied, Master...what can be done?'

He scratched at his bare chest with his left hand and belched. 'In this life, a man is always the servant of his servants.'

That night she could not go to sleep from anxiety. What if the advocate cheated her out of her pay too?

'For you!' One morning, Karthik tossed a letter onto the rice-winnower. Jayamma shook the grains of rice off it and tore it open with trembling fingers. Only one person in the world ever wrote her letters – her sister-in-law in Salt Market Village. Spreading it out on the ground, she put together the words one by one.

'The advocate has let it be known that he intends to move to Bangalore. You, of course, will be returned to us. Do not expect to stay here long; we are already looking for another house to dispatch you to.'

She folded the letter slowly and tucked it into the midriff of her sari. It felt like a slap to her face: the advocate had not bothered to tell her the news. 'Well, let it be, who am I to him, just another servant woman.'

A week later, he came into the storage room and stood at the threshold, as Jayamma got up hurriedly, trying to put her hair in order. 'Your money has been sent already, to your sister-in-law in Salt Market Village,' he said.

This was the usual agreement anywhere Jayamma worked; the wages never came to her directly.

The advocate paused.

'The boy needs someone to take care of him... I have relatives in Bangalore...'

'I only hope for the best for you and for Master Karthik,' she said, bowing before him with slow dignity.

That Sunday, she had collected all her belongings over the past year into the same suitcase with which she had come to the house. The only sad part was saying goodbye to the baby Krishna.

The advocate was not going to drop her off; she would walk to the bus stop herself. The bus was not due till four o'clock, and she walked about the back yard, amidst the swaying garments on the clothesline. She thought of Shaila – that girl had been running around this back yard, her hair loose, like an irresponsible brat; and now she was a married woman, the mistress of a household. Everyone changed and moved up in life, she thought. Only I remain the same: a virgin. She turned to the house with a sombre thought: this is the last time I will see this house, where I have spent more than a year of my life. She remembered all the houses she had been sent to, these past forty years, so that she could fatten other people's children. She had taken back nothing from her time at all those houses; she was still unmarried, childless, and penniless. Like a glass from which clean water had been drunk, her life showed no trace of the years that had passed – except that her body had grown old, her eyes were weak, and her knee joints ached. Nothing will ever change for me till I die, thought old Jayamma.

All at once, her gloom was gone. She had seen a blue rubber ball, half hidden by a hibiscus plant in the back yard. It looked like one of the balls Karthik played cricket with; had it been left out here because it was punctured? Jayamma had brought it right up to her nose for a good examination. Although she could not see a hole anywhere, when she squeezed it next to her cheek, she felt a tickling hiss of air on her skin.

With a servant's instinct for caution, the old cook glanced around the garden. Breathing in deep, she tossed the blue ball to the side of the house; it smacked against the wall and came back to her with a single bounce.

Good enough!

Jayamma turned the ball over and examined its skin, faded but still with a nice blue sheen. She sniffed at it. It would do very nicely.

She came to Karthik, who was in his room, on the bed: Bip! Bip! Bip! She thought how much he resembled the image of his mother in photographs when he beetled his brow to concentrate on the game; the furrow in his brow was like a bookmark left there by the dead woman.

'Brother...'

'Hm?'

'I'm leaving for my brother's home today... I'm going back to my village. I'm not coming back.'

'Hm.'

'May the blessings of your dear mother shine on you always.'

'Hm.'

'Brother...'

'What is it?' his voice crackled with irritation. 'Why are you always pestering me?'

'Brother...that blue ball out in the garden, the one that's punctured, you don't use it, do you?'

'Which ball?'

'...Can I take that with me for my little Brijju? He loves playing cricket, but sometimes there's no money to buy a ball...'

'No.'

The boy did not look up. He punched at the buttons on his game.

Bip!

Bip!

Bip!

'Brother…you gave the lower-caste girl a gold necklace…
can't you give me just a blue ball for Brijesh?'

Bip!

Bip!

Bip!

Jayamma thought with horror of all the food she had fed
this fat creature, how it was the sweat of her brow, dripping
into the lentil broth in the heat of that little kitchen, that had
nourished him until here he was, round and plump, like an
animal bred in the back yard of a Christian's house. She had a
vision of chasing this fat little boy with a meat-cleaver; she saw
herself catch him by the hair and raise the cleaver over his
pleading head. Bang! She brought it down– his tongue spread
out, his features bulged out, and he was…

The old lady shuddered.

'You are a motherless child, and a Brahmin. I don't want to
think badly of you…farewell, brother…'

She went out into the garden with her suitcase, shooting a
final glance at the ball. She went to the gate and stopped. Her
eyes were full of the tears of the righteous. The sun mocked
her from between the trees.

Just then, Rosie came out of the Christian's house. She stop-
ped and looked at the suitcase in Jayamma's hand. She spoke.
For a moment Jayamma couldn't understand a word, then the
Christian's message sounded loud and clear in her mind:

Take the ball, you Brahmin fool!

*

Swaying coconut palms rushed past. Jayamma was on the bus back to Salt Market Village, sitting next to a woman who was returning from the sacred city of Benares. Jayamma could pay no attention to the holy lady's stories about the great temples she had seen...her thoughts were all on the thing she was concealing in her sari, tucked against her tummy...the blue ball with the small hole...the one she had just stolen... She could not believe that she, Jayamma, the daughter of good Brahmins of Salt Market Village, had done such a thing!

Eventually the holy woman next to her fell asleep. The snoring filled Jayamma with fear for her soul. What would the gods do to her, she wondered, as the bus rattled over the dirt road; what would she be in the next life? A cockroach, a silver-fish that lived in old books, an earthworm, a maggot in a pile of cowshit, or something even filthier.

Then a strange thought came to her: maybe if she sinned enough in this life, she would be sent back as a Christian in the next one...

The thought made her feel light-headed with joy; and she dozed off almost at once.

Day Five (Evening): THE CATHEDRAL OF OUR LADY OF VALENCIA

It cannot be easily explained why the Cathedral of Our Lady of Valencia still remains incomplete, despite so many attempts to finish the work in recent years and so much money sent by expatriates working in Kuwait. The original baroque structure dating to 1691 was entirely rebuilt in 1890. Only one bell tower was left incomplete, and it remains incomplete to the present day. Scaffolding has covered the north tower almost continuously since 1981; work resumes fitfully and stops again, either because of a lack of funds, or the death of a significant priest. Even in its incomplete state, the cathedral is considered Kittur's most important tourist attraction. Of particular interest are the frescoes of the miraculously preserved corpse of St Francis Xavier painted on the ceiling of the chapel, and the colossal mural entitled *Allegory of Europe Bringing Science and Enlightenment into the East Indies* behind the altar.

George D'Souza, the mosquito-man, had caught himself a princess. Evidence for this claim would be produced at sunset, when work ended on the cathedral. Until then George was only going to suck on his watermelon, drop hints to his friends, and grin.

He was sitting on a pyramid-shaped mound of granite stones in the compound in front of the cathedral, with his metal backpack and his spray-gun to one side.

Cement mixers were growling on both sides of the cathedral building, crushing granite stones and mud, and disgorging mounds of black mortar. On a scaffolding, bricks and cement were being hoisted up to the top of the northern bell tower. George's friends Guru and Michael poured water from plastic one-litre bottles into the cement mixer. As the machines dripped into the red soil of the compound, rivulets of blood-red water cascaded down from the cathedral, as if it were a heart left on a piece of newspaper to drain.

When he was done with his melon, George smoked beedi after beedi. He closed his eyes and at once construction workers' children began to spray each other with pesticide. He chased them for a while, then returned to the pyramid of stones and sat on it.

He was a small, lithe, dark fellow who seemed to be in his early forties – but since physical labour accelerates ageing, he might have been younger, perhaps even in his late twenties. He had a long scar under his left eye, and a pockmarked face which suggested a recent bout of chickenpox. His biceps were long and slender: not the glossy rippling kind bulked up in expensive gyms, but the hewed-from-necessity sinews of the working poor, stone hard and deeply etched from a lifetime of having to lift things for other people.

At sunset, firewood was piled up in front of George's stone pyramid, a flame lit, and rice and fish curry cooked in a black pot. A transistor radio was turned on. Mosquitoes buzzed. Four men sat around the flickering fire, their faces burnished, smoking beedis. Around George were his old colleagues – Guru, James, and Vinay; they had worked with him on the construction site before his dismissal.

Taking his green notebook from his pocket, he opened it to the middle page, where he had kept something pink, like the tongue of an animal he had caught and skinned.

It was a twenty-rupee note. Vinay fingered the thing in wonder; even after it was gently prised away from him by Guru, he could not take his eyes off it.

'You got this for spraying pesticide in her house?'

'No, no, no. She saw me do the spraying and I guess she was impressed, because she asked me to do some gardening work.'

'If she's rich, doesn't she have a gardener?'

'She does – but the fellow is always drunk. So I did his work.'

George described it – removing the dead log from the path of the gutter in the back yard and carrying it a few yards away, removing the muck that had been sedimented in the gutter, allowing the mosquitoes to breed. Then trimming the hedges in the front yard with a giant clipper.

'That's all?' Vinay's jaw dropped. 'Twenty rupees for that?'

George blew smoke into the air with a luxuriant wickedness.

He put the twenty-rupee note back in the notebook, and the notebook in his pocket.

'That's why I say: she's my princess.'

'The rich own the whole world,' said Vinay, with a sigh that was half in rebellion and half in acceptance of this fact. 'What is twenty rupees to them?'

Guru, who was a Hindu, generally spoke little and was considered 'deep' by his friends. He had been as far as Bombay and could read signs in English.

'Let me tell you about the rich. Let me tell you about the rich.'

'All right: tell us.'

'I'm telling you about the rich. In Bombay, at the Oberoi Hotel in Nariman Point, there is a dish called 'Beef Vindaloo' that costs five hundred rupees.'

'No way!'

'Yes, five hundred! It was in the English newspaper on Sunday. Now you know about the rich.'

'What if you order the dish and then you realize you made a mistake and you don't like it? Do you get your money back?'

'No, but it doesn't matter to you if you're rich. You know what the biggest difference is, between being rich and being like us? The rich can make mistakes again and again. We make only one mistake and that's it for us.'

After dinner, George took everyone else out to drinks at the arrack shop. He had drunk and eaten off their generosity since being fired from the construction site: the mosquito-spraying, which Guru had arranged for him through a connection in the city Corporation, was only a once-a-week job.

'Next Sunday,' Vinay said, as they headed out of the arrack shop at midnight, dead drunk. 'I'm coming to see your fucking princess.'

'I'm not telling you where she lives,' George cried. 'She's my secret.' The others were annoyed, but didn't press the issue. They were happy enough to see George in a good mood, which was a rare thing, since he was a bitter man.

They went to sleep in tents at the back of the cathedral construction site. Since it was September, there was still the danger of rain, but George slept out in the open, looking at the stars and thinking of the generous woman who had made this day a happy one for him.

The following Sunday, George strapped on his metal backpack, connected the spray-gun to one of its nozzles, and walked out into Valencia. He stopped at every house along his route, and wherever he saw a gutter or puddle, and at sewage holes he found, he fired his gun: tzzzk...tzzzk...

He walked the half-kilometre from the cathedral and then turned left, into one of the alleys that slide downhill from Valencia. He took the route down, firing his gun into the gutters by the side of the road: tzzzk...tzzzk...tzzzk...

The rain had ended and muddy raucous torrents no longer gushed downhill, but the twinkling branches of roadside trees and the sloping tiled roofs of the houses still dripped into the road, where the loose stones braided the water into shining rivulets that flowed into the gutters with a soft music. Thick green moss coated the gutters like a sediment of bile, and reeds sprouted up from the bedrock, and small swampy patches of stale water gleamed out of nooks and crannies like liquid emeralds.

A dozen women in colourful saris, each with a green or mauve bandana around her head, were cutting the grass at the sides of the road. Swaying in concert as they sang strange Tamil songs, the migrant workers were down in the gutters, where they scraped the moss and pulled the weeds out from between the stones with violent tugs, as if they were taking them back from children, while others scooped out handfuls of black gunk from the bottom of the gutters and heaped it up in dripping mounds.

He looked at them with contempt and he thought: but I have fallen to the level of these people myself!

He grew moody; he began to spray carelessly; he even avoided spraying a few puddles deliberately.

By and by, he got to 10A, and realized that he was outside his princess's house. He unlatched the red gate and went in.

The windows were closed; but close to the house he could hear the sound of water hissing inside. She is taking a shower in the middle of the day, he thought. Rich women can do things like this.

He had immediately guessed, when he saw the woman the previous week, that her husband was away. You could tell, after a while, with these women whose husbands work in the Gulf: they have an air of not having been around a man for a long time. Her husband had left her well compensated for his absence: the only chauffeur-driven car in all of Valencia, a white Ambassador in the driveway, and the only air conditioner in the lane, which jutted out of her bedroom and over the jasmine plants in her garden, whirring and dripping water.

The driver of the white Ambassador was nowhere around.

He must be off drinking somewhere again, George thought. He had seen an old cook somewhere in the back the previous time. An old lady and a derelict driver – that was all this lady had in the house with her.

A gutter led from the garden into the back yard and he followed its path, spraying into it: tzzzk…tzzzk… The gutter was blocked again. He got down into the filth and muck of the blocked gutters, carefully applying his gun at different angles, pausing periodically to examine his work. He pressed the mouth of the spray-gun against the side of the gutter. The spraying sound stopped. A white froth, like the one that is produced when a snake is made to bite on a glass to release its venom, spread over the mosquito larvae. Then he tightened a knob on his spray-gun, clicked it into a groove on his backpack canister, and went to find her once again with the book she had to sign.

'Hey!' a woman peeped out a window. 'Who are you?'

'I'm the mosquito-man. I was here last week!'

The window closed. Sounds came from various parts of the house, things were unbolted, slammed, and shut, and then she was before him again – his princess. Mrs Gomes, the woman of house 10A, was a tall woman, approaching her forties now, who wore bright red lipstick and a Western-style gown that exposed her arms nine-tenths of the way up her shoulder. Of the three kinds of women in the world – 'traditional', 'modern', and 'working' – Mrs Gomes was an obvious member of the 'modern' tribe.

'You didn't do a good job last time,' she said and showed

him red welts on her hands, then stepped back and lifted up the edge of her long green gown to expose her ravished ankles. 'Your spraying didn't do any good.'

He felt hot with embarrassment, but he also did not dare take his eyes off what he was being shown.

'The problem is not my spraying, but your back yard,' he retorted. 'Another twig has blocked the gutters, and I think there's a dead animal of some kind, a mongoose maybe, blocking the flow of water. That's why the mosquitoes keep breeding. Come and see if you don't believe me,' he suggested.

She shook her head. 'The back yard is filthy. I never go there.'

'I'll clean it up again,' he said. 'That will get rid of the mosquitoes better than my spray-gun.'

She frowned. 'How much do you want to do this?'

Her tone annoyed him, so he said: 'Nothing.'

He went around to the back yard, got into the gutter, and began attacking the gunk. How these people think they can buy us like cattle! – How much do you want to do this? How much for that?

Half an hour later, he rang the bell with blackened hands; after a few seconds he heard her shout: 'Come over here.'

He followed the voice to a closed window.

'Open it!'

He put his blackened hands to a small crack between the two wooden shutters of the window and pulled them apart. Mrs Gomes was reading in her bed.

He stuck his pencil into the book and held it out.

'What should I do with the book?' she asked, bringing the smell of freshly washed hair with her to the window.

He held his dirty thumb on one line. House 10A: Mr Roger Gomes.

'Do you want some tea?' she asked, as she forged her husband's signature on his book.

He was dumbfounded; he had never been offered tea before on his job. Mostly out of fear of what this rich lady might do if he refused, he said yes.

An old servant, perhaps the cook, came to the back door and regarded him with suspicion as Mrs Gomes asked her to get some tea.

The old cook came back a few minutes later, a glass of tea in her hand; she looked at the mosquito-man with scorn and put the glass down on the threshold for him to pick up.

He came up the three steps, took the cup, and then went back down and took another three steps further back, before he began to sip.

'How long have you been doing this job?'

'Six months.'

He sipped the tea. Seized by a sudden inspiration, he said: 'I have a sister in my village whom I have to support. Maria. She is a good girl, Madam. She can cook well. Do you need a cook, Madam?'

The princess shook her head. 'I've got a very good cook. Sorry.'

George finished his tea and put the glass down at the foot of the steps, holding it an extra second, to make sure it didn't fall over as he left it.

'Will the problem in my back yard start again?'

'For sure. A mosquito is an evil thing, Madam. It causes

malaria and filaria,' he said, telling her of Sister Lucy in his village, who got malaria of the brain. 'She said she was going to flap-flap-flap her wasted arms like a hummingbird until she got to Holy Jerusalem'; using his arms, and gyrating around the parked car, he showed her how.

She let out a sudden wild laugh. He seemed a grave and serious man, so she had not expected this burst of levity from him; she had never heard a person of the lower classes be so funny before. She looked him over from head to toe, feeling that she was seeing him for the first time.

He noticed that she laughed heartily, and snorted, like a peasant woman. He had not expected this; women of good breeding were not meant to laugh so crudely and openly, and her behaviour confused him.

In a weary voice, she added: 'Matthew is supposed to clean the back yard. But he's not even here often enough to do the driving, forget about the back yard. Always out, drinking.'

Then her face lit up with an idea: 'You do it.' she said. 'You can be a part-time gardener for me. I'll pay you.'

George was about to say yes, but something within him resisted, disliking the casual way the job had been offered.

'That's not my kind of work. Taking shit out of back yards. But I will do it for you, Madam. I will do anything for you, because you are a good person. I can see into your soul.'

She laughed again.

'Start next week,' she said, vestiges of the laugh still rippling on her face, and closed the door.

When he was gone, she opened the door to her back yard. She rarely went out there: it was strong with the smell of fecund black soil, overgrown with weeds, the air tinged with sewage. She smelled the pesticide; it drew her out of the house. She heard a sound and recognized that the mosquito-man was still somewhere in her neighbourhood.

Tzzzk...tzzzk; in her mind she followed it as it sounded from round the neighbourhood – first at the Monteiros' house; then to Dr Karkada's compound; then at the Valencia Jesuit Teachers' College and Seminary: tzzzk...tzzzk...tzzzk – before she lost track of it.

George was on the pile of stones, waiting for other men who felt about their work as he did, and then they would move together to an arrack shop close by, to start drinking.

'What's got into you?' the other guys asked him later that evening. 'Hardly a word out of you.'

After an initial hour of raucousness, he had become sullen. He was thinking of the man and the woman – the ones he had seen on the cover of his princess's novel. They were in a car; the wind was blowing through the woman's hair and the man was smiling. In the background, there was an aeroplane. Words in English, the title of the novel, in silver letters, hovered over the scene, like a benediction from the God of good living.

He thought of the woman who could afford to spend her days reading such books, in the comfort of her home, with the air conditioner on at all times.

'The rich abuse us, man. It's always, here, take twenty rupees, kiss my feet. Get into the gutter. Clean my shit. It's always like that.'

'There he goes again,' Guru chuckled. 'It was this talk that got him fired in the first place, but he hasn't changed at all. Still so bitter.'

'Why should I change? Am I lying?' George shouted back: 'The rich lie in bed reading books, and live alone without families, and eat five-hundred-rupee dishes called…what was that thing called? Vindoo? Vindiloo?'

That night he could not sleep. He left the tent and went to the construction site, gazing at the unfinished cathedral for hours and thinking about that woman in 10A.

The next week it was clear to him she had been waiting for him. When he came to her house, she stuck her arm out, rotating it from side to side until he had seen the flesh from 360 degrees.

'No bites,' she said. 'Last week was much better. Your spray is finally working.'

He took charge of her back yard. First, walking with his spray-gun out and his left hand adjusting a knob on his backpack canister, he went down on his knees and drizzled germicide over her gutters. Then, as she watched, he put some order into her long-neglected yard: he dug, and sprayed, and cut, and cleaned for an hour.

That evening, the guys at the construction site could not believe the news.

'It's a full-time job now,' George said. 'The Princess thinks I'm such a good worker she wants me to stay there and sleep in a shed in the back yard. She's paying me double what I get now. And I don't have to be a mosquito-man any more. It's perfect.'

'We'll never see you again, I bet,' Guru said, flicking his beedi to the ground.

'That's not true,' George protested. 'I'll come down to drink every evening.'

Guru snorted. 'Sure, you will.'

And he was right: they did not see much of George after that.

Every Monday, a white woman dressed in North Indian salwar kameez arrived at the gate and asked him, in English: 'Madam is in?'

He opened the gate, and bowed, and said: 'Yes. She is in.'

She was from England; she had come to teach yoga and breathing to Madam. The air conditioner was turned off and George heard the sound of deep breathing from the bedroom. Half an hour later, the white woman emerged and said: 'It's amazing, isn't it? Me having to teach you yoga.'

'Yes, it's sad. We Indians have forgotten everything about our own civilization.'

Then the white woman and Madam walked around the garden for a while. On Tuesday mornings, Matthew, his eyes red and his breath reeking of arrack, drove Madam to the Lion Ladies' meeting at the club on Rose Lane. That seemed to be the extent of Mrs Gomes's social life. When they drove out, George held the gate open: as the car passed him, he saw Matthew turn and glare.

He's frightened of me, George thought, as he went back to trimming the plants in the garden. Does he think I will try to take over from him as driver one day?

It was not a thought he had entertained until then.

When the car came back, he looked at it with disapproval: its sides were filthy. He hosed it down and then wiped the outsides with a dirty rag, and the insides with a clean rag. The thought came to him as he worked that cleaning the car was not his job, as gardener, he was doing something extra – but of course Madam wouldn't notice. They never have any gratitude, the rich, do they?

'You've done a very good job with the car,' Mrs Gomes said in the evening. 'I am grateful.'

George was ashamed of himself. He thought: this rich woman really was different from other rich people.

'I'll do anything for you, Madam,' he said.

He kept a distance of about five or six feet between them whenever they talked; sometimes, in the course of conversation, the distance contracted, perfume made his nostrils expand, and he would automatically, with little backward steps, re-establish the proper radius between mistress and servant.

The cook brought him tea in the evenings and chatted to him for hours. He had not yet gone inside the house, but from the old woman he came to realize that its share of wonders went far beyond an air conditioner. That enormous white box he saw whenever the back door opened was a machine that did washing – and drying – automatically, the old cook said.

'Her husband wanted her to use it and she didn't. They never agreed on anything. Plus,' she said in a conspiratorial whisper, 'no children. That always causes problems.'

'What drove them apart?'

'That way she laughs,' the old woman said. 'He said she

laughed like a devil.'

He had noticed it, too: high-pitched, savage, like the laugh of a child or an animal, gloating and wanton. He always stopped work to listen when it ricocheted from her room; and he often heard it elsewhere even in the creak made by the opening of a door, or the particular cadence of an unusual bird-cry. He understood what her husband had meant.

'Are you educated, George?' Mrs Gomes asked one day, in a surprised tone. She had found him reading the newspaper.

'Yes and no, Madam. I studied till the tenth standard, Madam, but I failed the SSLC.'

'Failed?' she asked with a smile. 'How can anyone fail the SSLC? It is such a simple exam…'

'I could do all the sums, Madam. I passed Mathematics with sixty marks out of hundred. I only failed Social Studies, because I could not mark Madras and Bombay on the map of India that they gave me. What could I do, Madam? – we had not studied those things in class. I got thirty-four in Social Studies – one mark fail!'

'Why didn't you take the exam again?' she asked.

'Take it again?' He uttered the words as if he did not understand them. 'I began working,' he said, because he did not know how to answer her. 'I worked for six years, Madam. The rains were bad last year and there was no agriculture. We heard there were jobs for Christians at the construction site – the cathedral, I mean – and a bunch of us from the village came up here. I was working as a carpenter there, Madam. Where was the time to study?'

'Why did you leave the construction site?'

'I have a bad back,' he said.

'Should you be doing this kind of work, then?' she asked. 'Won't it hurt your back? And then you'll say that I broke your back, and make a fuss about it!'

'My back is fine, Madam. My back is fine. Don't you see me bent over and working every day?'

'So why did you say your back was bad?' she demanded. He said nothing, and she shook her head and said: 'Oh, you villagers are impossible to understand!'

The next day he was waiting for her. When she came out into the garden after her bath, wiping her wet hair dry with a towel, George approached her and said: 'He slapped me, Madam. I slapped him back.'

'What are you talking about, George? Who slapped you?'

He explained: he had got into a fight with his foreman. George pantomimed the exchange of palms, hoping to impress upon her how fast it had been, how reflexive.

'He said I was making eyes at his wife, Madam. But that was untrue. We are honest people in my family, Madam. We used to plough in the village, Madam,' he said. 'And we would find copper coins. These are from the time of Tippu Sultan. They are over a hundred years old. And those coins were taken from me and melted down for copper. I wanted so much to keep them, but I handed them over to Mr Coelho, the landlord. I am not dishonest. I do not steal, or look at another man's woman. This is the truth. Go to the village and ask Mr Coelho. He'll tell you.'

She smiled at this; like all villagers, his manner of defending his character was naïve, circuitous, and endearing.

'I trust you,' she said and went in, without locking the door. He peered into the house and saw clocks, red carpets, wooden medallions on the walls, potted plants, things of bronze and silver. Then the door closed again.

She brought tea out herself that day. She put the glass down on the threshold and he scampered up the steps with a bowed head, picked it up, and scampered back down.

'Ah, Madam, but you people have it all and we people have nothing. It's just not fair,' he said, sucking on the tea.

She let out a little laugh. She did not expect such directness from the poor; it was charming.

'It's just not fair, Madam,' he said again. 'You even have a washing machine that you never use. That's how much you have.'

'Are you asking me for more money?' She arched her eyebrows.

'No, Madam, why should I? You pay very well. I don't do things in a roundabout way,' he said. 'If I want it, I'll ask for money.'

'I have problems you don't know about, George. I have problems too.' She smiled and went in. He stood outside, hoping vainly for an explanation.

A little later it began to rain. The foreign yoga teacher came, with an umbrella, through the heavy rain; he ran up to the gate to let her in and then sat in the garage, by the car, eaves-dropping on the sound of deep breathing from Madam's bedroom. By the time the yoga session was over, the rain had ended and the garden was sparkling in the sun. The two women seemed excited by the sun – and the garden's carefully tended condition. Mrs Gomes talked to her foreign friend with an arm on her hip; George noticed that, unlike the European woman, his employer had retained her maidenly figure. He supposed it was because she did not have any children.

The lights came on in her bedroom at around six-thirty, and then the noise of water flowing. She was taking a bath; she took a bath every night. It was not necessary, since she bathed again in the morning, and anyway she smelled of wonderful perfume, yet she bathed twice – in hot water, he was sure, coating herself in lather and relaxing her body. She was a woman who did things just for her pleasure.

On Sunday, George walked uphill to attend mass at the cathedral; when he came back, the conditioner was still purring. 'So she does not go to church,' he thought.

Every other Wednesday afternoon, the Ideal Mobile Circulating Library came to the house on a Yamaha motorbike; the librarian-cum-driver of the bike, after pressing the bell, would untie a metal box of books strapped to the back of his motorbike, and place it on the back of the car for her to inspect. Mrs Gomes peered over the books and picked out a couple. When she had made her selection and paid, and gone back inside, George went up to the librarian-cum-driver, who was retying the box to the back of his Yamaha, and tapped him on the shoulder.

'What sort of books does Madam take?'

'Novels.'

The librarian-cum-driver stopped and winked at him. 'Dirty novels. I see dozens like her every day: women with their husbands abroad.'

He bent his finger and wiggled it.

'It still scratches, you know. So they have to read English novels to get rid of it.'

George grinned. But when the Yamaha, kicking up a cloud of dust, turned in a circle and left the garden, he ran to the gate and shouted: 'Don't talk of Madam like that, you bastard!'

At night he lay awake; he wandered about the back yard quietly, making no noise. He was thinking. It seemed to him, when he looked back on it, that his life consisted of things that had not said yes to him, and things that he could not say no to. The SSLC had not said yes to him, and his sister he could not say no to. He could not imagine, for instance, abandoning his sister to her own fate and trying to go back and complete his SSLC examination.

He went out, he walked up the lane and along the main road. The unfinished cathedral was a dark shape against the blue coastal night sky. Lighting a beedi, he walked in circles around the mess of the construction site, looking at familiar things in an unfamiliar way.

The next day, he was waiting for her with an announcement: 'I've stopped drinking, Madam,' he told her. 'I made the decision last night – never another bottle of arrack.'

He wanted her to know; he had the power now, to live any way he wanted. That evening, as he was out in the garden, trimming the leaves on the rose plant, Matthew unlatched the gate and came in. He glared at George, then he walked away into the back yard, to his quarters.

Half an hour later, when Mrs Gomes needed to be driven

to the Lion Ladies' meeting, Matthew was nowhere to be seen, even after she yelled into the back yard six times.

'Let me drive, Madam,' he said.

She looked at him sceptically: 'Do you know how to drive?'

'Madam, when you grow up poor, you have to learn to do everything, from farming to driving. Why don't you get in and see for yourself how well I drive?'

'Do you have a licence? Will you kill me?'

'Madam,' he said, 'I would never do anything to put you in the slightest danger.' A moment later he added: 'I would even give my life for you.'

She smiled at that; then she saw that he was saying it in earnest and she stopped smiling. She got into the car and he started the engine, and he became her driver.

'You drive well, George. Why don't you work full-time as my new driver?' she asked him at the end.

'I'll do anything for you, Madam.'

Matthew was dismissed that evening. The cook came to George and said: 'I never liked him. I'm glad you're staying, though.'

George bowed to her. 'You're like my elder sister,' he said and watched her beam happily.

In the mornings he cleaned and washed the car, and sat on Matthew's stool, his legs crossed, humming merrily, and waiting for the moment Madam would command him to take her out. When he drove her to the Lion Ladies' meetings, he wandered about the flagpole in front of the Club, watching the buses go by, around the municipal library. He looked at the buses and the library differently: not as wanderer, a manual

worker who got down into gutters and scooped out earth –
but like someone with a stake in things. He drove her down to
the sea once. She walked towards the water and sat by the
rocks, watching the silver waves, while he waited by the car,
watching her.

As she got out of the car, he coughed.

'What is it, George?'

'My sister Maria.'

She looked at him with a smile, encouraging him.

'She can cook, Madam. She is clean, and hard-working, and
a good Christian girl.'

'I have a cook, George.'

'She's not good, Madam. And she's old. Why don't you get
rid of her and have my sister over from the village?'

Her face darkened.

'You think I don't know what you're doing? Trying to take
over my household! First you get rid of my driver and now my
cook!'

She got in and slammed the door. He smiled; he was not
worried. He had planted the seed in her mind; it would germ-
inate, in a little time. He knew now how this woman's mind
worked.

That summer, during the water shortage, George showed Mrs
Gomes that he was indispensable. He was up at the top of the
hill, waiting for the water-tanker to come along; he brought the
buckets down himself, filling up her flush and commodes so
she did not have to go through the humiliation of rationing her
flushes, like everyone else in the neighbourhood. As soon as he

heard a rumour that the Corporation was going to release water through the taps for a limited time (they sometimes gave half an hour of water every two or three days), he would come rushing into the house, shouting: 'Madam! Madam!'

She gave him a set of the keys to the back door, so that he could come into the house anytime he heard that the water was going to be on and fill up the buckets.

Thanks to his hard work, at a time when most people couldn't bathe even once every other day, Madam was still taking her twice-a-day pleasure baths.

'How absurd,' she said, one evening, coming to the back door with her hair wet and falling down her shoulders, rubbing it vigorously with a white towel. 'That in this country, with so much rain, we still have water shortages. When will India ever change?'

He smiled, averting his eyes from her figure and her wet hair.

'George, your pay will be increased,' she said and went back inside, closing the door firmly.

There was more good news for him too, a few evenings later. He saw the old cook leaving, a bag under her arm. She looked at him with baleful eyes as their paths crossed and hissed: 'I know what you're trying to do to her! I told her you'll destroy her name and reputation! But she's fallen under your spell.'

A week after Maria joined the household of 10A, Mrs Gomes came to George as he was tinkering with the engine of the car.

'Your sister's shrimp curry is excellent.'

'Everyone in our family is hard-working, Madam,' he said and got so excited he jerked up his head, whacking it against the bonnet. It stung, but Mrs Gomes had begun to laugh – that sharp, high-pitched animal laugh of hers – and he tried to laugh along with her, while rubbing the red bump on his skull.

Maria was a small, frightened girl who came with two bags, no English, and no knowledge of life beyond her village. Mrs Gomes had taken a liking to her and allowed her to sleep in the kitchen.

'What do they talk about, inside the house, Madam and that foreign woman?' George asked her, when Maria came to his one-room quarters with his evening meal.

'I don't know,' she said, ladling out his fish curry.

'Why don't you know?'

'I wasn't paying attention,' she said, her voice small, scared, as always, of her brother.

'Well, pay attention! Don't just sit there like a doll, saying "Yes, Madam" and "No, Madam"! Take some initiative! Keep your eyes open!'

On Sundays, he took Maria along to mass at the cathedral; construction stopped in the morning, to let people in, but as they emerged, they could see the contractors getting ready to resume work in the evening.

'Why doesn't Madam come to mass? Isn't she a Christian too?' Maria asked, as they were leaving church.

He took a deep breath. 'The rich do as they want. It's not for us to question them.'

He noticed Mrs Gomes talking to Maria; with her open, generous nature, which did not distinguish between rich and poor, she was becoming more than just a mistress to Maria, but a good friend. It was exactly as he had hoped.

In the evenings he missed his drink, but he filled the time by walking about, or by listening to a radio and letting his mind drift. He thought: Maria can get married next year. She had a status now as a cook in a rich woman's house. Boys would line up for her back home in the village.

After that, he figured, it would be time for his own marriage, which he had put off so long, out of a combination of bitterness, poverty, and shame. Yes, time for marriage, and children. Yet regret still gnawed at him, created by his contact with this rich woman, that he could have done so much more with his life.

'You're a lucky man, George,' Mrs Gomes said one evening, watching him rub the car with a wet cloth. 'You have a wonderful sister.'

'Thank you, Madam.'

'Why don't you take Maria around the city? She hasn't seen anything in Kittur, has she?'

He decided that this was a clear opportunity to show some initiative. 'Why don't we all three go together, Madam?'

The three of them drove down to the beach. Mrs Gomes and Maria went for a walk along the sand. He watched from a distance. When they returned, he was waiting with a paper cone filled with roasted groundnuts for Maria.

'Don't I get some too?' Mrs Gomes demanded, and he hurried to pour some nuts out, and she took them from his hands, and that was how he touched her for the first time.

*

It was raining again in Valencia, and he knew he had been at the house almost a year. One day, the new mosquito-man came for the back yard. Mrs Gomes watched as George directed the fellow around the gutters and canals in the back, to make sure not a spot was missed.

That evening, she called him to the house and said: 'George, you should to do it yourself. Please spray the gutter yourself, like last year.'

Her voice became sweet, and though it was the same voice she used to make him move mountains for her, this time he stiffened. He was offended that she would still ask him to perform such a task.

'Why not?' She raised her voice, angrily. She shrieked. 'You work for me! You do what I say!'

The two of them stared at each other, and then, grumbling and cursing her, he left the house. He wandered aimlessly for some time, then decided to visit the cathedral again, to see how the old fellows were doing.

Nothing much had changed in the field by the cathedral. The construction had been held up, he was told, because of the rector's death. It would start again soon.

His other friends were missing – they had left the work and returned to the village – but Guru was there.

'Now that you're here, why don't we—' Guru made the gesture of a bottle being emptied down a throat.

They went to an arrack shop and there was some fine drinking, just like in old times.

'So how are things with you and your princess?' Guru asked.

'Oh, these rich people are all the same,' George said, bitterly. 'We're just trash to them. A rich woman can never see a poor man as a man. Just as a servant.'

He remembered his carefree days, before he was tied down to a house, and to Madam – and he became resentful at having lost his freedom. He left early, shortly before midnight, saying that he had something to take care of, at the house. On the way back, he staggered drunkenly, singing a Konkani song; but another pulse had started to throb beneath the light-hearted film number.

As he drew near the gate, his voice dropped down and died out, and he realized he was walking with exaggerated stealth. He wondered why and felt frightened of himself.

He opened the latch of the gate soundlessly and walked towards the back door of the house. He had been holding the key in his hand for some time; bending down to the lock, and squinting at the keyhole, he inserted it. Opening it carefully and quietly, he walked into the house. The heavy washing machine lay in the dark, like a nightwatchman. In the distance wisps of cool air escaped from a crack in the closed door of her bedroom.

George breathed slowly. His one thought, as he staggered forward, was that he must avoid walking into the washing machine.

'O God,' he said, suddenly. He realized that he had banged his knee into the washing machine and the damn machine was reverberating.

'O God,' he said again, with the dim, desperate consciousness that he had spoken too loudly.

There was a movement; her door opened and a woman with long loose hair emerged.

A cool air-conditioned breeze thrilled his entire body. The woman pulled the edge of a sari over her shoulder.

'George?'

'Yes.'

'What do you want?'

He said nothing. The answer to the question was at once vague and full of substance, half-obscure but all too present, just as she herself was. He almost knew what he wanted to say; she said nothing. She had not screamed or raised the alarm. Perhaps she wanted it too. He felt that it was now only a matter of saying it, or even of moving. Just do *something*. It will happen.

'Get out,' she said.

He had waited too long.

'Madam, I—'

'Get out.'

It was too late now; he turned around and walked quickly.

The moment the back door closed on him, he felt foolish. He thumped it with his fist so hard that it hurt. 'Madam, let me explain!' He pounded the door harder and harder. She had misunderstood him – completely misunderstood!

'Stop it,' came a voice. It was Maria, looking at him fearfully through the window. 'Please stop it at once.'

At that moment, the immensity of what he had done struck George. He was conscious the neighbours might be watching. Madam's reputation was at stake.

He dragged himself up to the construction site and fell

down there to sleep. The next morning, he discovered he had been lying, just as he had done months before, on top of a pyramid of crushed granite.

He came back, slowly. Maria was waiting for him by the gate.

'Madam,' she called, as she went into the house. Mrs Gomes came out, her finger deep into her latest novel.

'Maria, go to the kitchen,' Mrs Gomes ordered, as he walked into the garden. He was glad of that; so she wanted to protect Maria from what was coming. He felt gratitude for her delicacy. She was different from other rich people; she was special. She would spare him.

He put the key to the back door on the ground.

'It's okay,' she said. Her manner was cool. He understood now that the radius had increased; it was pushing him back every second he stood. He did not know how far back to go; it seemed to him he was already as far back as he could be and hear what she was saying. Her voice was distant and small and cold. For some reason, he could not take his eyes off the cover of her novel; a man was driving a red car, and two white women in bikinis were sitting inside.

'It's not anger,' she said. 'I should have taken greater precautions. I made a mistake.'

'I've left the key down here, Madam,' he said.

'It doesn't matter,' she said. 'The lock is being changed this evening.'

'Can I stay, until you find someone else?' he blurted out. 'How will you manage with the garden? And what will you do for a driver?'

'I'll manage,' she said.

Until then, all his thoughts had been for her – her reputation in the neighbourhood, her peace of mind, the sense of betrayal she must feel – but now he understood: she was not the one who needed taking care of.

He wanted to speak his heart out to her and tell her all this, but she spoke first.

'Maria will have to leave as well.'

He stared at her, his mouth open.

'Where will she sleep tonight?' His voice was thin, and desperate. 'Madam, she left everything she had in our village and came here to live with you.'

'She can sleep in the church, I suppose,' Mrs Gomes said calmly. 'They let people in all night, I've heard.'

'Madam,' he folded his palms. 'Madam, you're Christian like us, and I'm begging you in the name of Christian charity, please leave Maria out of–!'

She closed the door; then he heard the sound of it being locked, and then double-locked.

He waited for his sister at the top of the road, and looked in the direction of the unfinished cathedral.

Day Six (Morning): THE SULTAN'S BATTERY

The Sultan's Battery, a large black rectangular fort, appears high up to your left as you go from Kittur to Salt Market Village. The best way explore the fort is to ask someone in Kittur to drive you up here; your host will have to park the car by the main road, and then the two of you have to walk uphill for half an hour. When you pass through the arched doorway, you find that the fort is in an advanced state of decay. Although a plaque of the Archeological Survey of India declares this a protected site, and speaks of its role in 'enshrining the memory of the patriot Tippu Sultan, Tiger of Mysore', there is no evidence of any attempt to preserve the ancient structure from the onslaught of creepers, wind, rain, erosion, and grazing animals. Giant banyan trees have germinated on the walls of the fort; their roots smash between the stones like gnarled fingers reaching into a mouse-hole. Avoiding the thorns and piles of goat droppings, you should walk to one of loopholes in the walls of the fort; here, hold an imaginary gun in your hands, close an eye, and pretend that you are Tippu himself, firing down on the English army.

He walked quickly towards the white dome of the Dargah, a fold-up wooden stool under one arm, and in the other a red bag with his album of photographs and seven bottles full of white pills. When he reached the Dargah, he walked along the wall, not paying any attention to the long line of beggars: the lepers sitting on rags, the men with mutilated arms and legs, the men in wheelchairs and the men with bandages covering their eyes, and the creature, with little brown stubs like a seal's flippers where he should have had arms, a normal left leg, and a soft brown stump where he should have had the other leg, who lay on his left side, twitching his hip continuously, like an animal receiving galvanic shocks, and intoning, with blank, mesmerized eyes: 'Al-lah! Al-laaaah! Al-lah! Al-laaah!'

He walked past this sorrowful parade of humanity and went behind the Dargah.

Now he walked past the vendors squatting on the ground in a long line that extended for half a mile. He passed rows of baby shoes, bras, T-shirts bearing the logo 'New York Fucking City', fake Ray-Ban glasses, fake Nike shoes and fake Adidas shoes, and piles of Urdu and Malayalam magazines. He spotted an opening between a counterfeit-Nike seller and a counterfeit-Gucci seller, unfolded his stool there, and placed on it a glossy black sheet of paper with gold lettering.

The golden words read:

RATNAKARA SHETTY
SPECIAL INVITEE
FOURTH PAN-ASIAN CONFERENCE ON SEXOLOGY

The young men who had come to pray at the Dargah, or to eat lamb kebabs in one of the Muslim restaurants, or simply to watch the sea, began making a semi-circle around Ratna, watching, as he added to the display on the stool, the photo album and the seven bottles of white pills. With grave ceremony, he then rearranged the bottles, as if their position had to be exactly right for his work to begin. In truth, he was waiting for more onlookers.

They came. Standing in pairs or alone, the crowd of young men had now taken on the appearance of a human Stonehenge; some stood with their hands folded on a friend's shoulder; some stood alone; and a few crouched to the ground, like fallen boulders.

All at once, Ratna began to talk. Young men came quicker, and the crowd became so thick that it was two or three men deep at each point; and those at the back had to stand on their toes to get even a partial glimpse of the sexologist.

He opened the album and let the young men see the photos in plastic folders inside. The onlookers gasped.

Pointing at his photographs, Ratna spoke of abominations and perversions. He described the consequences of sin: he demonstrated the passage of venereal germs up the body, touching his nipples, his eyes, and then his nostrils, and then closing his eyes. The sun climbed the sky and the white dome of the Dargah shone more brightly. The young men in the semi-circle pressed against each other, straining to get closer to the photographs. Then Ratna went in for the kill: he shut the book and held up a bottle of white pills in both of his hands. He began shaking the pills.

'With each bottle of pills you will receive a certificate of authenticity from Hakim Bhagwandas of Daryaganj in Delhi. This man, a greatly experienced doctor, has studied the wise books of the pharaohs, and has used his scientific equipment to create these magnificent white pills that will cure all your ailments. Each bottle costs just four rupees and fifty paise! Yes, that is all you need to pay to atone for sin and earn a second chance in this life! Four rupees and fifty paise!'

In the evening, dead-tired from the heat, he boarded the 34B bus with his red bag and fold-up stool. It was packed at this hour, so he held on to a strap and breathed in and out slowly. He counted to ten, to recover his strength, then dipped a hand into the red bag, taking out four green brochures, each of which bore the image of three large rats on the cover. He held the brochures up high in one hand, in the manner of a gambler holding up his cards, and spoke at the top of his voice:

'Ladies and gentlemen! All of you know that we live in a rat race, where there are few jobs, and many job applicants. How will your children survive, how will they get the jobs you have? For life in this day and age is a veritable rat race. Only in this booklet will you find thousands of useful general knowledge data, arranged in question and answer form, that your sons and daughters need to pass the civil service entrance examination, the bank entrance examination, the police entrance examination, and many other exams which are needed to win the rat race. For instance' – he took a quick breath – 'the

Mughal Empire had two capitals; Delhi was one of them. Which was the other? Four capital cities of Europe are built on the banks of one river. Name that river. Who was the first king of Germany? What is the currency of Angola? One city in Europe has been the capital of three different empires. Which city? Two men were involved in the assassination of Mahatma Gandhi. Nathuram Godse was one of them. Name the other man. What is the height of the Eiffel Tower in metres?'

Holding the pamphlets with his right hand, he staggered forward, bracing himself as the bus bumped over the potholes of the road. One passenger asked for a pamphlet and handed him a rupee. Ratna walked back and waited near the exit door; when the bus slowed down, he dipped his head in silent thanks to the conductor and got off.

Seeing a man waiting at the bus stop, he tried to sell him a collection of six coloured pens, first at a rupee a pen; then at two pens a rupee; finally offering three for a rupee. Although the man said he would not buy, Ratna could see the interest in his eyes; he took out a large spring that could give much amusement to children, and a geometrical set that could make wonderful designs on papers. The man bought one of the geometrical sets for three rupees.

Ratna headed away from from the Sultan's Battery, taking the road towards Salt Market Village.

Once he got to the village, he went to the main market, took out a handful of change and sorted it out on the flat of his palm as he walked; he left the coins on the counter of a shop, taking in exchange a packet of Engineer beedis, which he put into his suitcase.

'What are you waiting for?' The boy in charge of the shop was new to the job. 'You have your beedis.'

'I usually get two packets of lentils too, included in the price. That's the way it's done.'

Before entering his house, Ratna ripped open one of the packets with his teeth and poured its contents onto the ground near his door. Seven or eight of the neighbourhood dogs came running and he watched them crunch the lentils loudly. When they began digging at the earth, he tore open the second packet with his teeth and scattered its contents on the ground too.

He walked into his house without waiting to see the dogs devour this second lot of lentils. He knew they would still be hungry, but he could not afford to buy them a third packet every day.

He hung his shirt on a hook by the door, as he scratched his armpits and hairy chest. He sat down on a chair, exhaled, muttered: 'O Krishna, O Krishna', and stretched out his legs; even though they were in the kitchen, his daughters knew at once that he was there – a powerful odour of stale feet went through the house like a warning cannon shot. They dropped their women's magazines and busied themselves with their work.

His wife emerged from the kitchen with a tumbler of water. He had begun smoking the beedis.

'Are they working in there – the maharanis?' he asked her.

'Yes,' the three girls, his daughters, shouted back from the kitchen. He did not trust them, so he went in to check.

The youngest, Aditi, crouched by the gas stove, wiping the leaves of the photo album with a corner of her sari. Rukmini, the oldest sister, sat beside a mound of white pills, which she was counting off and pouring into bottles; Ramnika, who would be married off after Rukmini, pasted a label on each bottle. The wife was in the kitchen, making noise with plates and pots. After he had smoked his second beedi, and his body had visibly relaxed, she built up the courage to approach him: 'The astrologer said he would come at nine.'

'Uhm.'

He burped, and then lifted a leg and waited for the fart. The radio was on; he placed the set on his thigh and slapped his palm against his other leg to the beat of the music, humming all the while and singing the words whenever he knew them.

'He's here,' she whispered. He turned off the radio, as the astrologer came into the room and folded his palms in a namaste.

Sitting down in a chair, he took off his shirt, which Ratna's wife hung for him on the hook next to Ratna's. While the women waited in the kitchen, the astrologer showed Ratna the choice of boys.

He opened an album of black and white photos; they gazed at the faces of one boy after another, who looked back at them out of tense, unsmiling portraits. Ratna scraped one with his thumb. The astrologer slid the photo out of the album.

'Boy looks okay,' Ratna said, after a moment's concentration. 'The father does what for a living?'

'Owns a firecracker shop on Umbrella Street. A very good business. Boy inherits it.'

'His own business,' Ratna exclaimed, with genuine satisfaction. 'It's the only way ahead in the rat race: being a sales-man is a dead end.'

His wife dropped something in the kitchen; she coughed and dropped something else.

'What's going on?' he asked.

A timid voice said something about 'horoscopes'.

'Shut up!' Ratna shouted. He gestured at the kitchen with the photo – 'I have three daughters to marry off and this damn bitch thinks I can be choosy?' – and he tossed the photo into the astrologer's lap.

The astrologer drew an 'X' across the back of the photo.

'The boy's parents will expect something,' he said. 'A token.'

'Dowry.' Ratna gave the evil its proper name in a soft voice. 'Fine. I've saved money for this girl.' He breathed out. 'Where I'll get dowry for the next two, though, God alone knows.'

Gritting his teeth in anger, he turned towards the kitchen and yelled.

The following Monday, the boy's party came. The younger girls went around with a tray of lemon juice, while Ratna and his wife sat in the drawing room. Rukmini's face was whitened by a thick layer of Johnson's Baby Powder, and garlands of jasmine decorated her hair; she plucked the strings of a veena and sang a religious verse, while looking out of the window at something far away.

The prospective groom's father, the firecracker merchant, was sitting on a mattress directly opposite Rukmini; he was a huge man in a white shirt and a white cotton sarong, with thick tufts of glossy, silvery hair sticking out of his ears. He moved his head to the rhythm of the song, which Ratna took as an encouraging sign. The prospective mother-in-law, another enormous and fair-skinned creature, looked around the ceiling and the corners of the room. The groom-to-be had his father's fair skin and features, but he was much smaller than either of his parents, and seemed more like the family's domestic pet than the scion. Halfway through the song, he leaned over and whispered something into his father's hairy ears.

The merchant nodded. The boy got up and left. The father held up his little finger and showed it to everyone in the room.

Everyone giggled.

The boy came back and squirmed into place between his fat father and his fat mother. The two younger girls came with a second tray of lemon juice, and the fat firecracker merchant and his wife took glasses; as if only to follow them, the boy also took a glass and sipped. Almost as soon as the juice touched his lips, he tapped his father and whispered into his hairy ear again. This time the old man grimaced; but the boy ran out.

As if to distract attention from his son, the firecracker merchant asked Ratna, in a rasping voice: 'Do you have a spare beedi, my good man?'

Searching in the kitchen for his packet of beedis, Ratna saw, through the grille in the window, the bridegroom-to-be, urinating copiously against the trunk of an Ashoka tree in the back yard.

Nervous fellow, he thought, grinning. But that's only natural, he thought, feeling already a touch of affection for this fellow, who was soon going to join his family. All men are nervous before their weddings. The boy appeared to be done; he shook his penis and stepped away from the tree. But then, he stood as if frozen. After a moment he craned his head back and seemed to gasp for air, like a drowning man.

The matchmaker returned that evening to report that the firecracker merchant seemed satisfied with Rukmini's singing.

'Fix the date soon,' he told Ratna. 'In a month, the rental rates for wedding halls will start to…' – he gestured upwards with his palms.

Ratna nodded, but he seemed distracted.

The next morning, he took the bus to Umbrella Street, walking past furniture and fan shops until he found the firecracker merchant's place. The fat man with the hairy ears sat on a high stool, in front of a wall of paper bombs and rockets, like an emissary of the God of Fire and War. The groom-to-be was also in the shop, sitting on the floor, licking his fingers as he turned the pages of a ledger.

The fat man kicked his son gently.

'This man is going to be your father-in-law, aren't you going to say hello?' He smiled at Ratna: 'The boy is a shy one.'

Ratna sipped tea, chatted with the fat man, and kept an eye on the boy all the time.

'Come with me, son,' he said, 'I have something to show you.'

The two men walked down the road, neither of them saying a word, till they got to the banyan tree that grew beside the Hanuman temple on Umbrella Street; Ratna indicated that they should sit down in the shade of the tree. He wanted the boy to turn his back to the traffic, so that they faced the temple.

For a while Ratna let the young man talk, only observing his eyes, ears, nose, mouth, and neck.

Suddenly, he seized the fellow's wrist.

'Where did you find this prostitute that you sat with?'

The boy wanted to get up, but Ratna increased the pressure on his wrist to make it clear that there would be no escape. The boy turned his face to the road, as if pleading for help.

Ratna increased the pressure on the boy's wrist.

'Where did you sit with her? At the side of a road, in a hotel, or behind a building?'

He twisted harder.

'By the side of a road,' the boy blurted out; then he looked at Ratna with his face close to tears. 'How do you know?'

Ratna closed his eyes; breathed out and let go of the boy's wrist. 'A truckers' whore.' He slapped the boy.

The boy began to cry. 'I only sat with her once,' he said, fighting back his sobs.

'Once is enough. Do you burn when you pass urine?'

'Yes, I burn.'

'*Nausea?*'

The boy asked what the English word meant, and said yes once he understood.

'What else?'

'It feels like there is something large and hard – like a rubber ball – between my legs all the time. And then I feel dizzy sometimes.'

'Can you get hard?'

'Yes. No.'

'Tell me what your penis looks like. Is it black? Is it red? Are the lips of your penis swollen?'

Half an hour later, the two men were still sitting at the foot of the banyan tree, facing the temple.

'I beg you...' The boy folded his palms. 'I beg you.'

Ratna shook his head.

'I have to cancel the wedding, what else can I do? How can I let my daughter get this disease too?'

The boy stared at the ground, as if he had simply run out of ways to beg. The drop of moisture at the tip of his nose gleamed like silver.

'I'll ruin you,' he said quietly.

Ratna wiped his hands on his sarong. 'How?'

'I'll say that the girl has slept with someone. I'll say that she's not a virgin. That's why you had to cancel the wedding.'

In one swift motion, Ratna seized the boy's hair, yanked back his head, held it for a moment, and then slammed it against the banyan tree. He stood up and spat at the boy.

'I swear by the god who sits in this temple before us, I will kill you with my own hands if you say that.'

He was in fiery form that day at the Dargah; thundering, as the young men gathered round him, about sin, and disease, and about how germs rise from the genitalia, through the nipples, into the mouth, and eyes, and ears, until they reach the nostrils. Then he showed them his photos: images of rotten and reddened genitalia, some of which were black, or distended, or even appeared charred, as if acid-burned. Above each photo was one of the face of the victim, his eyes covered by a black rectangle, as if he were a victim of torture or rape. Such were the consequences of sin, Ratna explained: and expiation and redemption could come only in the form of magic white pills.

Three months or so went by. One morning, he was at his

spot behind the white dome, bellowing at the Stonehenge of worried young men, when he saw a face that made his heart stop.

Afterwards, when he was done with his lecture, he saw the face again, right in front of him.

'What do you want?' he hissed. 'It's too late. My daughter's married now. Why have you come here now?'

Ratna folded the stool under his arm, dropped his medicines into his red bag, and walked fast. A flurry of footsteps followed him. The boy – the firecracker merchant's son – panted as he spoke.

'Things are becoming worse by the day. I can't piss without my penis burning. You must do something for me. You must give me your pills.'

Ratna gnashed his teeth. 'You sinned, you bastard. You sat with a prostitute. Now pay for it!'

He walked faster, and faster, and then the footsteps behind him were gone and he was alone.

But the following evening, he saw the face again and the quick steps followed him all the way to the bus stop, and the voice said, again and again: 'Let me buy the pills from you', but Ratna did not turn around.

He boarded the bus and counted to ten; producing his brochures, he spoke to the passengers of the rat race. As the dark outline of the fort appeared in the distance; the bus slowed down and then stopped. He got down. Someone else got down with him. He walked away. Someone walked behind him.

Ratna spun around and seized his stalker by the collar. 'Didn't I tell you? Leave me alone. What has got into you?'

The boy pushed Ratna's hands away, and straightened his collar, and whispered: 'I think I'm dying. You have to give me your white pills.'

'Look here, none of those young men is going to be cured by anything I sell. Don't you get it?'

There was a moment of silence and then the boy said: 'But you were at the Sexology Conference...the sign in English says so...'

Ratna raised his hands to the sky.

'I found that sign lying on the platform of the station.'

'But the Hakim Bhagwandas of Delhi...'

'Hakim Bhagwandas, my arse! They're white sugar pills that I buy wholesale from a chemist on Umbrella Street – right next to where your father has his shop; my daughters bottle them and stick labels on them at my house!'

To prove his point, he opened his leather case, unscrewed the top from a bottle, and scattered the pills across the ground, as if broadcasting seed on the earth. 'They can do nothing! I have nothing for you, son!'

The boy sat on the ground, took a white pill from the earth, and swallowed it. He got down on all fours and scooped up the white pills, which he began swallowing in a frenzy, along with any dirt attached to them.

'Are you mad?'

Getting down on his knees, Ratna gave the boy a good shake and asked the same question again and again.

And then, at last, he saw the boy's eyes. They had changed since he last observed them; teary and red, they were like pickled vegetables of some kind.

He relaxed his grip on the boy's shoulder.

'You'll have to pay me, all right, for my help? I don't do charity.'

Half an hour later, the two men got off a bus near the railway station. They walked together through streets that become progressively narrower and darker, until they reached a shop whose awning was marked with a large red medical cross. From inside the shop, a radio blared out a popular Kannada film song.

'Buy something here and leave me alone.'

Ratna tried to walk away, but the boy clutched his wrist.

'Wait. Pick the medicine for me and then go.'

Ratna walked quickly in the direction of the bus stop, but again he heard the footsteps behind him. He turned, and there was the boy, arms laden with green bottles.

Regretting that he had ever agreed to bring him here, Ratna walked faster. Still he heard the light, desperate footsteps again, as though a ghost were following him.

For several hours that night Ratna lay awake, turning in his bed and disturbing his wife.

The next day, in the evening, he took the bus into the city, back into Umbrella Street. When he reached the firecracker shop he stood at a distance, with his arms folded, waiting until the boy saw him. The two of them walked together in silence for a while and then sat down on a bench outside a sugarcane juice stall. As the machines turned, crushing the cane, Ratna said: 'Go to the hospital. They'll help you.'

'I can't go there. They know me. They'll tell my father.'

Ratna had a vision of that immense man with the tufts of

white hair growing out of his ears, sitting in front of his arsenal of firecrackers and paper bombs.

The following day, as Ratna was folding his wooden stand and packing his case, he was conscious of a shadow on the ground in front of him. He walked round the Dargah; past the long line of pilgrims waiting to pray at the tomb of Yusuf Ali, past the rows of lepers, and past the man with one leg lying on the ground, twitching from the hip and chanting: 'Al-lah, Al-laaah! Al-lah!'

He looked up at the white dome for a moment.

He went down to the sea, and the shadow followed him. A low stone wall ran along the sea's edge and he put his right foot up on it. The waves were coming in violently; now and then water crashed against the wall, and thick white foam rose up into the air and spread out, like a peacock's tail emerging from the sea. Ratna turned around.

'What choice do I have? If I don't sell those boys the pills, how will I marry off my daughters?'

The boy, avoiding his gaze, stared at the ground and shifted his weight uncomfortably.

The two of them caught the number 5 bus and took it all the way into the heart of the city, descending near Angel Talkies. The boy carried the wooden stool, and Ratna searched up and down the main road, until he located a large billboard of a husband and a wife standing together in wedding clothes:

HAPPY LIFE CLINIC
CONSULTING SPECIALIST: DOCTOR M. V. KAMATH
MBBS (MYSORE), B.MEC. (ALLAHABAD), DBBS

(Mysore), M.Ch. (Calcutta), G.Com. (Varanasi).
SATISFACTION GUARANTEED

'You see those letters after his name?' Ratna whispered into
the boy's ear. 'He's a *real* doctor. He'll save you.'

In the waiting room, a half-dozen lean, nervous men sat on
black chairs, and in a corner one married couple. Ratna and the
boy sat down between the single men and the couple. Ratna
looked curiously at the men. These were the same ones who
came to him – older, sadder versions; men who had been
trying to shake off venereal disease for years, who had thrown
bottle after bottle of white pills at it, to find no improvement –
who were now at the end of a long journey of despair, a
journey that led from his booth at the Dargah, through a long
trail of other hucksters, to this doctor's clinic, where they
would be told at last the truth.

One by one, the lean wasted men went into the doctor's
room, and the door shut behind them. Ratna looked at the
married couple and thought: at least they are not alone in this
ordeal. At least they have each other.

Then the man got up to see the doctor; the woman stayed
back. She went in later, after the man had left. Of course they
are not husband and wife, Ratna told himself. When he gets
this disease, this disease of sex, every man is alone in the
universe.

'And who are you in relation to the patient?' the doctor asked.

They had taken their seats, at last, at his consulting desk. On
the wall behind the doctor a giant chart depicted a cross-
section of a man's urinary and reproductive organs. Ratna

looked at it for a moment, marvelling at the diagram's beauty, and said: 'His uncle.'

The doctor made the boy take off his shirt; then he sat next to him, made him put his tongue out, peered into his eyes, and put his stethoscope to the boy's chest, pressing it to one side and then the other.

Ratna thought: to get a disease like this, on his very first time! Where was the justice in that?

After examining the boy's genitals, the doctor moved to a washbasin with a mirror above; he pulled a cord and a tube-light flickered to life above the mirror.

Letting the water run in the basin, he gargled and spat, and then turned off the light. He wiped a corner of the basin with his palm, lowered a blind over the window, inspected his green plastic wastebasket.

When he ran out of things to do, he returned to his desk, looked at his feet, and practised breathing for a while.

'His kidneys are gone.'

'Gone?'

'Gone,' the doctor said.

He turned to the boy, who was trembling hard in his seat.

'Are you unnatural in your tastes?'

The boy covered his face in his hands. Ratna answered for him.

'Look, he got it from a prostitute, there's no sin in that. He's not an unnatural fellow. He just didn't know enough about this world we live in.'

The doctor nodded. He turned to the diagram and put his finger on the kidneys, and said: 'Gone.'

Ratna and the boy went to the bus station together at six in the morning, the following day, to catch the bus to Manipal; he had heard that there was a doctor at the Medical College who specialized in the kidneys. A man with a blue sarong, sitting on the bench in the station, told them that the bus to Manipal was always late, maybe fifteen minutes, maybe thirty, maybe more. 'Everything's been falling apart in this country since Mrs Gandhi was shot,' the man in the blue sarong said, kicking his legs about. 'Buses are late. Trains are late. Everything's falling apart. We'll have to hand this country back to the British or the Russians or someone, I tell you. We're not meant to be masters of our own fate, I tell you.'

Telling the boy to wait for a moment by the bus stop, Ratna returned with peanuts in a paper cone which he had bought for twenty paise, and said: 'You haven't had breakfast, have you?' But the boy reminded him that the doctor had warned against eating anything spicy; it would irritate his penis. So Ratna went back to the vendor and exchanged the peanuts for the unsalted kind. They munched together for a while, until the boy ran to a wall and began to throw up. Ratna stood over him, patting his back, as the boy retched again and again. The man in the blue sarong watched with greedy eyes; then he came up to Ratna and whispered: 'What's the kid got? It's serious, isn't it?'

'Nonsense; he's just got a flu,' Ratna said. The bus arrived at the station an hour late.

It was late on the way back as well. The two of them had to stand in the densely crowded aisle for over an hour, until a pair of seats became empty beside them. Ratna slid into the window seat and motioned for the boy to sit down next to him.

'We got lucky, considering how crowded the bus is,' Ratna said with a smile.

Gently, he disengaged his hand from the boy's.

The boy understood too; he nodded, and took out his wallet, and threw five-rupee notes, one after the other, into Ratna's lap.

'What's this for?'

'You said you wanted something for helping me.'

Ratna thrust the notes into the boy's shirt pocket. 'Don't talk to me like that, fellow. I have helped you so far; and what did I have to gain from it? It was pure public service on my part, remember that. We aren't related: we have no blood in common.'

The boy said nothing.

'Look! I can't keep on going with you from doctor to doctor. I've got my daughters to marry off, I don't know where I'll get the dowry for—'

The boy turned, pressed his face into Ratna's collarbone and burst into sobs; his lips rubbed against Ratna's clavicles and began sucking on them. The passengers stared at them, and Ratna was too bewildered to say a word.

It took another hour before the outline of the black fort appeared on the horizon. The man and the boy got off the bus together. Ratna stood by the main road and waited as the boy blew his nose and shook the phlegm from his fingers. Ratna looked at the black rectangle of the fort and felt a sense of despair: how had it been decided, and by whom, and when, and why, that Ratnakara Shetty was responsible for helping this firecracker merchant's son fight his disease? Against the black rectangle of the fort, he had a vision, momentarily, of a white dome, and he heard a throng of mutilated beings chanting in unison. He put a beedi in his mouth, struck a match and inhaled.

'Let's go,' he told the boy. 'It's a long walk from here to my house.'

Day Six (Evening): BAJPE

Bajpe, the last area of forested land in Kittur, was marked out by the founding fathers as one of the 'cleansing lungs' of the town, and for this reason was for thirty years protected from the avarice of real-estate developers. The great forest of Bajpe, which stretched from Kittur right up to the Arabian Sea, was bordered on the town side by the Ganapati Hindu Boys' School and the small adjacent temple of Ganesha. Next to the temple ran Bishop Street, the only part of the neighbourhood where houses had been allowed. Beyond the street stood a large wasteland, and beyond that began a dark lattice of trees – the forest. When relatives from the centre of town visited, the residents of Bishop Street were usually up on their terraces or balconies, enjoying the cool breezes that blew from the forest in the evening. Guests and hosts together watched as herons, eagles, and kingfishers flew in and out of the darkening mass of trees, like ideas circulating around an immense brain. The sun, which had by now plunged behind the forest, burned orange and ochre through the interstices of the foliage, as if peering out of the trees, and the observers had the distinct impression that they were being observed in return. At such moments, guests were wont to declare that the inhabitants of Bajpe were the luckiest people on earth. At the same time, it was assumed that if a man built his house on Bishop Street, he had some reason to want to be so far from civilization.

Giridhar Rao and Kamini, the childless couple on Bishop Street, were one of the hidden treasures of Kittur, all their friends declared. Weren't they a marvel? All the way out in Bajpe, on the very edge of the wilderness, this barren couple kept alive the all-but-dead art of Brahmin hospitality.

It was another Thursday evening, and the half a dozen or so members of the Raos' circle of *intimates* were making their way through the mud and slush of Bishop Street for their weekly get-together. Ahead of the pack, moving with giant strides, came Mr Anantha Murthy, the philosopher. Behind him was Mrs Shirthadi, the wife of the Life Insurance Company of India man. Then Mrs Pai, and then Mr Bhat, and, finally, Mrs Aithal, always the last to descend from her green Ambassador.

The Raos' house was all the way down at the end of Bishop Street, just yards away from the trees. Sitting right on the forest's edge, the house had the look of a fugitive from the civilized world, ready to spring into the wilderness at a moment's notice.

'Did everyone hear that?'

Mr Anantha Murthy turned around. He put a hand on his ear and raised his eyebrows.

A cool breeze was blowing in from the forest. The *intimates* came to a halt, trying to hear what Mr Murthy had heard.

'I think it's a woodpecker, somewhere in the trees!'

An irritated voice boomed down: 'Why don't you get up here first and listen to the woodpeckers later! The food has been prepared with a lot of care and it's getting cold!'

It was Mr Rao, leaning down from the balcony of his house.

'Okay, okay,' Mr Anantha Murthy grumbled, picking his way down the muddy track again. 'But it's not every day a man gets to hear a woodpecker.' He turned to Mrs Shirthadi. 'We tend to forget everything that's important when we live in towns, don't we, Madam?'

She grunted. She was trying to make sure she didn't get mud on her sari.

The philosopher led the *intimates* into the house. When they had done scraping their chappals and shoes on the coconut-fibre mat, the visitors found old Sharadha Bhatt squinting at them. She was the proprietor of the place, a widow whose only son lived in Bombay. It was understood that the Raos stayed on in their cramped apartment, so far from the heart of town, partly out of concern for Mrs Bhatt – she was a distant relative. A suggestion of intense religiosity clung to the old lady. The visitors heard the drone of M. S. Subbalakshmi singing Suprabhatam from a small black tape recorder in her room. Sitting with her legs folded on a wooden bed, she struck at her thighs alternately with the front and back of her left palm as she followed the rhythm of the holy music.

Some of the visitors remembered her husband, a celebrated teacher of Carnatic music who had performed on All India Radio, and paid their respects, politely nodding towards her.

Done with their obligation to the ancient lady, they hurried up a wide stairwell to the Raos' quarters. The childless couple occupied a crushingly small space. Half the living area consisted of a single drawing room, cluttered with sofas and chairs. In a corner, a sitar was propped up against the wall, its shaft having slid down to a 45 degree angle.

'Ah! It's our *intimates* once again!'

Giridhar Rao was neat, modest, and unpretentious in appearance. You could tell at once that he worked in a bank. Since his transfer from Udupi – his hometown – he had been the deputy branch manager at the Corporation Bank's Cool Water Well Branch for nearly a decade now. (The *intimates* knew that Mr Rao could have risen much higher had he not repeatedly refused to be transferred to Bombay.) His wavy hair was flattened with coconut oil and parted to one side. A handlebar moustache – the one anomaly in his demure appearance – was neatly combed and curled at the ends. Mr Rao had now thrown a short-sleeved shirt over his singlet. The fabric of the shirt was thin: inside its dark silk, the thick singlet glowed like a skeleton in an X-ray.

'How are you, Kamini?' Mr Anantha Murthy asked in the direction of the kitchen.

The drawing room furniture was a motley mix – green metal seats discarded from the bank, a torn old sofa, and three fraying cane chairs. The *intimates* headed for their favourite seats. The conversation began haltingly; perhaps they sensed, once again, that they were as haphazard a collection of people as the furniture was. None was aware of any blood relation to the other. By day, Mr Anantha Murthy was a chartered accountant catering to Kittur's rich. In the evenings he became a committed philosopher of the Advaita school. He found Mr Rao a willing (if silent) listener to his theories of the Hindu life – and that was how he had become part of the circle. Mrs Shirthadi, who usually attended without her busy husband, had been educated in Madras and espoused several 'liberated' views. Her English was exceptionally fine, a marvel to listen to. Mr Rao had asked her to speak on the subject of Charles Dickens at the bank a few years ago. Mrs Aithal and her husband had met Kamini at a violin concert the previous May. The two of them were originally from Vizag.

The *intimates* knew that the Raos had selected them for their distinction – for their delicacy. They realized that they bore a responsibility upon entering that cosy little garret. Certain topics were taboo. Within the wide circumference of acceptable conversation – world news, philosophy, bank politics, the relentless expansion of Kittur, the rainfall this year – the *intimates* had learned to meander freely. Forest breezes came in from a balcony, and a transistor radio precariously balanced on the edge of the parapet emitted a steady patter of the BBC's evening news service.

A late arrival – Mrs Karwar, who taught Victorian literature at the university – threw the house into chaos. Her vivacious five-year-old, Lalitha, charged up the stairs shrieking.

'Look here, Kamini' – Mr Rao shouted at the kitchen – 'Mrs Karwar has smuggled your secret lover into the house!'

Kamini rushed out of the kitchen. Fair-skinned and shapely, she was almost a beauty. (Her forehead was protuberant and her hair thinnish at the front.) She was famous for her 'Chinese' eyes: narrow slits that were half closed beneath the curve of heavy eyelids, like prematurely opened lotus buds. Her hair – she was known to be a 'modern' woman – was cut short in the Western style. Ladies admired her hips, which, never having been widened by childbirth, still sported a girlish slimness.

She went up to Lalitha. She hoisted the little girl into the air, kissing her several times.

'Look, let's wait till my husband's back is turned, and then we'll get on my moped and drive away, huh? We can leave that evil man behind us and drive away to my sister's house in Bombay, okay?'

Giridhar Rao put his hands to his waist and glared at the giggling girl.

'Are you planning on stealing my wife? Are you really her "secret lover"?'

'Hey, keep listening to your BBC,' Kamini retorted, leading Lalitha by the hand into the kitchen.

The *intimates* acknowledged their keen delight in this pantomime. The Raos certainly did not lack the skill to keep a child happy.

The voices of the BBC continued from the radio outside – a gravy of words that the *intimates* dipped into when their conversation ran dry. Mr Anantha Murthy broke one long pause by declaring that the situation in Afghanistan was getting out of hand. One of these mornings the Soviets would come streaming over Kashmir with their red flags. Then the country would regret having missed its chance to ally itself with America back in 1948.

'Don't you feel this way, Mr Rao?'

Their host had never anything more to express than a friendly grin. Mr Murthy did not mind. He acknowledged that Mr Rao was not a 'man of many words' – but he was a 'deep' fellow all the same. If you ever wanted to check little details of world history – like for instance, who was the American president who dropped the bomb on Hiroshima – not Roosevelt, but the little man with the round glasses – then you turned to Giridhar Rao. He knew everything; he said nothing. That kind of fellow.

'How is it you remain so calm, Mr Rao, despite all this chaos and killing that the BBC is always telling you about? What is your secret?' Mrs Shirthadi asked him, as she often did.

The bank manager smiled.

'When I need peace of mind, Madam, I just go to my private beach.'

'Are you a secret millionaire?' Mrs Shirthadi demanded. 'What's this private beach you keep talking about?'

'Oh, nothing, really.' He gestured towards the distance. 'Just a little lake, with some gravel around it. It's a very soothing place.'

'And why haven't we all been invited there?' demanded Mr Murthy.

The guests sat up. A triumphant Mrs Rao entered the drawing room bearing a plastic tray whose multiple compartments brimmed with the evening's first offerings: dried walnuts (which looked like little shrunken brains), juicy figs, sultana raisins, chopped almonds, slices of desiccated pineapple…

Before the guests had recovered, the next assault followed: 'Dinner is ready!'

They went into the dining room – the only other room in the house (it led into a little alcove-kitchen). An enormous bed, plump with cushions, lay in the middle of the dining room. There was no pretending not to see the conjugal site. It lay there, brazenly open to view. A small table was pulled up right next to it, and three of the guests hesitantly took their seats there. Their embarrassment disappeared almost immediately. The informality of their hosts, the voluptuous softness of the bedding beneath them – these things soothed their nerves. Then dinner rolled out of Kamini's little kitchen. Course after course of fine tomato saaru, idli, and dosas flowed out of that factory of gustatory treats.

'This kind of cooking would amaze people even in Bombay,' proposed Mr Anantha Murthy, when Kamini's pièce de résistance– fluffy North Indian rotis, lined inside with chilli powder – arrived on the table. Kamini beamed and protested: he was all wrong, she had so many inadequacies as a cook and a housewife!

When the guests rose, they realized that their buttocks had left wide, warm, and deep markings on the bed, like an elephant's footprints in clay. Giridhar Rao brushed aside their apologies: 'Our guests are like gods to us; they can do no wrong. That's the philosophy in this house.'

They stood in line outside the washroom, where water flowed from a green rubber pipe twisted into a loop around the tap. Then back to the drawing room for the highlight of the evening – almond kheer.

Kamini brought out the dessert in breathtakingly large tumblers. The shake – served warm or cold, according to each guest's pleasure – was so full of almonds that the guests protested that they had to *chew* the drink! When they looked into their tumblers, they held their breath in wonder: shiny flecks, strands of real saffron, floated between the pieces of almond.

They left the apartment silently, heeding Mr Rao's request not to disturb the sleeping Sharadha Bhatt. (The old lady turned restlessly on her wooden bed as they departed; in the background the religious music droned on.)

'Do come next week!' Mr Rao had said from the terrace. 'It's the week of the Satya Narayana Pooja! I'll make sure Kamini does a better job with the cooking next week, unlike tonight's disaster!' He turned into the house and raised his voice: 'Did you hear that, Kamini? The food had better be good next time, or you're divorced.'

There had been a laugh and a high-pitched scream from inside: 'You'll be the one to get divorced, unless you shut up!'

Once at a safe distance, the *intimates* burst into chatter.

What a pair! The man and woman such complete opposites! He was 'bland'; she was 'spicy'. He was 'conservative', she was 'modern'. She was 'quick', he was 'deep'.

Still picking their way along the muddy road, they began to discuss the forbidden topic, with all the excitement and eagerness of people who were discussing it for the first time.

'It's obvious,' said one of the women, Mrs Aithal or Mrs Shirthadi, 'Kamini is the one "at fault". She wouldn't have *the operation*. No wonder her life is racked by guilt. Don't you see how she throws herself on any available child in a storm of frustrated maternity, showering them with kisses and blandishments and caramel chocolates? What does that signify, if not guilt?'

'And why did she refuse the operation?' demanded Mr Anantha Murthy.

Obstinacy. The women were sure of it. Kamini simply

313

refused to acknowledge that the fault was hers. Some of Kamini's stubbornness, to be sure, came from her privileged background. She was the youngest of four sisters, all fair as buttermilk, the darling children of a famous eye-surgeon in Shimoga. How she must have been spoiled as a child! The other sisters had married well – a lawyer, an architect, and a surgeon, and they all lived in Bombay. Giridhar Rao was the poorest of the brothers-in-law. You could be sure that Kamini was not the kind of woman to let him forget this. Haven't you seen how defiantly she rides about town in her Hero Honda moped, as if she were the lord of their household?

Mr Anantha Murthy raised several objections. Why were all the womenfolk so suspicious of Kamini's 'sportiness'? How rare to find such a free-thinking woman! The fault was surely *his*. Haven't you seen him refuse promotion after promotion just because he would have to move to Bombay? What does that tell you? The man is lethargic.

'If only he would show…some more *initiative*…the problem of childlessness could easily be solved…' Mr Murthy said, giving his bald head a sad philosophical shake.

He even claimed to have given Mr Rao the names of doctors in Bombay who could solve his lack of 'initiative'.

Mrs Aithal reacted indignantly. Mr Rao had more than enough 'spunk' in him! Didn't he have such thick facial hair? And didn't he ride an entirely masculine red Yamaha motorcycle to the bank every morning?

The women enjoyed romanticizing Mr Rao. Mrs Shirthadi irritated Mr Murthy by suggesting that the modest little bank manager was also in secret 'a philosopher'. Once she had caught him reading the 'religious issues of the day' column on the last page of *The Hindu*. He seemed embarrassed at this discovery, and parried her inquiries with jokes and puns. Still, the feeling had grown that beneath all his joking, he was undeniably 'philosophical'.

'How else can he be so calm all the time, even without children?' Mr Aithal demanded.

'He has a secret of some kind, I'm sure,' Mrs Murthy suggested.

Mrs Karwar coughed and said: 'Sometimes I fear that she might be thinking of divorcing him' – and everyone looked concerned. The woman certainly was 'modern' enough to think of trying something like that…

But they had reached their cars now, and the group broke up, and drove away one after the other.

Later in the week, though, the Raos were observed as they circled the Cool Water Well Junction on his Yamaha bike. Kamini sat on the backseat holding on to her husband tightly, and the observers were surprised to see how the two of them looked like a real couple just then.

Next Thursday, when the *intimates* returned to the Raos' residence, they found Sharadha Bhatt herself opening the door for them. The old woman's silver hair was disarrayed and she glared at her tenants' guests.

'She's having trouble with Jimmy – you know, her architect son in Bombay. She's asked him again if she can come to stay with him, but his wife won't allow it,' Kamini whispered, as she led them up the stairs.

Because of the anticipation of an extraordinary meal this

evening, Mr Shirthadi was putting in a rare appearance alongside his wife. He spoke passionately about the ingratitude of today's children, and said he sometimes wished he had stayed childless. Mrs Shirthadi sat nervously – her husband had almost crossed the invisible circumference.

Then Mrs Karwar arrived with Lalitha, and there was the usual shouting and shrieking between Kamini and the 'secret lover'.

After the sherbet, Mr Anantha Murthy asked Mr Rao to confirm a piece of gossip – had he turned down another offer to be posted to Bombay?

Mr Rao confirmed this with a nod.

'Why don't you go, Giridhar Rao?' demanded Mrs Shirthadi. 'Don't you want to rise in the bank?'

'I'm happy out here, Madam,' Mr Rao said. 'I have my private beach, and my BBC in the evenings. What more does a man need?'

'You are the perfect Hindu man, Mr Giridhar,' said Mr Murthy, who was growing restless for dinner. 'Which is to say, you are almost completely contented with your fate on earth.'

'Well, would you still be contented if I ran away with Lalitha?' Kamini shouted from the kitchen.

'My dear, if you ran away, then I'd be truly contented,' he retorted.

She shrieked out in mock outrage and the *intimates* applauded.

'Well, what about this private beach that you keep talking about, Mr Rao – when are we going to see it, exactly?' Mrs Shirthadi asked.

Before he could reply, Kamini came scampering out of the kitchen and leaned over the bannister.

A stertorous breathing grew louder. Sharadha Bhatt's face became visible, as she limped up, one stair at a time.

Kamini was agitated.

'Should I help you up the stairs? Should I do something?'

The old woman shook her head. Half out of breath, she stumbled onto a chair at the top of the stairs.

The conversation stopped. This was the very first time the old woman had joined the weekly dinners.

In a few minutes the *intimates* had learned to ignore her.

Mr Anantha Murthy clapped his hands when Kamini came out with the appetizer tray.

'So, what's this I hear about your taking up swimming?'

'And if I am?' she snapped, putting a hand to her waist. 'What's wrong with that?'

'I hope you are not going to wear a bikini like a Western woman?'

'Why not? If they do it in America, why can't we? Are we less than them in any way?'

Lalitha giggled furiously as Kamini announced plans for the two of them to buy the scandalous swimsuits right away.

'And if Mr Giridhar Rao doesn't like it – then the two of us are going to run away and live together in Bombay, aren't we?'

Giridhar Rao glanced nervously at the old woman, who was gazing at her toes.

'All this "modern" talk isn't getting you upset, is it, Sharadha-amma?'

The old lady breathed heavily. She curled her toes and stared at them.

Mr Anantha Murthy ventured a comparison between the barfi that Kamini had put out on the appetizer tray and the barfi served in the best café in Bombay.

Then the old lady spoke in a hoarse voice: 'It is written in the Scriptures…' She paused for a long time. The room went silent. '… that a man…a man who has no son may not aspire to enter the gates of Heaven.' She breathed out. 'And if a man doesn't enter Heaven, neither can his wife. And here you are talking of bikinis and wikinis, and cavorting with "modern" people, instead of praying to God to forgive your sins!'

She breathed heavily for another moment, then got to her feet and hobbled down the stairs.

When the *intimates* left – it was a truncated evening – they found the old lady outside the house. Sitting on a suitcase bursting with clothes, she was bellowing at the trees.

'Yama Deva, come for me! Now that my son has forgotten his mother, what more is there for me to live for?'

As she called to the Lord of Death, she struck at her forehead with the stems of her fists, and her bangles jangled.

Feeling Giridhar Rao's hand on her shoulder, the old woman burst into tears.

The *intimates* saw Giridhar Rao gesture for them to leave. The old lady had exhausted her histrionics. Her head sank onto Kamini's breast and she convulsed in sobs.

'Forgive me, mother… The gods have given us each our punishment. They gave you a uterus of stone, and they have smashed the heart in my son's chest…'

After they had put the old lady to bed, Mr Rao let his wife climb the stairs first. When he joined her, she was lying on the bed, with her back turned towards him.

He walked onto the verandah and turned the radio off.

She said nothing as he picked up his helmet and headed back down the stairs. The kick-starting of his engine rent the quiet of Bishop Street.

In a few minutes, he was heading down the road that went through the forest towards the sea. On either side of the speeding bike, serried silhouettes of coconut palms bristled against the blue coastal night. Hanging low over the trees, a bright moon looked as though it had been cleaved by an axe. With its top right corner sliced off, it hung in the sky like an illustration of the idea of 'two-thirds'. After a quarter of an hour, the Yamaha bike swerved off the road into a muddy track, thundering over stones and gravel. Then its engine went dead.

A lake, a small circle of water inside the forest, came into view, and Giridhar Rao stopped his bike, leaving his helmet on the seat. Fishermen had cleared a small shore around the lake, which was bounded on the far side by more coconut trees. At this hour, there would be nets all over the lake, but there was not another soul to be seen. A heron, walking through the shallow water at the edge of the lake, was the only other living thing in sight. Giridhar had stumbled upon his lake years ago, on a drive through the forest at night. He had no idea why no one came here; but a small town is like that, full of hidden treasures. He walked beside the lake for a few minutes, then sat down on a rock.

The water, its glossy surface broken by black ripples, looked like sheets of molten glass settling one on top of another.

The heron flapped its wings and rose into the air. Now he was all alone. He hummed softly, a tune from his bachelor days in Bangalore. A yawn expanded his face. He looked up. Three stars had emerged from the tatters of a grey cloud; together with the two-thirds moon they composed a quadrilateral. Mr Rao admired the structure of the night sky. It pleased him to think that the elements of our world were not cast about at random. Something stood behind them: an order.

He yawned again and stretched his legs out from the rock.

His peace was broken. It had begun to drizzle. He wondered if he had remembered to fasten the windows above their bed; the rain might strike her face.

Leaving his private beach behind, he sprinted to his motorbike, donned his helmet, and kicked the machine to life.

One morning in 1987, all of Bishop Street woke to hear the dull thack-thack-thack of axes hacking away at the trees. In a few days, chainsaws were buzzing, and cranes were scooping up huge portions of black earth. And that was the end of the great forest of Bajpe. In its place, the inhabitants of Bishop Street now saw a giant pit filled with cranes, lorries, and an army of bare-chested migrant workers carrying stacks of bricks and cement bags on their heads like ants moving grains of rice. A giant sign in Kannada and Hindi proclaimed that this was to be the site of the 'Sardar Patel Iron Man of India Sports Stadium. A Dream Come True for Kittur'. The racket was incessant, and dust swirled up from the pit like steam from a geyser. Outsiders who returned to Bajpe thought the neighbourhood had become a dozen degrees warmer.

Day Seven: SALT MARKET VILLAGE

If you want a servant you can trust, a cook who won't steal sugar, a driver who doesn't drink, you go to Salt Market Village. Although it has formed part of Kittur Corporation since 1988, Salt Market remains largely rural and much poorer than the rest of the town.

If you visit in April or May, you must stay to watch the local festival known as the 'rat hunt' – a nocturnal ritual in which the women of the suburb march through the rice fields bearing burning torches in one hand, as they pound the earth with hockey sticks or cricket bats in the other hand, shouting all the time at the tops of their voices. Rats, mongooses, and shrews, terrified by the noise, run into the centre of the field, where the women pound the encircled rodents to death.

The only tourist attraction of Salt Market Village is an abandoned Jain basadi, where early Kannada epics were written by the poets Harihara and Raghuveera. In 1990, a portion of the Jain basadi was acquired by the Mormon Church of Utah, USA, and turned into an office for its evangelists.

Murali, waiting in the pantry for the tea to boil, took a step to his right and peeped through the doorway.

Comrade Thimma, who was sitting beneath the framed Soviet poster, had begun to grill the old woman.

'Do you understand the exact nature of the doctrinal differences between the Communist Party of India, the Communist Party of India (Marxist), and the Communist Party of India (Marxist-Maoist)?'

Of course she doesn't know, Murali thought, stepping back into the pantry and switching off the kettle.

No one on earth did.

He put his hand into a tin box full of sugar biscuits. A moment later, he was out in the reception area with a tray holding three cups of tea and a sugar biscuit next to each cup.

Comrade Thimma was looking up at the wall opposite him, where it was pierced by a grilled window. The evening light illuminated the grille; a block of light glowed on the floor, like the tail of an incandescent bird perched in the grille.

The Comrade's manner strongly suggested that the old woman, considering her state of complete doctrinal ignorance, was unworthy to receive assistance from the Communist Party of India (Marxist-Maoist), Kittur branch.

The woman was frail and haggard; her husband had hanged himself two weeks ago from the ceiling of their house.

Murali placed the first cup before Comrade Thimma, who picked it up and sipped the tea. This improved his mood.

Once again looking high up at the glowing grille, the Comrade said: 'I will have to tell you of our *dialectics*; if you find them acceptable, we can talk about help.'

The farmer's wife nodded, as if the word 'dialectics', in English, made perfect sense to her.

Without taking his eyes from the grille, the Comrade bit into one of the sugar biscuits; the crumbs fell around his chin, and Murali, after handing the old woman her tea, went back to the Comrade and wiped the crumbs off with his fingers.

The Comrade had small, sparkling eyes, and a tendency to look high up and far away, as he delivered his words of wisdom, which he always did with a feeling of suppressed excitement. This gave him the air of a prophet. Murali, as prophets' sidekicks often are, was physically the superior specimen: taller, broader, with a large and heavily creased forehead, and a kind smile.

'Give the lady our brochure on *dialectics*,' the Comrade said, speaking straight to the grille.

Murali nodded and moved purposefully towards one of the cupboards. The reception area of the Communist Party of India (Marxist-Maoist) was furnished with an old tea-stained table, a few decrepit cupboards, and a desk for the secretary-general, behind which hung a giant poster, from the early days of the Soviet Revolution, depicting a group of proletarian heroes climbing a ladder up into heaven. The workers bore mallets and sledgehammers, while a group of oriental gods cowered at their advance. After digging into two of the cupboards, Murali found a pamphlet with a big red star on the cover. He brushed it with a corner of his shirt and brought it to the old woman.

'She can't read.'

The soft voice came from the woman's daughter, who was

sitting in the chair next to her, holding on to her teacup and untouched sugar biscuit. After a moment's hesitation Murali let the daughter have the brochure; keeping the teacup in her left hand, she held the pamphlet between two fingers of her right, as if it were a soiled handkerchief.

The Comrade smiled at the window grille; it was not clear if he was reacting to the events of the past few minutes. He was a thin, bald, dark-skinned man with sunken cheeks and gleaming eyes.

'In the beginning we had only one party in India, and it was the true party. It made no compromise. But then the leaders of this true party were seduced by the lure of bourgeois democracy; they decided to contest elections. That was their first mistake and the fatal one. Soon the one true party had split. New branches emerged, trying to restore the original spirit. But they too became corrupted.'

Murali wiped the cupboard shelves and tried to realign the loose hinge of its door as well as he could. He was not a peon; there was no peon – Comrade Thimma would not allow the exploitative hiring of proletarian labour. Murali was certainly not proletarian – he was the scion of an influential landowning Brahmin family– so it was okay for him to perform all kinds of menial work.

The Comrade took a deep breath, took off his glasses and rubbed them clean with a corner of his white cotton shirt.

'We alone have kept the faith – we the members of the Communist Party of India (Marxist-Maoist). We alone remain true to the dialectics. And do you know what the strength of our membership is?'

He put his glasses back on and inhaled with satisfaction.

'Two. Murali and me.'

He gazed at the grille with a wan smile. He appeared to be done; so the old woman placed her hands on her daughter's head and said: 'She is unmarried, sir. We are begging of you some money to marry her off, that is all.'

Thimma turned to the daughter and stared; the girl looked at the ground. Murali winced. I wish he'd have more delicacy sometimes, he thought.

'We have no support,' the old woman said. 'My family won't even talk to me. Members of our own caste won't—'

The Comrade slapped his thigh with his palm.

'This caste question is only a manifestation of the class struggle: Mazumdar and Shukla definitively established this in 1938. I refuse to accept the category of "caste" in our discussions.'

The woman looked at Murali. He nodded his head, as if to say: 'Go on.'

'My husband said, the Communists were the only ones who cared about people like us. He said that if the Communists ruled the earth there would be no hardships for the poor, sir.'

This seemed to mollify the Comrade. He looked at the woman and the girl for a moment, and then sniffed. His fingers seemed to lack something. Murali understood. As he went to the pantry to boil another cup of tea, he heard the Comrade's voice continue behind him: 'The Communist Party of India (Marxist-Maoist) is not the party of the poor – it is the party of the proletariat. This distinction has to be understood, before we discuss assistance or resistance.'

After turning the kettle on once more, Murali was about to toss the tea leaves in; then he wondered why the daughter had not touched her tea. He was seized by the suspicion that he had put too much tea into the kettle – and that the way he had been making tea for nearly twenty-five years might have been wrong.

Murali got off the number 67c bus at the Salt Market Village stop and walked down the main road, picking his way through a bed of muck, while hogs sniffed the earth around him. He kept his umbrella up on his shoulder, like a wrestler keeps his mace, so that its metal point wouldn't be sullied by the muck. Asking a group of boys playing a game of marbles in the middle of the village road for directions, he found the house: a surprisingly large and imposing structure, with rocks placed on the corrugated tin roof, to stabilize it during the rains.

He unlatched the gate and went in.

A handspun cotton shirt hung on a hook on the wall next to the door; the dead man's, he assumed. As if the fellow were still inside, taking a nap, and would come outside and put it on to greet his visitor.

At least a dozen framed multi-coloured images of gods had been affixed to the front wall along with one of a pot-bellied local guru with an enormous nimbus affixed to his head. There was a bare cot, its fibres fraying, for visitors to sit down on.

Murali left his sandals outside and wondered if he should knock on the door. Too intrusive for a place like this – where death had just entered – so he decided to wait until someone came out.

Two white cows were sitting in the compound of the house. The bells round their necks tinkled during their rare movements. Lying in front of them was a puddle of water in which straw had been soaked to make a gruel. A black buffalo, snippets of fresh green all over its moist nose, stood gazing at the opposite wall of the compound, chewing at a sack full of grass that had been emptied on the ground in front of it. Murali thought: these animals have no concern in the world. Even in the house of a man who has killed himself, they are still fed and fattened. How effortlessly they rule over the men of this village, as if human civilization had confused masters and servants. Murali was transfixed. His eyes lingered on the fat body of the beast, its bulging belly, its glossy skin. He smelled its shit, which had caked on its backside; it had been squatting in puddles of its own waste.

Murali had not been to Salt Market Village in decades. The previous time was twenty-five years ago, when he had come searching for visual details to enrich a short story on rural poverty that he was writing. Not much had changed in a quarter-century; only the buffaloes had grown fat.

'Why didn't you knock on the door?'

The old woman emerged from the back yard; she walked around him with a big smile and went into the house and shouted: 'Hey, you! Get some tea!'

In a moment the girl came out with a tumbler of tea, which Murali took, touching her wet fingers as he did so.

The tea, after his long journey, felt like heaven. He had never mastered the art of making tea, even though he had been boiling it for Thimma for nearly twenty-five years now. Maybe it was one of those things that only women can truly do, he thought.

'What do you need from us?' the old woman asked. Her manner had become more servile; as if she had guessed the purpose of his visit only now.

'To find out if you are telling the truth,' he replied, calmly.

She summoned the neighbours so he could interview them. They squatted around the cot; he insisted that they sit on the same level as him but they remained where they were.

'Where did he hang himself?'

'Right here, sir!' said one old villager with broken, paan-stained teeth.

'What do you mean right here?'

The old man pointed to the beam of the roof. Murali could not believe it: in full public view, he had killed himself? So the cows had seen it; and the fat buffalo too.

He heard about the man whose shirt still hung from the hook. The failure of his crops. The loan from the moneylender. At 3 per cent per month, compounded.

'He was ruined by the first daughter's wedding. And he knew he had one more to marry off – this girl.'

The daughter had been lingering in a corner of the front yard the whole time. He saw her turn her face away, in slow agony.

As he was leaving, one of the villagers came running after him: 'Sir...sir...I mean, an aunt of mine committed suicide two years ago... I mean, just a year ago, sir, and she was virtually a mother to me...can the Communist Party...'

Murali seized the man's arm and pressed his fingers deeply

into the flesh. He peered into the man's eyes: 'What is the name of the daughter?'

Slowly he walked back to the bus station. He let the tip of his umbrella trail in the earth. The horror of the dead man's story, the sight of those fat buffaloes, the pain-stricken face of that beautiful daughter – these details kept churning in his mind.

He thought back twenty-five years, when he had come to this village with his notebook and his dreams of becoming an Indian Maupassant. As he walked down the twisting streets, crowded with streetchildren playing their violent games, fatigued day-labourers sleeping in the shade, and with thick, still, glistening pools of effluent, he was reminded of that strange mixture of the strikingly beautiful and the filthy which is the nature of every Indian village – and the simultaneous desire to admire and to castigate that had been inspired in him from the time of his first visits.

He felt the need, as he had before, to take notes.

Back then, he had visited Salt Market Village every day for a week, jotting down painstakingly detailed descriptions of farmers, roosters, bulls, pigs, piglets, sewage, children's games, religious festivals, intending to juggle them into a series of short stories that he crafted in the reading room of the municipal library at night. He was not sure if the Party would approve of his stories, so he sent a bundle of them under a nom de plume– 'The Seeker of Justice' – to the editor of a weekly magazine in Mysore.

After a week, he received a postcard from the editor, summoning him from Kittur for a meeting. He took the train to

Mysore and waited half a day for the editor to call him into his office.

'Ah, yes…the young genius from Kittur.' The editor searched his table for his glasses and pulled the folded bundle of Murali's stories from their envelope, while the young author's heart beat violently.

'I wanted to see you' – the editor let the stories fall on the table – 'because there is talent in your writing. You have gone into the countryside and seen life there, unlike ninety per cent of our writers.'

Murali glowed. It was the first time anyone had mentioned the word 'talent' when speaking of him.

Picking up one of the stories, the editor silently scanned the pages.

'Who is your favourite author?' He asked, biting at a corner of his glasses.

'Guy de Maupassant.'

Murali corrected himself: 'After Karl Marx.'

'Let's stick to literature,' the editor retorted. 'Every character in Maupassant is like this…' – he bent his index finger and wiggled it. 'He wants, and wants, and wants. To the last day of his life he wants. Money. Women. Fame. More women. More money. More fame. Your characters' – he unbent his finger – 'want absolutely nothing. They simply walk through accurately described village settings and have deep thoughts. They walk around the cows and trees and roosters and think, and then walk around the roosters and trees and cows and think some more. That's it.'

'They do have thoughts of changing the world for the

better…' Murali protested. 'They desire a better society.'

'They *want* nothing!' the editor shouted. 'I can't print stories of people who want nothing!'

He threw the bundle of stories back at Murali. 'When you find people who want something, come back to me!'

Murali had never rewritten those stories. Now, as he waited for the bus to take him back to Kittur, he wondered if that bundle of stories was still somewhere in his house.

When Murali got off the bus and walked back to the office, he found Comrade Thimma with a foreigner. It was not unusual for there to be strangers in the office; lean, fatigued men with paranoid eyes who were on the run from nearby states going through one of their routine purges of radical Communists. In those places radical Communism was a real threat to the state. The fugitives would sleep and take tea at the office for a few weeks, until things cooled down and they could return home.

But this man was not one of those hunted ones; he had blond hair and an awkward European accent.

He sat next to Thimma, and the Comrade was pouring his heart out, as he gazed at the distant light in the grille up on the wall. Murali sat down and listened to him for half an hour. He was magnificent. Trotsky had not been forgiven, nor had Bernstein been forgotten. Thimma was trying to show the European that even in a small town like Kittur men were up to date with the theory of dialectics.

The foreigner had nodded a lot and written everything down. At the end, he capped his ballpoint pen and observed: 'I find that the Communists have virtually no presence in Kittur.'

Thimma slapped his thigh. He glared at the grille. The Socialists had had too much influence in this part of South India, he said. The question of feudalism in the countryside had been solved; big estates had been broken up and distributed among peasants.

'That man Devraj Urs – when he was leader of the Congress – created some kind of revolution here,' Thimma sighed. 'Just a pseudo-revolution, naturally. The falsehood of Bernstein once again.'

Murali's own land had been subjected to the socialist policies of the Congress government. His father had lost his land; in return, the government had allocated compensation. His father went to the municipal office to receive his compensation, but he found that someone, some bureaucrat, had forged his signature and run away with his money. When Murali heard this, he had thought: my old man deserves this. I deserve this. For all that we have done to the poor, this is fit retribution. He realized, of course, that his family's compensation had not been stolen by the poor, but by some corrupt civil servant. Nevertheless this was justice of a kind.

Murali went about his regular end-of-day tasks. First he swept the pantry. As he reached with his broom under the sink, he heard the foreigner say:

'I think the problem with Marx is that he assumes human beings are too…decent. He rejects the idea of original sin. And maybe that is why Communism is dying everywhere now. The Berlin Wall…'

Murali crawled under the sink to the hard-to-reach places; Thimma's voice resonated oddly in the enclosed space beneath the sink: 'You have completely misunderstood the dialectical process!'

He paused, and waited under the sink for Comrade Thimma to come up with a better response.

He swept the floor, closed the cupboards, turned off the unwanted lights to save on the electricity bill, tightened the taps to save on the water bill, and went to the bus station to wait for the number 56B to take him home.

Home. A blue door, one fluorescent lamp, three naked electric bulbs, ten thousand books. The books were everywhere; waiting for him like faithful pets on either side of the door when he walked in, coated in dust on the dinner table, stacked against the old walls as though to buttress the structure of the house. They had taken all the best space in the house and had left him a little rectangular area for his cot.

He opened the bundle that he had brought home with him: 'Is Gorbachev straying from the True Path? Notes by Thimma swami, BA (Kittur), MA (Mysore), secretary-general, Kittur regional politburo, Communist Party of India (Marxist-Maoist)'.

He would add them to the notes he was collecting on Thimma's thoughts. The idea was to publish them one day and hand them out to the workers as they left their factories.

This evening, Murali could not write for long; the mosquitoes bit him and he swatted them. He lit a coil to keep the mosquitoes away. Even then he could not write; and then he realized it was not the mosquitoes that were disturbing him.

The way she had averted her face. He would have to do something for her.

What was her name? – Ah, yes. Sulochana.

He began to rummage in the mess around his bed, until he found the old collection of short stories that he had written all those years ago. He blew the dust off the pages and began to read.

The photograph of the dead man hung on the wall, beside the portraits of the gods who had failed to save him. The guru with the big belly, perhaps taking all the blame, had now been dismissed.

Murali stood at the door, waited, and knocked slowly.

'They're working in the fields,' the old neighbour with the broken red teeth shouted.

The cows and the buffalo were missing from the courtyard; sold for cash, no doubt. Murali thought it was appalling. That girl, with her noble looks, working in the fields like a common labourer?

I've come just in time, he thought.

'Run and get them!' he shouted at the neighbour. 'At once!'

The state government had a scheme to compensate the widows of farmers who had killed themselves under duress, Murali explained to the widow, making her sit down on the cot. It was one of those well-intentioned rural improvement schemes that never reached anyone, because no one knew about it – until people from the city, like Murali, told them about it.

The widow was leaner, and sunburned; she sat there wiping her hands constantly against the back of her sari; she was ashamed of the dirt on them.

Sulochana brought out the tea. He was amazed that this girl, who had been working in the fields, had still found time to make him tea.

When he took the cup from her, touching her fingers, he quickly admired her features. Having just come from a day's hard labour in the fields, she was still beautiful – in fact, more beautiful than ever before. There was that simple, unpainted elegance to her face. None of the make-up, lipstick or false eyebrows you see in cities these days.

How old was she? he wondered.

'Sir...' The old woman folded her hands. 'Will the money really come?'

'If you sign here,' he said. 'And here. And here.'

The old lady held the pen and grinned idiotically.

'She can't write,' Sulochana said; so he placed the letter on his thigh and he signed for her.

He explained that he had brought another letter; one to be delivered to the central police station near the Lighthouse Hill, demanding prosecution of the moneylender for his role in instigating the man's death through usury. He wanted the old woman to sign that too, but she joined her palms together and bowed to him.

'Please, sir, don't do that. Please. We don't want any trouble.'

Sulochana stood by the wall, looking down, silently reinforcing her mother's plea.

He tore up the letter. As he did so, he realized that he was now the arbiter over this family's fate; he was the patriarch here.

'And her marriage?' he said, indicating the girl leaning against the wall.

'Who will marry this one? And what am I to do?' the old woman wailed as the girl retreated into the dark of the house.

It was on the way back to the bus station that the idea came to him.

He pressed the metal tip of his umbrella to the ground and trailed a long, continuous line through the mud.

And then he thought: why not?

She had no other hope, after all...

He boarded the bus. He was still a bachelor, at fifty-five. After his time in jail his family had disowned him, and none of his aunts or uncles had tried to fix an arranged marriage for him. Somehow, in the midst of distributing pamphlets and spreading the word to the proletariat and collecting Comrade Thimma's speeches, he had never found time to marry himself off. He had not had any great desire to do so, either.

Lying in bed, he thought: but this is nowhere for a girl to live. It is a filthy house, filled with old editions – books by veterans of the Communist Party and nineteenth-century French and Russian short-story writers – that no one reads any more.

He had not realized how badly he had been living until he tried to imagine living with someone else. But things would change; he felt a great hope. If she came into his life everything could be different. He lay down on his cot and stared at the ceiling fan. It was switched off; he rarely turned it on, except in the most oppressive summer heat, so that he wouldn't increase the electricity bill.

All his life he had been dogged by a restlessness, a feeling that he was meant for some greater endeavour than could be found in a small town. After his law degree from Madras, his father had expected him to take over his law practice. Instead, Murali had been drawn to politics; he had begun attending Congress party meetings in Madras, and continued doing so in Kittur. He took to wearing a Nehru cap and keeping a photo of Gandhi on his desk. His father noticed. One day there was a confrontation and shouting, and Murali had left his father's house and joined the Congress party as a full-time member. He knew what he wanted to do with his life already: there was an enemy to overcome. The old, bad India of caste and class privilege – the India of child marriage, of ill-treated widows; of exploited subalterns – it had to be overthrown. When the state elections came, he campaigned with all his heart for the Congress candidate, a young lower-caste man named Anand Kumar.

After Anand Kumar won, he saw two of his fellow Congress workers sitting outside the Party office every morning. He saw men approach them with letters addressed to the candidate; they took the letters and a dozen rupees from each supplicant.

Murali threatened to report them to Kumar. The two men turned grave. They stepped aside and invited Murali to go right in.

'Please complain at once,' they said.

As he went and knocked on Kumar's door, he heard laughter behind him.

Murali joined the Communists next, having heard that they were incorruptible. The larger factions of the Communists turned out to be just as rotten as the Congress; so he changed his membership from one Communist Party to the other, until one day he entered a dim office and saw, beneath the giant poster of heroic proletarians climbing up to heaven to knock out the gods of the past, the small dark figure of Comrade Thimma. At last – an incorruptible. Back then the party had seventeen member-volunteers; they ran women's education programmes, population control campaigns, and proletarian radicalization drives. With a group of volunteers, he went to the sweatshops near the Bunder, distributing pamphlets with the message of Marx and the benefits of sterilization. As the membership of the party dwindled, he found himself going alone; it made no difference to him. The cause was a good one. He was never strident like the workers from the other Communist parties; quietly, and with great perseverance, he stood by the side of the road, holding out pamphlets to the workers and repeating the message that so few of them ever took to heart: 'Don't you want to find out how to live a better life, brothers?'

He thought that his writing, too, would contribute to that cause – although he was honest enough to admit that perhaps only his vanity made him think so. The word 'talent' was now lodged in his mind, and that gave him hope; but even as he was wondering how to improve his writing, he was sent to jail.

The police came for Comrade Thimma one day. This was during the Emergency.

'You are right to arrest me,' Thimma had said, 'as I freely and openly support all attempts to overthrow the bourgeois government of India.'

Murali had asked the policemen: 'Would you mind arresting me as well?'

Jail had been a happy time for him. He washed Thimma's clothes and hung them out to dry in the mornings. He had hoped all the free time in jail would concentrate his mind, and help him reshape his fiction, but he had no time for that. In the evenings, he took notes as Thimma dictated. Thimma's responses to the great questions of Marxism. The apostasy of Bernstein. The challenge of Trotsky. A justification for Kronstadt.

He collected the responses faithfully; then he pulled a blanket over Thimma's face, leaving his toes out in the cool air.

He shaved him in the morning, as Thimma thundered to the mirror about Khrushchev's defiling of the legacy of Comrade Stalin.

It was the happiest period of his life. But then he had been released.

With a sigh, Murali rose from his bed. He paced around the dark house, looking at the mess of the books, at the decaying editions of Gorky and Turgenev, and saying to himself, again and again: what do I have to show for my life? Just this broken-down house...

Then he saw the face of the girl again and his whole body lit up with hope, and joy. He took out his bundle of short stories and read them again. With a red-ink pen he began to delete details of his characters, quickening their motives, their impulses.

It came to Murali one morning, on his way to Salt Market Village: 'They're avoiding me. Both mother and daughter.'

Then he thought: no, not Sulochana – it's only the old woman who's gone cold.

For two months now, he had been catching the bus to Salt Market Village on a variety of fictitious premises, only to see Sulochana's face again, only to touch her fingers when she brought him his cup of scalding-hot tea.

He had tried to put it to the old lady that they should marry – hints could be delivered, and the topic would insinuate itself into the woman's mind. That had been his hope. Then, purely out of social responsibility, he would agree, despite his advanced age, to marry her.

But the old lady had never divined his desire.

'Your daughter is excellent in the household,' he had said once, thinking that enough of a hint.

The following day, when he arrived, a strange young girl came out to meet him. The widow had moved up in life; she had now hired a servant.

'Is Madam in?' he asked. The servant nodded.

'Will you go and get her?'

A minute passed. He thought he heard the sound of voices behind the door; then the servant came out and said: 'No.'

'No what?'

She turned her gaze towards the house again. 'They...are not here. No.'

'And Sulochana? Is she in?'

The servant girl shook her head.

Why shouldn't they avoid me, he thought, trailing his umbrella on the ground as he returned to the bus station. He had done his work for them; he was not needed any more.

This is how people in the real world behaved. Why should he be hurt?

In the evening, pacing around his gloomy home, he felt he had to agree with the old woman's judgement: surely this is no fit habitation for a young girl like Sulochana. How could he bring a woman into it?

Yet the next day, he was back on the bus to Salt Market Village, where, once again, the servant girl told him that no one was home.

On the way back, he rested his head against the grille and thought: the more they snub me, the more I want to fall down before that girl and propose marriage.

At home he tried writing a letter. 'Dear Sulochana: I have been searching for a way to tell you. There is so much to say...'

He went back every day for a week, and was refused entry every day. 'I will never come back,' he promised himself on the seventh evening, as he had for six evenings before. 'I really will never come back. This is disgraceful behaviour. I am exploiting these people.' But he was also angry with the old woman and Sulochana for treating him like this.

On the journey home, he stood up and shouted to the conductor: 'Stop!' He had remembered, out of the blue, a story he had written twenty-five years ago, about a matchmaker who worked in the village.

He asked the children playing marbles for the matchmaker; they directed him to the shopkeepers. It took an hour and a half to find the house.

The matchmaker was an old, half-blind man sitting in a chair smoking a hookah; his wife brought a chair for the Communist to sit in.

Murali cleared his throat and cracked his knuckles. He wondered what to say, what to do. The hero in his story had walked around the matchmaker's house and then left; he had never come this far.

'There is a friend of mine who wishes to marry that girl. Sulochana.'

'The daughter of the fellow who...?' The matchmaker pantomimed a hanging.

Murali nodded.

'Your friend is too late, sir. She has money now, and so she has a hundred offers,' the matchmaker said. 'That is the way of life.'

'But...my friend...my friend has set his heart on her...'

'Who is this friend?' the matchmaker asked, and with a dirty, omniscient gleam in his eyes.

He caught the bus in the mornings, as soon as his work was over at the Party office, and waited for her at the market. She came in the evenings to buy vegetables. He would follow her slowly. He looked at the bananas, at the mangoes. He had been buying fruit for Comrade Thimma for decades. He was expert at so many women's tasks; his heart skipped a beat when he saw her choose an over-ripe mango; when the vendor tricked her, he wanted to run over and yell at him and protect her from his avarice.

In the evenings, he stood waiting for the bus back to Kittur. He observed the way people lived in villages. He saw a boy cycling furiously, a block of ice strapped to the back of his bicycle. He had to make it in time before the ice melted; it was already half gone, and he had no aim in life but to deliver the rest of the ice in time. A man came with bananas in a plastic bag and looked around; there were large black spots on the bananas already, and he had to sell them before they rotted. All these people sent Murali a message. To want things in life, they were saying, is to recognize that time is limited.

He was fifty-five years old.

He did not take the bus back that evening; instead, he walked to the house. Rather than approach the front door, he entered through the back. Sulochana was winnowing rice; she looked at her mother and went inside.

The servant went in to bring a chair, but the old woman said: 'Don't.'

'Look here; you want to marry my daughter?' she asked.

So she had found out. It was always like this; you make an effort to conceal desire and then it is out in the open. The greatest fallacy: that you can hide from others what you want from them.

He nodded, avoiding her eyes.

'How old are you?' she asked.

'Fifty.'

'Can you give her children at your age?'

He tried to respond.

The old woman said: 'Why would we want to get you into our family, in any case? My late husband always told me, Communists are trouble.'

His jaw dropped. Was this the same husband who had praised the Communists? Had this woman just made all that up?

344

Murali understood now; her husband had said nothing about the Communists. In their wanting they became so cunning, these people!

He said: 'I bring many advantages to your family. I am a Brahmin by birth; a graduate of—'

'Look here!' The widow got up. 'Please leave – or there will be trouble.'

Why not? Maybe I can't give her children, at my age, but I can make her happy, certainly, he thought, on the bus back home. We can read Maupassant together.

He was an educated man, a graduate of the Madras University; this was no way to treat him. Tears flooded his eyes.

He sought out books of fiction and poetry, but it was the words of a film song he had heard on the bus which seemed to express his feelings best. So this is why the proletariat go to the cinema, he thought. He bought a ticket himself.

'How many?'

'One.'

The ticket-seller grinned. 'Don't you have any friends, old man?'

After the movie, Murali wrote a letter and posted it to her.

The next morning he woke up wondering if she would ever read it. Even if it reached the house, wouldn't her mother throw it away? He should have hand-delivered it!

It is not enough to make an honest attempt. That was enough for Marx and Gandhi – to have tried. But not for the real world, in which he suddenly found himself.

After considering the matter for an hour, he wrote the letter

345

again. This time he paid an urchin three rupees to deliver the message into the girl's hands.

'She knows you come here to look for her,' the vegetable seller said, the next time he came to the market. 'You've scared her away.'

She is avoiding me – his heart felt a pang. Now he understood so many more film songs. This is what they meant, the humiliation of being avoided by a girl you have come a long way to see...

He thought the vegetable sellers were all laughing at him.

Even ten years ago – in his forties – there would have been nothing unseemly about approaching such a girl, he thought, as he headed home. Now he was a dirty old man; he had become the stock figure whom he had worked into several of his stories – the lecherous old Brahmin, preying on an innocent girl of a lower caste.

But those fellows were just caricatures, class-villains; *now* he could flesh them out so much better. When he climbed into bed at night, he took a piece of paper and wrote: 'Some thoughts that a lecherous old Brahmin might *actually* have.'

Now I know enough, Murali thought, looking at the words he had written. I can become a writer at last.

The next morning order and reason returned. There were the comb on his hair, the breathing exercises before the mirror, the slow steady gait out the front door, the business of cleaning the Party headquarters and making tea for Thimma.

But, by afternoon, he was on the bus to Salt Market Village again.

He waited for her to come to the market and then walked behind her, examining potatoes and brinjals and stealing glances at her. All the time he could see the vendors mocking him: dirty old man, dirty old man. He thought with regret of a man's traditional prerogative in India – in the old, bad India – to marry a younger woman.

The next morning, back in the pantry at the Party head-quarters, boiling tea for Thimma, everything around him seemed dingy, and dark, and unbearable – the old pots and pans, the filthy spoons, the dirty old tub out of which he scooped sugar for the tea: the embers of a life that had never flared, never flamed.

'You've been fooled,' everything in the room said to him. 'You've wasted your life.'

He thought of all his advantages: his education, his sharper wit, his brains, his gift for writing. His 'talent' – as that Mysore editor had said.

All of that, he thought as he brought the tea out into the reception area, wasted in the service of Comrade Thimma.

Even Thimma had wasted himself. He had never remarried after his wife's early death; he had dedicated himself to his life's goal – uplifting the proletariat of Kittur. Ultimately it was not Marx; it was Gandhi and Nehru who were to blame. Murali was convinced of that. A whole generation of young men, deluded by Gandhianism, wasting their lives running around organizing free eye clinics for the poor and distributing books for rural libraries, instead of seducing those young widows and unmarried girls. That old man in his loincloth had turned them mad. Like Gandhi you had to withhold all your lusts. Even to know what you wanted in life was a sin; desire was bigotry. And look where the country was, after forty years of idealism? A total mess! Maybe if they had all become bastards, the young men of his generation, the place would be like America by now!

That evening he forced himself not to take the bus to the village. He stayed on, cleaning the Party headquarters twice over.

No – he thought, as he strained to clean under the sink the second time – it was not a waste! The idealism of young men like him had changed Kittur and the villages around it. Rural poverty was halved, smallpox had been eradicated, public health was a hundred times improved, literacy was up. If Sulochana could read, it was because of volunteers like him, because of those free library projects...

He paused in the darkness under the sink. A voice growled inside him: 'Fine, she can read – and what does that do for you, you idiot?'

He rushed back into the light, into the reception area.

The poster now came to life. The proletarians climbing up to heaven to overturn the gods began to melt and change form. He saw them for what they were: a subaltern army of semen, blood, and flesh rebelling inside him. A revolution of the body proletariat, long suppressed, but now becoming articulate, saying:

We want!

The Communists were finished. The European visitor had said as much; and all the newspapers were saying the same thing. The Americans had somehow won. Comrade Thimma would talk on and on. But there would soon be nothing to talk about; because Marx had become mute. Dialectics had become Dust. So had Gandhi; so had Nehru. Out in the streets of Kittur, the young people were driving brand-new Suzuki cars, blaring pop music from the West; they were licking raspberry ice-cream cones with red tongues and wearing shiny metal watches.

He picked up the pamphlet and threw it at the Soviet poster, startling a gecko that had been hiding behind it.

Do you think privilege has no place in Indian life? Do you think a Madras University man – a Brahmin – can be tossed aside so lightly?

In his hand, as the bus rocked, Murali held a letter from the state government of Karnataka that announced that another instalment of the money was due to arrive for the widow of the farmer Arasu Deva Gowda, provided she signed. Eight thousand rupees.

Asking for directions, he found the house of the money-lender. He saw it: the biggest construction in the village, with a pink façade and pillars up the front supporting a portico – the house that 3 per cent interest, compounded monthly, had built.

The moneylender, a fat, dark man, was selling grain to a group of farmers; by his side, a fat, dark boy, probably his son, was making a note in a book. Murali stopped to admire it all: the sheer genius of exploitation in India. Sell a farmer your grain. Get rid of your bad stock this way. Then charge him a loan for buying that grain. Make him pay it back at 3 per cent a month. Thirty-six per cent a year. No, even more – much more! Compound interest! – how diabolical, how brilliant! And to think, Murali smiled, that he had assumed that Communists had brains.

When Murali went up to him, the moneylender was sticking his hand deep into the grain; when he brought it out, the chocolate-coloured skin was coated with a fine yellow dust, like a bird's pollen-covered beak.

Without wiping his arm, he took the letter from Murali. Behind him, in an alcove in the wall of his house, sat a giant red statue of the pot-bellied Ganesha. A fat wife, with fat children around her, was sitting on a charpoy. And from behind them wafted the odour of a feeding, defecating beast: a water buffalo, without doubt.

'Did you know that the government has paid the widow another eight thousand rupees?' Murali told him. 'If you have debts outstanding, you should collect them now. She is in a position to pay.'

'Who are you?' the moneylender asked, with small suspicious eyes.

Hesitating for a moment, Murali said: 'I am the 55-year-old Communist.'

He wanted them to know. The old woman and Sulochana. They were both in his power now. They had been in his power from the day they had walked into his office.

When he returned to his house, there was a letter from Comrade Thimma under the door. Probably hand-delivered, since there was no one else to deliver anything now.

He tossed it away. He realized, as he did it, that he was casting away for good his membership of the Communist Party of India (Marxist-Maoist). Comrade Thimma, his mouth thirsting for tea, would deliver lectures alone, in that dim hall, denouncing him. He joined Bernstein and Trotsky and the long line of apostates.

At midnight he was still awake. He lay staring at the ceiling fan, whose fast-rotating blades were chopping the light from the halogen streetlamps outside the bedroom into sharp white glints: they showered down on Murali like the first particles of wisdom he had received in his life.

He stared at the brilliant blur of the fan's blades for a long time: then, with a jerk, he got up from the bed.

CHRONOLOGY

1984

31 October

News reaches Kittur via the BBC that Mrs Indira Gandhi, prime minister of India, has been assassinated by her own bodyguards. The town shuts down in mourning for two days. Mrs Gandhi's cremation, broadcast live, proves a major boost to the number of TVs sold in Kittur.

November

General elections. Anand Kumar, the Congress (I) candidate and a junior minister in Indira Gandhi's cabinet, retains his seat. His majority of 45,457 votes over Ashwin Aithal, his BJP opponent, is the largest in Kittur's history.

1985

Reflecting the growing interest in the stock market, the *Dawn Herald* begins publishing a daily report on the activities of the Bombay Stock Exchange on page 3.

Dr Shambhu Shetty opens Happy Smile Clinic, Kittur's first orthodontic clinic.

1986

A giant rally held by the Hoyka community in Nehru Maidan pledges to build the first temple 'for, by, and of Backward Castes' in Kittur.

The first video lending library opens in Umbrella Street.

Construction of the north bell tower, delayed for over a century, is resumed at the Cathedral of Our Lady of Valencia.

1987
The Cricket World Cup is held in India and Pakistan. Interest in cricket proves a major boost to the demand for colour TVs.

Riots break out between Hindus and Muslims in the Bunder. Two people are killed. Dawn-to-dusk curfew in the port.

Kittur is reclassified by the state government of Karnataka from 'town' to 'city', and the town municipality becomes a 'City Corporation'. The first act of the new Corporation is to authorize the cutting down of the great forest of Bajpe.

The arrival of migrant Tamil workers, drawn by the construction boom in Bajpe and Rose Lane, is believed to be the cause of a severe outbreak of cholera.

1988
Mabroor Ismail Engineer, generally believed to be the richest man in town, opens the first Maruti-Suzuki car showroom in Kittur.

The Rashtriya Swayamsevak Sangh (RSS) holds a march from Angel Talkies to the Bunder. Marchers call for India to be declared a Hindu nation, and for a return to traditional social values.

Elections held to the City Corporation. The BJP and the Congress divide the seats almost exactly.

Construction of the north bell tower, delayed for a year by the death of the rector, is recommenced at the Cathedral of Our Lady of Valencia.

1989
General elections. Ashwin Aithal, the BJP candidate, upsets cabinet minister and Congress candidate Anand Kumar to become the first non-Congress candidate ever to win the seat of Kittur.

The Sardar Patel Iron Man of India Stadium opens in Bajpe. The construction of houses in the neighbourhood proceeds rapidly, and by the year's end the old forest is almost entirely gone.

1990
A bomb explodes during a chemistry class at St Alfonso's Boys' High School and Junior College, leading to its temporary closure. The *Dawn Herald* runs a front-page editorial asking: 'Does India need martial law?'

The first computer lab in Kittur is opened at St Alfonso Boys' High School and Junior College. Other schools follow within the year.

The Gulf War breaks out, leading to the loss of expatriate remittances from Kuwait. A severe economic crisis follows. However, the broadcast of the war on CNN, available only to those TVs with a dish antenna, proves a great boost to sales of satellite TV dish antennas in Kittur.

With its funding frozen, construction work on the north bell tower of the cathedral once again comes to a halt.

1991
21 May
News reaches Kittur via CNN of the assassination of Rajiv Gandhi. The town is shut down in mourning for two days.